PRAISE FOR SH...
AND *THE D...*

P9-DNW-946

"History, philosophy, religion, murder and mayhem combined with a sharply defined sense of time and place, original characters and a magnificently medieval plot—there is little else one can ask for in a book."
—*Ellis Peters Appreciation Society Journal*

"Sharan Newman's medieval mysteries use scholarship, subtlety and humor to investigate the universal labyrinths of murder and morality, heart and soul. Her fresh, provocative view of women's roles in the medieval milieu offers a background as richly detailed as fine stained glass."
—Carole Nelson Douglas, author of the *Irene Adler* series

"Fans of Brother Cadfael should rejoice at this new find."
—*Deadly Pleasures*

"Strong characters, sparkling dialogue, sound scholarship, and rich historical setting (the same time period as the Brother Cadfael Chronicles) make this series one to read and collect."
—*Poisoned Pen*

"Top-notch sleuthing."
—*Kirkus Reviews*

"Newman skillfully depicts historical figures and issues in a very different age, one in which piety and great beauty coexist with cruelty. The intriguing medieval material informs the entire novel with a vivid sense of the past."
—*Publishers Weekly*

The Devil's Door

Sharan Newman

A TOM DOHERTY ASSOCIATES BOOK
NEW YORK

This is a work of fiction. All the characters and events portrayed in this book are either fictitious or are used fictitiously.

THE DEVIL'S DOOR

Copyright © 1994 by Sharan Newman

Cover art by John Howe

A Forge Book
Published by Tom Doherty Associates, Inc.
175 Fifth Avenue
New York, N.Y. 10010

Forge® is a registered trademark of Tom Doherty Associates, Inc.

ISBN: 0-812-52295-8
Library of Congress Card Catalog Number: 94-119

First edition: May 1994
First mass market edition: September 1995

Printed in the United States of America

0 9 8 7 6 5 4 3 2 1

This book is for my mother, Dr. Betty Donoghue, with all my love.

I want it clearly understood that the reason I can write such horrid mothers is because she's always been such a wonderful one. Thanks, Mom!

Acknowledgments

I would like to thank all the scholars who helped me with their expertise, especially Dr. Mary M. Mc-Laughlin, who took time from her work *Héloïse at the Paraclete: Ductrix et Magistra* to send me several chapters in manuscript, along with answers to a number of questions; Fr. Chrysogonus Waddell who supplied me with information on the Paraclete and monastic life as well as reading the manuscript in its roughest form and offering excellent suggestions for improvements. I owe both these people more that I can hope to repay.

I am also grateful to Dr. John Riddle, of North Carolina State, who provided me with copies of his work on the efficacy of herbal remedies in the Middle Ages; Dr. Barbara Newman, Northwestern University, who shared her insights on Héloïse with me; Dr. Brian McGuire, for help with St. Bernard; Rabbi Gelman of Santa Barbara for advice on Jews in the twelfth century; Dr. Richard Hecht, both for providing me with the Hebrew translation and for teaching a great class on Jews in the Middle Ages. Prof. Michel Bur of Nancy for information on Champagne; Dr. Bert Hall of Toronto and Gavin Faulkner (as well as an unsung graduate student) for hunting up information on medieval mining practices. Dr. Harold A.

Drake for Catullus, among other things; Dr. Georgia Wright for being on call to explain architecture, and for being charitable about mistakes in the first book. Jennifer Russell for reading the manuscript and telling me what she liked as well as noting errors. And, of course, Dr. Jeffrey Russell for who no question was too obscure. They all did their best to keep me honest. Any errors are my own perversity.

I would also like to thank Fran Halpern, Louise Ramsey and Brenda Loree, for emotional support and for keeping me from taking myself too seriously. (Also because they said that if I didn't thank them, they wouldn't ask me out to lunch any more.)

TWELFTH-CENTURY FRANCE

One

The convent of the Paraclete, Feast of Saint Benedict,
Thursday, March 21, 1140

Haec quippe prima sapientiae clavis definitur, assidua scilicet seu
frequens interrogatio; . . . Dubitando enim ad inquisitionem
venimus; inquirendo veritatem percipimus. . . .

Assiduous and frequent questioning is indeed the first key
to wisdom . . . for by doubting we come to inquiry;
through inquiring we perceive the truth. . . .

—Peter Abelard,
Introduction to *Sic et Non*

Sister Bertrada was snoring like a woman possessed. The snorts, trills, gasps and sudden silences, each followed by a piercing screech, bespoke a hideous battle with the forces of evil. To Catherine, wide awake in the next bed of the dormitory, it appeared that evil was winning. She tried covering her ears with her pillow but it was far too thin. How could the others stand it? Catherine peered down the row of narrow cots but could see no signs of wakefulness from the rest of the women.

Beside her, there was a minor explosion as when wine ferments too long in the cask and suddenly erupts from the bung hole. Sister Bertrada should be grateful the pillows were so flimsy for Catherine was sorely tempted to smother her with one.

Outside the rain dripped gently from the roof. It was the deepest part of night, Compline long past and Vigils nowhere near. All the women slept. Catherine lay awake and wondered why she had come back to the convent from Paris.

She had not wanted to venture out of the cloister in the

first place, but had gone at the request of the abbess, Héloïse. However, in following that request Catherine had found that the world was something she could not hide from, however inexplicable or frightening it might be. And it had been both. In the three months she had been away, her world had been turned inside out. Her family, whom she thought she knew as well as the lines of her own hand, had proved to be strangers. People she loved and trusted had dark, unsettling secrets. Even, no, especially, her own parents.

My mother has gone insane and believes me risen to heaven and worthy of her prayers and my father is a Jewish apostate. She tried thinking it calmly, but she couldn't yet. How could anyone? It was too absurd to even say aloud. Oh, why had she ever left the cloister? Outside the walls of the Paraclete, life had so many complications.

Of course, one of the complications she had found had been Edgar. And that was not something she wished to avoid.

She smiled in the darkness, remembering the reaction of the convent to her announcement of her intention to marry Edgar. Mother Héloïse had been warned in advance in a letter from Master Abelard. She was doubtful, but sympathetic. But others were not so kind.

"You think because you've gone and become betrothed that I will give up trying to save your soul," Sister Bertrada had told her the day she returned. "You are mistaken again, Catherine. Until you are wrapped tight in the marriage bed, I will keep up the struggle."

Sister Bertrada had kept her word, watching Catherine every moment, catching every fault; catching faults that didn't exist; berating her for folding her hands incorrectly at prayer, for appearing at None in a torn robe. To remind her that there was no place for frivolity in a discussion of Saint Veronica, Catherine spent a day away from her books, embroidering the white crosses on the veils of the consecrated virgins instead.

"You see what you'll lose by this willful act?" the novice mistress asked, holding up the veil Catherine had just completed. "Marry now, and even if you crawl back to us, as I believe you will, you will never be able to consecrate your virginity to God. You'll always be less than perfect in his eyes."

Catherine forbore reminding her that their own Abbess Héloïse had been married and borne a son before she became a nun. Did God love her less for that?

Perhaps, a voice in her mind had whispered. *How do you know who God loves?*

Catherine had admitted to herself that the affections of the Almighty were not known to her and held her tongue.

Every day had been a new diatribe, every night a cacophonous concert. Sister Bertrada was a foretaste of purgatorial torment. And yet, Catherine was happy she had returned to the Paraclete before her marriage. She needed the wisdom of Mother Héloïse and her sisters in Christ to help her come to terms with all she had learned. The revelations about her father's ancestry, the pathetic madness of her mother, what would they mean to her life? And Roger, the uncle she had loved and who had shown himself possessed by an insanity even worse than her mother's, what if it should touch her, too? Would Edgar still want to marry her?

No sane man would, her voices said. *So it's likely he's possessed by his own kind of lunacy. Have you told him yet that your own mind argues with you?*

Catherine desperately tried to squelch such traitorous thoughts. One of her greatest desires was to control the doubts that tormented her as greatly as Sister Bertrada's snoring.

The sounds from the next bed began to take on the fury of a tempest, one that might toss a ship like a toy upon the waves. Even now, Edgar might be somewhere on that dark water, making his way back to her from his family in Scotland, tossed and spun at the whim of Nature.

Catherine sat up. This would not do. Another hour between Sister Bertrada and her own unruly mind would certainly cause the dementia she feared. Better to make her body work, instead. She stuck a stockinged toe out from under the cover. The cold sent a shock through her and she drew her foot back under the blanket and felt around with

her hands for her slippers. Quietly she put them on and
eased from the cot, keeping the blanket wrapped about her,
her unbelted skirts trailing the wooden planks of the floor.

The darkness was almost complete but Catherine knew
the way. At the end of the dormitory was a narrow staircase
down to the cloister, only a step from the oratory where the
sisters prayed and recited the office. She would go down
now. In the silence and the darkness, she would pray for the
serenity and forbearance she so lacked. If the bell rang for
Vigils while she was still there, perhaps her nocturnal devotion would impress Sister Bertrada.

Not likely, her voices reminded her. *She'll be more inclined
to say you need extra prayers more than the others and make you
do this every night.*

Catherine sighed as she came to the top of the steps to
the cloister. It didn't seem fair that her own thoughts,
trained to question, should spend all their time questioning
the ideas that would give her the most peace. It was even
worse in that they were often right.

Reaching the bottom of the staircase, she froze as a sudden light flashed across her eyes. Someone was coming
across the cloister in a great hurry, the lantern she carried
swinging dangerously as she ran.

Knowing that wandering about alone at night was unsuitable behavior, Catherine stepped back into the shadows
as Sister Thecla, the portress, rushed by on her way to the
cell of Abbess Héloïse.

Forgetting rules in her intense curiosity, Catherine followed the portress out into the rain, stopping only to stick
her feet into a pair of wooden *sabots* from the row kept by
the door. She must find out what was going on. What sort
of visitor would arrive in the middle of the night? It could
only be something serious, a missive of terrible urgency.
Irrationally, she thought of Edgar. His ship had been lost;
brigands had cut his throat. Worry for him was so much on
her mind that she didn't stop to think that she was not important enough for someone to come racing through the
night to relay such a thing to her.

The abbess appeared only a moment after Sister Thecla
had entered. She wrapped her scarf around her head as she

followed the portress through the cloister, out into the yard
and into the portress's lodge by the gate.

Catherine knew the trouble she would be in if she were
discovered, but she followed them all the same. She covered her head with the blanket, slinking after them like a
misplaced shadow, trying to keep her feet from squelching
in the mud.

The two women entered the gatehouse. Catherine crept
up to the door to hear what was going on.

"She must have someone with her constantly," a man's
voice commanded. "Have the priest within call for last
rites. I don't know how she survived this long with what
those bastards did to her."

"She will not be left alone for a moment, my lord,"
Héloïse said softly. "We will see that she is well taken
care of."

"Good," the voice answered, as if dismissing her. "And
I will do the same for Walter of Grancy."

"Are you quite sure it was Walter?" she heard Héloïse
ask.

"He was seen escaping. We found her soon afterwards,
in the woods just outside the castle. Not," he added, "that
it is any concern of yours."

Catherine's mouth dropped open. How dare this man
speak to the abbess so rudely! She thought she recognized
the man's voice and half expected the roof to open and a
well-aimed divine curse to fall upon Raynald of Tonnerre.

She was so outraged that she didn't hear the next words
and wasn't prepared for the door to be suddenly thrown
open. Catherine found herself face to face with the man
who had spoken. Startled, she tried to step back, but the
sabot was stuck where she had been standing and she fell
backwards into the mud.

Raynald, Count of Tonnerre, stepped over her with complete indifference. He pulled on his gloves, fastened his
cloak and went down the path to the stables by the guesthouse.

As Catherine struggled to get up, another figure appeared in the doorway. The lamp illumined the face of
Mother Héloïse. Normally its expression was gentle, if a

bit sad. But Catherine took one look at her now and knew to the depths of her soul what it must be like to face the wrath of God.

The abbess stood over her. With some difficulty Catherine released herself from the grip of the earth and got up. She was hampered by her efforts to get her foot back into the still-stuck *sabot* and, at the same time, cover her head with her blanket. She opened her mouth to explain. Héloïse cut her off with a gesture.

"There is nothing you can say to excuse your being here, at this hour, and in such a state, so don't waste my time trying," she said.

"No, Mother; yes, Mother. I'm sorry, Mother," Catherine stuttered.

One corner of Héloïse's mouth twitched. Catherine exhaled in relief. No punishment was worse than Mother Héloïse being angry with her.

"I know very well that you are sorry only at being found in such a state, not for the curiosity that brought you to it," Héloïse continued. "We will discuss your correction tomorrow.

"For now," she added as Catherine turned to go back to the dormitory, "you can utilize your wakefulness in being of service. Go wash as much of yourself as you can and change into clean robes. Come to the infirmary when you are fit for Christian eyes."

"Yes, Mother," Catherine gulped. The water would be as cold as Lucifer's heart but worth enduring to find out what all this was about. In the brief glimpse, she had confirmed her guess that the man was Raynald. And, she was also certain that under his cloak had been the gleam of chain mail. But who had he brought for the nuns to take care of and why at such an hour?

Several icy minutes later she presented herself, shivering and damp, but clean, at the door of the infirmary.

Sister Thecla admitted her and then went out, back to her station. Catherine took a step into the room and stopped in astonishment.

Abbess Héloïse was sitting at the side of a bed on which lay a woman. Her head was swathed in bandages, her face swollen and dark with bruises. The arm that lay across the coverlet was also wrapped tightly, her fingers white and still. The two lay sisters who had carried her to the infirmary were just leaving with the litter.

"Come over here and sit down," Héloïse told her. "Sister Melisande is upstairs preparing the medicine she will need. It will take her a few more minutes. As long as you are awake, Catherine, I want you to remain here and give any help that is needed. I will send one of the other lay sisters also. Can you remain alert until Matins?"

"Yes, Mother." Suddenly Catherine felt the urge to yawn. She suppressed it as she brought her stool to the side of the bed. Hesitantly, she reached toward the injured woman's hand.

"It's the Countess Alys, isn't it?" she asked.

Héloïse nodded. "She was brutally attacked, as you can see, a few days ago as she was returning from a visit to her mother in Quincy. The count thought she could be better cared for here. He has the right. When she gave us lands five years ago, the countess specifically requested that she be allowed to retire to our convent someday or at least, if that were not possible, to be buried with us."

"You don't think she'll live?"

"It doesn't seem very likely," Héloïse answered. "She hasn't woken since she was found. Her arm was broken, the bones are splinters in her flesh. You can see how her face was battered. I understand that the rest of her body is also badly bruised."

The abbess bent over to tuck in the coverlet more securely. In the lamplight, Catherine saw the tears glitter.

"You should use the time to prepare rags to replace the bandages," Héloïse said steadily. "You may have to use them before anyone comes. The countess also miscarried as a result of this attack. The women at the castle haven't been able to stop the bleeding. Call Sister Melisande if you feel unequal to the task."

"I know what to do," Catherine assured her.

After Héloïse had left, Catherine sat staring at the unconscious woman. The little oil lamp cast shadows across the bed, making the bandages seem grotesque. Only the rasp of her breath showed that the Countess Alys still lived. Catherine took a cloth and dipped it in a cup of water mixed with vinegar. She pressed it against the woman's dry lips and dampened as much of her face as was visible. She felt so useless. There was nothing more she could do.

"*Sanctissime confessor Domini,*" she asked Saint Benedict. "*Monachorum pater et dux, Benedicte, intercede pro sua salute.*"

She started to stroke the uninjured hand, but at the first touch, Alys jerked away with a cry.

"Allder!" Her scream was harsh but weak, the words garbled through her battered face, a string of syllables Catherine couldn't understand, then, "*Harou!* No! Lord, lord! No!"

Nervously, Catherine tried to calm her. Alys would injure herself more if she didn't stop moving about. Catherine lifted the coverlet to smooth it. A red stain had blossomed like a rose onto the sheet. Catherine swallowed. She wasn't upset by the mess but she was terrified that she would jolt the countess while cleaning her and cause her to become worse.

As she stood staring down at the sheet and wondering if she should interrupt the infirmarian to ask for help, Catherine suddenly felt a tap on her shoulder.

"Arrp!" She inhaled a shriek and turned.

The woman standing behind her signed an apology, but she was clearly amused at Catherine's reaction.

"Paciana!" Catherine whispered. "I didn't hear you come in. I'm glad you're here; I need help changing her bedding."

The laughter in the lay sister's face vanished as she looked beyond Catherine to the woman on the bed. She closed her eyes a moment, blessed herself and then rolled up her sleeves and went to work.

Paciana's touch produced a much more soothing effect than Catherine's. The countess Alys lay still and limp while they moved her as gently as possible and peeled off the blood-soaked rags. The lay sister signed to Catherine when she needed help, and Catherine, for once, was quiet too, although her most frequent infraction was breaking the rule of silence. While Paciana lifted Alys, Catherine washed her and applied clean rags. No wonder the poor woman had miscarried, the bruises on her stomach were worse than those on her face. There were cuts, too, which ought to be cleansed.

"That's odd," Catherine said, forgetting silence again. "Look at this, Paciana. Do you see?"

The lay sister leaned over to look. A spasm of anger flashed across her face, then she took a deep breath and regained her customary calm. The body of the countess was ribboned with thin white lines of scars, along with raised welts of mishealed flesh.

"These wounds weren't made at the same time," Catherine continued. "There are bruises here that have almost healed and these marks on her legs and buttocks must be from something long ago. It looks as though she's been whipped, over and over. See how they overlap?"

Catherine felt a spasm of anger, too. But she didn't try to control it. Swiftly, she finished her job. The two women wrapped and settled the countess, Catherine's jaw set in fury. Who could have treated the poor woman so? She turned to the lay sister.

"Have you ever met the count of Tonnerre?" she asked.

Paciana shook her head.

Across the cloister the bell was ringing for Matins. Catherine washed her hands.

"You'll stay with her?" she asked.

Paciana nodded, then her fingers made the sign for the number seven and seven again. Catherine sighed.

"I know that one should forgive seventy times seven, but only those who sin against us. And the sinner should first repent, I think. Mine is a righteous anger, Paciana. The proud and haughty need to be brought low, especially the haughty count Raynald."

Catherine followed the sound of the bells to the chapel, but she stumbled often in her recitation of the office. The only thing she wanted to pray for was the swift smiting of the count of Tonnerre. What sort of man would beat his wife and then try to pass it off as the work of someone

else! They found her outside the castle! Who would believe that? Why would she have been travelling alone?
Where were her guards? Did Raynald think the nuns were
incapable of noticing the difference in the scars? Well, he
wouldn't be allowed to continue in his wicked schemes.
Mother Héloïse would learn of this.

The office of Matins flowed into Lauds, and from Lauds
until the office of Prime, at dawn, the sisters worked quietly by candlelight on sewing or study. Catherine usually
read for these hours, the most pleasant of the day for her.
But this morning she went over to the abbess's chair and,
kneeling next to it, whispered that she must speak with her
about the countess. At first Héloïse frowned, then she
whispered back.

"You may come to my room, after Prime. We can discuss it then fully."

When they had finished singing the office, Catherine
followed Héloïse to her room. The abbess sat down at a
table covered with papers, which she regarded wearily.
Catherine could tell they were not devotional reading without looking at them. Only the convent accounts caused the
abbess to look so tired. Héloïse picked one up and began
to read through it.

"Catherine," she said without looking up. "If we are
given the rights to berries and apples in the wood between
the convent and the monastery of Vauluisant, and fallen
trees for fire, but may not cut any standing trees and must
maintain the road through as well as leave all acorns for
the pigs belonging to the monks, do we have a profit or a
liability?"

She handed the paper to Catherine.

Catherine studied for a moment. "There isn't enough information here," she said at last. "How do we feed the
men who clear the road? What is the fruit harvest and who
gathers it? And how much damage do the pigs do?"

She gave the paper back.

"The pigs!" Héloïse exclaimed. "I knew I was forgetting something. They can turn a road into a morass in no
time at all. It would be our responsibility if a cart lost a
wheel or a horse stepped in a hole and broke its leg. And

we haven't even been given the tolls to that road. Prioress Astane felt there was something suspicious about this offer. Wait until we meet again with the prior of Vauluisant!"

She stopped. "But that's not why you've come. What is troubling you so that you felt the need to speak to me during the Great Silence?"

"Mother, I've found out something dreadful." Catherine told her what she had discovered.

Héloïse listened gravely.

"You are making a very serious accusation," she told Catherine. "What proof do you have that any of the wounds suffered by that poor woman were caused by the count?"

"Who else had the power to use her so severely for so long? Many of those scars were long ago healed over."

Héloïse began to gather up the accounts.

"I can think of many others, her parents or guardians. I don't remember all of her early history. I believe she has a mother and a stepfather. She may have been a recalcitrant child."

"Mother! No child is wicked enough to deserve such treatment!"

Catherine thought of her parents and how recalcitrant a child she had often been. She had endured her share of punishments, but no one had ever hurt her like that.

Héloïse nodded. "I agree. I am only pointing out that there may be other explanations for the scars. Some may even have been self-inflicted. She may have felt the need to subdue the flesh. I do not approve of that practice, either." She forestalled Catherine's objection. "I am simply putting forth another possibility."

Catherine was outargued, but not convinced. She shook her head.

"I understand what you are saying, Mother. I formed a conclusion without studying all possible rational hypotheses. But I feel I am right."

"Ah, my dearest Catherine," Héloïse smiled. "That is the worst fault of the human philosopher. When logic fails, we feel. Or we twist the logic to fit our emotions."

"Then I should ignore my feelings?" Catherine asked.

"Not at all." Héloïse turned back to her desk as she replied. "Often our feelings are sound. But you must analyze them fully and find a rational basis for them. If you can find none, then you must learn to put them aside. The dialectic I have taught you is not for use in the classroom alone. Just because you dislike Count Raynald is not good enough reason to assume he is a monster. You may go."

"Yes, Mother." Catherine waited. "Would you like me to come back before Compline and help with the accounts?"

"No, they can wait."

Héloïse piled up the stacks of papers with little interest. Under the accounts were a few pages of a letter. Catherine only glimpsed the salutation. *"Heloisae ancillarum dei, ductrici ac magistrae . . . frater Petrus humilis Cluniacensium abbas, salutem a deo . . ."* Peter, abbot of Cluny. Why would he be writing Héloïse?

No doubt you feel you should be informed of all business between the abbey of Cluny and the Paraclete? Catherine's voices said scornfully.

Feeling well-chastised and completely frustrated, Catherine turned to go.

"Catherine."

She stopped. "Yes, Mother?"

"Whatever horrible things have happened to Countess Alys, you have my word that, as long as she is under my care, I will see to it that no one ever hurts her again."

Catherine closed her eyes and swallowed hard.

"Thank you, Mother Héloïse."

But her heart still cried for the countess and her mind still insisted that whoever had hurt her should not be left to God alone.

Two

The coast of France, Feast of the Annunciation
to the Blessed Virgin,
Monday, March 25, 1140

Forthon nu min hyge hweorfeth ofer hretherlocan
min modsefa mid mereflode
ofer hwæles ethel hweorfeth wide,
eorthan sceatas, cymeth eft to me
gifre ond groedig gielleth anfloga
hweteth on hwæweg hrether unwearnum
ofer holma gelagu.

And still my mind wanders within me. My spirit, with
the tide across the whale road, wanders far upon the
earth's surface, and comes back to me eager and greedy,
the lone flier calls, inciting the unwary heart on to the
whale road and across the wide sea.

—The Seafarer 11.58–64

dering from the cold, swam the boat out past the breakers.
They hoisted themselves aboard and rowed back to the
ship, ready to sail on for Boulogne when the tide turned.

Edgar didn't look back as he left the channel behind him
and strode inland to the village. He paid no attention to his
fellow passengers, either. They had spent most of the trip
moaning and praying. His excellent health and obvious en-
joyment of the rolling of the ship had not endeared himself
to them. He shifted the books to his other shoulder and felt
once again for the roll of cloth tied about his waist. Sewn
in it were thirty bezants, pure gold. Apart from the books,
they were his entire fortune. He wondered how his brother,
Egbert, had come by them. Like many things concerning
his brother's activities, it was better not to know. They were
his now, honestly acquired, a bride-price to prove his worth
to Catherine's father, a merchant more impressed by ability
and moveable wealth than lineage, especially when the lineage consisted of land in a country at the northern end of the
world and a claim to a title usurped by the Norman invaders three generations ago.

He fixed his thoughts inland, down through Flanders and
Picardy to the edge of Champagne, to the Paraclete, where,
he prayed, Catherine still waited for him. He had been gone
less than four months, from Paris to Scotland and back
again, resenting every moment wasted in waiting for tides
or safe passage through the war in England. There had been
no time to send or receive word, but he refused even to consider that she had changed her decision. His step quickened.
His father had raged at his plans and his stepmother had
warned him against competing with God for a woman's affections. But he had placed his faith in Catherine, in the
promise she had given him, and, yes, in the certainty that
the intense need he felt to be with her was returned.

Thinking of Catherine made him feel more wobbly than
any ship could and he had an intense need for a long gulp
of beer or even the sharp pear cider they fermented in Picardy. Edgar was glad to see the roofs of the town of Saint-
Valéry and to remember that hard by the church was a fine
inn which specialized in slaking the thirst of wandering
scholars and pilgrims.

The inn was ancient, the dirt floor swept down well below the level of the street. Edgar could imagine Roman soldiers sitting at these same plank tables and speculating on the chances of invading Britain. He knew that soldiers of William of Normandy had drunk there seventy-five years ago, waiting for the order for their own invasion of England. But the soup was hot and the cider cheap and none of the innkeepers of the last thousand years had allowed politics to interrupt business.

Edgar sniffed his way through the windowless room to the hearth, handed over his money, filled his bowl and mug and trusted that his shins would find an empty stool where he could sit until his eyes adjusted to the gloom.

"Here, man. You can sit next to me." A hand guided him to a resting place. "You just off the boat from England?"

Edgar downed the cider. "This is the first drink I've had in two days that didn't taste of bilge and tar."

He pulled out his spoon and started on the soup. His companion went back to his meal. Edgar relaxed. Only thieves and *trigoleres* made idle conversation with strangers.

"*Salve, amice!* Going to Paris with those books?" another voice startled him.

Edgar amended his thought; thieves, degenerates and vagabond students. He turned to the group at the end of the table.

"Going *back* to Paris," he told them, to forestall any of the wild tales gullible new students were treated to.

"Anything good in your book pack?" the boy nearest him asked. He couldn't have been more than sixteen. Edgar, at twenty-five, felt quite paternal toward him.

"Not really," Edgar said. "The *Letters* of Hildebert, a Macrobius, Seneca's *Naturales Quaestiones* and a *Life* of Saint Cuthbert."

The boy groaned, "Just the sort of plodding stuff my master wants me to study. I'd have carried it to the bottom of the sea."

Edgar laughed and got up for another draught of cider. When he returned to the table, the two young students had gone outside to relieve themselves and then to try to follow the innkeeper's directions to the nearest brothel. One man was left. He looked up briefly as Edgar sat. Something about his face in the flicker of the lamplight was familiar.

"Don't I know you?" Edgar asked. "Did we meet in Paris?"

The man looked up again, startled. "Shouldn't you have tried that speech with the boys?" he replied.

Edgar cringed. Every father in Christendom warned his sons about the prostitutes and their procurers who pretended to be from one's home town and then fleeced the poor homesick students of all they had.

"Sorry," he muttered. "For a moment you looked like someone else. I meant no offense."

"None taken," the man answered. "What's the news from England?"

"The truce with King David still holds," Edgar answered, "or I wouldn't have been able to cross from the north. But King Stephen has a talent for creating enemies. He made Philippe d'Harcourt bishop of Salisbury for about a week before Bishop Henry of Winchester stopped him and appointed his own man. I don't see how the king hopes to maintain his authority. After all, if Stephen's own brother, Henry, is against him, who will be next? I forget who's bishop now. It's nothing to me, in any case. No one has suggested putting a Saxon in the see again, just another bloody Norman."

"Don't glare at me!" the man laughed. "I'm Breton. It was your people who drove mine out of Britain five hundred years ago. No one's suggested giving anything back to us, either."

Edgar looked at him more closely.

"I had a friend from Britanny once," he said. "A stone carver named Garnulf. He came from Le Pallet."

"You knew Garnulf?" The man stared at him doubtfully. "What are you called?"

"Edgar, of Wedderlie, in Scotland," Edgar answered. "And you?"

The man hesitated, then spoke. "I am also of Le Pallet. Garnulf did the altar carvings for my uncle, Dagobert, when he had the chapel rebuilt about ten years ago. He went on to work on Abbot Suger's church, I heard, and died in a fall from one of the towers."

Edgar nodded. "I was there."

The man studied his face carefully. Then, to Edgar's relief, he changed the subject.

"I'm on my way to Paris with those two nurslings. You may join us, if you like," he said. "I have a mule that can bear the weight of a few more books."

"I had hoped to travel with a better-armed party," Edgar began.

"It's almost Holy Week," the man reminded him. "The roads will be full of pilgrims and merchants going to the shrines and faires. I've arranged to join a group of Flemish cloth sellers."

Edgar felt the weight of the gold against his skin and thought of cut throats. But then he thought of Catherine. He wondered if he could have one coin made into gold bells for her ears. How they would shine against her dark hair!

Suddenly he felt hotter than Saint Lawrence on the gridiron. "If you're leaving at once," he said, "I'll come with you. I need to be in Paris as soon as possible."

"Neither of my charges have enough coin for more than a small taste of the delights of the flesh. They should be back shortly. If we leave before noon, we should be able to take advantage of the hospitality of the monks of Saint-Riquier tonight. With luck and good weather, we can celebrate Palm Sunday at Saint-Germain-des-Prés."

Edgar agreed. The man returned to his own dish and Edgar concentrated on finishing his soup. Damn. He hated making a fool of himself, but the man *had* seemed familiar. Even his tricks of speech and his cool disdain had reminded Edgar of someone. Not Garnulf, though. The poor old stone carver had been a model of gentleness and his tongue full of the rough gallic speech of the Bretons.

His thoughts were interrupted by the return of the two young students. They tumbled into the inn like half-grown puppies, bumping against the tables and benches.

"They wouldn't take our money," one whined. "Said the *jaels* were all busy with the knights from that ship. We have to wait until they're finished."

"Then you'll have to wait a few more days," their keeper told them. "We're leaving at once for Saint-Riquier. But no doubt the monks will provide more edifying entertainment."

"But As—tro—labe!" The boy's whine rose as his voice squeaked in frustration.

Astrolabe gave a quick glance toward Edgar, saw the gleam of recognition at his name, and sighed.

"Get your things and meet me at the stables," he ordered. "Are you coming with us?" he asked Edgar.

Edgar nodded, his face expressionless. Inside he was grinning, though. Now he knew where he'd seen that face. Edgar had spent the past few years attending the lectures of Master Abelard. He should have seen it at once. Astrolabe's face was a younger version, not worn by adversity, sorrow and illness, but with the same high cheekbones and long nose, the same air of assuredness. No wonder he didn't want to give his name. Only one couple in France had been so uncaring of convention as to name their son after a navigational device, Héloïse and Abelard. Edgar wondered how he'd have felt if his father had named him Protractor or Anvil.

He got up, wiped out his bowl and spoon and put them back in his pack. He filled his cup once more, for the journey. Although intensely curious about his new travelling companion, he vowed to wait for the man to talk about himself. Astrolabe must have passed his life answering the same questions that had leaped to Edgar's mind. What was it like for all the world to know that your father had seduced your mother and been castrated for it by her furious family? Since Abelard and Héloïse had married after his birth, Edgar supposed that also made Astrolabe a bastard. Well, he'd known plenty of those, many of whom had legitimate bloodlines longer than his arm.

Perhaps it was only the striking resemblance to his father that made Edgar warm to him, but he felt that the time spent studying Astrolabe would be worthwhile. He began to look forward to the journey.

The conversation on the road dwelt on general topics; the unrest in England, in Toulouse, the Holy Land. The possibility of the battle for the English throne affecting business in France. One could count on feuds and minor wars for discussion with strangers. The boys, still sulking over their missed opportunity for debauchery, wanted to have a proper philosophical debate. Astrolabe gave them the old rhetorical question, "Is a pig led to market held by the man or the rope?" They dove into it as if the solution were of vital importance. Astrolabe fell back to walk with Edgar.

"I shouldn't laugh," Edgar admitted. "Ten years ago I was as green and as much a *bricon* as they."

"And now that you are old and learned, you know that to the pig it doesn't matter a fig what's holding him," Astrolabe said. "For no matter how he travels, the end of the journey is still the butcher's knife." He sighed. "You wouldn't be one of those acolytes who buzz around my father like bluebottles, would you?"

"I've been known to," Edgar admitted. "How is he? There were rumblings against his *Theologia Christiana* last autumn, but I've heard nothing more. Has something happened since I left in January?"

"Only the usual outcries about his writing, that his application of logic to the study of dogma is unsound, even heretical. He has made many enemies. The canons of Saint-Victor are not fond of him, as I'm sure you know, nor are the monks of Saint-Denis," Astrolabe told him. "And some Cistercians find his theories bordering on blasphemy. I am more concerned about his health, though; that and his insistence on finding a place to publicly debate Bernard of Clairvaux on these recent charges."

"The master would defeat Abbot Bernard easily," Edgar said. "That's nothing to concern yourself with. He's bested every teacher in Paris."

"Your words are confident, but not your tone." Astrolabe glanced ahead at the boys, who were still wrangling over the pig. "You know what I fear, don't you?"

Edgar dodged the pile the mule had just left in the road.

"Master Abelard and Abbot Bernard are like spring and autumn constellations," he admitted. "They don't belong in the same sky."

"Yes, my father will argue brilliantly, using every rhe-

torical device, but only the most brilliant of his listeners
will understand him," Astrolabe said. "Bernard speaks
with the mouth of a poet and the heart of a saint. He'd
make the devil himself weep. Even my mother said that,
on his visit to the Paraclete, he preached like an angel.
How can one counter passion with logic? They have no
meeting place."

Edgar didn't answer at first. If ever passion and logic
met, it was in the person of Peter Abelard. But he was not
the one to argue the point with Abelard's son.

"So you're going to Paris to convince him to abandon
his challenge?" he said.

Astrolabe snorted. "Hardly. There's only one person in the
world who might do that. No, I'm going to ask him to accompany me to see Mother. I've written her about it and she
agrees. She says it would be fitting for the three of us, just
once, to be together at the celebration of the Resurrection."

"Oddly enough," Edgar said. "I was also planning on
being at the Paraclete for Easter."

Astrolabe showed no surprise.

"There are many who would come from farther than
Scotland to hear my father preach an Easter sermon. And
many," he added, "who would travel even farther to silence him. I shall be glad of your company."

Edgar wrapped his cloak more tightly. Until today, all his
thoughts had been for Catherine, of earning the right to
marry her and then doing so with all due speed. He suddenly
wondered if she had been so single-minded. This news
would have been brought to the Paraclete long ago, and just
as much as he, she was a disciple of Peter Abelard. Would
she put aside her devotion to him and, even more, to
Héloïse, just because he had finally come to claim her?

The road to Paris stretched on interminably.

Catherine had volunteered to sit by the Countess Alys for
the length of the Great Silence, from Compline at sunset, to
Prime. She felt that somehow the time of quiet and darkness
was more dangerous than the bustle of the day. Perhaps that
was why the blessed Saint Benedict had made the night of-

fice the longest. The sleeping world needed more protection from the servants of Evil, from the Angel of Death.

Despite all their efforts, a faint, nauseating scent was starting in the swollen broken arm. The bone had been snapped through the skin. There was no way to stop the infection once it had started. Catherine knew that Alys would lose the arm, if not her life. Her attacker was not a spirit sneaking through the night, though. It had been a human demon who walked proudly under the sun.

Her anger billowed inside her. On the other side of the cot, Paciana watched her. Catherine felt her gaze and looked up, blushing. Paciana raised her thumb to her lips and moved her fingers slightly, then signed three and six.

"Oh, Paciana," Catherine said, then looked about guiltily for Sister Bertrada. She smiled and kissed her fingertips then blew on her opened palm, thanking the lay sister.

Psalm Thirty-six: "Do not fret because of the wicked . . . *spera in Domino et fac bonum.*" That was easy for Paciana, her faith was firm and she never did anything but good. It wasn't so easy for someone without a natural leaning toward docility. All the same, Catherine recited the words under her breath and tried to push her anger aside.

Count Raynald had neither returned since he had left his wife six days before nor sent to know if she still lived. Alys's mother had not come from Quincy, only a short ride away. She lay here dying among strangers.

Why does this matter so to you? her voices asked. *Christian pity is well and good, but making yourself her defender and chief mourner is arrogant.*

Catherine shook her head. She didn't know why the plight of the poor woman had affected her so strongly. Perhaps it was her own uncertainty. She was forsaking this place of order and peace for marriage, for the world. When Edgar had been beside her, it had seemed the only choice, but now. . . . She tried to sign her thoughts to Paciana, but it took so long and she was so clumsy at it, she finally gave up and whispered.

"It's only that she's here alone, no family, no one familiar."

Paciana shook her head, her arm moved in a circle, encompassing them all.

"Yes, or course, we all love her as one who would be our sister in Christ, but still . . ."

Paciana sighed and gestured again, with some reluctance.

"Me . . . secular . . . blood . . . sister," Catherine interpreted. "You're her real sister?"

Her voice had gone up. Paciana leaned across the bed and put her fingers firmly over Catherine's lips. She looked as stern as Wrath, itself.

Her hands shaking, Catherine signed, "Then how can you forgive what's been done to her?"

The lay sister smiled sadly and bent to kiss the countess's forehead.

"God forgives," she signed. "I accept. Say nothing."

"If you wish," Catherine nodded reluctantly.

But why not? Mother Héloïse and Prioress Astane must know already. Paciana couldn't have been admitted to the convent without the approval of her family. It struck Catherine that she knew the background of every one of the other sisters. Many came from local families; some were part of the original group that were driven with Héloïse from Argenteuil. Abelard's own nieces, Agate and Agnes, were here, too. Only a few were like her, drawn from farther away by the Paraclete's reputation for learning. Paciana had always seemed so much a part of the convent that Catherine had never thought of her anywhere else. But now she wondered. She had presumed Paciana was not of the nobility. But if she were Alys's sister, she must be, unless she were illegitimate, and that alone wouldn't be enough to keep her from a proper place in the convent. But, if Paciana were wellborn, then why hadn't she become a choir nun, to copy books and sing the office? Lay sisters were the drudges of the convent. They did the laundry and carried the water buckets.

The only answer Catherine could think of was that Paciana had been ordered to perform some long, hard penance.

But what could she have done? And why was she so clearly terrified of anyone knowing that she was sister to Countess Alys?

Three

The Paraclete,
Friday, March 29, 1140

*Iusto enim vita ista carcer est: mors huius carceris solutio. Nemo
enim his adeo iustus est: ut perfectam possit hic consequi
iusticiam.*

For the just, life itself is a prison: death is the solution
to this prison. Truly, no one on earth is so just that
he is able to attain perfect justice.

—Serlo of Savigny,
Sermons

*H*oly Week was fast approaching; the time of darkness and fasting would soon be over. Even the weather brightened. The constant drizzle gave way to sunshowers with dazzling rainbows or brief curtains of huge, lazy snowflakes that fell glistening onto the green shoots in the garden before melting into the soft earth.

Catherine hardly noticed the world waking up around her. She moved through the patterned days, drawing comfort from the familiar prayers and duties, but her mind was always in the infirmary. Even her fears for Edgar were pushed aside for this present pain.

Paciana must know who beat Alys before, she thought for the hundredth time. *She ought to tell us. One can bring a criminal to justice and still forgive him. It would be for the good of his soul to have him face his wickedness now, while he can still repent.*

But when Catherine tried to question her further, Paciana refused even to sign. Her eyes stayed focused on her work, her hands busy sweeping or scrubbing.

In desperation, Catherine went to her friend Emilie,

whose family was connected in one way or another with most of the nobility of Champagne, Burgundy, Blois and Lorraine. She would know, if anyone did. The only difficulty was that, while Catherine had been gone the previous autumn, Emilie had taken her final vows. As someone who was no longer even a novice, but more of a special boarder, Catherine had little to do with the choir nuns. The only time she was with them was in groups, in the refectory or the oratory, and in neither place was there opportunity for private talk.

Except on Saturday. That was the day for hair washing. If she volunteered to help, pouring the warm water and towelling the short curls dry, she might have a few moments to arrange a longer meeting.

"Wash hair?" Sister Bertrada pursed her lips in annoyance. "Do you even know how? You'd probably rub soap in everyone's eyes and leave tangles impossible to comb out. The younger girls get very upset at that."

Catherine stifled a sigh. She had forgotten about the students like herself and the novices, whose hair had yet to be cut. "I would be very careful, Sister. I have not done my share of manual labor since I returned."

"As if you ever did." But Sister Bertrada gave grudging, suspicious permission.

So Catherine, dressed in a shift and apron, with her sleeves tied above the elbow, spent Saturday morning being splashed with suds by squealing fourteen- and fifteen-year-olds. Despite her initial reluctance, she found herself smiling and splashing back. She and her sister, Agnes, had once played so, bent over the sink at the house in Paris, their long hair dripping puddles on the rushes. Outside, they could hear cursing as the soapy water ran down the pipe onto the boots of some passerby. A long time ago, it seemed.

The choir nuns came last, quietly as befitted their rank. It only took a moment for each shorn head to be washed. Catherine rubbed the towel briskly over Emilie's blonde cap.

"I must speak with you," she whispered.

It was like Emilie that she wasted no time with inconsequentials.

"After None, I will be g ... grinding herbs in the infirmary," she answered, her voice shaking with the energy of Catherine's drying. "I think I'm d ... done now. Thank you."

The apothecary room, where the infirmarian, Sister Melisande, slept, was upstairs from the infirmary proper. On one wall were the shelves of oils and powders from distant lands that were bought each year at the faire at Troyes. Hanging from the ceiling were herbs grown and dried at the convent. On a long table in the center of the room were clay bowls and wooden pestles, as well as vials for measuring. When Catherine entered, Emilie was bent over these, grinding at something which scraped against the bowl in a way that set Catherine's teeth on edge.

"Will you do this a while?" Emilie asked. "I'm trying to make a powder of cinnamon and eggshells to mix with fennel and pomegranate juice for Alys."

"What will that do?" Catherine asked as she took the pestle and went to work.

"Fennel may help bring the fever down and I hope the rest will keep the bleeding from starting again," Emilie answered. "Oh, that's better. My arm was aching."

"Emilie, do you know who attacked the countess?"

Emilie took down a bottle labeled πεπλισ. Catherine recognized it as one that her father had brought. She tried to remember enough of the Greek Mother Héloïse had taught her to sound out the word. Emilie opened it and sniffed before adding it to another bowl.

"Walter of Grancy, of course," she finally answered. "Everyone knows that. He and Raynald have been feuding for years."

"But this wasn't the first time," Catherine insisted. "She's been beaten before."

"Who hasn't?" Emilie didn't look up from her work.

"Not like this, Emilie." The cinnamon shattered under Catherine's anger. "Not over and over to leave scars, laced across each other. What do you know of her family?"

"Her father married twice," Emilie said after a moment's thought. "The first marriage lasted only a few years. His wife died quite suddenly. There was a child, I think, who also died. Alys is from the second marriage. After he died, Alys's mother married again."

Catherine sorted it out. Paciana must have been very young when her mother had died, but why would Emilie think she had died, too? She opened her mouth to ask, then held her tongue with difficulty, remembering her promise to Paciana.

"Mother Héloïse said that Alys's property came from her father's family," Catherine told her. "What happened to the dower of his first wife?"

"I don't know." Emilie stopped stirring and closed her eyes, trying to trace out all the family connections. "Let me think. Alys's father was a castellan of Count Thibault. He had control of several towns when he died and I'm sure much of the land was heritable. I don't know much about the first wife. She died before I was born. I think she was some relation to Count Thibault, which was why they did so well. I remember my mother mentioning that the count gave her the tithes of five mills and a vineyard near Troyes as a wedding gift. Alys's father may have kept them or they may have reverted to Thibault. Mother Héloïse might know, or Sister Bietriz. She's niece to Thibault's former seneschal, André de Baudement, you know."

"I had forgotten that," Catherine said. "Perhaps I'll ask her. It's odd that a count like Raynald, with his connections, would marry the daughter of a castellan."

"If enough land or money came with her, and if the connection with Count Thibault were strong enough, I don't suppose Raynald would care."

"No, I suppose not." Catherine was doubtful. The count of Tonnerre struck her as a man proud of his lineage. And Tonnerre was not a poor area. Still . . . "I wonder what she did bring to the marriage and where it goes if she dies childless."

Emilie shrugged. "I no longer have an interest in such things."

Catherine bent over the mortar in embarrassment. "I'm sorry to ask you about them. It is not appropriate to your new status to be drawn into gossip."

"Do you imagine yourself a tool of Satan?" Emilie laughed. "I will confess in chapter this week that I have been speaking idly and take my penance. But I don't think you asked for idle reasons. And I am your true friend. I always will be. Do you think my taking the veil could change that?"

"I am leaving soon," Catherine said. "We won't be sisters after all. I thought it might make a difference."

Emilie leaned across the table and gently pushed a loose curl back under Catherine's scarf.

"We will always be sisters," she said.

Edgar, Astrolabe and the two Norman students entered Paris on the morning of Palm Sunday and the streets were already crowded with people come to take part in the procession. All of them seemed to be heading toward the Île. The travellers pushed their way down the Rue Saint-Martin and across the Grand Pont, letting the crowd carry them along.

"Where is Master Abelard staying?" Edgar asked.

"With the monks at Sainte-Geneviève," Astrolabe told him. "Aren't you coming with us?"

"I have to see someone first," Edgar said. "When do you think we'll leave for the Paraclete?"

"Tomorrow, Tuesday at the latest. It depends on the weather and my father's health."

"I'll find you this evening," Edgar promised.

"Very well," Astrolabe agreed. "Come along, children," he added to his charges. "I'm going to deliver you to your new keeper."

He did look as though he were leading a pair of tame bears. The boys, fresh from the country outside London, stumbled through the crush of people, gawking at the pilgrims, tumblers and hawkers of trinkets and not noticing where they stepped. Astrolabe drew them along behind him. In a moment, they were lost among the crowd.

The procession moved on across the Île, turning left to

the churches of Saint-Christophe, then Saint-Etienne, to conclude at Sainte-Marie-Nôtre-Dame. Before the crowd turned, Edgar slipped away and went into the Juiverie. Unlike the other streets, the area around the synagogue was quiet. A few men, loaded with parcels, walked purposefully, glancing about with every step. When they saw Edgar, each faltered a second, taking his measure and judging the likelihood of his using a concealed knife. Satisfying themselves that he was harmless, they continued on their way.

It took Edgar a while to find the right door. He realized with some embarrassment that he had never entered through the front of the house, at least not while conscious. He hoped they would receive him. He hoped they were there. The whole street had the look of a place shut down for the winter, or until some great storm passed.

At first there was no response to his knock. Then he heard a swish of skirts upon the rushes and a narrow slot was pushed back. A brown eye focused on him then looked beyond, as if checking for companions.

"What do you want?" It was a woman's voice, young but trying to sound old and brusk.

"My name is Edgar," he said gently. "I'm a friend of Solomon, of this house, and of Hubert LeVendeur. I've just returned to Paris and wished for word of them."

His stomach tightened as he spoke. He didn't give a rat's ass about Solomon and Hubert. Catherine! He wanted to shout it. Tell me if Catherine is safe. Tell me that everything is as it was, that we are still betrothed, and I'll leave you in peace!

But he only stood quietly at the door as the eye examined him once again. The slot closed.

It seemed he stood there for days as other eyes watched him from slots up and down the narrow street. Finally, the door opened a few inches and a hand pulled him in.

He was suddenly smothered in a soft, maternal bosom then pushed to arm's length. Catherine's aunt Johannah greeted him.

"You look better than the last time you were here," she laughed. "How's the arm?"

"Fine," he gasped. He had not expected to be welcomed. He straightened and bowed properly.

"May the Lord bless all who dwell here," he said, remembering at the last minute not to go on to the Virgin and the saints.

"And you," Johannah smiled again. "Come in, wash the road from your hands and face. I will have Dulce bring you some wine and cheese. Eliazar is out, but I expect him soon."

It was hard to endure the customs of civilization when operating on basic feelings, but Edgar managed to survive until Catherine's uncle Eliazar returned.

"Yes," Edgar answered him. "It is good to see you again, also. I am fully recovered, thanks to your kind attentions. My family is well. My trip was uneventful, except . . . I was able to sell my land to provide a bridal gift. Please tell me, do I still have a bride?"

Eliazar leaned back in his chair and laughed, his stomach shaking. He ran a hand through his beard and his expression softened to sympathy.

"As far as I know," he said, "my brother has not changed his mind about allowing you to marry his daughter. Of course, those nuns may give you a fight for her soul. But why don't you simply go ask Hubert? Why come here and now, of all times?"

Then Edgar realized why the houses were all locked and barred. He had been so caught up in his own life that he had missed the obvious. This was Holy Week. Every day from now until Easter, good Christians were reminded in sermon, play and procession of Christ's passion and death. More than any other time of the year, the ancient guilt and continued intransigence of the Jews in their midst was made apparent to them.

"I'm sorry," he said. "I didn't think . . ."

Eliazar shrugged. "Why should you? You are not the one they throw stones and fishheads at. Still, you could have gone to my brother's. He has made a reputation as a good Christian. No one in Paris knows he was born a Jew."

Edgar hung his head. He felt like a just-thrashed schoolboy. In his part of the world, Jews were mythical beings inhabiting only the Old Testament or Easter sermons. He still found it difficult to associate them with the people of Paris who looked and acted just like everyone else. He had forgotten the shame of Hubert LeVendeur's family connections and remembered only the kindness they had shown him when his life was in danger.

Why had he come to Eliazar first? The reasons that came into his mind could not be spoken. Because I felt more likely to be taken in here. Because I wanted someone to be on my side when I see Catherine's family. Because your wife reminds me of my stepmother and it comforts me to see her. He felt like an idiot and knew that whatever he said would cause laughter or offense. He took a deep breath and decided to tell the truth.

"I didn't want to appear at Catherine's door like a beggar or an abductor," he explained. "Also, I wasn't sure how I would be received there. Perhaps Hubert has decided that Catherine should remain in the convent, if only for her mother's sake. You know her mother believes that Catherine has risen bodily into heaven and is now a saint?"

Eliazar nodded. "His wife's condition is one of Hubert's greatest sorrows. Yes, it would be difficult if you appeared at family dinner. Madeleine would not take kindly to your intentions."

"Exactly," Edgar said. "If Hubert were not there, I didn't know how I would explain myself, or to whom. But you know me."

"Yes," Eliazar smiled. "We have had a short but illuminating acquaintance. For most of it, you were unconscious, as I recall."

Edgar grimaced. "Yes, that's true. I suppose I came here because I know you. You were kind to me. I would have gone directly to the Paraclete and met Catherine there, avoiding the whole problem," he added, "but I don't want to be accused of abduction."

"Very commendable." Eliazar smiled. "Especially since they would not be likely to let you anywhere near my niece without her father's permission. Well then, as far as I know, my brother is in Paris. Madeleine is at Vielleten-

euse with Catherine's brother and his family and so safely
out of the way. If you want word of Catherine, or a formal
contract made up, I think you should go see Hubert. I
would send a messenger to him, but I won't risk anyone
this week."

"I understand," Edgar got up. "Thank you."

Johannah came in just as he was leaving. "Are you going without eating? We do allow Christians at our table."

"You have given me something better than food," Edgar
said. "I will not intrude upon you further."

When he had gone, Johannah turned to her husband.

"That boy is still in love with Catherine," she said.

"And what's wrong with that?" Eliazar asked.

"Love should come after marriage, not before," she answered firmly. "It's something that happens in spite of
knowing a person's worst habits. Putting it first will only
cause trouble."

"If you feel that way, I'm very glad you didn't love me
when we got married."

Johannah patted Eliazar's stomach. "You foolish man,
I've loved you since I was six years old."

Eliazar shook his head. "Then I hope you will forgive
me, I've only loved you since you were ten."

Johannah sighed. "Those poor children, from opposite
ends of the world. It's a miracle they even met. I hope
nothing prevents their happiness."

"My dearest, that's what life does," he answered sadly.
"I only hope they taste a little joy before things go
wrong."

Despite Eliazar's advice, Edgar went in the opposite direction from Hubert LeVendeur's house at the Grève on the
northern bank of the river. Instead he crossed the Petit
Pont and headed west, to Sainte-Geneviève. On the other
side of the Seine the crowds were rowdier, younger, much
more drunk. He pulled his hood far down over his face
and elbowed his way through. He could feel hands groping
him, hunting for a purse, he hoped. He had none. He had
sent the books and his pack on with Astrolabe. He felt a
sudden thud against his side, as if someone had thrown a

rock, but in this crush it was impossible. A voice muttered, *"Aversier ou serjens? Par le cors Saint Omer! Fils a batart avoutre!"*

Edgar looked down in time to see a knife flash away from him, the tip bent. He rubbed his side. There was a tear in his *chainse* that had slit the cloth underneath. He could feel the smooth gold revealed. He covered it with his hand and wrapped his cloak more tightly. With renewed energy, he shoved himself away from his assailant and hurried on, repeating under his breath, *"Deo gratias, Mariae gratias!"* over and over.

"And thank you, too, Egbert," he added. "For paying me in good thick bezants."

By the time he reached Sainte-Geneviève, his side was aching fiercely. He would have one beautiful bruise from this, but it made him shaky to think how close he had come to having his stomach gutted. He had passed twice through an England in the middle of civil war and had not come so close to death.

As he climbed the steps to the abbey, he began to wonder about it. The man had not tried to cut a purse. He had thrust at his left side, under the rib cage. He had wanted to murder him in the crowd and be gone. Why? Edgar felt a cold hand on his neck and shuddered violently, turning. There was no one there.

This was insane, Edgar told himself. There was no reason for someone to single him out for murder. He had no importance. His family's feuds were confined to the area between Northumbria and Edinburgh. It was unlikely anyone would follow him here for revenge. Apart from a difference of opinion with Catherine's uncle Roger, now mercifully dead, he had made no enemies that he knew of. His attacker was most likely mad, someone with a grudge against all clerics. Perhaps a student had seduced his wife or cheated him at dice. It was unnerving and painful, but nothing to become morbid about. Cities bred madness; it was a well-known fact.

Astrolabe was sitting by the fire in the monastery hostel. The bag of books and a smaller sack of clothes and writing tools were beside him. Edgar shook himself, forcing the fear from his limbs. There was no point in recounting the tale. Certainly not here, at least, where his explanation for being saved by his belt of gold coins might be overheard.

"What are your plans? Are we leaving soon?" Edgar asked Astrolabe, as he went through the sack for his drinking cup. "Is there any ale?"

"The barrel is in the corner. There's a monk guarding it," Astrolabe answered. "My father wants to leave at first light tomorrow."

Edgar stopped in his quest for a drink. Astrolabe seemed as upset as he was himself. "That worries you?"

Astrolabe rubbed his forehead. "He is much worse. He's gaunt as if on a perpetual fast. His skin is some part red, some part pale as your own. He barely has the strength to stand."

"Is he well enough to ride the mule?"

Astrolabe frowned. "I have no idea. It certainly is the proper mount for an abbot and he clings to the perquisites of his office. He has little more." He covered his face with both hands. "I just don't know if he could even stand that much jolting. Which would anger my mother more, if I let him use the last of his strength to reach her or if I risked his dying where she could not reach him?"

"I haven't met your mother," Edgar said. "But I do know Master Abelard. The decision will be his."

"Exactly." A hand descended heavily onto Edgar's shoulder. At first he thought it was a blow of reprimand, then he realized that, if he moved, Abelard would fall. Edgar looked around slowly. His eyes widened in shock.

In the four months he had been gone, Abelard had aged ten years, it seemed. His hair was nearly white and the skin was stretched over the bones of his face like leather on a new drum. The hand gripping Edgar's shoulder, however, was iron strong.

"I will spend Easter at the Paraclete," he announced. "It is my duty to see to the welfare of my daughters in Christ. Then, I must see the archbishop of Sens."

"Father . . . !" Astrolabe began. Then he stopped and shook his head in resignation. "Then I'm going to see about getting you a horse. The mule has too uneven a gait.

And don't make any objection," he added as he got up and put on his cloak. "I may not have your gift for argument, but I'm as stubborn as you and Mother put together."

Abelard eased himself onto the stool Astrolabe had vacated. He smiled at him fondly.

"I think a horse would be an excellent idea," he said. "Thank you, son."

His agreement seemed to alarm Astrolabe even more. Muttering that the Day of Judgement must surely be at hand, he went out.

Edgar finally went for his drink, getting another for Master Abelard. When he returned, he found the master staring blankly into the fire. He roused himself to take the offered cup.

"Do you ever see images in flames?" he asked Edgar.

Startled, Edgar answered, "No, never."

Abelard sighed. "Neither do I. God grants me no such visions. I see only what logic and common sense tell me is there. It might be better if I saw dragons or visions of damned souls. Instead, I see only something burning to create warmth. One would think a heretic would feel some premonition upon regarding fire."

Edgar looked at the glowing coals and tried to decide if he was supposed to see something or not. After a few minutes, Abelard spoke again, in a different tone.

"So, are you still determined to steal away one of Héloïse's charges for the trials of married life?"

Edgar grinned. "Yes, Master, if she'll still have me."

"I will not lecture you on the subject again," Abeleard assured him. "Although the ability to enjoy carnal union has been taken from me, I remember it well enough and know the force with which it can overcome us."

"Neither of us has taken any other vows," Edgar reminded him. "It isn't the easiest road to salvation, I know, but . . ."

"You intend to marry this woman, don't you?" Abelard asked sharply. "You intend to live with her and honor her and engender children upon her who will be raised in the faith. Is that correct?"

"Yes, of course," Edgar answered, though he hadn't actually thought too far beyond the initial consummation as yet.

"Then I see no reason for you to alter your plans. The apostle would not have told couples to pay each other the marriage debt if it were a sin. I believe that no such natural pleasure of the flesh, such as that which is necessary to continue the human race, should be called a sin. Nor should it be considered a fault if we take pleasure from the act in marriage when the pleasure is unavoidable."

"I remember your lecture on that, Master," Edgar said. "So you feel that I should not consider it a sin if I prefer marriage to burning."

"Precisely," Abelard replied. He set down his cup, serious again. "I wonder if that is among the list of heresies the former abbot of Saint-Thierry is making from my writings."

"I don't understand this new controversy." Edgar said fiercely. "Haven't they persecuted you enough? After Soissons, didn't they realize how ridiculous these charges of heresy were?"

"That was many years ago," Abelard answered. "Since then, I have achieved even more respect and renown for my theological studies. Little minds fear me. They are in terror of the influence I might have. My books are read even in Rome. William of Saint-Thierry was once my friend. He must know my faith is as strong and orthodox as his own. But I intend to settle this matter once and for all."

"How?" Edgar wasn't sure he wanted to hear the answer.

"Henry Sanglier, archbishop of Sens, is holding a display of relics on the octave of Pentecost. He has invited the king, the count of Champagne and a number of bishops and nobles. The following day I propose to debate William's champion, the abbot of Clairvaux, on these matters that he considers counter to dogma. I will prove my case before everyone."

Abelard sank back on the stool, exhausted. Edgar didn't know what to say. He believed completely that his teacher was no heretic, that he was the most brilliant scholar in

France, or anywhere else. but he did not believe that Abelard, in his present state of health, was strong enough to debate anyone, especially someone with the passion and certainty of Bernard of Clairvaux. But, as Astrolabe had said, there was only one person who could outargue Peter Abelard.

"You say we'll leave for the Paraclete at first light?" he asked. "I must go now to make arrangements with Catherine's father. Where shall I meet you?"

"At the Devils' Fart," Abelard answered. "Be there before the sun strikes the spire of Saint-Jean, or we'll leave without you."

Four

Paris, at a house on the right bank near the Grève,
Palm Sunday and the eve of the Feast of All Fools,
March 31, 1140

*Brutescent homines si concessi dote priventur eloquii, ipsaeque
urbes videbuntur potius pecorum quasi saepta quam coetus
hominum nexu quodam societatis foederatus, ut participatione
officiorum et amica invicem vicissitudine eodem iure vivat.*

Deprived of their gift of speech, men would degenerate
to the condition of brute animals, and cities would seem
like corrals for livestock, rather than communities
composed of human beings united by a common bond for
the purpose of living in society, serving one another
and cooperating as friends.

—John of Salisbury,
Metalogicon

$\mathcal{T}$he open field of the Grève was still cluttered with stalls and celebrants when Edgar arrived that evening. He waded through the broken laurel branches, carried in lieu of palms by most of the people in the processions. The scent of pine mingled with that of stale beer, incense and the sharp tang of freshly tanned hides. Edgar inhaled deeply. It reminded him of home. He wondered if he should buy another draught of beer to fortify him for the meeting with Catherine's father.

A woman was lounging against the keg.

"How much to fill a cup this size?" Edgar asked, holding up his drinking mug.

The woman smiled and straightened. "It depends on what I fill it with," she said, wrapping an arm about his waist.

It was only then that Edgar noticed the bright yellow belt the woman wore. As she brushed against him, he also realized that her *chainse* was laced up so loosely that one could see her naked skin showing between the ribbons from armpit to thigh. She must have been cold without her shift. But he didn't have the time, money or inclination to warm her.

"Sorry," he said, backing off quickly. What if she had felt the gold?

"You should be," she answered. "A night with me is worth a day of penance, cleric."

Edgar doubted it. The skin he had touched had been greasy and her hair had smelled of a hundred unwashed men.

Catherine's hair smelled like summer rain.

He made his way through the detritus to the door of the house of Hubert Le Vendeur, merchant.

Catherine's father was just finishing the evening meal and was thinking seriously about taking a cup of mulled wine and going to bed when Edgar was announced.

"By the vats of Saint Vincent!" he exclaimed. "You've come back!"

"Yes, sir," Edgar said. He wasn't sure if this greeting were a welcome or a curse.

The room was empty, except for a small trestle table near the fire, where Hubert was seated. An oil lamp, hanging from the ceiling, gave the only light.

"Where is everyone?" Edgar asked.

Hubert shrugged. "I sent my men-at-arms to spend Holy Week with their families. The rest of the household is at my son's home at Vielleteneuse. I have business that keeps me here. And you?"

He didn't ask Edgar to sit, or offer him wine. Common manners should have required that much. Edgar's nervousness suddenly turned to anger. Who was this man to glare at him and treat him like a serf? He lifted his chin and glared back.

"I have business here, too," he answered. "Four months ago you agreed to my betrothal to your daughter, Catherine. The *desponsatio* having been approved by both you and the lady in question, I returned to my father's home to acquire his permission and to obtain a dower. Since you did not wish her to be burdened with land in a foreign country, I have brought her dower in gold."

He reached beneath his shift and untied the belt he had worn for so many miles. He then laid it on the table in front of Hubert.

Catherine's father didn't even glance at it. He poured another cup of wine from the pitcher.

"And what did your father say when you told him you were returning to France to marry a woman who was meant to marry Our Lord?"

Until that moment, Edgar was unaware of the generations of aristocratic arrogance hidden deep in his being.

"My father was not at all concerned by that," he said. "He was much more appalled that I would forfeit my right to become abbot of the family monastery and then bishop of Glasgow. It was only to that end that I was sent to study in Paris."

Hubert nodded slowly and drained the cup. He looked at Edgar again, this time with deep sadness.

"It's not too late to fulfill your father's wishes," he said.

Edgar blinked. His stomach lurched. Hubert had not touched the gold.

"What are you trying to tell me?" he asked, his voice faltering slightly. "What has happened while I was gone? Has Catherine . . ."

"No," Hubert said. Finally he stood.

"Come over here, son. Sit. Drink. Catherine is well. Her letters speak mostly of her concerns for you. I have spent many wakeful nights reviewing my decision to grant her to you. I truly expected your father to forbid you to return. I thought, Well, she will be unhappy a while and then realize that the Paraclete is the best place for her."

Edgar's hand froze as he reached for the pitcher.

"And now?" he asked.

Hubert poured wine for them both. He gestured to the half-finished bread and meat, then gazed into the shadows lurking beyond the small circle of lamplight.

"I came to Paris from Rouen thirty-five years ago. The Christian merchant who raised me had given me the job of providing the Norman lords of the area with wine from Francia and Burgundy. In executing this commission, I acquired wealth and connections of my own. One was with

a knight of Blois, Raoul de Boisvert. The family had little
money but they were distantly related to the counts of
Blois and could trace their line back to Richard le
Justicier. Raoul had a daughter. He was amenable; she was
obedient. I married her."

Edgar remembered the only time he had seen Madeleine, daughter of Raoul. Catherine had been so ill, she
had fallen from her horse outside the castle keep. He had
rushed up to catch her but Madeleine had pushed him
away and started raving about the sickness being a punishment or a penance. Catherine had already told him how
her mother spent most of every day praying and visiting
the local shrines.

Hubert sighed. "Pay attention, boy. I'm telling you the
story for a purpose. I want you to understand why I'm
doing this, so you know what to expect from me. I bought
Madeleine from her father. I was fond enough of her, but
mostly I cared for her family. Her ties to nobility would
improve my social position and increase my wealth. It was
a perfectly normal arrangement.

"Then there were the stillbirths, the children taken by
fever their first winter, our second son crushed by the cart.
She began to suspect that my conversion to Christianity
had not been genuine, that I still adhered to the faith of my
ancestors. She withdrew from me and replaced me with
the saints. Finally, the saints alone mattered, even more
than our remaining children. But nothing she does for
them brings her peace. Look what these fears have done to
her. What I did. I keep thinking that, if I had loved her, I
would have noticed sooner that her piety was beyond the
normal. I could have reassured her as to my faith. Perhaps
it would have made a difference."

From what Edgar knew of Madeleine's family, he
doubted that her madness could have been prevented. Her
brother Roger had certainly been insane. Was Hubert
warning him against marrying into a family of lunatics? It
could work both ways. Edgar hoped they never had a visit
from his uncle Ethelraed.

Hubert refilled his cup. "I'm almost finished," he promised. "They say that physical lust is the worst possible rea-

son for a marriage and I can see, as can everyone else, by the way, how you and my daughter lust after each others' bodies. All I can hope is that you also share a love encompassing the mind and heart that will see you through to the end of your days. If you don't, if one day you regret not making a career in the Church, then release her. Let her go back to the nuns and be happy. Don't make her stay with you for pride's sake or honor.

"I love Catherine the most of all my children," he added. "I would rather see her happy than countess of Champagne. That's all."

Edgar picked up the gold and laid it in Hubert's lap.

"I will not buy your daughter," he said. "This is my promise that, with or without me, she will be taken care of. Catherine is more a part of me than any friend I have ever had. And I think I would make a most unholy abbot."

Hubert untied the cloth and counted out the bezants. He held one up to the light.

"I'll have Ullo make up a bed for you when he's cleared the table. You can sleep here by the fire tonight. Later, when you have been properly wed, I'll have the room above the counting house made up for you and Catherine. She'll want to be near the books."

Then he called for another pitcher of wine.

Edgar was standing next to the Devil's Fart the next morning at first light. He leaned against it as he waited, rubbing his back against the scratches on the ancient megalith. No one knew who had built it or why it had been so named. It had been done by pagans, of course, long before the Romans, long before Christ. But the people of Paris seemed happy enough to leave it standing, once its evil influence had been countered by the church of Saint-Jean, built next to it. Large and easy to spot, it was a convenient gathering place. Many a pilgrim had etched his mark on the old Fart before setting out for Jerusalem or Compostela.

The sun touched the spire of Saint-Jean and the bells of the town began ringing Prime. Edgar felt his mended *chainse* and was reassured by the crackle of vellum. It was worth as much to him as the gold that had been there before. Hubert Le Vendeur had written a letter in his own hand, authorizing the abbess of the Paraclete to release his daughter, Catherine, if she agreed, to Edgar of Wedderlie for the purpose of honorable matrimony. Hubert had also noted that she was to be under the care of Abbot Peter Abelard until she was returned to Paris for the nuptials. It was as clear a contract as they needed. Permission had been granted. The bride-gift had been paid. All that remained was to collect the bride.

The sun climbed higher above Paris. The bells he heard ringing now were from the street, not the churches. Vendors, lepers and pigs all made noise to warn or attract passersby. The road to the Porte Baudoyer was thick with people these days. Ever since the artisans and merchants had started spilling from the Île into Monceau-Saint-Gervais on the right bank to avoid the high tariffs and expensive housing, the streets around the Fart had begun to resemble the faires at Troyes and Lendit. Edgar fidgeted as he was pushed farther from a clear view of the road.

Finally, he saw them, Astrolabe leading his father, who was riding a white palfrey with easy skill. Edgar smiled. Despite all his adversities, Abelard never quite forgot that he was the son of a knight. He would never sit a horse like a mealbag scholar.

With them was Edgar's English friend John, who had gone to study at Chartres that winter, and another man, a cleric, whom Edgar thought he should recognize.

"I apologize," Astrolabe said as soon as he was within hearing range. "We left early, but it seemed that half of Paris needed to have 'just one word' with my father. You'd have thought his purse was laden with benefices, the way the clerks trailed him."

"I presume you are referring to me, young Astrolabe?"

The man who spoke was grey, well past sixty, Edgar judged, but still vigorous. He was not tonsured and wore the robes of a priest, but had an air of authority and humor that wasn't often found among parish clergy.

Astrolabe flushed. "Of course not, sir," he said. "Not at all! Edgar, perhaps you already know Master Gilbert, late chancellor of Chartres?"

"Only by reputation." Edgar now knew why Astrolabe was so embarrassed. "I have not had the fortune to attend one of your lectures but hope to do so now that I have returned to Paris."

Master Gilbert laughed. "You know my repute and still you wish to hear me speak? Brave man! I have as many crows circling me these days as Master Abelard."

Edgar glanced toward Abelard, who was speaking with John and another student. He lowered his voice.

"Are there still so many who would pick his bones?"

Master Gilbert grew serious. "Too many. They can't forgive him for wanting to apply the rules of logic to theology."

They were jostled and sworn at by a milk vendor on his way to the Pierre au Lait to set up his stall. The canon drew Edgar out of the path.

"What worries me most," Gilbert continued, "is this insane plan to have Henry Sanglier arrange for Abelard to debate Abbot Bernard."

"You think he would lose?" Edgar asked. "No one can outargue Master Abelard."

"Don't be so loyal," Gilbert told him. "Astrolabe told me you have already discussed it. This debate would serve no purpose and might do great harm. When they condemned Abelard's work at Soissons nineteen years ago, it nearly killed him to have to put his own books into the flames. What do you think it would do to him now, in his state of health?"

"But he has many powerful friends," Edgar protested.

"Many of whom also owe favors to the abbot of Clairvaux," Gilbert answered. "I wouldn't want to count on them to protect Abelard from him. Please, ask Héloïse to make him see reason."

Edgar sighed. "I will ask, Master Gilbert, but from what I have heard of her, she will do what she decides, and no one's words will sway her."

* * *

The Paraclete was busy during the last days before Easter.
There were extra prayers, fasts and alms. Catherine had always felt it a joyous season, but this year she was no
longer truly a part of the convent. Her mind was not fixed
on heaven, but on things of the earth, on carnal desire. Her
own for Edgar, she admitted it. But her thoughts also
gnawed on the other base passions; anger, pride, fear. Living in the world meant facing those, too. Was she strong
enough? Watching over the broken body in the infirmary,
Catherine wasn't sure. Despite the rapidly spreading infection, the countess Alys still lived. It was as if she were
struggling to accomplish one more thing before she let go.
To name her true attacker? Catherine hoped so. But how
much longer could she survive?

It was Holy Thursday after None, and Héloïse knelt
with the other sisters in the cloister wing to wash the feet
of twelve poor women. After this symbolic ritual, the
women would be given new shoes and cloaks and a warm
meal.

"Careful of my corns, Lady Abbess!" one old woman
winced. "Scrub any harder, you'll have them bleeding, and
then how will I manage?"

"Just as you always do, Hrotruda," Héloïse smiled.
"Your feet will get you from your son's door to ours and
we'll both see that you're cared for."

Hrotruda leaned forward so that her face was even with
Héloïse's. "Do you think Our Lord mocked the poor beggars who came to Him for comfort?"

Héloïse's smile wavered. She looked directly at the old
woman and spoke without a trace of mockery. "Do you
imagine for a moment, my honored guest, that I believe
myself in any way equal to Our Lord?"

Suddenly there was a clattering and thumping. Both
women looked toward the noise. Sister Ermelina came
running down the east wing of the cloister, beating on a
wooden board with a mallet, the signal for the sisters to
gather at the bedside of the dying.

"Mother Héloïse! Come quickly! Everyone, hurry!"

Héloïse rose with a startled gasp. She swayed and Hrotruda reached out a hand to steady her.

"Careful, my lady," she said. "I expect you to be here to do better next year."

Héloïse caught her balance. "Thank you," she said. "Agate, will you explain what is happening to the women and see that they are served before you join us? This takes precedence. Emilie, tell one of the lay sisters to run for Father Guiberc. Tell him the countess is dying. We need to prepare for the Last Rites."

The nuns gathered quickly in the oratory. Father Guiberc, carrying the Host in a chalice, and the sacristan with the holy oils were waiting to begin the procession to the infirmary. Catherine took her place near the end.

They all filed in through the open door. As she entered, Catherine was hit with a stench that almost drove her back outside. With an effort, she controlled her stomach and forced herself to keep her place.

The infirmarian had hung bunches of rosemary and valerian at the windows and over the bed. She had also put scented oil in the lamps, but nothing could overcome the odor of putrefaction and approaching death. As each woman entered, a lay sister handed her a scarf that had been dipped in wine vinegar. Catherine tied it at once over her nose and mouth and found she could at least breath without gagging. She looked across at the countess Alys.

A pair of terrified blue eyes stared back at her.

For a moment, Catherine thought the countess was already dead, then the eyes blinked. They searched the room until they found Paciana, standing in the shadows. Alys tried to lift her hand.

"Bele suer, duce amie," she whispered. " 'Ciana!"

Paciana stumbled through the crush of people and knelt at the bedside as Father Guiberc began the rite.

"She's conscious!" he exclaimed. "Miraculous!"

Sister Melisande shook her head. "Not enough of a miracle, Father. She will not last the night, I fear, but at least she can have the comfort of the sacrament.

Sadly, Father Guiberc continued with the anointing. Paciana helped support Alys so that she could sit up

enough to receive and swallow the Viaticum. Then she
sank back into the pillow. The priest stepped away.

Alys tried feebly to reach out to him. "No!" she rasped.
"More. Mother! You promised!"

The effort started her choking. Paciana wrung a few
drops of wine from a cloth into her mouth and she lay
back again, breathing shallowly.

The priest looked at Héloïse in bewilderment. What
more could there be?

"The countess Alys wants to be admitted to our order,"
Héloïse answered. "When she donated to us, the countess
made it a condition of her gift that she be allowed to take
the veil here before she died."

"But we can't; we need the bishop to consecrate her!"
Father Guiberc protested. "There isn't time to summon
him, even if Hatto would come."

"She's not asking to be a *sanctimonialis*, Father,"
Héloïse said. "The bishop is necessary only for the conse-
cration of virgins. You are permitted to witness her profession and give her the veil."

"Are you sure?" he asked. "On whose authority?"

"Bishop Ivo of Chartres," Catherine answered angrily.

"Catherine!" Héloïse said sharply. "It is not your place
to speak. Did you think I might not know?"

"I'm so sorry, Mother." Catherine was horrified at herself. "Please, forgive me."

Héloïse nodded. "I will speak with you later. She is
quite right, Father. Ivo, following the decretals of Pope
Gelasius, permits a priest to veil and give the benediction
to a widow or wife. Bishop Hatto has simply always been
here to do so before."

Alys's eyes had closed again. Her ragged breath was the
only sound in the crowded room.

The priest was still doubtful. "I believe you, of course.
But I don't wish to imperil her soul now or my own by
doing the wrong thing. She is a married woman. We must
have the approval of her husband before the marriage bond
can be broken."

This time Catherine bit her tongue. The bond would be

broken by death soon enough, while the old priest, whom she had liked up until now, dithered about procedure.

Héloïse considered. Then she looked at Catherine again.

"The charter," she said. "Catherine, here, run to my room and open the chest where we keep the records. Here is the key. Count Raynald's consent must be in the charter."

Alys stirred again. "My veil . . ."

Catherine pushed her way out and ran as ordered, only tripping once in the mud. She fumbled through the box of documents. Yes, there it was. She scanned it quickly: ". . . *sub presentia et cum laude et voluntate conjugis sui Raynaldi comitis de Tornordoro,*" ". . . in the presence, and with the consent and will of her husband, Count Raynald of Tonnerre." Catherine stuffed the parchment in her sleeve and rushed back.

"There it is," she said as she handed the paper to Héloïse. "Mother, shouldn't we ask her about her attacker?"

She looked so anguished that Héloïse didn't have the heart to reprimand her.

"Catherine, dear," she said. "This is not the time to seek vengeance. She wants to die a member of this house. That is all that matters. Father, can we proceed?"

"Yes, of course."

Hersende, the wardrobe mistress, laid a length of black cloth over his arm. As Héloïse supported her, the priest arranged it lightly about Alys's face, since she was unable to do it for herself as prescribed.

"*Accipe,* ah . . . *domina, pallium quod perferas sine macula ante tribunal Domini nostri Jesu Christi. . . . Effunde, Domine, caelestem benedictionem super hanc famulam tuam, Aleydem. Amen.*"

He spoke haltingly, not sure of the form in this situation. But Héloïse seemed satisfied.

With great effort, Alys moved her hand up to feel the rough wool cloth against her face. "*Ah, Jesu,*" she breathed.

Her eyes turned upward and she gave a long sigh, which turned into a rattling in the back of her throat. Hurriedly,

Father Guiberc began the prayers for the dying. The sisters began chanting the responsory.

Alys lay still. She was free.

Catherine sat outside Héloïse's room, waiting for her punishment. She felt completely drained of feeling. Even now, the corpse of Alys, once countess of Tonnerre, was being cleaned and wrapped. She had been grateful that her offer to help had been turned down. The sight and smell of that poor, scarred body would have been too much for her to bear. Alys seemed so easily disposed of. Because it was already late afternoon of Holy Thursday, there would not even be a funeral Mass before the burial. It would have to wait until after Easter.

At least, Catherine thought, *she didn't die alone. But why should she have died at all? Why? She should have told us who killed her.*

To satisfy your curiosity, Catherine? her conscience asked. *Were you planning to seek revenge? Start a blood feud? Isn't it more important that she died in a state of grace?*

Catherine buried her face in her hands. She wanted to scream her anger and frustration, but she was too worn. It wasn't right simply to bury Alys and forget how she died. Just because she was now in a better world didn't mean one should ignore the horrors she had endured in this one.

The door opened and Héloïse appeared.

"Come in, Catherine," she said. "I have chosen to speak with you here, instead of in chapter. But you must apologize there next time and take your reprimand."

"Of course, Mother," Catherine said. She waited.

Héloïse sat and rubbed her eyes.

"I realize that, for some reason, the plight of the countess . . . of our sister Alys has affected you strongly. You know that we did all we could for her."

Catherine sighed. "Yes, Mother, I know. But I wish we could have done more, before she was hurt. I don't know why, but I feel it's important, necessary, that we discover if she were really attacked by Walter of Grancy and, even more, who it was who beat her so many times before."

"Catherine, how can that help her now?"

Héloïse was clearly exhausted. Catherine felt terribly guilty for adding to her burdens. She reached for an acceptable reason for her belief. She was too tired; she could only stare with pleading eyes at this woman who had become her mother. Without warning, she began to cry. Héloïse took her in her arms and rocked her like a baby.

"Catherine, Catherine," she murmured. "You can't grieve like this for a woman you never knew. One can't hurt so easily when there is so much pain in the world. Alys had a sorrowful life, it seems. But she would not want your pity for her to make your life more sad."

Catherine took a deep breath and wiped her eyes.

"I'm so sorry, Mother. I feel foolish and I know I'm not really crying for Alys. She has found peace."

She paused.

"Mother, . . ." She tried to think of a way to ask this. "Do you know why Paciana became a lay sister?"

"Yes," Héloïse said. "She confessed to me when she entered the Paraclete."

"Then you know who she is?"

"Yes."

Catherine was feeling her way now, as through a dark forest. But she was beginning to understand her own intense reaction to the countess's death.

"If I had decided to stay and take my vows," she said slowly, "instead of marrying Edgar, *(Oh, please send him soon!)* I wonder what I would do if my sister, Agnes, were brought here in this way, if she had been beaten so horribly, with no one near to protect her. How would I feel? could I forgive them? Could I forgive myself? Perhaps I'm not a good Christian, but I would want such people punished. Why won't Paciana tell us who hurt Alys? That is what worries me so."

Héloïse continued rocking, one finger twisting an errant curl escaped from Catherine's scarf.

"I don't know," she said at last. "Perhaps Paciana is a better Christian than either of us. You know I cannot betray her confidence. She only told me of her own life, not her sister's. I have my speculations but I cannot break my word to her any more than you can."

Catherine gave one last sniff. "No, but ... Oh, Mother Héloïse, I am so confused."

To her surprise, Héloïse laughed. "My dearest Catherine, have I never told you? Confused is the natural state of every true scholar."

Alys was buried immediately before Vespers that afternoon. The traditional sadness of the day was intensified by this new sorrow, and an extra candle was lit, beside Our Lady's altar, for her soul.

Catherine fell into bed that night, more tired than she had ever been in her life.

"Dear Lord," she prayed, "let me sleep until Edgar comes. I'm so tired of hurting alone."

Five

Near the Paraclete,
Good Friday, April 5, 1140

Quid Salomone sapientius? Attamen infatuatur amoribus feminarum.

Was ever man wiser than Solomon? Yet love for woman made even him foolish.

—Saint Jerome,
Letter to Rusticus

*D*ense fog filled the valley as the three travellers made their way down the road from Nogent. Edgar and Astrolabe were warm from walking, but Abelard shivered as the mist coalesced and dripped from the hood of his cloak and down his neck. Astrolabe touched his hand. It was cold and trembling.

"Perhaps we should find a house to rest in and dry ourselves," Edgar suggested.

"Father?" Astrolabe said.

Abelard looked through the fog, at someone neither Edgar nor Astrolabe could see.

"You can't expect everyone to comprehend on faith alone," Abelard pleaded. "They must be gently guided to belief by simple logic. We are not all saints, after all. If we were, Our Lord's sacrifice would have no meaning. You must see that. Why won't you admit it?"

Astrolabe touched him again, trying to call him back from his wandering.

"Father!" Astrolabe bit his lip. "You're not well. Per-

haps we shouldn't go any further. We could stop for the
night at Saint-Aubin."

"You are called 'saint,' even 'angel,' " his father
shouted into the air. "It is not so. You're only a man,
whatever your repute. How dare you correct me!"

"There's an inn at Saint-Aubin," Edgar said. "We
should at least get him warm and calm him, if we can. After that, it's only another mile or two to the Paraclete.
They can care for him there better than anywhere else."

"You're right, of course," Astrolabe said. "I'm as bad as
he, thinking more of his dignity than his health. It's only
that the nuns revere him so. I fear that he might not want
them to see him in such a state."

"I don't think their respect for him would be diminished
if they saw him ill," Edgar told him.

Suddenly, echoing faintly in the fog, came the sound of
a wooden clapper, which called clerics to prayer instead of
the bells, from the Gloria of the Mass of Maundy Thursday to the Gloria of the Mass of the Easter Vigil. Edgar
turned his head, hunting for the source.

"Listen! It must be None," he said. "I'd lost all sense of
time in this cloud."

At the sound, Abelard first started in surprise, then quieted and bowed his head.

"*Parasceve,*" he whispered. "I had forgotten! How
could I be so full of my own persecution?" Softly, he
began to chant, "*Nona, qua vera lux penam finierit, sub-
tractam lucem hanc mundo restituit....*"

" 'At the ninth hour, when the true light ended his torment, he restored to this world the light that had been
lost,' " Edgar translated. "I don't know that hymn."

"It's Father's," Astrolabe said. "He wrote it for the Paraclete, for Mother. He made one for almost every office of
the last days of Holy Week."

They listened without moving until Abelard fell silent.

"How much farther?" he asked.

Edgar looked up. Master Abelard smiled at him. His
eyes were red and his hands still shaking, but he had returned to them.

"A couple of miles," Astrolabe told him. "Do you feel well enough to continue?"

"Of course. I am ashamed of myself. In my own anger over my troubles, I had forgotten the day. How can I complain of those who torment me, when I think of what Our Lord suffered at this very hour for speaking his truth?"

He set his horse at a brisker pace. Astrolabe and Edgar soon had no breath for conversation, but neither suggested they slow down. Edgar was glad that the redness of his face could be put down to the exercise, but he was also ashamed. He had known well enough that it was Good Friday but, instead of remembering the passion and death of Christ, he had only been thinking of his own passion for Catherine. It was just as well he had decided not to become a bishop.

They began to hear another sound, growing rapidly, that of hooves beating against the dirt road. Without warning, a party of knights galloped out of the fog, giving them no time to move out of the way. Edgar managed to hold onto the neck of Abelard's horse as the party raced by, not even seeming to see them, but Astrolabe was thrown to the side of the road.

Abelard rose in his stirrups. *"Questres!"* he shouted at them. *"Fis des lisses!* If you've no care for your own worthless necks, think of your horses!"

Edgar ran to Astrolabe, who was trying to untangle himself from a thornbush.

"Don't worry," he assured them. "Apart from scratches, I'm fine. What incredible *bricons*! Who would be insane enough to ride at top speed in weather like this?"

"Perhaps," Abelard said, "they've had a divine summons and were hurrying to join the brothers of Clairvaux."

Astrolabe looked at his father and then at Edgar. He relaxed and then began to laugh much more than the joke allowed.

"You're feeling better, Father," he said at last. "I stand rebuked. Who are we to keep the converted from hastening to their new life?"

"That's right, my son," Abelard answered. "Of course,

as they journey, we might piously wish that they will soon
discover how the mighty may be humbled."

"Still," Edgar added, "I would feel better if I knew
where they were really going. There isn't much along this
road besides the Paraclete."

The three men looked at each other, considering Edgar's
observation. Without speaking, they started off again, even
more quickly than before.

The clapper sounded also at the Paraclete. Barefoot, the
nuns headed to the oratory. But Catherine was not among
them. She knelt on the hard floor of the infirmary. Her
hands were raw and her nose running. She dipped the
brush into the bucket again and splashed the soapy water
onto the wall. The scent of death still lingered in the room
despite all the scrubbing and censing.

They had taken down all the dried flowers and herbs
and put them in a brazier in the center of the room, where
they were slowly burning. The smoke seared Catherine's
lungs and eyes. Kneeling beside her on the floor, Paciana
rubbed at the oaken planks with her scrub brush as if attempting to cut through them. She kept her head down.
Catherine had given up trying to talk with her.

Together in silence, they wiped up the water and opened
the door to let out the smoke.

In silence they changed their wet robes. In silence they
walked to the chapter house for the daily conference, a
practice not omitted at the Paraclete even on Good Friday.
Catherine sat silently next to Paciana in the back with the
lay sisters. Her decision to return to the world had removed her from a place with the other nuns. But all here
could listen to the conference, a short spiritual talk given
by Héloïse or one of the other sisters.

Héloïse entered and all the women rose.

"I had planned today," she started, "to speak to you on
the Book of Luke. However, my original thoughts have
been superceded."

She smiled at them tenderly.

"We are a young house and have lost few of our own
since our founding, for which we thank God. Yesterday, a

woman died among us. She was only one of our community for a moment. Yet she was our sister, and our benefactress, and it is right that we mourn her on this solemn day and also rejoice that she came to us in time to die surrounded by our love and prayers."

Catherine felt the resentment rising to her throat again.

Stop this, Catherine! her voices rang in her head. *Charity, forgiveness! Anyway . . . you're being hypocritical, admit it. It's not what was done to Alys that upsets you. It's the fear that it might happen to you.*

No! Edgar would never hurt me! Catherine thought.

Of course not. She knew he wouldn't. It was true they had only spoken a dozen times, but the circumstances had been optimal for complete understanding. She hated those voices, that part of her that had been trained to line up arguments on both sides of every question. They bored through everything she said to comfort herself and illuminated the smallest shred of doubt.

"Therefore," the abbess concluded, "on this day of grief and hope, let us all pray that the soul of our sister Alys be granted the true peace, which is unknown to any of us still on this earth."

Héloïse handed the list of daily duties to the prioress and left. Catherine looked about, embarrassed. She had missed most of what the abbess had said. Catherine took a deep breath, the first all day that didn't smell of smoke or decay. Peace. There were small sounds in the room; the creak of the wooden chapter seats, the rustle of clothing, a gentle click of beads, the patient elderly voice of Prioress Astane, who had grown up in a convent and come with Héloïse from Argenteuil, going over a few rubrical details concerning the Good Friday afternoon liturgy.

This was contentment. This was what she knew, where she belonged. To Catherine, heaven was a convent, one with no novice mistress and an infinite number of books.

And Edgar?

"By the thundering vengeance of Saint Emerentiana, stop!"

"Catherine!" Prioress Astane stared at her reproachfully. Sister Bertrada started toward her, stick raised.

Catherine looked up in horror, half expecting a thunderbolt to strike her down and half hoping one would. Those stupid voices, changing sides on her so suddenly that she had spoken aloud. She was too embarrassed even to apologize. She just buried her face in her hands and hunched over. Someone nearby giggled.

Thwack! The giggle was replaced by a yipe of pain.

Catherine felt a wisp of comfort. God may choose his own time and place for revenge, but the blows of Sister Bertrada were swift and certain.

As they left the chapter, Catherine managed to pass near Emilie and Sister Bietriz. Emilie shook her head at her, trying not to laugh.

"If you must carry on arguments with demons, Catherine," she teased, "couldn't you at least use a softer voice?"

Catherine sighed. "The demons were winning this time."

Bietriz put a hand on Catherine's shoulder. She was a tall woman who moved with more resolve than grace. Her face was all wrong for the standard of beauty extolled in the songs of the *jongleurs*. Her nose was straight and large, her hair almost as dark as Catherine's own, and her eyebrows so thick that a lady of the court would have plucked them to almost nothing. Her chin was also firm and decided. All the same, as the niece of the seneschal of the count of Champagne, she could have made a good marriage, had she wanted to. Catherine admired her greatly, but always felt a little bit in awe of someone so completely undistracted by imagination.

Bietriz smiled. "Emilie tells me that you are concerned about the death of Sister Alys. No, I correct myself, it is her life that troubles you."

"Yes," Catherine said. "She suffered greatly."

"It is a mystery why some have lives of so much pain and others, who seem no more deserving, have so little," Bietriz said sadly. "The Book of Job has never seemed to me to give an adequate answer to this paradox. But I trust that there is one, if only our minds were capable of comprehension."

"No doubt, Sister," Catherine answered. "I understand that you may know something more about the mystery of Countess . . . of Sister Alys's family."

Bietriz nodded. "Oh, that's no mystery. We all know her family. She is the child of Gerhard of Quincy's second wife, Constanza. Constanza is the daughter of Norbert, who was the second son of Hugo, lord of Neuvry. Her brother is Robert, prior of Vauluisant. Constanza's second husband is a man named Rupert, of no discernible family whatever, as far as I know. I can't imagine why she chose him.

"Now, let me think, . . ."—she was arranging the family on her fingers—"a sister of Constanza married into a family in Flanders that supposedly was involved in the murder of Charles the Good, although they try to keep that quiet. Then, through the marriage of her aunt, she's related to the . . ."

"Wait," Catherine stopped her. "I can't remember all of this unless we write it down. Would you do that for me?"

Bietriz seemed uncomfortable. "I don't know. It's terribly worldly. Some might think all this no more than idle gossip. You know that nothing of the world should matter here."

"I know that well. And it doesn't matter here," Catherine agreed. "But it matters a great deal outside."

But Bietriz had already repented her lecture in genealogy. "Then perhaps," she said, "when you are out there again, you can ask someone who has taken no vow to renounce the world. Family connections no longer exist for me. We are all only one family, equal in the eyes of Our Lord."

She strode across the cloister, leaving Catherine and Emilie standing sheepishly at the door to the chapter.

"Sorry, Catherine," Emilie said. "I tried. She is right, though. I know you only ask because you were so affected by the countess's suffering. But she's dead. You can't help her. Leave the matter to her family to sort out. I still think Walter of Grancy was responsible."

Catherine nodded. There was no point in going into her theories here. Somehow, now that Alys was dead, it seemed even more improper to discuss the cruelty she had endured. Emilie smiled and hugged her.

"Don't let this distress you any longer," she told Catherine. "Alys is free now. And Sunday is Easter; we can all rejoice in that."

"That's true," Catherine sighed. "And it *will* be nice to be given two meals a day again."

Emilie laughed and agreed. "I need to finish some work in the infirmary this afternoon. Our supply of compound for fever is very low. What will you be doing?"

"What?" With difficulty, Catherine pulled herself back from her thoughts. Why had Emilie called Alys free? Of the earth, life, temptations? Or was there something more Emilie knew and refused to tell?"

"Daily labor?" Emilie prompted.

"Oh, yes," Catherine said firmly "I'm to go to the hostel and help with the distribution of alms."

"That will be good for you," said Emilie. "I always liked that, especially when there are children. You see, that's something else a good cloistered *sanctimonialis* can no longer do."

It did cheer Catherine to be part of the almsgiving. Bread and leftover vegetables were usually all they had to give, since the Paraclete was not a rich establishment like Cluny or Fontevraud. But today a local peasant had made a gift from the last of the winter roots and so they could also give each recipient a few fresh turnips. The sick were sent to Sister Melisande.

"The coughing sickness must be very bad this spring," Catherine said to the doorkeeper, Sister Thecla, whom she was helping with the food distribution. "That's the fifth person I've sent to Sister Melisande."

Sister Thecla pursed her lips. "Perhaps," she said. "It has been a hard winter. But it is odd that almost no one came to us for coughing until Melisande concocted her new remedy of honey and red wine."

The thought of a spoonful of such medicine almost made Catherine want to start coughing. It had been months since she had tasted anything sweet. And it had been a hard winter. The convent survived on tithes from mills and fishponds and the harvest from the eighth parts of fields. A bit of land, a strip of wood, a few *denarii* given by one of the local castellans; these were uncertain sources to feed thirty people and still allow for charity.

"The fog's finally lifting," the doorkeeper said. "I can see a bit down the road now, even make out some shapes. Men on horseback, knights, I'd guess. No carts; they're not with a merchant party. They're riding hard, and . . . well armed."

She put down the basket of bread.

"Catherine, dear," she said carefully. "Go ask the prioress if we can spare a few more turnips. Have Brother Baldwin carry them out to me. You go back to the cloister."

"But . . ." Catherine started. Then she saw the doorkeeper's face. "Yes, Sister."

She found Brother Baldwin in the vegetable garden just outside the convent walls.

"There is a group of knights approaching," she told him. "Sister Thecla sent me to ask the prioress to give you more turnips for the poor, but I don't think that's why she wants you out there with her."

The lay brother shouldered his hoe. "Don't worry. I'll go see to her. You'd better go on in to the prioress."

He squared his shoulders and strode toward the main gate. Catherine felt reassured. Before renouncing the world, Brother Baldwin had been in the service of the last king, Louis the Alert, and his father, Philippe the Bigamist. He had survived the Great Crusade and, on his return, had fought on through the interminable sieges and squabbles of the nobility. Although nearly seventy now, he could still swing a hoe with deadly skill.

"Breaking the peace during Holy Week," he muttered as he left. "What is this world coming to?"

She found Prioress Astane checking on the preparations for the Good Friday offices. Her jaw tightened as Catherine told her of the knights.

"Don't worry, I think I know who it is," she told Catherine. "But Sister Thecla is quite right. With those men

about, you and all the other young girls should be somewhere safe. Tell Sister Bertrada to gather up the students
and the *sanctimoniales* and take them to the chapter house.
Bar the door, if necessary."

Catherine gave Sister Bertrada the message and even
helped shepherd the younger girls into the chapter. But she
had no intention of staying cooped up in there, ignorant
and helpless. By now, she too had a good idea of whose
knights were at the gate and she wanted to know why
Raynald of Tonnerre needed an armed escort to come and
mourn his wife.

The five men who had accompanied Count Raynald
were still mounted when Catherine returned to the gate.
The count had apparently been admitted to the gatehouse,
but either Brother Baldwin's hoe or Sister Thecla's tongue
had kept the others from forcing their way in. They brightened when they saw Catherine.

"Eh! *Bele!*" one leered. *"Folez o me le vendange?"*

"Leceres!" Brother Baldwin raised his hoe and stepped
in front of Catherine. "What the hell are you doing here?"
he fumed at her. "Everything was fine until you came
out."

"I'm sorry." Catherine tried to see around him. "I only
wanted to ... Brother Baldwin, there are more of them
coming down the road, look! Oh, no, it's not, it's ... Master!"

Everyone turned to look where Catherine was pointing.
Out of the fog rode a man sitting straight as a lord on a
white horse. At either side walked a servant, but no one
noticed them.

"Abelard?" the knight who had propositioned Catherine
asked. Another man nodded.

"The eunuch?" the same man whispered.

"Yes."

They all fell silent, twitching nervously in their saddles.
Philosophy could not intimidate them, but the sight of a
man who had paid the ultimate price for stolen passion
was terrifying.

Abelard took in the situation and bent down to say

something to one of his servants. The man nodded and hurried on ahead, his hood falling back as he did.

"Astrolabe!" Catherine cried in delight, stepping out from behind Brother Baldwin. She held out her hands to her old friend.

"Catherine!"

The voice came not from Astrolabe, but from the other servant. Catherine swayed and her hands dropped. Only one person in the world said her name like that, with the "th" soft as a lisp.

"Catherine?"

I'm crying! she thought. *What a stupid thing to do!*

Go to him, her voices chided. *You know that's what you most desire. You have no argument for that.*

"I can't move," she whispered. "I'm afraid."

Astrolabe had reached the group. He bowed formally to the knights.

"My father wishes to know why you are waiting at the gate of the Paraclete," he said. "You must have mistaken this door for the one leading to the church. You've come for evening services, haven't you? You will stay through Easter? I'm sure his sermon will be most edifying for you."

With one hand, he pulled Catherine into motion.

"I've brought someone to see you," he laughed. "I knew him at once from your description, but I haven't told him yet that we've been friends for years."

Edgar kept walking forward only because he was holding the bridle of the horse. She wasn't dressed the way she had been when he last saw her. Her hair was completely covered now, not a tendril showing. Why did Astrolabe have to drag her? Had she changed her mind? Edgar knew that he cut a poor figure next to the Almighty. He had hoped she wouldn't notice.

As she came closer, he saw that the hem of her robe was muddy and she had a bruise on the back of her left hand. She would wave them about when arguing. Why, by all the saints, should he find such things so incredibly compelling? Edgar didn't need disputatious voices to an-

swer him. It was because mud and bruises were a part of
what Catherine was and she was what he loved.

Abelard waited patiently as Astrolabe brought Catherine
to her betrothed. She looked nothing like Héloïse but, even
after twenty-five years and a host of disasters, he remembered how he had felt. Poor Edgar!

Catherine tried to match the man standing before her
with the Edgar of her memory. Had he always been so
pale? His flaxen hair was straight and almost to his shoulders. Well, at least he hadn't decided to be tonsured and
come only to say good-bye.

"*Diex te saut,*" Catherine greeted him. "How was your
journey?"

"*Diex te saut,*" he answered. "I encountered no trouble.
I've seen your father in Paris. He sends you his love."

"Thank you," she said. "Are you here to celebrate
Easter with Master Abelard?"

Abelard started laughing. He couldn't help it. They were
so young and so absurd. The other three stared at him.

"I apologize," he said. "Edgar, answer the question."

Edgar looked at Catherine and grinned.

"I am always honored to spend time with Master
Abelard," he said. "But no, you know the reason very
well. I came to the Paraclete for you."

For the first time in her life, Catherine had no words.
She held out her hands and Edgar took them.

Six

A few minutes later, in the guesthouse

Hic ingenio ... phylosophus construxit cenobium ... quod Paraclitum nominavit. Quibus sanctimonialis quandam uxorem suam, religiosam feminam et literis tam Hebraicus quam Latinis adprime eruditam, prefecit abbatissam.

This philosopher [Abelard] cleverly constructed a cell, which he named the Paraclete. One of the nuns, who was once his wife, he made abbess, a devout woman, exceedingly learned, literate in both Hebrew and Latin [Héloïse].

—Robert of Auxerre,
Chronicles of Saint Mariani

Peter is here. No, young man, you will *not* go with her!"

"Yes, Sister."

Héloïse wanted desperately to close her eyes and rub her aching temples, but this was not a time for weakness.

"Don't think you can get away with this trick," Count Raynald said icily. "I've told you that I'll leave money for you to pray for her soul, but you only had the *usufruct* of that property, not full possession!"

"Unless she became a member of our community before her death," Héloïse said softly. "The wording of the charter is clear, my lord. But this isn't something we should be discussing now, while you are still overcome by your sudden loss."

The count's jaw tightened. Whatever his inner grief, only anger showed. Before he could make more accusations, Héloïse stood and moved toward the door.

"Because of the season, we will not be able to have a funeral Mass for Sister Alys until next week. But I'm sure you will want to join us for the Easter Vigil, at which we will remember her."

"I'll be damned first!" Raynald nearly spit the words in her face. "You were supposed to care for her, instead you chopped off her hair and wrapped her in one of your filthy robes and let her die so you could get her donation. Don't think you'll profit from your greed, Lady Abbess. I will see to that!"

He wheeled about and stomped out of the room. Héloïse watched him go, stunned. It would be all right, she told herself. He would calm down and realize they had done nothing except follow the countess Alys's wishes. She covered her eyes with her hands and pressed her thumbs against the pain in her head. She couldn't even remember which of the donations he was so angry about losing. Land? A tithe from a bridge? Two-thirds of a mill? Nothing they had been given was enough to be greedy about. Not for a man like Raynald. But to the convent, every vine, every egg, every arpent of land mattered. There was never enough to keep all their dependents.

"Mother, are you ill?"

Héloïse looked up. "It's nothing, Catherine. The count and his men will not be staying, I think. But I want you to remain inside the cloister until they go. Catherine, do you understand me?"

What was the matter with the girl now? She looked radiant, almost beatified.

"Oh, Mother, Edgar's come back for me!" Catherine said.

Héloïse nearly laughed, despite her pounding headache and sense of disquiet. Catherine's exaltation was so obvious. The only other time Héloïse had ever seen the girl that thrilled was the first Latin lesson in which she had correctly identified an ablative absolute.

"I'm glad for you, my child," she said. "You do seem to be certain that this is the correct choice."

The light in Catherine dimmed. "I am not certain that I am correct, Mother. But I know it is the choice my heart has made and I must follow it."

Héloïse closed her eyes, seeing back more than twenty years.

"Yes, Catherine, you must," she said. "Has your Edgar come alone, or did your father send a suitable guardian?"

"Oh, Mother Héloïse!" Catherine's hand flew to her mouth. "I'm so sorry. Yes, he did. Prioress Astane sent me to tell you that Master Abelard had arrived. He is resting in his old room."

Héloïse's face showed no radiance, no sudden aberration of the pulse. She had learned her lessons in twenty years.

"Thank you, Catherine," she said. "you may go to the oratory now to prepare for Vespers."

Héloïse didn't run. At one time she had, disregarding custom and propriety. At one time the most famous philosopher in Paris had written love songs for her and raced through his lectures in his haste to return to her bed. It was a long time ago. But, as she walked, it seemed there was a man in the twilight running toward her. For a moment she felt dizzy, thrust back in time, then she recognized him. The same, but not the same, and yet loved with the

same tenderness. Forgetting her age and position, she ran
to him.

"Astrolabe!" She hugged him tightly.

"Hello, Mother," Astrolabe said.

"My dearest son," Héloïse kissed him. "I'm so glad
you're here."

His face lit. "Are you? I have often thought that with so
many daughters, you might not miss me. . . ." He trailed
off. He had always believed that it was his shameful birth
that had set in motion all her sorrows.

She hugged him tightly. "Astrolabe, you will always be
beloved to me. Never forget that."

"I brought Father, as I promised," Astrolabe paused.
"He's not well, Mother. A slight fever, perhaps nothing
more. It seems to come and go without warning. But I fear
that these renewed attacks on his philosophy have weak-
ened him."

"He has survived worse," Héloïse answered. "I'm sure
he only needs rest."

Astrolabe didn't answer. She would know when she saw
him.

"And how are my cousins?" he asked as they resumed
walking.

"Sisters Agate and Agnes are well. They'll be delighted
to see you again. I understand you brought Catherine's Edgar with you. What's he like?"

"He suits her," Astrolabe answered.

"Oh, dear," Héloïse laughed as she opened the door.

Edgar sat on a stool next to the bed, watching Abelard
as he slept. The cool spring light illuminated him and he
had turned away from its harshness. But each line across
his face was deeply etched. Héloïse froze in the doorway.
It was as if someone with a mailed fist had hit her in the
stomach as hard as he could.

"Oh, my dear," Héloïse whispered. "Astrolabe, you and
Edgar must be tired and hungry from your journey. If you
go to the guesthouse, Sister Ermelina will have something
sent to you."

She barely noticed them go. She sat down on the stool
and hesitantly touched the hand lying on the blanket.

It was still his hand, twice the size of hers, with long supple fingers, strong enough to pound rhetoric into the dullest head. It had always been a marvel to her how incredibly gentle his hands could be. But his face was so thin and his hair had gone almost white, only a few streaks stayed stubbornly black. When had that happened? He had never changed before, not even during those first long years when he had refused to see her. Somehow she had believed he would remain thirty-five until she caught up with him. But she had long since passed that year and he had entered his sixties. He had survived physical attacks and the battering of disputation. He had been driven from one place to another. It was not surprising that he should be ill and worn. But . . .

"Peter," she breathed. "You promised me you would be immortal. I'm holding you to that. It's hard enough to live each day, knowing you're somewhere else, that you can never stay with me. But if I lose even the hope of seeing you again, I will die."

Slowly his eyes opened and he smiled at her.

"Dilectissima," he said, "I *will* be immortal. Do you think an intellect such as mine can be extinguished so easily? Are you now becoming like those grey vultures who expect me to humbly bow before their superior faith? Ridiculous! I intend to outlive them all."

Héloïse's eyes filled but her voice remained steady.

"That's better," she said.

"I don't know what the lady abbess was thinking of," the lay brother Baldwin said as he ladled the last of the turnip soup out for Edgar and Astrolabe. "It's Good Friday; you boys should be fasting. Bad enough that those men of the count's demanded the last of the wheat bread and then wanted fish, as if we had any."

"There's nothing in the vivarium?" Astrolabe looked out the window to the spot in the river netted on three sides so that fish coming downstream would be trapped.

"There haven't been many yet this spring; what we salted from the gift of Felix of Bossenay is almost gone.

Those *mesels* wouldn't have wanted it anyway. They prefer the taste of blood."

"Just so it isn't ours," Edgar said as he ate his soup. "Why are they here, in any case?"

"It's convent business, I shouldn't tell outsiders," Baldwin said. He took out some barley bread and began cutting it. They waited. "Of course, you aren't really outsiders. . . ."

Edgar smiled; Astrolabe kicked him under the table.

"Of course not," he said. "What's been happening here? When I mentioned that Father was ill, Prioress Astane told me the infirmary was not yet fully cleansed. What has happened?"

"Oh, the smell is something dreadful! It was horrible; there were maggots in her living flesh! I haven't seen an infection that bad since I left the Holy Land. I don't believe her people did anything to help her until they brought her here."

"The poor woman!" Astrolabe crossed himself. "Who was she?"

"The wife of the count of Tonnerre. And now Count Raynald is trying to cause scandal in the convent, shouting that we forced his wife to take the veil just to steal her property. As if the lady Héloïse would stoop to such a thing! He's just like his father! No respect for the Church!"

Brother Baldwin rose, jabbing with his bread knife as if the count were there to be sliced.

Edgar and Astrolabe looked at each other gloomily. Edgar shook his head.

"Is there nothing concerned with your family that doesn't involve scandal?" he asked.

"My parents do seem to attract it," Astrolabe admitted. "But our notoriety needn't bother you. You are simply here to retrieve your bride."

Edgar was glad he wasn't holding a breadknife.

"Do you imagine that either Catherine or I could return to Paris with the Paraclete threatened and Master Abelard sick and beset by enemies?" Edgar's voice rose. "We have already proved our loyalty, how dare you doubt it!"

"We?" Astrolabe's eyebrows rose. "Not even married and already you speak for her. What would Catherine say to that?"

"That he was right, Astrolabe."

Both men started.

"Catherine! How long have you been here?" Astrolabe recovered first.

"Only a moment. I'm supposed to be hiding in the chapter until the count has left," she said as she came and sat down next to Edgar.

Brother Baldwin looked at her askance and stood behind them as chaperon. Under the table, Edgar took Catherine's hand. She sighed happily. He had spoken just as she would have. Her fears were ridiculous. No one who understood her that well would ever hurt her.

Those are the ones who can hurt you the most, the voices taunted. She clenched her teeth and ignored them

"There must be something we can do," she said. "I believe Count Raynald is afraid we'll discover that he caused his wife's death."

"Did he?' Astrolabe asked.

"He must have," Catherine said. "In one way or another. He's cruel and proud. He didn't care if she died. He only wanted a reason to attack Walter of Grancy."

"Catherine,"—Edgar removed his hand—"I can't see that it would be worth killing one's wife just to provoke a blood feud. Laming a horse is excuse enough."

"He probably cared too much for his horse," Catherine sniffed.

"And he didn't have to bring Alys to the Paraclete," Astrolabe added. "He could have let her die at her own home."

"Yes, but there might have been more questions then," Catherine countered. "It would seem a pious act, bringing her here. How could he know she would awaken? That was a kind of miracle."

"Yes, there is reason in that," Edgar said. "But not enough for an accusation. How can we prove it?"

"And what difference would it make to the countess's bequest?" Astrolabe added.

Catherine frowned. "He couldn't keep her dower if he had murdered her, could he? I don't know the law; would it be decided at the court of Count Thibault? He would never make a judgement against Mother Héloïse."

"I don't think so," Edgar said. "Isn't Tonnerre a fief of the king's?"

"But Raynald only holds it from his father, William of Nevers, so it would be . . . no, the property couldn't be decided in his own father's court, could it?" Catherine shook her head. "I can never remember who holds what from whom. It may be that the whole matter should be decided by Archbishop Henry. I think we should first find out what really happened to Alys and let the law sort itself out."

"But how?" Astrolabe asked.

The three of them stared in deep concentration at the empty soup bowls until Brother Baldwin made a pointed comment about getting ready for the afternoon service, which was already later than usual, due to the interruptions. But none of them had formed a brilliant plan. With a guilty start, Catherine got up quickly to go and then swayed dizzily.

"Catherine? Are you ill?" Edgar was glad of an excuse to hold her.

Astrolabe gently pulled her away and set her on her feet.

"When did you last eat?" he asked.

"Eat? I don't remember." She tried to think. "I couldn't face the bread last night. I kept imagining maggots. I drank my water. I suppose I ate Wednesday."

"Catherine! And you let me sit here gorging on turnip soup!" Edgar said. "Brother Baldwin, Catherine is starving, give her some bread, at least."

"No, Brother Baldwin," Catherine said firmly. "I am still a member of this community and I wish to abide by the Rule. After the service we will have bread and water. I doubt I'll die of hunger before then."

"You won't stand with me in the church transept, then?" Edgar asked. "You intend to stay with the nuns?"

Catherine took his hands.

"I have made my choice to marry you, Edgar, and I do

not regret it," she smiled and lowered her eyes. "In fact, I'd like to begin at once."

"Well, then ..." He began to pull her to him.

"But," she added, "I would like to share the service with my sisters one last time, as far as I am permitted. I will see you tomorrow and then, after Easter, I never want to be apart from you again. Can you understand that?"

"The last part, very easily." His arms went around her waist.

Astrolabe spent a moment studying the design of a water pitcher while Catherine became further convinced that there were many compensations for giving up the convent.

"You're going to be late for the service," Brother Baldwin warned her again, when it began to appear that Catherine was more in danger of suffocation than starvation. He placed a hand heavily on Edgar's shoulder.

Reluctantly, Edgar let her go.

Catherine reached the cloister just in time to get in line at the end, behind the lay sisters. Silently, they all filed into the choir. The consecrated virgins came in first, with the other *moniales* behind them and then the lay sisters. Héloïse and Prioress Astane stood in front, one on each side. Hersende, the chantress, faced them. The choir screen running across the nave, just behind the transept, hid them from the view of the people of the town of Saint-Aubin who had come to the service and stood in the left side of the transept.

There was a rustle of whispers from the other side of the screen and Catherine wished she could see what was happening. She strained to hear what the voices were saying, but she was too far away.

On the other side of the screen, Astrolabe and Edgar stood with the townspeople. In their worn woolen cloaks, they blended in easily. The convent church was really only an oratory, too small to hold large numbers of worshippers. It reminded Edgar of the local church at home, with children sitting on the floor at their parents' feet, thumbs in their mouths, quieted with threats or promises. These weren't querulous, sophisticated Parisians who demanded

entertainment with their devotions, but peasants and craftsmen for whom the plain ritual of Holy Week was enough
to comfort and refresh.

Astrolabe nudged him from his reflections.

"Isn't that Count Raynald?" he asked, pointing to the
man leaning against the transept wall, looking bored. "I
thought he was leaving."

"Apparently not," Edgar said. "I've never seen him before, but he fits Catherine's description. He doesn't look as
though he's here to make peace with the abbess."

"If he tries to interrupt the service, I'll . . ." Astrolabe
stopped. The door to the sacristy had opened and the
clergy entered the sanctuary.

The people around them began whispering in pleased
excitement. They had not known that Abelard was visiting.

Father Guiberc chanted the opening collect. Then, giving his arm to Abelard, he helped the master to the lectern.
Abelard bowed his head a second, then began: *"Haec dicit
Dominus: In tribulatione sua mane consurgent ad me: Ve-
nite, et revertamur ad Dominum, quia ipse cepit, et sanabit
nos; percutiet, et curabit nos, . . ."*

Catherine listened to the melodic voice and realized it
was Master Abelard. She couldn't believe he had recovered
so quickly. The world was full of small miracles. "Come,
let us return to the Lord, for it is he who has wounded and
he will heal us, he has struck us down and he will bind us
up, . . ." God healed Abelard so that he could perform the
service for his daughters in Christ once more. But, Catherine remembered at once, no one had healed Alys; she had
been struck down and no one had lifted her up.

Catherine's anger began to burn again. The words of
Hosea rolled through her without meaning until the end of
the passage.

*"Quia misericordiam volui, et non sacrificium; et
scientiam Dei plus quam holocausta."* "For I desire compassion and not sacrifice; and understanding of God more
than burnt offerings."

As the chantress rose to intone the tract from Habakkuk
which followed, Catherine felt properly chastised.

Edgar kept a close watch on Count Raynald throughout

the long service. The count took no part in the prayers or responses. He didn't seem moved by Abelard's sermon on the Passion or by the unearthly beauty of the singing of the sisters. Why was the man there? What did he want? For a moment Edgar had the wild thought that Raynald was attending on the chance of hearing something heretical to help destroy Abelard and the Paraclete with him. But that was nonsense. Edgar doubted the count could follow the sermon, much less take notes on it. The man must be plotting some revenge. When, at the end of the service, Raynald left the church, Edgar resolved to follow him.

After the service, the nuns went to the refectory for their one meal of the day. Catherine ate her bread slowly, afraid her stomach would reject it. The stench of the sickroom still lurked in her nose. While the bread was deciding what it would do, Catherine noticed Paciana leave the lay sisters' side of the room. She signaled a request to go also, indicating that she was not feeling well, and hurried after her.

Paciana was not returning to the building where the lay sisters slept. She had gathered up her skirts and was heading outside the convent to the tiny graveyard.

When Catherine saw where she was going, it occurred to her that perhaps she shouldn't follow. It was a private grief. It was not her right to intrude.

She slowed her steps and hid behind a tree. Watching wasn't as bad as intruding, she told herself.

Her voices were too outraged to comment.

Paciana knelt by the new grave. The ground was lumpy with clods left behind by the diggers. She threw herself forward, lying on her face across the mound of earth. She made no sound although her face was streaked with tears and dirt. She pushed herself up and, ripping open her tunic, she dug her fingernails into her chest, clawing across her breasts until there were deep streaks of blood.

"We have to stop her!" a voice hissed in her ear.

Catherine nearly cried out. Edgar put his fingers to her lips.

"You shouldn't be here," she hissed back.

"Neither of us should," he answered. "Who is she?"

"Her name is Paciana," Catherine said. "You're right. We must keep her from hurting herself. But she will be furious if she knows we've been watching. Why did you follow me?"

"I didn't," Edgar said. "I followed him."

Catherine looked where he was pointing. At the edge of the cemetery stood Count Raynald.

"You! Woman!" he shouted. "What do you think you're doing here?"

Stunned, Paciana quickly covered herself before she looked up.

Count Raynald moved closer to her in the twilight.

"Don't think you can fool me with some fake show of grief," he sneered. "All you want from Alys is her property. That abbess of yours has no business . . ."

His voice stopped as if snuffed out. He had seen her face.

" 'Ciana!" he said. "Oh, Paciana!"

Catherine listened in astonishment. She had never heard the count speak with a trace of emotion before, and now . . .

He was almost crying. "Dear God, 'Ciana, they told me you were dead!"

Paciana remained kneeling in the soft earth, one hand holding her ripped tunic against her chest. Her face showed no emotion and she rose to her feet and backed away from Raynald.

For the last time in her life, Paciana spoke.

"I am dead," she said.

Seven

The cemetery of the Paraclete,
twilight, Good Friday, April 5, 1140

*Habet effrenis elatio hoc amplius surperbia ut, cum hec
superioritatem, illa nichilominus dedignetur paritem . . .*

He who has unbridled conceit is worse than one who is
proud, for the latter thinks no one is his superior, while the
former believes no one is his equal . . .

—Abbot Suger,
Vita Ludovici Grossi Regis

$\mathcal{P}$aciana turned and walked slowly back toward the convent. Raynald moved as if to follow her, then shook his head and stumbled in the opposite direction, toward the town. In their hiding place, Catherine and Edgar watched in astonishment.

"What just happened?" Edgar asked.

"I'm not sure," Catherine said. "In all the time I've been here, Paciana has never made a sound. She must have been terribly upset to break her vow. I swore I would say nothing about her, Edgar. I promised, so I can't explain why I believe this. But I'm sure she knows what happened to Raynald's wife."

"Her grief was not that of a stranger," Edgar said.

"No, she knew the countess," Catherine admitted. "But I don't understand this at all. What is she to the count? I thought she had been here since long before his marriage to Alys. Oh, Edgar, why are people's lives so tangled? Things should move in straight lines, nice and clear, from birth to heaven, without all this pain."

Edgar held her more tightly, his cheek against the curls that had once again tumbled loose onto her forehead.

"So they should," he said. "so ours should. But I have no power to make it happen. I wish I did, *min leoffæst.*"

Catherine sighed and then smiled as she felt the roughness of his jaw against her face. She ran her fingers across the stubble on his chin.

"I'm glad you don't," she said. "You'd be insufferable if you were omnipotent."

"Catherine." He kissed her again, thoroughly enough that she began to wonder whether the ground were very uncomfortable and whether a bit more mud on her robes would be that obvious. With an effort, she broke away.

"Edgar, it's Easter Vigil," she reminded them both.

"Yes, yes." He inhaled deeply to clear his head. "You are quite right, and the rain seems to have started again. We should return at once."

They hurried back to the guesthouse, but not quickly enough. Prioress Astane stood at the door, arms crossed.

"Catherine," she said. "I saw you leave the cloister. And now you return alone with this man! I cannot allow such flouting of the rules of proper behavior. You gave no thought to the reputation of your community. I'm ashamed of you."

Edgar stepped in front of Catherine.

"She is not a member of your community any longer, Sister," he said. "She is my betrothed and we have done nothing dishonorable."

Astane nodded. "I'm glad to hear it. Nevertheless, Catherine, Sister Bertrada has instructed me that you will stay with Sister Melisande in the infirmary until you leave us. She has felt all along that you shouldn't be allowed to remain in the dormitory with those who have dedicated their lives and chastity to Our Lord."

Catherine's heart sank, but she nodded acquiescence. Edgar started to protest.

"No, Sister Bertrada is right," Catherine said. "I was only allowed to stay with the other sisters because of Mother Héloïse's kindness and because there was nowhere else for me. It's not an expulsion, Edgar. I've made my choice. I don't mind."

Edgar gave in. "I'll go find Astrolabe. And tomorrow, you can stand next to me in the transept and not hide from the world in the choir anymore."

He turned to go, then stopped and took a small leather bag from around his neck.

"I almost forgot," he said. "I brought you a present. It's not much but I thought you might like it because the old one that Garnulf made for you was lost. Take it now, as a talisman."

He tossed the bag to her as Sister Astane opened the gate and led her in.

"We're not really angry with you, you know," she whispered to Catherine. "He seems a nice boy. Master Abelard speaks very highly of him. But you must think of our reputation."

"I know, Sister. I am sorry," Catherine told her.

Sister Melisande was at Compline when Catherine arrived at her small room above the infirmary. A pallet had been made up on the floor and Catherine took possession of it at once, knowing that the infirmarian would otherwise insist on giving up her own bed.

So, her voices began. *You've finally crossed the Rubicon. About time, too. Aren't you ashamed?*

We didn't do anything, yet! Catherine protested.

Only because you couldn't find a dry place to throw yourselves! they taunted. *But that's what you wanted to do, Catherine, and intention is what matters. At least be honest. Somehow you thought you could be a part of the convent without obeying the Rule. That's the worst hypocrisy. Admit that the door to the cloister is now closed to you and start living a decent secular life, if that's possible for you!*

Catherine put her hands over her ears. It was true. The sin was not in her desire of the body as much as in the dishonesty of believing she could continue to enjoy the benefits of the convent without trying to control that desire.

No more.

The bag Edgar had given her was still in her hand. A

talisman, not a love token. That was like him. She reached in and felt something hard. Not a ring. That was a relief. She wasn't fond of rings; they got in the way of the pen when writing. She took it out.

It was a cross, about two inches long, made of bone or ivory. There was a delicate tracing across it, patterns and swirls, with occasional eyes and hands appearing and vanishing in the design. It was beautiful. In the center of the crosspiece there was a clear space. She squinted. In the center of that was an ornate ℭ, blending into an ℗. A hole had been bored in the top and the silver chain passed through it.

"A talisman, truly. Oh, Edgar, wherever did you find it?" she whispered, and she slipped it around her neck and tucked it inside her *chainse*. She lay down and, despite the hardness of the bed, fell asleep at once.

She was wakened in the night by the bells calling the sisters to the night office. She had gotten up and was out the door before she realized that there was no longer a place for her in the choir. Slowly, she returned to her bed. She lay awake a long time, clutching the ivory cross until the pattern of it was etched into her hand.

Edgar and Astrolabe were quite happy to stay in the guesthouse. The comfort there was no worse than a monastery hostel and better than many inns. The guesthouse, like the hostel for pilgrims and paupers, was managed by the lay brothers. These were the men who tilled the fields, repaired the buildings and did the other manual labor that was too difficult for the sisters. They were from all classes; all had promised the abbess obedience unto death.

Brother Baldwin came to see that they had everything they needed. The old man fascinated Edgar. Despite his gnarled hands and rough clothing, he still carried the aura of the warrior he had been for so many years.

"We're fine," he told the brother. "We noticed Count Raynald at the service. Are he and his men in the hostel tonight?"

"Not they," Baldwin snorted. "Nothing we could offer would be good enough for them. No, the count has gone to Quincy, to stay with the family of his poor countess. Weaklings, all of them. Need feather cushions or they can't sleep. They wouldn't have lasted long at the siege of Antioch."

"You were there, on the Great Crusade, then?" Edgar asked, his eye as wide as a child's.

The old man nodded. "More than forty years ago, it was. Funny, the stories I hear about the crusade all tell of the glory of Jerusalem, the towers and the holy places. But all I remember now is the dust and the blood and what I would have given for a mug of cold ale."

"You fought with King Louis, afterwards, didn't you?" Astrolabe asked.

"And his father, King Philippe, before," Baldwin said. "Against the English king and the count of Meulan. I was in the Auvergne and at the siege of Clermont. We burnt most of the town at Montferrand in that campaign, as I recall. Smoke and ashes everywhere. I was as thirsty as Shadrach, Meshach and Abednego in the fiery furnace!"

"I never realized that war dried the throat so," Edgar commented.

"More important than food," Baldwin told him. He was about to elaborate on other parched battles when Astrolabe interrupted.

"You don't happen to remember who was lord to Count William of Nevers, do you?" he asked.

"Duke of Burgundy," Baldwin answered without hesitation.

So that's who would decide the crimes of Raynald. Edgar tried to remember what he had heard of Duke Hugh.

"Of course, sometimes Nevers fought for Louis," Baldwin added. "Burgundy aids the crown if it's in their interest to. And Nevers is part of the archdiocese of Sens, of course, which contains Paris." He scratched at a louse in his beard. "It changed all the time, really. Look at Count Thibault. One minute he was against Louis and with Henry of England. Then the next he was with Louis against Meulan. And, of course, now he's not happy about the affair between his cousin's husband and the queen's sister. He refused to help young Louis put down the com-

mune at Poitiers. I'm not sure liege loyalties matter much
to Thibault. Now his father, and even more, his mother . . .
ah, well, that's another story."

He got up reluctantly.

"You boys have everything you need?" he asked them.
"I have duties to perform yet tonight. I'll look in on you
again before I go to bed."

He took his lantern. Edgar leaned from his bed and blew
out the candle.

"Not much help there," Astrolabe said.

"What do you think he has to do?" Edgar wanted to
know. Compline was over. Everyone should be in bed by
now.

"Check the locks, perhaps." Astrolabe wasn't interested.
"Why? do you think we should follow him? He's been
here for years. Mother and Prioress Astane trust him."

"Sorry. I seem to have become less trusting lately," Edgar answered. "I shouldn't be so suspicious of everyone."

"Yes, you should," Astrolabe said. "You'll live longer.
But I think we can assume Brother Baldwin has genuine
work to perform."

"Very well." Edgar sat a moment as his eyes slowly adjusted to the night. "So, what should we do?"

"Sleep?"

Edgar ignored that.

"What about Master Abelard?" he said. "Do you think
your mother can convince him to abandon his debate with
Bernard of Clairvaux?"

"She seems to think it would be wrong to try to stop
him." Astrolabe's voice was tired. "I don't think she real-
izes how ill he is."

"Could this problem with the count of Tonnerre affect
him?" Edgar asked. "If we try to accuse someone other
than Walter of Grancy of attacking countess Alys, could it
anger someone who might revenge himself on Master
Abelard?"

Astrolabe was silent a long time. "I'm not sure," he said
at last. "It would be bishops and abbots who judged the
debate, but they all have families they are loyal to, as well.
For instance, if Peter of Cluny came, he might vote in Fa-

ther's favor, if only because he feels Abbot Bernard defines orthodoxy too narrowly. And, if we prove that Raynald of Tonnerre was responsible for the death of his wife, Peter might be even more inclined to help because his brother, Ponce, is abbot of Vézeley and Raynald's father has been fighting with the monks there for years."

"And Hugh of Auxerre is not only bishop under Raynald's brother, the count of Auxerre, he's also a distant relation of Abbot Bernard and a former monk of Cîteaux," Edgar added. "Any meddling on our part to discredit Raynald might only make things worse in his opinion."

"It seems as if we'll be damned whichever way we go." Astrolabe didn't sound very concerned.

"Then we may as well continue as we planned," Edgar yawned.

There was the sound of scratching from Astrolabe's side of the room.

"I think," he said mildly, "I'll mention to Mother that, now that Lent is over, Brother Baldwin should be encouraged to change the straw in this bed."

"I remember a bathhouse in Paris where the *estuveresses* sing as they wash your hair," Edgar said, half asleep. "I'll take you there when we get back."

"Do you think Catherine would approve?" Astrolabe laughed.

The image came to Edgar of a huge wooden tub filled with streaming water and Catherine sitting next to him, clothed only in the dark disorder of her curls, soapy and smiling.

"Edgar?"

Edgar was grateful for the darkness. His imagination was affecting his body strongly. Suddenly, he was wide awake.

"Approve?" he said. "Why not? They'd just wash our hair. But what about this business here? We can't ignore it. Catherine definitely wouldn't approve of that."

"But where could we start?" Astrolabe asked. "We can't simply accuse Raynald of murder and demand trial by combat."

Edgar shuddered as the thought. He'd seen enough of those at home.

"We could try to eliminate Walter of Grancy as a suspect," he suggested. "Or prove his guilt. He probably has a group of friends and tenants all willing to swear to his innocence, but we could ask locally about where he was when the countess was attacked. People are more likely to tell the truth when they're not asked to swear to it in public."

"Yes, that would be a good start," Astrolabe said. "First we take my father and Catherine back to Paris and then we'll set out on our own private crusade. *C'est tes acors?*"

"C'est mes acors," Edgar agreed. He wondered how Catherine would feel about being left behind in Paris. He wondered how he would feel about leaving her. Both speculations were unsettling.

"How many locks does the Paraclete have?" he asked suddenly. "Brother Baldwin has been gone a long time."

"Maybe we should go see if he needs any help," Astrolabe said.

Edgar agreed. They stopped at the hostel to see if Brother Baldwin was there, but there was no sign of him. Growing worried, Edgar picked up a stout iron-tipped hoe from the toolroom, just in case.

Catherine heard the whispers for some time before she woke enough to realize what they were. There were men hissing in the herb garden under the infirmary window. Yes, men, of course, not the snakes and dragons of her dream. Sister Melisande slept the sleep of the hard-working and pure of thought. She didn't stir when Catherine crept closer to the window to make out the words.

"It's your duty, old man," someone said. "There's a traitor in there."

"Whom did they betray?" The voice was Brother Baldwin's. "One of your lords? That's nothing to me. I have no earthly allegiance now. I only serve God and his daughters here."

"And what if one of them broke the laws of God?" the man insisted.

"Then I would leave her to his justice," Baldwin answered. "Now go from this place. you have no business prowling about here like the soldiers at Christ's tomb. The night is for grave robbers and heretics."

"We'll have her," the other man said, "if we have to burn this place down to do it."

"God won't let you." Baldwin's voice rose. "And neither will I."

Through the shutter, Catherine saw the glint of a dagger being raised and pointed at Brother Baldwin. She reached for the first heavy object she could lay her hands on. A solid earthenware pot.

"I hope there's nothing expensive in this," she thought as she pushed the shutter open and dropped it on the head of Baldwin's attacker.

There was a thump and a cry. The knife dropped. Baldwin picked it up with a swiftness that belied his new profession.

"What did I tell you?" he said calmly. "God has spoken. If I slit your throats right here, I've no doubt I'll be doing his will. I cut enough of them at Antioch and Jerusalem and the pope himself blessed me for it. Are you ready to meet your creator?"

Catherine couldn't make out the faces in the dark, but she could tell that there were two men facing Baldwin. Their ages combined were probably half his, but the charisma of the crusader was on him and they were uncertain as to their next move.

"Brother Baldwin!" someone called.

The men turned. Edgar and Astrolabe had followed the intruders over the garden hedge and were running toward them. Catherine heard the sound of steel being unsheathed. She knew neither Edgar nor Astrolabe were trained to fight and she feared neither one had a weapon. She felt around. What else was there to throw?

"*Montjoie et Saint Denis!*" Brother Baldwin gave the old battle cry as he leaped at the men who were now advancing upon Astrolabe and Edgar.

"*Hâlig Cuthbert ond Ædward Cyning!*" Edgar shouted back as he charged the knights with the hoe.

Catherine added to the confusion by throwing as many small objects as she could reach from the shelf next to the window.

Caught by sudden attacks from two sides and above, the knights veered suddenly and made for their horses, tethered to a tree outside the hedge.

Edgar and Astrolabe reached Brother Baldwin as the knights rode off.

"Did they hurt you?" Edgar asked.

"Hardly," Baldwin responded, tucking the knife in his rope belt. "I had them well in hand and only spared them for Our Lord's sake, of course. That was some advance you made, young man. I wouldn't have thought one of you scholars would have enough *pendans* to fight."

"My father would have been surprised, too," Edgar said.

"I wasn't," Catherine announced.

They all looked up.

"Was that you showering rocks at us?" Baldwin said. "I haven't been so pelted since the siege of Antioch."

"Have we wakened the whole convent?" Astrolabe asked.

"I don't think so," Catherine said, remembering to lower her voice again. "The dorter is on the other side of the cloister. Even Sister Melisande hasn't stirred. What did those men want, Brother Baldwin?"

"Robbery and rape, most likely," Baldwin said.

"I heard more than that," Catherine told him. "They were looking for a particular woman."

"Catherine, we can't discuss this here, shouting up at you," Astrolabe reminded her.

"You're right, I'll come down," Catherine answered. "It's not far. If I hang from the window, will one of you catch me?"

"Catherine! You can't do any such thing!" Edgar was as horrified as Sister Bertrada would have been. "It's the middle of the night!"

"I know that," she said as she climbed over the sill. "And all the gates are locked and barred. But I really must get out somehow and not just to talk to you. I have a definite problem. I just discovered that the first thing I threw at those men was the infirmary chamberpot."

With that, she dropped into Edgar's waiting arms.

"Now," said Catherine when she had returned after taking care of immediate business, "It sounds to me as if the count sent someone back to see that Paciana never revealed what she knew about the countess Alys."

Edgar agreed. "The abbess should be warned. What if they come back and bring a larger troop?"

Brother Baldwin seemed more perturbed by the troop standing around him.

"The other brothers and I can fight off such men," he insisted. "Or we'll send to Anseau of Trainel for aid. But there really can't be any danger. Think of what you're saying, son. No one would attempt to attack a convent, at least not openly. Especially not this one. Not a house in Christendom would be open to such a man."

That was true. Not since the days of the heathen invaders, hundreds of years ago, had a convent been destroyed by force. Even in tales like *Raoul de Cambrai*, such an act was done only by the greatest villain and was punished most horribly by God and man. The walls of the convent were not for defense. They were a symbol of the division between the worlds of the sacred and the profane. As Catherine had proved, it was not difficult to leave and anyone determined to enter could, welcome or not.

"Still, my mother and father must be told," Astrolabe said. "The protection of the Paraclete is their duty."

"Of course," Catherine said. "But I don't think Count Raynald will lay siege to the Paraclete. He only wanted to remove one woman, and quietly, by night, it seems."

"Then this is not the place to look for the answers," Astrolabe said.

"No, we have to find out what happened some other way," Catherine agreed. "Edgar, do you think we could wait until after Ascension to be married? I want to see Alys's mother, Constanza, and it would be easier to go alone."

"Forty days more!" Edgar forgot to keep his voice down. "Why not wait until Pentecost or Michaelmas or Christmas? Perhaps you'd like to forget the whole idea?"

For an instant, Catherine was startled by his reaction.

For another instant, she was angry. Then she realized what he was really saying.

"Then why not tonight, now?" she asked. "Consent is all that's required and we have that."

"Well, unless you can think of a way to get back into the infirmary tonight, that might be the best idea," Astrolabe said.

"Oh, no!" Brother Baldwin interrupted. "I don't think much of almost-consecrated nuns leaving the convent for marriage, but if you do it, you go out by the front gate, with the blessing of the abbess and the sisters. I have the keys and I'm taking you back now. What you do tomorrow or Michaelmas is not my responsibility, but tonight, it is."

He took Catherine roughly by the elbow and marched her to the little door leading from the garden to the infirmary. He unlocked it and unceremoniously pushed her inside, making sure to lock the door after her.

"Now, let's have no more sacrilege done tonight," he said when he returned to Edgar and Astrolabe. "Not in all my years here have I had such an evening."

"Reminds you of the old days, does it?" Astrolabe asked.

"Ah, yes," Brother Baldwin smiled. "I could have run those *avoutres* through the heart as easy as slicing bread. It's shameful how they're training men these days. A knight who loses his concentration just because a pot falls on his head won't last long in this world."

Edgar paid them little attention. Forty days! He'd already waited four months. That was enough. And what did Catherine have in mind regarding the mother of the countess? Did she intend to disguise herself as a laundress and uncover secrets among the dirty sheets? Did she think for a moment that he would let her go alone into a place that might harbor a murderer?

Edgar stopped. Of course she did. For the first time, he realized why Catherine's father had sighed when he accepted the dower for her. He had thought it was a sigh of regret. But now he knew it was relief.

Despite himself, Edgar grinned. Life with Catherine was going to be fun.

Eight

The Paraclete,
dawn, Easter Sunday, April 7, 1140

Inde est, quod omnes credimus:
illo quietis tempore,
quo gallus exsultans canit,
Christum redisse ex infernis.

And so it is, as we all believe, that at this quiet
moment, when the cock crows in exultation,
Christ returned from hell.

—Prudentius,
Cathemerinon

$\mathcal{T}$he entire community stood on the hill outside the convent to greet the Risen Savior. Father Guiberc and Abelard came first. Then the sisters arrived in procession, Abbess Héloïse leading, their faces illuminated by the candle each one carried. The tiny drops of light flickered through the mist of the morning twilight like splinters of hope. Sister Hersende raised her hands. There was a long silence as everyone watched her. She gave the signal and all the candles were extinguished by the joyous breath of the Alleluia given at the first ray of dawn.

Many of the townspeople of Saint-Aubin had come to attend this Easter service, which was special to the Paraclete. Edgar and Astrolabe looked them over carefully to be sure none of Raynald's men were among them. But only local people made up the gathering; peasants, craftsmen, and the minor knights and their families, hardly better dressed than those who tilled the fields.

Catherine stood with them, participating in the responses of the laity. She knew all these people, from the poor knight, Felix, who gave them the fish from his pond at Bossenay, to Walter the bargeman, who gave the convent land and tithes, to Paul and Emmelina the vintners, who had brought their children, still half-asleep. The family set aside an arpent of vines every year to make wine for the nuns. Even Emma Rebursata had come, her bristly hair covered as well as possible. Catherine had always felt a certain comradeship with Emma, whose hair was so untamable that the children called her Emma Hedgehog. All these people were as much a part of the Paraclete as the nuns. They tithed themselves to support the convent and depended on it for prayers and comfort.

So it was not so foreign on this side of the choir, after all. Catherine went with the town into the church by the common door, her hand resting lightly in the crook of Edgar's arm.

She cried through the entire services of Easter Lauds, not noisily, but as snow melts in the sunlight. When it was over, she had mourned her old life and knew she was ready to rejoice in the new one.

"Are you going to do that at our wedding?" Edgar asked as they left.

"Very likely," Catherine admitted, returning her sodden handkerchief to her sleeve. "Ceremonies always make me cry. But I feel absolutely wonderful when I've finished."

"I won't wait until Ascension," he told her.

"I must find out about Countess Alys," she said.

"We'll find a way to do it together," he answered. "We should start as we mean to go on."

"And what of the accusations against Master Abelard?" Catherine asked.

Edgar shook his head. "We can do nothing about those except to be prepared to stand with him should he continue in his determination to debate Abbot Bernard."

"Together?"

"Yes. Do you doubt me?" Edgar asked.

Catherine looked away. "I think that you mean it at this moment. But a part of me is still afraid. In law you will have the power to beat me and to forbid me what I want most. Other men do this."

Edgar considered that. Technically, his father had that

same power over him, his brothers and his stepmother. It had never occurred to Edgar that he would have any more luck exercising that power than his father had.

"Do you know what Master Hugh of Saint-Victor says?" he asked.

"About beating your wife?" Catherine said. "What would he know about that?"

Edgar went on. "He says that Eve was made from Adam's rib to be his equal companion. If she were to have been his mistress, she would have been made from the head; if his slave, from the feet. He also says that marriage is a reciprocal compact in which we each become debtor to the other, and Catherine, I very much want to start paying my debt."

Catherine feared she might start crying again.

"Oh, Edgar," she said, "I'm so glad you're well read. I think we should be married the moment we get to Paris."

"That is an arrangement I can tolerate," he answered. "The very first moment."

"Agreed."

The next morning, as they were preparing to leave, Sister Thecla came to the infirmary to see Catherine.

"There's a man at the gate," she said. "He says he needs to see you and Master Abelard before you go."

"Do you know who he is?" Catherine asked.

"I've never seen him before. His accent is of Paris," she answered. "He says he's a messenger of your father's."

"Father?"

"I asked him to wait in the guest's entry, but he said he'd rather stay outside. He looks quite a bit like you," Sister Thecla added. "Don't you have a brother?"

"Yes, but he doesn't look . . ." Catherine got up. Not her brother, but her cousin, her Jewish cousin. Although she had known him all her life, she had only discovered their relationship the previous autumn. But that was something Sister Thecla wasn't ever to know. Her father would be ruined if anyone in Paris learned he had secretly returned to the faith of his parents.

"I'll come down at once," she finished.

Solomon was waiting with Edgar, Astrolabe and Master Abelard by the gate. They looked far too serious for a wedding party.

"*Diex te saut,*" Catherine greeted him shortly. "What's happened? Is my father all right?"

"He's well," Solomon answered. "He sent me to tell you that you mustn't come to Paris now. Your mother has returned home unexpectedly."

"Oh, dear, that is inconvenient." Catherine tried to think of an alternative. "Couldn't I come stay with Eliazar?"

"No," Solomon said. "Hubert thinks it would be too dangerous. Your sister tried to keep your mother under guard, but you know how she wanders from church to church. What if she saw you in the street?"

"From what I understand of your mother's condition," Abelard said, "she firmly believes that you ascended to heaven last Christmastide from the tower of your brother's castle and that you are among the blessed saints."

Glumly, Catherine nodded. "Agnes says that she's built a shrine to me up there between the bake oven and the guard's urinal."

"Just think what it might do to her, if she met you one night, walking through the Juiverie," Abelard reminded her. "She has found her own way to reconcile herself to losing you. She might not be strong enough to endure the joy of having you back."

"But it's so embarrassing," Catherine said. "And difficult. What can we do?"

"Your father has given me orders concerning that," Solomon told her. "I'm to take you to Troyes."

Catherine stared at him, shocked. She turned to Edgar. He looked at the ground and shuffled his feet. She made an attempt to control her anger. She failed.

"The only way you're taking me to Troyes is trussed up like one of your parcels, and you'd better gag me, too, or you'll hear what I think of you every step of the way!" she began. "How dare my father send me off like a horse to market!"

"Now Catherine," Edgar began.

"And aren't you going to do anything about this?" she

yelled at him. "Does one partner just stand there writing in the dust while the other one is stolen into slavery?"

"It's hardly that . . ." Solomon tried again.

"And what would you call it, if you were picked up and taken somewhere you didn't want to go, without any consultation?" she shouted.

"Catherine!" he shouted back. "Why do you think I'm here now? Have I ever had a say in where I go or what I do? I've been so long running from one faire and trading town to another that I haven't even had time to find a wife of my own. I just returned from Mainz; do you think I was eager to turn around without washing the dust from my clothes and race here to be abused by you?"

They stood nose-to-nose, mirror images of fury. Suddenly, Catherine's lip twitched. She started to laugh.

"Solomon," she giggled. "It's just like when we were children. We never could play without fighting." She pulled herself together quickly. "But I still won't go to Troyes."

The gate opened and Mother Héloïse came out.

"I'm sorry to lose your voice for the choir," she told Catherine. "It carries so well."

"Mother, do you know what they want me to do?" Catherine was still too upset to submit to the rebuke.

"I believe everyone from here to Nogent does," Héloïse replied. "I don't know all the particulars, but if you would consider following your father's request, there are some things I would like you to do for me in Troyes. Could we please come inside and discuss this?"

"Catherine, I had no intention of letting you go anywhere without me," Edgar said as they all went through the gate.

"You might have said so at once," Catherine muttered, but she was already ashamed of her outburst. She looked back at Solomon. His face was thin and drawn. She shouldn't have taken her anger out on him. It was as stupid as killing the messenger who carried bad tidings.

Solomon hesitated at the threshold, then shrugged in resignation and entered. Héloïse led them to the gatehouse. Abelard sat in the chair reserved for honored visitors and the others in a row on a bench against the wall. As always when worried, the abbess paced the room. When she stopped, her fine fingers still moved, lacing and unlacing themselves as she spoke.

"I have found a puzzle in the charters," she told them. "I need your help to explain it."

She turned to Master Peter. "You know our situation; the Paraclete exists on bits and pieces of things. People don't give us great tracts of land the way they do for the monks. We get eggs and cheese and a third of the grinding of a mill. Or the right to some woodland for fuel or building."

"I thought the people here had been generous to you," Abelard said. "Are you in need? Do they deny you subsistence because of your association with me?"

"Of course not," she said too quickly. "What I meant was that I am accustomed to many small donations, which together provide for us very well and in a true Christian spirit of sharing. Countess Alys gave us one such small piece of land, in the forest of Othe. We had the use of it in her lifetime and were to receive it in full if she died after making her profession here."

She paused. "At least, that is how I interpret the charter. Count Raynald disagrees with me. He wants us to return the land at once. I don't understand his vociferousness. The gift is not extensive and the land, as I recall, is extremely rocky. We have done nothing with it since the donation, as it's useless for farming or grazing."

"Then why is Count Raynald so determined not to let you have it?" Astrolabe asked.

"That's what I would like Catherine to find out in Troyes. I believe there are people there who will know why this unimportant bit of land is so valuable to Raynald," Héloïse answered. She turned to Solomon. "Where did Sieur Hubert plan on Catherine staying, at Nôtre-Dame-aux-Nonnains?"

Solomon was distinctly uncomfortable. He did not like being anywhere near a convent and he hated pretense. What should he tell her?

"I think Father had intended that I stay with a family of

his acquaintance," Catherine spoke up. "At least, I presume so. Another merchant who might be going back to Paris soon."

Héloïse looked from Catherine to Solomon.

"Are these people coreligionists of yours?" she asked. Solomon nodded.

"And they would take her in?"

He shrugged and nodded again.

"As you know, Mother," Catherine said, "my father has many business dealings with the Jews. Since, by their laws, they are not allowed to loan money to each other, he often acts as an intermediary."

"If her safety could be assured," Abelard spoke slowly, considering, "she would have much more freedom of movement there than if she went to another convent."

He faced Catherine. "You have made it clear that you do not wish to go to Troyes. Would you change your mind for our sake?"

Throughout the discussion, Edgar had sat staring at the floor, seemingly lost in his own thoughts. Now he took Catherine's hand.

"Master Abelard . . . Father Peter," he said, "Catherine and I, we seem to be constantly brought together only to be separated again. There is nothing I must do in Paris, unless you have a commission for me. If she must go to Troyes, I want to go with her . . . honorably."

"Oh, yes," Catherine said. "I think that would be the most logical thing to do. Edgar would be a great help, Mother. We work very well together. Master Abelard, we have all the contracts signed, everything we need. Will you please witness and bless our vows here, now?"

She waited for a chorus of disapproval, both from the people in the room and the voices inside her mind. No one spoke at all.

Abelard looked at Héloïse. She put her hands to her lips and stared back at him for the longest moment of Catherine's life. Was the abbess remembering the hasty and hidden wedding she had made, and all the sorrow that had come afterwards? Catherine had heard the story many times. She remembered that Héloïse had resisted, even af-

ter Astrolabe was born. She had been determined not to
ruin her lover's career by marriage. She had told people
she was proud to be Abelard's whore.

Could I do that for Edgar? she wondered. *It would be
a poor sort of love if I couldn't.*

And his would be a poor sort of love if he'd let you.

Ah, yes. She had feared those voices couldn't keep silent for long.

Finally Héloïse lowered her hands to her throat and
closed her eyes.

"Yes," she said. "It seems the best way."

"We should leave at once if we're to be at Troyes by
nightfall," Solomon reminded them.

"And Father and I wanted to reach Provins today," Astrolabe added.

"Very well," Abelard said. "We shall meet at the church
door. Catherine, go get your things."

As they left, Héloïse put a hand on Catherine's arm.

"Stay a moment," she said. "I wish to speak with you
alone."

Catherine waited until everyone had gone. She smiled
nervously.

"You have a last word of advice for me?" she asked.

Héloïse sighed. "No, my dear. I've given you all I can.
From now on you will have to discover life for yourself.
I asked you to wait because I have another commission for
you."

She took a small square of parchment from her sleeve.

"Some time ago, the convent made a loan to Peter of
Baschi, deacon of Saint-Aventin in Troyes. He has made
no effort to repay us. I have sent letters to him and to
friends in Rome who might have some influence over him,
but I've heard nothing." She stopped, seeming embarrassed. "It was twenty marks of silver and we need it."

"Twenty!" That seemed a huge sum to Catherine.

"Catherine," Héloïse continued, "these people you will
be staying with, ask them if they will undertake to recover
from Father Peter the money he owes us. I will be willing
to pay them half of it for their efforts."

"I don't know about that part of the business," Catherine said. "Father does little moneylending, except as I described. But I'll ask Solomon."

"Thank you," Héloïse smiled. "Now, I've kept you long enough. Get your things. We'll say our farewells after you're married."

Catherine hugged her and ran.

True to her promise, Catherine cried for the few moments it took to become Edgar's wife. It wasn't much of a ceremony; only the exchange of vows was required outside the church door. No one had remembered a ring. They were witnessed by Héloïse and Prioress Astane, Solomon and Astrolabe, as well as a few of the lay sisters and brothers who had seen them assemble and been curious as to the reason.

When Master Abelard closed the book and announced that she was married, Catherine felt quite unchanged. Shouldn't something have happened, some grand revelation or sense of loss? Mother Héloïse was kissing her cheek and wiping her eyes.

"You will always be welcome here, if you need us," she whispered. "Don't be afraid."

Catherine hugged her. "I'm not; I don't seem to feel anything. Why not?"

"It can be a great shock to get what you want most so suddenly." Héloïse smiled. "I assure you, feeling will return."

Out of the corner of her eye, Catherine noticed Paciana. The lay sister was standing on the pathway, her arms full of kindling. She turned away as soon as Catherine looked, but in that second, her expression hit Catherine with a sharp slap. There was no pity or forgiveness or sisterly love. Paciana was staring at her with murderous hate.

Catherine shuddered. Héloïse followed her glance.

"Catherine, you are not to worry about Paciana any longer," she said. "Go to Troyes and find out what you can about that land. And make that request for me. Nothing more. Do you understand?"

"Yes, Mother," Catherine said.

The men had gone to get the horses. Solomon had gone

to Saint-Aubin and purchased a mount for Edgar and Catherine to share. Héloïse went back to her duties, leaving Catherine to wait with Brother Baldwin. He leaned on his hoe as they watched the men load the packs for the journey.

"The boy over there,"—Brother Baldwin gestured— "you called him Solomon; he a Jew?"

"Yes," Catherine admitted. "The nephew of a man who trades with my father."

"Funny," Brother Baldwin said. "He doesn't look like the Jews I saw in the Holy Land. He looks just like us."

"How were they different?" Catherine asked.

"You know, darker, crafty-eyed," Baldwin said. He scratched his head. "Truth is, the Saracens looked like that, too. We couldn't tell them apart. Now that I think of it, even the Christians who lived there were dark and crafty-eyed."

Catherine stared at him.

"Then how did you know who to fight?"

"That was easy; we just killed everyone who lived there." Brother Baldwin went back to his hoeing. "After all, they were all pagans and heretics, so it didn't much matter."

Catherine had heard the stories and songs of the crusade. Somehow she had always imagined that a divinely empowered army would know who the enemy was. She looked at Solomon again. He probably would have been spared. He was as French as anyone.

Brother Baldwin was feeling reminisicent. He leaned on his hoe again.

"Of course, when I came back, it was harder," he mused. "When I was fighting for the old king. You figured that if you were besieging a place, anyone who came out was the enemy and everyone around was a friend. And, if you were inside the castle, you killed anyone who tried to come over or tunnel under the wall. But it didn't always work that way. Annoying, that was."

He shook his head and returned complacently to his work.

Catherine stared at him. Whatever his reasons for becoming a *conversus*, they didn't seem to include slaughtering fellow Christians.

As she was pondering this, the church door behind her opened a crack and a hand reached out and beckoned to her. Quickly, she slipped inside.

Emilie hugged her. "*Benedicite*, Catherine," she whispered. "Be happy in your life. You know I have nothing for a wedding gift, but I can give you a piece of information. Alys's mother, Constanza, is my second cousin; my mother's father and her father's mother were brother and sister."

Catherine absorbed this. "And . . . ?"

"We don't talk about it much; her grandmother was a bastard, but," Emilie continued, "Constanza has always tried to establish herself in the family. If you have any trouble meeting her, use my name. She'll have no choice but to admit you."

"Thank you, Emilie," Catherine said. "But I don't think I'll have the chance to meet her."

Emilie looked over her shoulder. "I have to hurry. I'm supposed to be copying a commentary on Romans II. I thought you were going to Troyes."

"I am, but . . ."

"Constanza always spends the month after Easter at her late husband's home in Troyes. It's near the Paris gate, not far from Saint-Remi. Anyone can direct you."

There was a noise from the shadows on the convent side of the church. The steady tapping of a wooden rod on a stone floor.

"Sister Bertrada," Emilie sighed. She hugged Catherine again. "Good luck! Don't forget me."

"Never," Catherine promised. "Good luck to you. Pray for me."

Emilie vanished into the shadows and Catherine stepped back into the sunlight.

Edgar and Solomon were waiting.

"Are you ready?" Edgar asked.

Catherine's hand touched the weathered paint of the church door. She hoped Sister Bertrada wouldn't punish Emilie too much.

"Yes," she answered.

Solomon steadied her as she swung up behind Edgar and wrapped her arms about him. His pale hair hung past his collar and tickled her nose, but she only tightened her grip.

"Do you feel married?" she asked him.

"Not yet," he said.

"I don't either," she said. "How long does it take, do you think?"

He twisted round in the saddle and kissed her, nearly causing them both to fall.

"I would say until ten minutes after we finally find a bed to ourselves," he answered.

"Oh."

Solomon rode ahead of them, trying not to listen. He foresaw a very boring journey that day, with little intelligent conversation. He resigned himself to a dull trip and only hoped that this sex business wouldn't permanently ruin two fairly good minds. With the way things were shaping up in Paris, as well as the problems here, he knew he would need as many clear-reasoning people around him as he could find.

Nine

Il se coucent ensanble quant nuis fu enserie,
L'une cars conut l'autre, Nature nes oublie;
L'uns rent l'autre son droit et font lor cortoisie
Qu'amors a estoré entre ami et amie
Quant ont lor volenté et lor joie aconplie,
Si n'est mais damoisele, ains est dame joïe.

When night had fallen they lay together,
Then one body knew the other. Nature does not
forget them.
The one renders the other her right and they make
the respect
That love has created between a man and woman.
When they have all their desire and their joy fulfilled
She is no more a maid but is now a happy wife.

—*Elioxe* 11.460–465

*C*ould you move a bit, Edgar?" Catherine asked. "There's a very sharp bit of this hay sticking straight into my back."

Obligingly, but with reluctance, Edgar lifted himself up and waited while she wriggled herself away from the offending fodder.

"This isn't exactly the wedding night I'd planned," he told her. "I had thought we'd have a feather bed and silken sheets."

"And all the relatives snickering at the door? I've heard enough about those to be glad we didn't," she said as she put her hands around his neck. "A blanket on straw is really more practical, considering. It's just as well the fog was too thick for us to reach Troyes last night. By the way, you don't have to hang above me like that anymore."

"I know," he smiled. "I just wanted to look at you. It was too dark last night to see clearly."

He proceeded to do so. Catherine felt herself blushing. She looked above him, to the bits of dim light penetrating the thatch of the roof. She could hear the scurry of the rats as they ran across the timber frame. A trickle of dust landed on Edgar's back. He didn't seem to notice. It embarrassed her to be so closely examined.

"The scar on my side is from falling out of a tree when I was seven," she said, trying not to watch him. "Everything else is just as God made me."

"I see nothing in his work to complain of," he said as he settled back down on her.

"Wait, get up again," she said. "Where did you get that?"

She pointed to the fist-sized bruise over the left side of his rib cage.

He'd almost forgotten about the knife attack, although the area was still tender to the touch and ached if he had to breathe heavily. Actually, it was aching a bit now.

"An accident in Paris," he told her. "Someone bumped into me. You know how the crowds are in Holy Week."

There was no point in worrying her, he told himself. It was near enough to the truth.

She brushed her hand lightly across the bruise, as if to erase it. Then she drew him back down against her.

"From now on," she said, "we must try to watch out for each other more."

His lips felt the scar on her throat, still red even four months after the incident. Watching out for Catherine was no easy task. She had already endured pain for his sake, and he had begun their life together by giving her more.

He lay quietly for a minute, as her fingers idly wandered across his back. Then he rolled over onto one elbow.

"Catherine," he said, "are you sorry this morning that you chose me? I hurt you. I tried not to, but I know I did. You can't deny it. I wanted so much not to hurt you."

She snuggled closer to him, pressing her ear against his chest to feel the certain pattern of his heartbeat. Then she smiled up at him.

"It's all right," she said. "It couldn't be helped. It's Eve's fault, not yours. Really, it wasn't as bad as I'd been told. The way some women talk, one would think slow evisceration was preferable to a bridal bed."

She considered a moment, then kissed the underside of his chin.

"I suspect," she added, "that they didn't approach the event with as much shameless desire as I did. And Mother Héloïse has assured me that each time will be better. She was quite emphatic about it."

"Bless her for that," Edgar said fervently. "I will do my best to fulfill her promise."

"I'm sure I could do better, too, with practice," Catherine said. "After all the advice I've been given, when the time came, I was so involved that I forgot most of it. I'm sorry; I didn't want to disappoint you."

"You didn't."

They lay quietly for a few moments, Edgar renewing his examination, this time with his fingers. Catherine closed her eyes.

"Edgar," she said. "Mother Héloïse's hypothesis about improving with practice may not be true in every case. I think we should start testing it . . . at once."

And, as a fellow seeker of knowledge, he could only agree to aid in the inquiry.

Solomon had spent a damp night rolled in blankets beneath a tree. It was uncomfortable but he preferred it to sharing the stable with Catherine and Edgar. He consoled himself with the thought that those two would very likely have some trouble riding their horse today. If day ever came, he amended. The fog was still as impenetrable as it had been last night.

Solomon hated fog. He needed to see the road before him for miles ahead. It was too easy to make a false step and crash into a chasm in the mist. It was too easy for one's enemies to hide in it and either attack or slip away. The fog was worse than darkness, for there were half-shapes in it that might be human or animal or a little of both. And one couldn't be sure if they were friends or demons until it was too late.

All the same, he wished Catherine and Edgar would forget that they were newly married and remember that he was outside, dripping, cold and with a task to be completed.

Catherine and Edgar had forgotten Solomon altogether and didn't think of getting up until rousted out by a good-natured but vulgar query from the owner of the stable. Catherine cringed in embarrassment but Edgar leaned over the side of the loft and grinned down at their host.

"Quite well, thank you," he said. "Any chance of a meal before we go?"

"Your friend ate some time ago," the man said. He seems impatient to be off. But I can get you some bread and cheese to take with you. And my wife makes a goose grease salve we could spare a bit of, if you need it."

He smirked up at Edgar.

"Why, thank you," he answered. "We are in great need of . . ." Catherine reached out and pinched the first bit of flesh she found. Edgar gave a small yelp. "Bread and cheese will be fine," he finished. "Any chance of beer?"

Solomon tried not to show his annoyance when they finally started, late in the morning. There was still only enough light for them to feel their way along the road. Occasionally they would overtake a cart loaded with a few boxes holding the last of the winter roots or be overtaken by a messenger on his way from Paris, but for the most part, the three of them were alone in the cloud.

To Solomon's secret amusement, Catherine shifted from side to side and finally slid off the horse early in the journey. He decided then that he would forgive her for making him wait.

"We're going so slowly that I might as well walk," she explained.

No one commented.

"It shouldn't take long to find out about the land that the countess Alys donated to the Paraclete," Catherine continued, after a few moments of silence. "Did Father say how long he wanted me to remain in Troyes?"

"He hoped your mother could be convinced to return to Vielleteneuse soon," Solomon answered. "The household in Paris is too small to spare someone to be with her constantly."

Conversation lapsed again. Catherine watched Solomon. He was worrying about something. He had the same look her father wore when he'd been forced to sell at a loss.

"You're keeping something from us, cousin," she said. "There's another reason for us not to return to Paris, isn't there? Are you sure my father isn't ill?"

"Yes, of course," he answered. "It's nothing to do with his health, or with you. It's business, we think. Someone unhappy with a trade or a debtor who won't pay. Maybe just another overzealous Christian."

"What is?" Edgar broke in. "Are you aware of how infuriatingly oblique you're being?"

"Your father didn't want you upset," Solomon said to Catherine.

By now she was more than upset. She grabbed the reins from Solomon and forced him to stop.

"By the sunburnt body of Saint Mary the Egyptian!" she shouted. "Tell us what's been going on!"

Solomon exhaled and dismounted. Edgar also got down.

"In this fog we could be ten yards from the gates of Troyes or ten miles," Edgar said. "We need to have this sorted out before we get there. You shouldn't have been so angry with the nice man who let us use the stable, Catherine. Along with the bread and cheese, he filled a skin with ale for us as a wedding present. Unless there's a bog on either side of us, I think we should sit, eat and let Solomon explain."

"I think he should explain before he gets anything to eat or drink." Catherine added.

"An excellent suggestion. Solomon?"

"Very well," Solomon answered. "There seems to be a tree over there and a rock beneath it. We can tether the horses and you two can beat my head against the rock until I talk. Will that make you happy?"

He looked so miserable that Catherine couldn't be angry, although she was thoroughly frightened by his half-told story. She took his hand and looked into the face that was so like her own.

"We have been worried about Master Abelard and about this threat to the Paraclete," she told him. "And, it is true, we have been absorbed in each other. But no one told us there was also something amiss in Paris."

Solomon felt unbelievably weary. He allowed Edgar to take his horse as Catherine led him to the rock and sat him down. He put his head in his hands, rubbing at his scalp.

"Everywhere I go, there's something amiss," he said. "The world is changing beneath my feet, it seems. I have the sense that, when the fog lifts, I'll be in a land I've never seen. It scares the hell out of me."

"Solomon," Edgar said. "If you don't come to the point, I might indeed start pounding your head against the rock."

"Last week, just after you left," Solomon said, "someone tried to murder Uncle Eliazar."

"What!"

"We thought at first it was just a robber, but he didn't try to cut Uncle's purse. The man simply stabbed him in the crowd and vanished."

Edgar rubbed at his side. Perhaps there was a cult of murderers arising in Paris.

"How is he now?" Catherine asked.

"Did he see who did it?" Edgar spoke at the same time.

"Recovering, we think," Solomon answered Catherine first. "He must have moved just as the man struck. The blade went through his side. It was a clean wound, beneath the ribs. As for who did it, the street was full. But Uncle heard him mutter. That's what made him suspect it was some Christian out to avenge the murder of his Savior."

The chill on the back of Edgar's neck had nothing to do with the weather.

"What did he say?"

"He said," Solomon concentrated. " 'This one's no *aversier*; he can die.' Don't you think that sounds like Easter polemic?"

"Poor Uncle Eliazar!" Catherine said. "Those priests don't think when they give their sermons. Every year someone decides they've been called to destroy the Jews in their midst."

Edgar said nothing. The chill spread down his spine. He had been coming from Eliazar's when he was attacked. But with his white-blond hair and fair skin, he couldn't imagine that anyone would have taken him for a Jew. Of course, his first years in Paris, the other students had taunted him, saying that he was a follower of the Evil One and had lost his color from hanging over vats of poisons and elixirs. But they had been more interested in learning the ingredients than in persecuting him. Still, the man who had tried to kill him had certainly been startled when the knife hadn't penetrated and had called him a demon. Could it have been the same person? He shivered.

"Have some ale." Solomon handed him the skin. "So you see, it has nothing to do with you, but it does provide another reason for Hubert to want you away from Paris. He didn't wish you to worry. I'm sorry to have told you of it, now. Shall we be going? The ale is warming but I keep having visions of hot soup and a blazing fire."

Catherine agreed and they started off again. This time she rode behind Edgar, clutching him carefully to avoid the bruise on his chest. She wondered if being married gave one an extra sense, for she felt decidedly ill at ease after Solomon's story. She was horrified by the attack on Eliazar, of course, but the panic she felt wasn't for him, but for Edgar.

You have no reason to fear for him. You're simply overwrought by recent experiences.

Catherine sighed. She had rather hoped she would lose her voices along with her virginity.

He didn't tell me what sort of accident he had in Paris, she worried. *He was far too quiet while Solomon was telling us the story. Something's wrong.*

There is a huge lacuna in your logic, the voices responded. Silence does not imply anything but a lack of speech. You have no basis for your conclusion other than a response colored by the least intellectual of all human actions.

Catherine shifted uncomfortably. She was not in a mood to argue, especially from a position of weakness, both intellectual and physical. Across from her, Solomon was singing softly. She leaned over at a dangerous angle to catch the words.

"Ast nos tristificis perturbat potio sucis, cum medus atque Caeres, . . ."

"Solomon! When did you learn Latin?" She was so startled she nearly fell. Edgar reached out an arm to pull her
upright again.

Solomon laughed. "I don't need to understand it to sing
it. With each stanza comes another round of drinks. After
a few of those, one becomes almost fluent. Since we've
finished the ale, it's particularly appropriate now. Care to
join me?"

And so, singing lustily of their need for more beer, the
trio approached the gates of Troyes.

A beam of light fell across the page. Héloïse looked up.
The fog was lifting, but not her mood. Spring, it seemed,
had finally come to Champagne. She heard laughter in the
cloister. Sister Bertrada would most likely arrive soon to
remind the women of decorum and dignity. And she would
be quite right. But for now, Héloïse let them rejoice. It
soothed her aching spirit.

"I ought not to set my sights on the things of the earth,"
she told herself firmly and picked up the pen once more.

But the only thing she saw was the image of all she
loved most leaving, and leaving her behind once more.

"Dear God," she pleaded, "I have tried to do my duty
and serve you, but I still love him more. Why won't you
give me peace?"

There was no answer. Héloïse had long ago stopped trying to change her heart. She could only hope that one day
she would be forgiven and God would change it for her.

Her mind strayed to Catherine. Dear, gawky, bright
child. Héloïse had a special fondness for her. It was a
shame she had been torn between the flesh and the mind,
but perhaps the way she had chosen was for the best.
There was no point in observing a life of outward piety
and rectitude if one were constantly yearning for an occa-
sion to sin.

"*Mea culpa,*" she sighed and got up from her desk.

And it was useful, she considered, to have Catherine
available to look into those matters she couldn't see to,
herself. Héloïse only hoped that marriage would bring the
child a stronger sense of caution. She was entirely too

prone to leaping into situations that mature reflection would have warned her to avoid.

"Lady Abbess?"

The voice through the door was that of Sister Thecla. Héloïse opened to her.

The elderly woman looked at her a moment with concern. Héloïse smiled, knowing that Thecla guessed her feelings.

"You know me too well, old friend," she said. "I'm fine, but I admit you were wise to interrupt my thoughts."

"Thoughts can become demons if we stay alone with them too long," Thecla said. "But I have no such fears for you. No, I'm sorry to say I've come because we have a visitor."

She paused portentously. Héloïse had a sudden image of a wrathful angel at the gate, righteously swinging a flaming sword around his head.

"Yes?" she prompted, firmly putting the idea away. "And who is it?"

"It's *that man*," Thecla said.

"Ah," Héloïse needed no more explanation. Robert, the prior of Vauluisant, come with another demand or complaint. Very well. She lifted her chin and straightened her spine. There was nothing like a good fight to take one's mind from gloom.

Prior Robert rose as she and Sister Thecla entered the guest room, but there was no respect in his attitude.

"I have just learned," he began without preamble, "that you allowed my niece, the countess Alys, to stay with you for over a week without showing me the courtesy of sending someone to tell me she was here. Is your anger against us so great that you would deny me the right to see her before she died!"

Héloïse's shoulders drooped. She put her palms together and pressed her fingers against her lips, lest she speak too hastily. She had forgotten the relationship entirely. The prior had every reason to be angry. But, she noted, like Raynald, all he showed was anger. Where was his grief? His demeanor was just the same as when he came to argue over his pigs. Poor Alys! It was obvious that Robert had another reason for being here. What was it? She lowered her hands. She would have to make him tell her.

"I beg your forgiveness, my brother," she said. "Truly, we were so concerned with the care of Countess Alys and the observance of Holy Week that we were unable to spare anyone to go to you. But if I had known that Lord Raynald had not sent word to you himself, I would have sent one of our lay brothers at once."

"Raynald has had quite enough to occupy himself with," the prior sniffed. "Finding and punishing his wife's murderer."

"Yes, of course," Héloïse nodded. "Surely that is why he did not return to visit or send anyone to inquire how she fared. We do our best to remove ourselves from such wickedness as revenge, which is best left to the Lord. We pray that her attackers are soon brought to His justice, though. As I'm sure you and the brothers of Vauluisant do."

"Naturally." The prior waved her comments aside.

Héloïse waited. Prior Robert was of an age with her and she had never felt intimidated by his ways, only exasperated. She looked at him steadily, which seemed to anger him even more.

"My niece's widower *has* sent word to me," he corrected her. "He has informed me that, because his poor wife died under your roof, you are now attempting to keep a donation of land that was never intended to be yours and for which you have no use."

The bequest again! What was so important about it? Héloïse hoped Catherine could find out soon. It was difficult to play this game in the dark.

"I have been through this with Count Raynald," she said. "Even though you are a member of her family, I cannot see how it concerns you. As I understand, the property *Sister* Alys left us comes from her father's side of the family. You are her mother's brother, I believe."

"I'm not here only as Alys's uncle," Robert answered.

Héloïse could readily believe that. She opened her eyes wider and inclined her head, inviting him to continue.

Her stare seemed to disconcert him. He moved back a

step, nearly bumping Sister Thecla, who sat in the shad-
owed corner. She moved her feet out of his way and he
jumped.

"*Harou!*" he yelped. "Saint Maurice's sword, woman,
you startled me! I'd forgotten you were there."

"I am not worth your notice, good prior," the portress
said. "I am only here because it would not be seemly for
our abbess to receive you unaccompanied."

"And yet, I understand Peter Abelard was just here,"
Prior Robert shut his mouth as soon as the words were out,
but they could not be recalled. He gave Héloïse a sidelong
glance. Her mouth was shut firmly.

Before she could speak, Thecla answered, "Ah, yes,
Master Abelard honored us with a visit. He gave the most
beautiful Easter sermon I have ever heard and inquired
most kindly as to my health. We are fortunate that, with all
his duties and his work, Abbot Peter finds time for his
daughters."

Héloïse blessed Thecla with all her heart. She had been
about to be as rash in her speech as Catherine ever had.
Prior Robert had known that his comment would anger
her. They had been sparring too many years. She took a
deep breath.

"You were saying?" she smiled politely. "Your niece?"

"I was saying," he paused to collect himself, "that I am
not here solely because she was my niece. This property is
in the forest of Othe, adjoining our land. As I said, you
have no use for it and it is not clear if you have any right
to it. However, in a spirit of charity and because of our
long association, I've been sent by my abbot to make you
an offer."

"Oh?" This was becoming more interesting every moment.

"I've been authorized to arrange for the Paraclete to
receive all the proceeds of our vineyards at Chablis, in return for which we will accept the uncultivated land in the
forest of Othe."

"The proceeds from the vineyards?" Héloïse asked.
"Your people will do all the work, care for the land, har-

vest the grapes and make the wine and then give us the profit?"

"Yes," he said.

"For how long are we to receive this?"

Prior Robert swallowed. "Because of our great respect for your piety and holiness, . . ."

A response seemed to be expected here. Héloïse smiled humbly.

"We are prepared to grant them to you in perpetuity," he finished.

Forever. Héloïse knew where the vines of Vauluisant were in Chablis. Those wines travelled as far as Carcassonne and Denmark. What could be hidden in the forest of Othe, the True Cross? She was greatly tempted to borrow a pair of trousers, dress as a charcoal burner, and set out herself to find out.

"That is a most generous offer," she said. "I will have to discuss it with the other nuns in chapter. We will let you know our decision. Sister Thecla, perhaps the good prior would like some dinner before he leaves?"

"Of course, Lady Abbess." Thecla clapped her hands and Brother Baldwin appeared in the doorway.

"Could you please show Prior Robert where he might wash?" she said. "I will have a meal brought to him here."

And, before he could do more than give an inarticulate protest, Prior Robert was led away in search of a wash he didn't need to prepare for a meal he didn't want.

Héloïse turned back to the portress.

"Thank you, Thecla," she said. "I almost lost control of my temper. Prior Robert has a talent for infuriating me."

Sister Thecla chuckled. "That's nothing to what you do to him, my dear abbess."

"What are you talking about?" Héloïse asked.

"You poor lamb,"—Thecla patted her cheek—"did you think that by putting on a wimple you stopped being a woman? Now, I know I shouldn't be speaking to you like this, but I've known you since you were a child. If you want me to repeat it in chapter, I'll do it and take my punishment. But you should be aware of things. That man is so drawn to you, he can barely keep from stuttering. He

probably goes back to his cell and sits on cold stones to
punish himself."

"That is absolute nonsense," Héloïse told her. "I'm
ashamed of you."

"I'm not the one with the lustful thoughts," Thecla said.
"I may have spent my life in a convent, my lady abbess,
but in my day we were taught to know the signs of a
man's attention straying to bodily temptations, if only to
avoid them. You are as beautiful now as you ever were
and Prior Robert is still a man, for all his vows."

Héloïse had known Sister Thecla too long to discount
her advice. She had been made portress partly because she
had shown herself a good judge of people. But Héloïse did
not need another complication in her dealing with
Vauluisant.

"Very well," she said. "I will keep your observation in
mind. For the moment, I need to speak with Prioress
Astane about this 'offer.' And we will discuss it in chapter.
Someone must know why this particular piece of woods is
so desirable. With all the interest in it, I can only assume
we've been given the site of the Garden of Eden."

Ten

Outside a house in the old Jewish quarter of Troyes,
late afternoon, Tuesday, April 9, 1140

The ancients who have preceded us have passed down the
following rules: that each will pay according to all his
fortune, with the exception of tools, houses, vines and
fields. As for the money of the Christians by which he
earns his bread, he only needs to pay on the capital.

—Rules for taxation in Troyes,
Rashi, responsa n. 248

*T*hey can't stay here," Joseph ben Meïr told Solomon firmly. "She might not be noticed, but that man with her is not only a Christian, but obviously a foreigner. My business is too delicate just now to have questions asked about my visitors."

"Our sort of business is always delicate," Solomon insisted. "The law of hospitality still holds. It's your duty to take us in!"

"Only you," Joseph answered. "Not them. I have no duty to outsiders."

"How much wine has my uncle Hubert bought from you this year?" Solomon asked. "And how much wool from your wife?"

"I can find another contact in Paris," Joseph sighed. "Peter of Baschi lives here in Troyes and that *culein* deacon will make my life impossible if he can find a reason to. He owes me forty marks and hasn't even paid the interest on it this year. If I have Christians in the house, he'll accuse me of proselytizing and refuse to pay at all."

Joseph rubbed at his chin beneath his beard and stared

at the table, apparently waiting for sympathy. But Solomon was not interested in financial problems; he heard enough of those at home.

Joseph slammed his palm against the table. "No," he repeated. "It's not worth the risk. I won't have those idolators in my house. Take them to their own people."

Solomon got up. He was sure that they could find someplace else in Troyes to stay, but that wasn't the point. Hubert had done too many favors for Joseph ben Meïr for him to announce that the arrival of Hubert's daughter and nephew was inconvenient to his business.

"Very well," he said. "I will take them elsewhere. But I hope you remember this when your priest decides to pay you back by heating those marks until they glow and shoving them up your *tabahie*, brother. You may wish you had made friends among the idolators, as well as debtors."

Catherine and Edgar were waiting outside in the shelter of the overhanging roof. Catherine was shivering even though Edgar was as close to her as possible and had wrapped her in his cloak as well as her own. She didn't notice his attentions at the moment. She was busy worrying about how she was going to find out about the land for Mother Héloïse and, at the same time, prove that Count Raynald had beat his wife to death. Edgar was thinking on a more immediate level, of a hot meal and then a steaming shared bath in a curtained wooden tub. He kissed her forehead, which happened to be the part closest to his mouth at the moment.

"I wonder if we can find a shop that sells perfumed soap," he whispered.

"From the stench of the tanneries, there must also be rendering and soapmaking done here," Catherine answered. "This place smells worse than Paris."

"Somehow, a hot bath sounds less appealing, after that thought," he moved away a pace.

"A hot bath?" Catherine stopped her musing and returned to the present. "You mean the two of us?"

"That was the thought," he answered, still annoyed.

"Oh, I'm sorry," she smiled. "I was thinking of something else. I'd like that. I could wash your hair; I've had lots of practice."

He smiled back. He wondered if she would sing, too, but decided to wait to suggest it.

They were still standing there grinning when the gate slammed behind Solomon.

"Avoutre!" he muttered. *"Fils de cochons."*

"Is there a problem?" Edgar asked.

"He won't take us," Solomon answered. "Afraid of the Gentiles."

"Then we'll have to stay at one of the hostels," Edgar sighed. "Stuck in a room with twelve other people. Come along, Catherine."

He began to lead their horse through the narrow street, past the church of Saint-Frobert, toward the Rue de la Cité, where, either in the old city or out in the new town, they might find a place for the night.

"If we could just find a hostel upwind of the tanneries," Catherine said, "I wouldn't mind anything else. I'm dreadfully tired."

"Didn't sleep well last night?" Solomon asked mildly.

They didn't answer him. All three of them were aware of their exhaustion as they trudged through the gate of the old city and crossed the bridge over the swampy bed of the river Seine, which had been diverted to create a canal around the expanded town. Catherine realized that the night before hadn't been the first sleepless one that week. Between caring for the countess, the duties of Holy Week and ruffians beneath her window, she couldn't remember a time when she hadn't been tired. Poor Edgar! She probably had disappointed him. She would have to do better the next time. If they could only find a private place to have the next time.

Edgar and Solomon were conferring about their options for a hot meal and a bed and didn't notice as Catherine fell behind. As usual, her thoughts were not on the road under her feet, and she didn't hear the sedan chair coming up behind her until the bearer cried out his warning. With a start, she jumped to the side of the road, tripped and slid headfirst into the dank weeds of the riverbed.

"Catherine!" Edgar heard the scream and knew, from experience, that it was not of fear but annoyance. Still, he hurried back to the edge of the ditch, prepared to descend and fetch his bride. He couldn't say that he hadn't been warned.

"*Leoffæst!*" he called. "Are you hurt? I'm coming!"

"No, don't!" Catherine called back. "It's horridly slimy here. I don't want to think about what I've landed on, but it was soft enough to break my fall. I'll climb up the side. Hold your nose with one hand and help me up with the other."

Catherine began climbing up the bank. She had lost her scarf and her braids were covered with bits of leaves and rushes, as well as the combination of mud, scum and garbage that she'd fallen into. Edgar ignored part of her order and leaned over the edge, holding out both hands to help her up.

"Give the man some help, Hugh!" The sharp and imperious voice was right at Edgar's ear and nearly caused him to slide in after Catherine. "Lupel, stop fussing about your hose and get the poor girl out!"

Two more hands reached out and grabbed one of Catherine's wrists. Edgar took the other, and together, he and the stranger pulled her back onto the street. Immediately, the stranger backed away, looking around frantically for something to wipe his hands on beside his own linen, furedged robe.

"Here, Lupel, don't be so fastidious. Take my scarf."

They all turned to the sedan chair, now resting in the road. Its occupant appeared oblivious to the fact that all the traffic now had to pass around her, with some difficulty. And none of those so inconvenienced seemed inclined to remonstrate.

"Are you hurt, girl?" The woman asked Catherine.

"No, my lady countess." Catherine recognized her at once and was so abashed she could hardly speak. "I am terribly sorry. It was all my fault. I wasn't watching the road."

Mahaut, countess of Champagne and Blois, wife of Count Thibault, daughter of Englebert, duke of Carinthia, sister to abbots and bishops and mistress of any situation, peered at Catherine. Beneath the mud, she noted that Catherine's cloak was good wool, and under that, the *bliaut* was linen and well made. She also saw the delicate carving on the ivory cross around her neck. She looked closer. Catherine returned her stare. In her dark, begrimed face, Catherine's blue eyes shone like lapis. The countess blinked.

"I know you girl," she said. "I've seen you before, I'm sure."

"My name is Catherine, daughter of Hubert Le Vendeur." Catherine tried vainly to wipe her face.

Mahaut suddenly began to laugh. "Of course! How could I forget the little girl who came with her father to my faire at Provins and managed to fall from a tree onto my son and his nurse, spill a pitcher of wine she was carrying to me and nearly be trampled by a bee-stung mule, all in one day." She tried to control her amusement, but the sight of Catherine was too much. "My dear, you haven't changed at all!"

Finally, she sobered. "But what are you doing here? I seem to recall your father asking me to sponsor your entrance into the Paraclete. If you've run off from Abbess Héloïse, I'll have you whipped and sent straight back. And who are these men?" she added, at last noticing Edgar and Solomon.

"This is my husband," Catherine said.

Edgar bowed.

"If this is true, you have my sympathy, sieur," the countess said. "If it's not, I'll have your . . ."

"Of course it is," Catherine interrupted. "Edgar, show her the contract."

Hurriedly, Edgar started rummaging in the pack. Countess Mahaut turned her attention to Solomon. "And this is your brother?"

"No," he answered. "Her cousin, Stephen, from Rouen."

He glanced a warning at Catherine, who for once held her tongue.

With a gasp of relief, Edgar found the contract and gave it to the countess. She studied it carefully.

"In French and Latin," she said at last. "Signed by Hubert Le Vendeur and witnessed by both Abelard and Héloïse. Even if Peter Abelard is a heretic, which I doubt, he should be competent to sanction a marriage. It seems official. And dated . . . yesterday?"

She studied them all, Catherine most closely. "Married at the convent, with only your cousin present. Rather unusual and hasty, I would say. Are you pregnant?"

"No, my lady!" Catherine said with indignation. "Of course not!"

"Then there must be a story in all this," the countess said. "I love a good story. Come with me, all of you. Lupel, run on back to the castle and see that a room is prepared for my guests. And start heating water for baths. A lot of water. Hurry."

There seemed no reason to argue. Edgar took Catherine's arm and he and Solomon led the horses in procession behind the countess's chair.

"This is a stroke of luck," Catherine said. "If the countess will help us, no one will dare deny our requests for information."

"Nearly getting yourself killed, yet again, is not lucky, Catherine," Edgar said. "And I don't like how noticeable we've suddenly become. Everyone in town now knows that we're here. What if the countess disapproves of our requests?"

He rubbed his aching side. Money and property, internecine greed and death, Catherine's uncle attacked in Paris just as he had been. He wondered if the man—it must be the same man—who had tried to stick his knife into Eliazar and himself had meant to kill them at all. It was odd to have two such inept attempts. Of course, he amended, Saint Guthlac may well have been watching out for him. But what saint would save a Jew? And always he worried about these whispers of heresy. Even now in Paris they were drawing up sides to condemn or defend Abelard. From the countess's comment, they were doing the same in Troyes. And how many there had actually read his work?

Edgar rubbed absently at his side. He should have gone

with Abelard to Paris. Now his place was at the side of his master, not entangled in some sordid plot of the champenois and burgundian nobility. What did their earthly struggles matter when Truth was being threatened?

Catherine noticed the gesture. That bruise must hurt more than he had said. She plodded along, filthy, exhausted, mortified at her continued clumsiness and wondering why she had left the convent.

You're walking beside the reason, Catherine. Stop whining.

That was true. In spite of her discomfort, Catherine smiled. She'd have taken Edgar's arm, but didn't want to smear his clothes any more than they had been. Hot water, soap, dry clothes, good food, a warm bed, Edgar. Hot water, soap, dry clothes . . . like a litany, Catherine hummed her desires. There was no room in her tired brain for further disquiet.

Solomon followed as ordered, hoping he would be allowed to wash alone. His faith would be evident the moment he dropped his pants. In the past, he had resorted to convoluted explanations to avoid being seen naked. And he did long for a hot soak. Beyond that, he refused to worry. He had long ago realized that his life was not his own. If the Almighty One was now telling him to dine with the countess of Champagne, who was he to question?

Countess Mahaut was a thorough hostess and they were all provided with whatever they needed. Edgar was dismayed to realize that the amenities didn't include a chance to indulge his steamy fantasy. He and Solomon were given the curtained tub and Catherine was sent to the women's rooms to have the countess's ladies heat the water, wash and braid her hair with ribbons and sew her into a pair of sleeves so tight they almost cut off the blood to her hands.

Catherine felt like a newborn butterfly in the borrowed finery. The linen *chainse* was a bright yellow and the silk *bliaut* over it was blue. The hem and neckline were embroidered with vines. Although Catherine had insisted that the *chainse* be laced tightly on the sides so that her skin was covered, the *bliaut* was done up loosely, so that the yellow cloth showed through. She had a belt of blue silk in a darker shade, with gold fringes at the ends that she found fascinating.

The countess came up to inspect her. Catherine stood nervously. Part of her was enchanted by the beauty and softness of the clothes. But another part was ashamed that these worldly things could give her such pleasure.

Mahaut pursed her lips. "I don't suppose you brought any jewelry from the Paraclete?" she asked. "No, of course not. I know Abbess Héloïse too well to think she would allow such things. I was one of her first patrons, did you know that?"

"Yes, my lady," Catherine said. "You've been very generous to us, I mean, them."

The countess let that pass. "Well, then, I have a fancy to see you dressed as a lady should be. It would be fun to dazzle that new husband of yours. Have the holes in your ears closed during your time at the convent?"

Catherine rubbed her earlobes. "I don't think so."

"Well, if they have, a hot needle will take care of it. I have a nice little pair of earrings, gold and set with beryl. You may have them as my wedding gift."

"Thank you, Lady Countess. You are very kind to me. I have no way to repay you," Catherine said.

"You can include me in your prayers," Mahaut answered. "And I may think of something else for you to do. Am I right in assuming that you were at the Paraclete when Alys of Tonnerre died?"

Startled, Catherine dropped the earring she was trying on into the rushes. With a sigh, one of the ladies knelt to hunt for it.

"Yes, I was," Catherine answered.

"Did she say anything before she died?"

"Only that she wanted to be made a member of our order," Catherine said. "She received the veil *ad succurendum*."

"I'm glad to hear that she died in the life she most desired," Mahaut said. "So. We still don't know."

Catherine started to ask what, then noticed that the woman hunting for the earring had stopped and was listening intently.

"I'm sure Our Lady will intercede for her in heaven and that she is now at peace," she said instead.

"*Deo volente,*" Mahaut said as she blessed herself. "Poor Alys. We will speak of her later."

Edgar was indeed dazzled by Catherine when she came down to the hall for dinner. But she was even more surprised by the change in him.

"Who are you?" she said as she took his offered hand.

He had been shaved and his hair trimmed, which altered his appearance somewhat, but from somewhere, he, too, had been transformed, from a student-cleric into a nobleman. His boots were of black leather, and his stockings and *braies* were also dark. His *chainse* was grey wool, embroidered at the neck in red flowers, and over it, his surcoat was red silk, with freshly goffered sleeves. He wore a gold chain around his neck and his surcoat was pinned with a brooch of gold twisted into a design similar to the one on her cross.

"Your husband," he said, with a smile that made her throat constrict. "I brought these to be married in, but there wasn't time to change. I hope you don't expect me to dress like this every day."

"I'd be afraid to get close to you if you did. We'd never get ink stains out of that."

He lowered his head to the level of her ear, as if to mutter endearments. "Catherine," he said, "Solomon and I have been talking with some of the men here about Walter of Grancy. It seems he was near Tonnerre on the night the countess was attacked. There were others besides the count's men who saw him."

She brushed her lips across his cheek. "That doesn't mean he did it. He may have been trying to rescue her."

"You have no facts upon which to establish that hypothesis," Edgar answered, kissing the tip of her nose.

"That's quite enough of that," Mahaut interrupted. "You cannot behave as if my home were the streets of Paris. Catherine, Gervais, here, will show you to your place. You, what's your name? Edgar, go with Richilde. Richilde, this young man has just married the daughter of an old friend of mine. Keep your hands above the table."

Catherine was rather glad to hear that. Richilde was radiantly blonde and fashionably flat-chested. Being loved by a man was too new an experience for Catherine to trust her ability to compete with someone like that. When she considered the situation, it seemed much more likely that Edgar would suddenly start up, announce he'd been enchanted by a witch but was miraculously healed and then hurry back to Scotland as fast as possible.

Richilde was pouting. "Is that one married?" she asked, pointing at Solomon.

He winked at her.

"I presume not," Mahaut said. "You may put him on your other side, Richilde, but my admonition holds for them both."

They had all been set at the lower tables. The countess of Champagne entertained at all times on a grand scale. Catherine guessed there were more people in the hall that afternoon than the convent maintained in a year. Gervais, the page, had put Catherine between two men of about her own age. The one on her left glanced at her, but she apparently did not meet his standards and he turned away.

The man on her right smiled at her. "I'm Lisiard. My father is provost of Château Saint-Thierry and I should warn you that my uncle, Isembard, is the count's cook."

"I would never criticize the food." Catherine assured him. "I'm Catherine Le Vendeur, of Paris, and I'm so hungry, I'd eat saltless gruel."

"Have no fear, Uncle will provide you with better than that. Wait, . . . Le Vendeur. Hubert's daughter?" Lisiard asked. "He sells wine to us."

"Does everyone know my father?" Catherine asked.

"Most people in this area, I would say." Lisiard grabbed a pitcher going by on a tray and poured wine for Catherine and himself. "It's rare to find a merchant who's honest, smart and Christian. Doesn't he also have connections with the abbey of Saint-Denis?"

Catherine nodded. She craned her neck along the side of the table to see how Edgar was doing. He and that Richilde seemed to be discussing something seriously. One of her hands was under the table, but she was relieved to see it was on Solomon's side.

"Do all these people eat here every day?" she asked Lisiard.

"Oh, no, it changes all the time. I don't know all of them. Most of the usual men have gone with Count Thibault and King Louis to put down the commune at Reims. You know about that, don't you?"

Yes, she knew, Catherine had a certain sympathy with the burghers at Reims, who, like many others recently, had formed groups to try to win tax and toll concessions from the local lords. Sometimes they got what they wanted, but other times their demands were refused. When that happened, too often the result was violent protest. The king had just crushed one such commune at Poitiers. Catherine felt it was his own fault in the case of Reims, though. If Louis hadn't allowed the episcopal see to stay empty so long, the townspeople wouldn't have taken matters into their own hands. However, she didn't want to get involved in a discussion about that. People tended to have strong opinions and express them forcibly.

"Are there any people here from Tonnerre?" she asked.

"I don't think so." He looked up and down the table. "The count's men usually dine with the lady Constanza, his mother-in-law. Of course, they are mourning the death of his wife, now. He would want them to join him in his prayers for her."

Catherine wondered how many prayers Count Raynald had authorized. Then her attention was distracted by the arrival of food. The pages had finally finished serving the high table and were passing out the trenchers of bread and slabs of meat, with dishes of sauces. It was all Catherine could do to keep from tearing into her share like a savage. Lisiard picked up his meat and let the juice drip into the bread as he continued.

"The man up there, last at the countess's table, is Nocher of Montbard. He is in the service of Walter of Grancy." Lisiard stopped and looked at her.

"Oh?" she asked, as she tried to rip the meat from the bone without splashing on her borrowed clothes.

"You have heard how Raynald of Tonnerre is saying that Walter killed the countess Alys?"

Catherine nodded. She picked up a napkin to wipe off the juice that was running down her hands to her wrists.

"Did he?" she asked.

"Well,"—Lisiard's voice lowered and Catherine leaned closer to hear—"I've heard that there were others closer to her who would have liked to see her dead, especially since she wasn't able to provide the count with an heir. Or perhaps that wasn't her fault. They say he has no bastards."

"But she . . ." Catherine caught herself. She hadn't considered that the baby Alys had miscarried might not have been her husband's.

"That is kitchen gossip, of course. The most reliable kind. You wouldn't believe what they hear in the kitchens." Lisiard smiled. "I have a friend there, and she tells me such things. She has a sister in the lady Constanza's service, and between them, I think they know everything that happens from here to Paris."

"And they know something about Walter of Grancy?" Catherine said, trying to sound uninterested. "And the countess of Tonnerre?"

Lisiard smiled and poured more wine. Some spilled on the tablecloth and it occurred to Catherine that he had started drinking before he had come to dinner.

"Walter is a good man," Lisiard said. "He was fond of Alys. And Raynald really wanted the other one, you know, Alys's half sister. But Constanza wouldn't hear of it. Just as well; the sister died years ago, a fever or something. Anyway,"—he gestured with his meat, leaving spots of grease on Catherine's arm—"anyway, Walter may loathe Raynald and argue with him over that blasted forest land, but he would never have hurt a woman."

Catherine could well believe that. There were rules, after all. But something else Lisiard had said caught her attention. "Forest land? What forest?"

Lisiard yawned. "You know, west of here. Makes no

sense to me. It's thick with oaks and thieves and were-wolves. I wouldn't kill anyone over it."

He yawned again and reached for the pitcher. As he did, he looked at the high table. Nocher of Montbard was frowning at him. When he caught Lisiard's eye, he motioned for him to leave.

With a sigh, Lisiard got up, stumbling a bit over the bench.

"I forgot to mention, I'm in service with Nocher for now. My older brother gets our castle, so I have to try to earn my own."

He leaned down to speak to her again. "I can tell you a lot more about Raynald of Tonnerre and his family, if you like gossip, too. Perhaps you'll sit with me again, to-morrow?"

"If the countess permits." Catherine smiled at him, then closed her eyes against the reek of his breath. She was already cataloging in her mind the information she had just been given, and could hardly wait to share it with Edgar.

The meal lasted well into the evening. At the end, *gastels* and dried honeyed apples were passed around, along with sweet raisin wine. A man came in with a *viele* and began to play and chant a story, but after a few lines, Catherine recognized the *Vie de Saint Alexis* and lost interest. With no one to talk to, she fiddled with her cup. The man on her left roused himself to offer to pour her more, but she shook her head. She didn't want to drink too much raisin wine, although she loved it. In case she and Edgar found a place together, she didn't want to fall asleep as soon as she lay down.

She looked down the table at him again. Richilde had turned her attention to Solomon. Edgar was looking back up the table at her. She tried to smile at him, but all at once her exhaustion, the wine and her longing were too much and she began to cry.

He was with her in a moment, settling into the place Lisiard had vacated.

"I liked the barn better," she sniffed.

"So did I," he answered. "Do you ever think we'll be alone again?"

"Oh, I hope so," Catherine answered.

She took his hand.

Even a seemingly interminable evening is eventually over. The countess signaled the end of the meal at last. Solomon got up and came over to where Catherine and Edgar were still seated.

"I'm going back to Joseph ben Meïr's tonight," he said. "That woman is entirely too friendly. She has brothers. Very large and stupid brothers. I don't think they would appreciate me."

"Will you be safe walking back?" Catherine asked.

"Yes; you didn't notice our path here," Solomon told her. "The Juiverie is almost in the shadow of the count's palace. And not by accident."

"Very well," Edgar said. "We'll meet you tomorrow on the steps of Saint-Frobert."

After Solomon had left, the page, Gervais, came up to them.

"Countess Mahaut has asked me to show you to your bed," he said with a flourish. He was about ten years old and full of his own importance.

"Did he say bed?" Catherine said hopefully.

He led them to an alcove between floors. It was small and curtained off. The boy tried to pull the curtain aside, but was too short. Edgar did it for him.

There, crammed into the space, a bed had been set up. A proper bed with a mattress covered by several feather beds. There were blankets and soft linen sheets and bolsters covered in fur. How they had managed to assemble it in such a small area, Catherine couldn't imagine.

"Thank you," Edgar told the boy, then propelled him back to the stairs and pulled the curtain shut firmly, hooking the edge to a ring in the wall. At once he began pulling off his boots and stockings. Catherine pulled the *bliaut* off over her head and started ripping the stitches out of her sleeves.

"How can we ever thank the countess?" she said as they finished undressing.

"We'll name our first daughter after her," Edgar said as he lifted the blankets and drew her into bed.

Some time later, Catherine woke up. A frantic search around and under the bed made her realize that the countess's servants had neglected to leave them a chamber pot. With a sigh of resignation, she wrapped herself in Edgar's cloak and set off to find the latrine.

She knew which side of the palace the canal was on, and the odds were that was where the garderobe would be, but on what level?

After a few trips up and down stairs, she finally found a small door set into the stone wall with the sound of water trickling below. She opened the door and went in, feeling her way.

There was a window high in the wall and enough starlight to guide her. As she sat, she felt a drop of something wet on her head. She rubbed her hair. It was damp and cold and sticky. She looked up.

Her eyes had adjusted to the darkness and in it she saw the sheen of a large, pale object, hanging above her. Then she recognized the curve of a back, a shoulder, another shoulder and, in between, a dark emptiness from which drops of blood were dripping slowly onto her upturned face.

Eleven

Roughly thirty seconds later,
the time it took for Catherine to make her legs move

Ille gladius carnalitate spoliat: hic carne. Quis mihi dabit sic
spoliari et sic suspendi?

This sword strips us of carnality: this one of flesh.
Who will aid me to be so stripped and so suspended?

—Gilbert of Hoyland,
Sermon on the Protomartyr Stephen

$\mathcal{E}$dgar, wake up," Catherine prodded at him. "Wake up, please. There's a body in the privy."

Edgar rolled over and pushed her hand from his side.

"Must have been the meat sauce," he mumbled. "Leave him alone."

"Edgar, listen to me." Catherine's words ran together. "There's a body hanging there like a gutted deer draining into the canal only it's not a deer, it's a man because it has skin and no fur and no head, just an empty hole and the blood is dripping out of it and I don't know what happened to his head. Edgar? Are you listening?"

He was awake now. She was shaking and her teeth were chattering. He put his arms around her.

"Sweet Jesus, Catherine, you're like ice! Let me warm you."

She pushed away. "Edgar we have to do something! There's a dead body in the privy!"

He sighed. "Of course there is. I don't suppose we could leave it there until morning? It doesn't sound as though we could give it any aid tonight."

"Edgar, there are murderers wandering the castle. Would you want to leave them free to kill us all?"

Slowly he swung his legs over the side of the bed.

"Help me find my *braies*," he said. "And my boots. This floor is cold as Lazarus's tomb."

She handed them to him and then found her own shoes and started putting them on.

"What are you doing?" he demanded, although he knew the answer quite well. "You stay in bed and get warm again."

"Oh, no," she said firmly. "I'm not staying anywhere alone until I find out where that man's head is."

"Very well," he said. "Which way is the garderobe, up or down?"

"Down," she said. "The second turn of the staircase, a small door in the wall."

He led the way, pausing to take an oil lantern from an iron hook at the first turn of the stairs.

"There," she said. "I must have left the door open when I ran out."

"Naturally," he answered.

Standing on the threshold, he shone the lantern into the tiny room. Catherine closed her eyes.

"Catherine?"

She opened them and looked in first at the floor and then up and up to the ceiling. There was nothing there.

"Edgar," she said with deceptive calmness, "it wasn't a nightmare. It wasn't a trick of the dark. There was a body there not ten minutes ago."

"I believe you," he said, to her great relief. "For two reasons. One, it's just the sort of thing that would happen to you, and two, you have blood on your face."

He wiped his fingers across her cheek. They came away red.

"And," he continued, "this blood is colder than you are. He must have been dead for several hours."

"What do we do now?" she asked, feeling the stickiness in her hair, as well. "We can't very well raise the watch to tell them a headless body has vanished and may be roam-

ing about the house, as well as its murderers. They'd laugh
or think us mad. Do we dare wake the countess?"

Edgar held the lantern close to the floor and the privy
seat.

"If there was blood here, it's been washed," he said.
"The only evidence is on you. I don't know. We're strangers here, even if the countess does know your father. It's
not good for visitors to notice trouble."

"Yes, but we can't ignore it." The shock was wearing
off now, leaving her feeling almost as drained as the body.
She shuddered. "And we still don't know where the head
is."

Edgar looked at her. Standing there, in only her shoes
and *chainse*, her face smudged with red, Catherine looked
about twelve years old. Her eyes were big and frightened
and her curls had come loose so that tangles fell across her
forehead. She looked completely lost and vulnerable and
he loved her so much that it hurt. He had no idea what
they should do. Spending the rest of the night wandering
about the castle, half dressed, searching for the missing
head to a missing body would only result in great embarrassment, if nothing worse. And, to be honest, he didn't
want to meet anyone strong and ruthless enough to kill a
man, decapitate him, gut him, and hang him up to season.
And why, he thought suddenly, had the body been removed?

"Catherine, when you saw this thing, did you scream?"
he asked.

She shook her head. "I was too frightened. I think I may
have croaked or wheezed, but nothing louder would come
out."

"Yes," he said. "That's what you sounded like when you
woke me. Then it's not likely that anyone heard you and
decided that it was too dangerous to leave the body there."

"How close is it to dawn?" she wondered.

"I'd have to see the stars to tell you," he said. "But,
you're right, that might be the reason it was taken. They
left it here to drain but had to remove it before the castle
awoke. You said the blood was dripping slowly. He must

have been brought here immediately after everyone went
to bed. I wish we had the head."

"So do I," Catherine said. "I'm not getting into bed
again until we've checked under it."

"No, I mean, then we might know how he was killed,
not to mention who he was." Edgar considered. "From
what you said, I'd guess he was strangled and then
brought here, where they trussed him up and eviscerated
him. Then everything was thrown into the canal, where it
would be washed down to the run off from the abattoir by
the tanneries."

"Yes, by morning no one would notice," Catherine
agreed. "But a human head . . ."

"Yes, that they would have to hide somewhere else." He
began leading her back up the stairs. "I think the first
thing we should do is wash your face and then return to
bed. There doesn't seem to be any point in waking anyone,
except to let those responsible know we've discovered
their work. The odds against making anyone else believe
this tale are too great to calculate. Even if we can't sleep
after this, at least we can be warm. Then, in the morning,
we should see if we can have a private audience with
Countess Mahaut."

They reached the niche where their bed was. Before re-
placing the lantern, Edgar checked under the bed and even
among the covers. Then he picked up one of her sleeves
from the floor, spit on it, and began cleaning Catherine's
face and hair.

"Edgar," she said as they climbed into bed, she making
sure she was nearest the wall. "I just thought, the countess
couldn't be involved in this, could she? Her piety is famous; they even say Count Thibault married her for it."

"The countess?" He paused, one knee on the bed, a foot
on the floor. "No, of course not. She might order someone's death in her court, if she had no alternative, but not
a murder in her own house. This is the work of someone
who makes his own justice."

He tucked the blankets around them and Catherine
wrapped herself around him, her head on his chest.

"Edgar?" she said.

"What?"

"I'm still frightened, are you?"

He started to say, "No, of course not," but that was a lie.

"Yes," he admitted. "This whole thing terrifies me. But I won't let anyone hurt you."

"I know that," she answered.

She was quiet a moment. Then she began to murmur something, almost in a drone. He turned her face upwards to catch it.

"Ecce enim Deus audivat me, et Dominus susceptor animae meae," she chanted.

"Averte mala inimicis meis, . . ." he responded.

They finished the psalm together. *"Quoniam ex omni tribulatione eripuisti me, et super inimicos meos despexit oculus meus."*

"Amen," Catherine said. "I will take care of you, and you of me, but it never hurts to have someone caring for us both."

And, holding each other so tightly that not a breath of evil could come between them, they both slept soundly until morning.

The bells awakened them. Troyes was full of bells, from Saint-Frobert, Saint-Pierre, the abbeys of Saint-Loup and Nôtre-Dame-aux-Nonnains, from Saint-Stephen, Saint-Urban and Saint-Remi. Catherine covered her ears against the tolling. It was as loud as Paris. She'd forgotten how insistent the bells could be, even when one wasn't required to recite the Divine Office.

They picked up their finery, sadly crumpled. and put on more serviceable clothing.

"What shall we tell the countess?" she asked Edgar as they made their way to the Great Hall.

" 'Thank you for your hospitality,' " he said.

"Nothing more?"

"We could ask if someone is missing," he considered. "But people seem to come and go rather causally here."

"Still, the man might have been one of the servants," Catherine said. "She should be told something!"

"Yes, but not before everyone," Edgar said. "Can you arrange to see her privately, to return the jewelry, perhaps?"

"I'll try. Goodness!" she said as she saw the angle of the sun through the window. "It's late. Solomon must have been waiting for us for hours. You should go and tell him what's happened. Then come back for me. We have a lot to do."

"Very well," he agreed. "But, if you tell the countess about what you saw last night, please notice who's listening."

"I will. Don't worry." She kissed him absently before he left, her mind already on the interview ahead.

This death has nothing to do with you, her voices intervened. *Tell the countess what you saw and leave the matter to her wisdom to handle.*

"Yes, of course," Catherine murmured. "But doesn't it seem odd that the poor man was hung at a place so near to where I was sleeping?"

Not at all; it was far from most of the other sleepers. A private place, they argued.

Catherine felt herself blushing. The countess was a very thoughtful woman. It seemed a shame to repay her kindness with trouble.

Catherine reached the top of the stairs to the countess's private rooms. She knocked timidly and the door was opened by one of the girls the countess was fostering. Past her, Catherine saw Mahaut seated by the window, her embroidery frame placed where it would receive the light. She looked and smiled as Catherine was let in.

"Ah, Catherine," she said. "How fortunate you've come at this time."

Her smile faded and she sorrowfully indicated the woman sitting next to her, a petite person in her forties, nicely rounded, with hair of a shade of blonde only achieved with assiduous use of saffron.

"This is Constanza of Quincy. The poor thing is desolate from the loss of her only child," Mahaut almost whispered. "Perhaps you can give her some comfort, since you were at the Paraclete when Alys died."

Catherine bowed to the woman, who extended a limp hand.

Saint Veronica's veil! What could she possibly say to Alys's mother? Why did you give your daughter to a cruel monster like Raynald? That didn't seem a good beginning.

You were taught manners, girl, Sister Bertrada's voice resounded in her head. *Would you have your behavior shame us?*

"We cared for her as best we could," Catherine blurted to Constanza. "She died a sister of the Paraclete, surrounded by our love."

Lady Constanza's lips tightened a fraction. "So my son-in-law has told me," she said. "What prayers have been arranged for her?"

"I don't know, Lady Countess," Catherine said. "But I'm sure Mother Héloïse will do everything for her that she would for any of our house."

Constanza turned to Mahaut. "You are very kind, my lady, but this visit has been difficult for me, so soon after losing my child. Still, I would like to hear more of the Paraclete and the place where poor Alys is buried. Perhaps you would allow this young woman to come to my home for the afternoon?"

"I would be happy to," Catherine broke in. This *was* fortunate. Now she had no need to create a reason to visit Constanza.

Countess Mahaut nodded agreement.

"But," Catherine added, "I would like to speak to you, my lady countess, before I go. Last night . . ."

"When you return," Mahaut interrupted. "Constanza is in no condition to wait through social trivialities."

"But . . ." Catherine tried again.

Her hostess shook her head decidedly. "Later," she said.

Catherine saw there was no use in trying to explain. But why wouldn't the countess allow her a moment? Did Mahaut already know about the body? Or did she think there was some other matter Catherine needed advice on, something more to do with marriage than murder? She gave up and followed Constanza down the stairs.

It wasn't until they had left the castle and were out in the street that Catherine remembered Edgar. But, she considered, Countess Mahaut would tell him where she had gone and he might have better luck telling the countess about the body. The chance to speak with Constanza about Alys was too important to risk losing.

Solomon sat on the steps of the church of Saint-Frobert, growing more and more impatient. Joseph and his wife had given him the minimum the law required, both of hospitality and information. They had made it clear that his habit of consorting with Christians would only lead to grief, and he was inclined to agree. But he feared that their custom of avoiding all contact with them outside of business would lead them to worse. His uncle Eliazar had taught him that the only way to survive was to treat everyone with respect. Even though it hadn't saved Eliazar's mother and sisters from the crusaders, he still believed in this. If nothing else, a man who lived so could face his maker with a clear heart.

Of course, that didn't mean Solomon intended to trust anyone.

He wondered why his uncles had really wanted him and Catherine away from Paris. They had to be involved in something dangerous. What could it be this time? The two of them were still sending him all over Christendom to gather material for Abbot Suger's church, even more so since the abbot wasn't as close to the king as he once had been. Louis doted on his queen, Eleanor, and she was doing her best to wean him from his monkish friends. With fewer reasons to be at the court, Suger could spend even more time on his building project. One would think that would be enough business for Hubert and Eliazar.

Solomon leaned back and arched over the stone steps. His back was full of kinks from the pallet he had been grudgingly given the night before. A sharp toe nudged his ribs. Instantly, he went for his knife.

"*Avoi!* Solomon! It's just me."

He looked up. Edgar was standing over him, grinning.

"And how was your night?" Solomon leered.

"Typical; Catherine got up to use the latrine and found a dead body." Edgar sat down next to him.

"Probably the meat sauce," Solomon said. "Anyone we know?"

"I have no idea," Edgar said. "His head was missing."

"I see," Solomon nodded. "Where is Catherine now?"

"Gone to tell Countess Mahaut about it."

"That should take some time. Shall we go have a beer?"

Edgar thought a moment. Catherine couldn't be ready in less than an hour. Men weren't allowed in the women's rooms, except for Count Thibault, of course. They could either wait here or find a stall with some bread and beer. His stomach growled.

"Just one," he told Solomon.

"Of course," Solomon agreed.

For such a small person, Constanza of Quincy had a great presence. She moved through the crowds oblivious of obstacles. And, for her at least, they didn't exist. Catherine followed in her wake, marvelling. Constanza managed the same air of being above the common world as Raynald of Tonnerre, and she did it without chain mail or a sword. There was a man walking half a step behind her. He bent to speak to her and she brushed him away. When she turned, Catherine saw the glint of tears on her cheek. The man dropped back to walk beside Catherine.

"Alys's death has upset her greatly," he said. "Especially since she lost not only a child, but a grandchild. Walter of Grancy has much to answer for."

Catherine wondered why everyone was so sure Walter was responsible. Certainly Alys's own family would have known how her husband treated her.

"Has Walter been found?" she asked.

The man shook his head. "Gone to earth somewhere," he said. "Not been seen since Alys was attacked. Raynald will find him. If he doesn't show up soon, we'll take his family hostage. That should bring him out."

"We? Are you one of the count's men?" Catherine asked.

The man seemed too mild to be a *bacelor*, fighting for hire. He was about the same age as Constanza, and not much taller, stooped as a scholar, with thinning grey hair.

He had been freshly shaved by a clumsy barber; his chin and neck had nicks in them. Catherine's question had the effect of making him stoop a little more, hunching his shoulders about his neck for all the world like a turtle retreating into his shell.

"Ah, no," he said, aiming his words at the dust beneath his feet. "I'm ... ah ... Rupert of Troyes, Constanza's husband."

"Oh, excuse me, my lord." Catherine bobbed belated respect. "Then you are the countess Alys's stepfather?"

"Ah ... yes." He seemed to need time to study the matter before he answered. "I raised her as if she were my own, of course. Constanza and I have not been blessed with children."

Catherine studied him more closely. This was the man Constanza had married after Gerhard of Quincy had died. Sister Bietriz had thought it odd, since he brought little to the marriage. Perhaps it had been purely out of affection. Rupert did not appear the sort who would inspire great devotion, but perhaps his retiring ways would appeal to some.

By the time they reached the house, Constanza seemed to have regained control of her emotions. Her voice was cool and steady as she ordered cakes and wine for them all and sent Catherine with a servant to wash her hands.

When she returned, Catherine found Rupert and Constanza seated in the solar. Realizing that she had not yet eaten that morning, Catherine looked with longing at the cakes, which were almost the same color as Constanza's hair. But the countess was determined to have information before feeding her guest.

"Who tended to my daughter?" she asked abruptly.

Catherine stood before her, feeling like a novice caught in the dormitory with an extra blanket.

"Sister Melisande is the infirmarian," she answered. "But we all sat with her. She was never left alone and the whole community was there, praying for her, when she finally died."

Constanza straightened in her chair. "Finally? I was

given to understand that she was near death when Raynald brought her to the convent."

Catherine remembered the poor battered body. "It seemed so," she said. "But Sister Alys was very strong. She was determined to survive until she could become one of our community."

"That is not true." Constanza's jaw clamped around the words. "If she did any such thing it is only because she was terrified into it by the closeness of death."

"Oh, no," Catherine assured her. "She put it in the charter when she gave us the property in the forest of Othe that she wished to retire to the Paraclete."

"She gave you what? In the forest? Who wrote this charter?" The countess seemed amazed at this news.

"I . . . I don't know, my lady." Catherine stepped back. She hadn't expected to have to defend the Paraclete. "But I have seen it. Count Raynald agreed to it. His consent is clear in the charter and it was properly witnessed. I have read it."

"Well, if so, it makes no difference. She had no right to give it away. That land was part of my dower."

Rupert seemed startled.

"From my first husband, Alys's father, of course." Constanza dismissed her second husband with a wave.

That land again, what *was* so special about it? Catherine was beginning to believe it must contain unicorns and griffons from the eagerness of all those vying for possession of it.

"I know nothing about such things," Catherine said. "But I came to care very much about your daughter's fate. I grieve with you. I wish I could have known her before she was hurt."

Constanza looked Catherine up and down.

"I doubt you would have enjoyed each other's company," she said. "Alys was not interested in spiritual matters."

A woman who would save her last breath to take the veil had no interest in spiritual matters! Catherine opened her mouth to refute that.

Say nothing, Catherine! The warning was so sharp that she

almost thought it came from a human voice. *She wants you to tell her all you know and she has given you no information at all.*

It was true. Catherine was used to arguing from a fixed point, by successive steps to the next point. Constanza had learned her rhetoric in another school.

"Perhaps we could have found another shared interest," Catherine replied instead.

"It is not likely," Constanza repeated. "Alys cared for clothes and dancing and other frivolous matters. She was very lucky to find a husband who would indulge her in such things."

Catherine didn't need her voices now. She knew what Alys's mother was doing. She wanted to know how much the convent knew about Alys's life. And Paciana? Did Constanza believe her first husband's daughter was dead or did she know Paciana was also at the Paraclete?

"Raynald even got her a monkey," Rupert added. "Nasty thing, bit everyone and shit everywhere."

"Rupert, really," Constanza said mildly. "It was foolish, but Raynald was so devoted to her."

Is that why he never came to see her? Catherine thought. *And why didn't you come to her? It's only a half hour's ride from Quincy to the Paraclete.*

"Perhaps, as you say," Catherine agreed, "the approach of death caused a change in her. We felt that Alys was very concerned about the fate of her soul and wished to do all she could in the few days that remained to her."

"And well she should, the . . ." Constanza stopped herself in horror. "That is, her life had not been all I might have desired in my concern for her soul. I'm glad if she repented and received your prayers and those of other sisters. But I'm sure you gave them without thought of earthly reward. Abbess Héloïse would not want anyone to conclude that she had taken in my daughter for her own profit, especially now, with Peter Abelard once again being tried for heresy."

"He's not!" Catherine insisted. "He has merely requested a debate with Abbot Bernard. He will prove his orthodoxy before everyone."

"No doubt," Constanza shrugged. "Still, I'm sure you'll remind the abbess that Master Peter needs no more scandal associated with him."

Scandal! Héloïse knew all about that. She needed no reminder. Catherine suddenly realized that Constanza didn't know she had left the convent permanently. Perhaps it was just as well that she didn't.

"I will be happy to convey any message you like to Mother Héloïse," she said, trying to be meek and nunlike. "Perhaps you would care to speak with her yourself. Now that Easter is past, we will have a proper funeral service for your daughter."

"That will be very nice," Rupert said, before Constanza could reply. "We would be happy to make a donation for her soul, and our own. Would you like a cake?"

Catherine practically leaped at the tray.

As she was taking the first bite, there was a clanking in the hall and Raynald of Tonnerre burst in, unannounced. Ignoring Catherine and Rupert, he strode over to Constanza's chair and grabbed her by the shoulders, pulling her up like a cloth doll.

"You bitch!" he shouted, his face almost touching hers. "You said she was dead! You lied to me so you could get me to take your own whelp."

He began shaking her, as Rupert and Catherine vainly tried to loose his hands. Constanza's head bobbed back and forth, at one point hitting Raynald so hard that his lip bled. He paid them no mind. His whole being was focused on his rage against Constanza.

"Raynald, I warned you!"

The voice was firm and seemed to pierce through Raynald's fury. He stopped shaking Constanza and dropped her, still bobbing, to the floor. Catherine, who had been pulling on Raynald's arm with no effect, was as suddenly thrown off balance. She stumbled back several steps and stopped, leaning against the wall. From this angle, she was able to take a long look at the man who had followed Raynald into the room.

He was taller than Raynald and older by twenty years, but much like him. He had the same look of the fighting man, or more, of one used to sending others to fight and expecting them to prefer death to disobedience.

Only Rupert seemed unperturbed by the incident. He righted his wife, brushed straw from her gown and bowed to his guests.

"Count William," he said. "We were having some wine and cake. Would you care to join us?"

"Father," Raynald said, "she has deceived us both. I tell you, I saw Paciana, alive, at the Paraclete. I was not mistaken."

William, count of Nevers, nodded to Rupert and took a chair.

"Wine," he said.

Rupert clapped his hands. Catherine looked around, but there was no servant. William raised an eyebrow in her direction. He didn't actually look at her, but the intent was plain. Catherine took the ewer and tried to pour without spilling. She handed him the cup and backed into the corner, for once not indignant at being too unimportant to be visible.

Constanza moved her head slowly, rubbing her neck in pain.

"How dare you touch me, *mesel*," she said, but the insult lacked force. "Wait. What did you say? Paciana? You *saw* her? You must be mad. She's dead. She's been dead ten years."

Raynald moved as if to strike her again, but his father stopped him.

"How do you know this, Constanza?" William asked. "Did you see her die?"

"No, of course not," Constanza answered. "It was a tertian fever. I had no desire to take it, myself. I went to Paris with Alys, to keep her safe. Paciana died at Quincy. She's buried there. We have a Mass every year on the anniversary. I tell you, she's dead."

"So she told me, not a week ago," Raynald answered. "I don't believe her, either."

"Rupert, you were there when she died,"—Constanza was still checking to be sure her head was attached—"tell Raynald he's raving."

"Paciana had a tertian fever," Rupert said quietly. "She died in the middle of the night. She received the Final Rites. We buried her two days later. You've seen the grave."

"No," Raynald said, but with less certainty. "I saw her. She's at the Paraclete."

"Well, Raynald," Rupert's voice was soothing, "we have a visitor here now from the Paraclete, come to tell us of poor Alys's last breath. Perhaps she'll convince you that you are mistaken."

Catherine looked at him in astonishment. All at once, everyone was staring at her, waiting. What was she to say?

She closed her eyes and wished with all her heart that she could be invisible again.

Twelve

... it was an obstinate custom with such people in matters
of which they were ignorant, to condemn others, without
discussion and without rational inquiry.

—Robert of Melun,
Sentences

Catherine was thinking more rapidly than she ever had in her life. What did these people know? Who was lying. Perhaps Paciana wasn't the sister of Alys. No, of course she was. Alys had recognized her, called her by name. But, if Paciana were of that family, then some relative must have known she was at the Paraclete. It was required that each entrant be sponsored and approved. The only answer was that someone had known. But who? She remembered the knights who had tried to enter the convent and the murderous look Paciana had given her as she left. Someone had sent them and Paciana knew who. Catherine made up her mind.

"There is no *monialis* at the Paraclete named Paciana," she said. That much was true. Paciana was a lay sister, not a nun.

"You're lying!" Raynald took a step toward her.

"I am not!" Catherine shot back. "I'm disobedient, prideful and clumsy, but I don't lie. You may ask Abbess Héloïse or Prioress Astane. They will tell you the same."

"There, you see," Constanza told him. "You were mis-

taken. Now you may apologize for your behavior. I'm
your mother-in-law, after all, not some *fame vilaine* to
abuse as you wish."

Raynald didn't bother to face her.

"Your daughter is dead, woman," he said. "You are
nothing to me now."

He looked directly at Catherine and she knew that he
would remember her the next time they met. She prayed
that she would not be alone when it happened.

"I must go now," she whispered. "The countess Mahaut
is expecting me."

Raynald nodded, his eyes fixed on her face.

"Go," he told her. "I will see that you and that abbess
of yours are punished for your deceits. Once they learn of
your perfidy, you may be sure that none of your powerful
patrons will dare intervene."

"Yes, girl, leave. You have no more business here." William of Nevers waved her out. Constanza and Rupert said
nothing, allowing the two powerful men to usurp the authority of their home.

Catherine backed out of the room and hurried from the
house. Whatever else those people were discussing, however important it might be to the Paraclete, she was not
prepared to stay another minute. As she struggled to open
the door, she realized that she was still holding the
squashed remains of the cake she had been given. The
gold of the spices had stained her *bliaut* and, most likely,
Raynald's silk surcoat. Oh, yes, he would definitely remember her if he saw her again.

She hurried down the street, past Saint-Remi, turning
right at the alley that led along the swampy bed of the
Seine to the gate to the old city. The southern wind carried the stench of the tanneries and the sound of shouting.
There must be something happening in the square between
the convent of Nôtre-Dame-aux-Nonnains and the church
of Saint-Urbain. Catherine paused to listen as she neared
the bridge. Perhaps it was some wandering preacher, or a
troop of tumblers. If so, they weren't being well received.
The voices were angry.

The shouts were growing louder and closer. Catherine

walked more quickly toward the bridge. On the other side was the palace of the count. As she crossed over, she could see the place where the waste of the palace emptied out into the dank weeds and sluggishly flowing water. Remembering her slide down the bank the day before, she was grateful that the bridge was upstream from the deposit.

As she reached the old town on the other side of the bridge, a crowd erupted from the narrow opening between Saint-Urbain and the square and poured down the Grand Rû to the canal. There was a crash as a peddler's stall was upended into the water. Catherine looked over her shoulder and started running for the palace. One look at the faces of the people pouring onto the bridge was enough to tell her that it wasn't a crowd; it was a mob.

The mug of beer had become two and then three. Edgar and Solomon sat outside a tavern on the Rue de la Cité, drinking, gnawing on hard black bread and trading stories of their travels.

"There's a loch north of my home." Edgar paused to belch. "There's a sea monster in it as long as a *meduœrn*, longer even. They say that Saint Columba destroyed it once, but that's not true; it's still there. I saw its head once on a grey, misty morning, poking up out of the loch. It had a huge selkie snout and a long, black serpent neck. A *seldlic* sight!"

Solomon put down his mug.

"I can't understand half you say," he told Edgar. "It's bad enough when you ramble on in Latin. At least that has the flavor of proper French, but your German words sound like you're choking on your bread."

Edgar laughed. "Saxon, not German. Sorry. To tell you the truth, my family doesn't even speak good Saxon anymore. I found that out when I went to England. They complain that we garble it with Norse and Gælic."

"And in your land there are monsters in the waters," Solomon said. "I've seen no monsters, myself, but I've often glimpsed strange shapes in the forests here, too often in the fog. Sometimes I think there are demons wandering the earth that only can be seen when the mist hangs on them."

He shuddered. "I'm sick to death of travelling through dark forests. All I want is to get some vines, a cottage, a few sheep, a nice wife with well-cushioned hipbones and never have to enter the wood again."

"I can just see you," Edgar laughed. "Solomon *rusticus*. It will never happen. You don't have the soul of a peasant."

Solomon stared deeply into his beer.

"Perhaps not," he admitted. "But I don't have the soul of a scholar, either. And, in my family, one either studies or trades."

"You could convert," Edgar suggested.

Solomon's face hardened.

"No," he said. "I couldn't."

Edgar said no more. He finished his cup and squinted at the sun.

"We should be returning to the palace," he said. "The bells for Sext will start soon and Catherine will be impatient to get on with her commission for the abbess."

Solomon stood, a bit unsteadily. He shook his head to clear it and then wiped his mug with the hem of his *chainse*. Edgar did the same. As they crossed the road to the palace, they became aware of angry shouting. The people in the street were scattering, trying to get out of the way of a mass of people who were shoving past the guard at the end of the bridge. Among the frightened townspeople, there was a woman in convent grey, trying to push her way through. She had almost reached the palace gate, when a man with a rack loaded with sausages knocked against her and threw her sideways. As she fell, one of her braids came loose and caught on a sausage hook. She screamed in sudden pain. Edgar and Solomon dropped their mugs and ran to her.

Edgar picked her up as Solomon unhooked her hair. The sausage man swore at all of them.

"Catherine! What are you doing here?" Edgar said as they dragged her back around the corner of the palace. "You were supposed to be with the countess Mahaut."

"I went to question Alys's mother." Catherine rubbed her sore head. "What's going on?"

The mob had reached the palace gate and were pounding on it.

"Justice!" someone yelled. "We have a murderer and we demand justice!"

"No!" a voice gasped weakly. "I killed no one. My shop! They've destroyed my shop!"

"Silence, you lying infidel!"

Solomon's head came up sharply. He heard the whack as the man was hit and started forward. Edgar grabbed him.

"Don't!" he said. "You'll get yourself killed. Go find your elders or leaders or whatever. The countess's men are coming. They'll restore order. But, if there really is a charge of murder, this man will need someone to speak for him."

Solomon took a deep breath and nodded. He edged his way around the crowd and disappeared in the crush.

By this time, people had arrived from everywhere in Troyes, curious and eager for diversion. A woman came out of the bakehouse on the corner and stopped next to Catherine.

"What's all the noise for?" she asked, wiping the flour from her hands. "I heard someone cry murder."

"I don't know," Catherine told her. "They came from the direction of the tanneries. They seem to have caught a felon."

"Ah, the guard has opened the palace gates," the woman said. "You're taller than I am. Can you see anything?"

Catherine stood on tiptoe, leaning on Edgar.

"Yes, the countess has sent her men. The knights are on horseback. That will make those people think again."

The crowd did move back as the mounted knights appeared in the open gateway, all but two men in tanning aprons, each holding the arm of a third man, whom they dragged up to the leader, Nocher of Montbard.

"This is Gershom, the Jewish butcher," one man announced. "It isn't enough for him that he sells his cast-off meat to us at exorbitant prices. Now he must slaughter a Christian man and hang him up just as he does his cattle!"

There was another commotion as the crowd reacted to the accusation. Nocher leaned over and said something to one of the other knights, who nodded. The woman beside Catherine cried out in horror.

"*Quel aborissement!* Isn't it enough that we let them live among us, even when they murdered Our Lord! Must they now murder us, too? Kill him!" she screamed. "Hang him now!"

Her cries were joined by others and the knights moved forward to stop the people from grabbing the prisoner and carrying out their own justice. They used their lances to separate the fainting butcher from his attackers and push him, half crawling, into the palace courtyard.

Catherine tugged on Edgar's sleeve. He turned to her. Her face was pale with fear.

"Edgar, do you think . . . ?"

"Yes," he said, "I do. Now the countess will believe your story."

"I never had a chance to tell it to her," Catherine said. "We must get in there. That man couldn't be guilty. He couldn't have gotten into the palace after dark."

"They'll never let us in again," Edgar worried. "They don't want trouble from the town and we look just the same as the rest of these people. Do you see anyone among the knights who knows us?"

"It's hard to tell with their armor on." Catherine scanned the dozen or so men. "Wait! Jehan!"

She started to wriggle her way through to the front of the crowd. "Jehan!" she called again. "It's Catherine!"

Edgar followed, but reluctantly. He remembered Jehan, too. The knight was in service to Count Thibault, but was also sometimes loaned to do jobs for Catherine's father. In their last meeting, before he and Catherine had been betrothed, Jehan and his fellow knight Sigebert had throttled him in an alley in Paris, dislocating his arm and nearly slitting his throat. He wasn't eager to renew the acquaintance.

But Catherine forged onward, pushing around anyone in

her way and occasionally jumping and waving to attract the knight's attention. Grimly, Edgar followed.

"Jehan!" Catherine called again, when she was closer. "Jehan! Let us in!"

Finally he noticed her. The others were already through the gate, taking the unfortunate butcher and his immediate accusers with them. Hearing his name, Jehan twisted in the saddle.

"Lady Catherine!" he said. "Saint Simeon's pillar! What are you doing here?"

"I can't explain now," Catherine said as they reached him. "Just let us in. We have to speak with Countess Mahaut."

Jehan looked down on them from the back of his horse. A flash of anger crossed his face as he recognized Edgar.

"We?" he said. "Not with him. My job is to protect you from his sort."

"My sort!" Edgar grabbed at the reins. "Does your protection include attacking an unarmed man in an alley? Come down here and face me, *questre!*"

"Edgar, not now!" Catherine stopped them. "Edgar and I are married, Jehan. You owe us both protection, if you are still the count's man."

Jehan regarded them both. Edgar felt at a distinct disadvantage, having neither horse nor armor. His fist itched to land just one good blow straight into that *mesel's* gut. But Catherine was right. Now was not the time.

"I have the marriage contract with me," he said mildly, instead. "It carries Hubert's mark. Would you like to read it?"

Edgar smiled politely. He knew that it was unlikely that Jehan could do more than make out the letters of his own name.

The knight glared at them for another moment before he grudgingly allowed them through the gate. As they passed through, Jehan signaled the guard to close it behind them. The people in the street muttered to each other, but no one dared challenge.

Inside the courtyard, the chaos was almost as great as in the street. The people of the palace, servants and guests milled about, getting and giving what little information they could find and inventing as they saw fit. Catherine and Edgar ignored them and headed for the Great Hall, where the countess would appear to judge the matter.

The hall was also full of people. They had pulled out all the dining tables and were sitting or standing on them. There was a balcony on the landing of the stairs to the women's quarters. Here several ladies sat with their sewing, waiting for the entertainment to begin. As she was jabbed in the ribs and back by those trying to get a good view, Catherine wished for a second that she were the sort of woman who could always command a comfortable chair.

You'd only trip over it and spill wine on the embroidery, Catherine.

She sighed. She wondered if Sister Bertrada's opinions would ever leave her head.

"They're bringing in the prisoner and the tanners now," Edgar said.

Catherine craned her neck to see. Gershom, the butcher, had his arms tied behind his back and was being guarded by two of the knights. The tanners stood on the opposite side of the room from him. They seemed both angry and awed by the situation.

Finally, Countess Mahaut entered, accompanied by her chamberlain, Girelme, and her chaplain, Conon. They stood behind her as she seated herself at the high table. The room quieted.

"In the absence of my husband, Count Thibault," she began, "it is my duty to see that the peace of Troyes is preserved. I will now hear the charges against this man."

Jehan stepped forward.

"My lady countess," he bowed. "The butcher, Gershom, has been accused of murder. These two men discovered the body."

The tanners were brought up to the table. Mahaut studied them, noting their filthy aprons and stained hands.

"Give your names," she said. "Your occupation and status are obvious."

The elder of the men stepped forward.

"I am Aymo, Your Excellency," he bowed. "This is my

apprentice, Heldric. I own the tannery east of Nôtre-Dame-aux-Nonnains, on the Grand Rû."

"Can someone vouch for this man?" the countess asked.

A man stepped forward.

"I can, my lady."

Mahaut hesitated, then Conon bent down and whispered something in her ear.

"Ah, yes," she said. "You are Peter of Baschi, deacon of Saint-Aventin?"

"Yes," the priest said. "I am acquainted with both these men. They have sold leather and vellum to me, of good quality and at a fair price. I believe them to be truthful and of good character."

Catherine lifted herself on the edge of someone's stool to get a better look at this man who had borrowed money from Abbess Héloïse and not repaid it. His robes were clerical, but not ascetic. His collar and gloves were embroidered and he wore several heavy rings. She was not disposed to trust or admire him. But the countess nodded, accepting his statement.

Mahaut returned to the tanners. "And you accuse Gershom, the butcher, of murder?" she asked. "Gershom?" The name finally registered. "The Jew? Have his own people been notified of this charge? Nocher?"

"Their leaders have been sent for," Nocher of Montbard told her.

"Very well," she said, but she seemed uncomfortable. She gestured for the prisoner to be brought forward.

"Gershom the butcher," she said, "I wish to decide if the charges against you have any basis in fact. Will you trust me to listen and judge fairly, on my honor as a Christian woman?"

"I killed no one!" Gershom drew himself up. "These idolaters have fouled my shop with human blood. I am the one wronged! I have no fear. The Holy One will protect me, for I have honored the Law."

Nocher gave the man a blow that sent him to the ground. "How dare you speak to the countess in that manner!" he shouted.

"Nocher!" Mahaut spoke quietly but her voice was cutting. "I will determine if I have been insulted. Now, Aymo, tell your story. And I want no interruptions."

Now that he was the center of attention, Aymo seemed to have difficulty beginning.

"Well, ah, it was this way, Your Excellency, . . ." He reached beneath his apron to scratch and then, realizing where he was, withdrew his hand in horror.

"That is," he began again, "Heldric and me, this morning, we went to Gershom's, like always, to see if he had any skins to sell. He said no, but he'd received a few sheep the day before and did we want any of the bits his people couldn't eat. We said we wouldn't mind. Mutton in spring is a rare treat, however come by."

He paused, glaring around the room, daring anyone to accuse him of planning apostasy.

"I'm sure we all like spring mutton," Mahaut said patiently. "Continue."

Aymo swallowed. "Well, then we all went into the storehouse, where Gershom had hung the meat. And there—" he swallowed again and his voice dropped "—there were the sheep, alright, hanging in a row and, at the end was something bigger. We all looked and, well, it was gutted and cleaned just right and hung proper, but it wasn't a sheep; it was a man. And a Christian man, too. He were naked. I could tell. A poor Christian lamb, slaughtered!"

Aymo had risen to the rhetorical height of his life with his last statement and it reduced him to weeping incoherence.

"It's true!" he cried over the noise of the audience. "I swear it on the skin of Saint Bartholomew!"

Catherine paid no attention to the outcry arising from this revelation. She was certain now, and she and Edgar had to get to the front to tell what they knew.

Mahaut shuddered and looked at Gershom with revulsion. She waited for the guards to restore order.

"This is a hideous deed!" she said. "A man treated as if he were nothing more than a carcass. What possible defense can you make?"

The butcher was frightened, but still angry. His indignation was apparent.

"I say again, I am a cutter of meat according to the Law. This accusation of murder is pure madness or spite. You have no right to bring me into your Christian sacrileges. Someone has done this to ruin my name in the city. I am respected and have many customers, including your own cook, my lady. Now the Christians will no longer buy from me. I know it!"

He pointed to his accusers, but his gaze included the rest of the room.

"You've destroyed me!" he shrieked. "You want a martyr? Someone to blame for your own filthy crimes? Take me, then. My life is worthless!"

He rent his *chainse* and clawed at his face, falling, sobbing, to the floor.

The countess was impressed, but puzzled.

"These men weep honestly, it appears to me," she said. "The butcher does not deny that a body was found in his shop. The tanners admit that is all they know. Because the man was hung like an animal, they presume he was killed like one. I feel there is more here than we first thought. Has this Christian body even a name?"

Aymo was still weeping and Gershom sobbing, so Heldric, the apprentice, answered with some relish.

"No name, my lady," he said. "No head."

The reaction to this was wondrous to behold. One of the ladies in the balcony screamed, either in horror or delight, and in a forgotten corner, a travelling poet feverishly tried to adjust an old *chanson de geste* to fit this new event.

Finally, Edgar managed to reach the space before the table.

"My lady countess," he bowed. "I believe my wife and I can add something to the testimony already given. We do not think that the butcher could have killed this man. Catherine discovered the body before dawn this morning, hanging here, in the palace."

Another woman shrieked, this time with more sincerity. The poet quickly rewrote a stanza in his head.

Mahaut waited again for everyone to quiet.

"Catherine?" she asked. "Would you care to tell us just how and where you made this discovery."

Edgar took Catherine's hand. He stood behind her, shielding her from curious eyes. Catherine took a deep breath and told her story.

"Edgar washed my face," she ended. "But there is still dried blood in my hair. I tried to tell you this morning."

Mahaut listened gravely. It was one thing to have to judge a crime committed by one's townspeople, quite another to have that crime brought inside one's own home.

Nocher stepped forward.

"This tale is nonsense," he stated. "The woman is hysterical and has invented the whole thing."

"For what purpose?" Mahaut asked. She forbore pointing out that Catherine was the only witness so far who hadn't dissolved into tears.

"We know her father, Hubert, has business with the Jews," Nocher said. "She is likely under instructions from him to protect them."

Gershom stopped his wailing to look at her curiously. Catherine moved closer to Edgar, trying to protect herself from so much attention.

Mahaut shook her head. "I find that unlikely," she said. "I have had business with Jews, myself. So have most of us in Troyes. But the charge that the man was killed in my house is a grave one and I would like to have proof of it. You say that, when you returned with your wife, there was no evidence of a body."

Reluctantly, Edgar nodded. "But as she said, there was blood on her face and in her hair. I believe her."

"We need more than your word, sieur," Mahaut said. "You are not known to us or to anyone here."

Catherine could tell that Edgar was angry at being addressed as lowborn. She feared he was about to recite all his ancestors back to Adam, which would not improve anything. There must be some way they could prove that the poor man had been gutted in the palace. She wrung her hands, thinking. They were still sticky from the cake and she rubbed them on her robe. Why could she never stay clean more than ten minutes? Blood in her hair, honey on her fingers, thank goodness she'd had a chance to wash after falling yesterday into that stagnant water.

All at once, she had a clear image of the pipes coming out of the stonework of the palace and of the still water beneath.

"My lady countess," she said, "Edgar and I think that the poor soul was hung up in the privy so that the, uh, entrails could be washed down into the Rû Corde. But the water is low and the place where the pipes drain is away from the main current. There might be some remains there still."

She closed her eyes, trying not to see them in her mind.

The countess showed no emotion.

"Nocher, take two of your men and search the water beneath the pipes," she ordered. "If you are worried about damage to your boots, take them off. And hurry.

"While we are waiting," she added, "bring me some wine. And open a barrel of beer in the courtyard for anyone who thirsts."

The room emptied rapidly, leaving only the butcher, the guards, the countess, and Catherine and Edgar. Mahaut shook her head.

"This is not how I would have had you repay my hospitality," she said to them.

Catherine leaned against Edgar, who put his arm around her.

"We are truly sorry, my lady," he said. "We had no wish to bring scandal to your house. But, if we are correct, this man before you is innocent of murder. Your guards would never have allowed him to enter the palace last night. You would not want such an injustice on your soul."

Mahaut stiffened. "I trust to divine guidance to prevent that from happening, although you and your wife seem strange instruments of the Lord. But I did not believe the butcher guilty, in any case."

Gershom looked up in surprise.

"I believe that Jews are infidels and damned for their refusal of Our Lord. I do not, however, believe they are, as a rule, stupid. Only a fool would kill a man in his own shop and then show the body to the first people to pass by. Does my reasoning surprise you, butcher Gershom?"

The man bowed. "I ask your pardon, my lady. I admit, I had not expected justice in a Christian court. Am I free to go?"

"Not yet," Mahaut answered. "You're still a part of this, and I don't know how you fit. Is this body still hanging in your shop?"

Gershom shuddered. "Unless the mob took it."

The countess signaled to one of the guards.

"Do you know where the shop is?" she asked. The guard nodded. "Take some men and go there. If the body is as they said, take it to Saint-Loup for the monks to prepare it for burial. Perhaps they will find some indication as to his identity."

Mahaut had barely had time to sip at her wine when the commotion began again outside. Her fingers tightened on the stem of the cup and some of the wine spilled onto the table. Watching her, Catherine realized the effort she was making to appear calm and dispassionate.

I could never do that, she thought with admiration.

Nocher and his men had returned. They entered the hall, trailed by an excited mass of people. One of the men carried a bucket. He held it as far out from his body as possible and kept his eyes steadily averted from the contents.

The countess saw the bucket and her face grew still.

"Did you search the pool?" she asked Nocher.

His face was pale and he spoke haltingly.

"We did, Lady Countess," he said. He stopped and looked at Catherine with an expression she could not read.

"The woman was correct," he continued. "Birds and vermin have been at work, but there are streaks of blood on the wall under the pipes and, in the pool, we found this."

He gestured for the man with the bucket to come forward.

"Please, sir!" the man begged.

"Show her," Nocher ordered.

Sweating profusely, the servant reached into the bucket, pulling out a long, white, slimy rope. He let it fall and then, gagging, held up a soft red piece of something, about as large as his fist.

"I have fought enough to know, my lady," Nocher said. "This is a human heart."

Catherine buried her head in Edgar's shoulder. In the corner, the poet abandoned his epic and quietly threw up his beer.

Thirteen

The Great Hall of the palace at Troyes, that evening

> *Cascuns fuit que mielx pour aler a garant,*
> *Et li gentis barnages les vas bien encauçant.*
> *Tous tans fierent sour aus a tas demaintenant,*
> *De sanc et de cervelle vont la terre jonçant—*
> *Aval les plains de Rames en vont li rui corant.*

> Each one was eager to go to into the fray,
> And the nobility goes avidly to the chase.
> They all strike at once in a great array,
> So that the earth is strewn with blood and brains—
> Flowing across the fields of Ramla in a stream.

—*Chanson de Jérusalem* 11.9489–9492

Catherine and Edgar sat together at dinner that night, the normal seating order being ignored by those who had the stomach to attend. Countess Mahaut sat in her place as usual, but even she was somewhat pale. When the joint was brought in, several people excused themselves abruptly.

"I don't think I'm very hungry," Catherine whispered to Edgar.

"Let me tear you some bread, at least," he replied.

Catherine took it and nibbled on the crust. She looked up and down the table.

"Who are you looking for?" Edgar asked.

"That man I sat next to last night, Lisiard," she said. "The cook's nephew. I told you about him. He seemed to know a lot about Alys's family. After meeting her mother and stepfather this morning, I'm curious about them. They weren't what I expected at all. But I don't see him here."

Edgar looked around, also. "Well, there are a number of people missing. Didn't you say he was in service with Nocher? I imagine his men are fairly busy tonight. Despite the countess's decree about the butcher, people are still muttering about the murder of innocent Christians."

"Yes, I suppose he might be with the guards," Catherine nodded absently. "I still don't understand why the countess didn't release the butcher. It's obvious that he knows nothing about the body."

"To you, perhaps," Edgar said. "And to me, and even to the countess, but without guarantees from his people, she doesn't dare let him go. And, after all, doesn't it seem odd to you that anyone would think of leaving a body in a place like that? It would be sure to be found."

"Perhaps the murderers thought the butcher would be so afraid of being accused that he would hide it for them," Catherine guessed.

"Perhaps," Edgar said. "Or they might have a grudge against the man, personally. He may know something and not even be aware of it. And, in that case, the countess's jail would be the safest place for him."

"Yes, I suppose so. But why hasn't Solomon come back?" Catherine worried. "If there is trouble for the Jews, I don't want him involved. He should stay here and pretend to be Stephen. It's all very disquieting. Where has everyone gone?"

"I'm still here," Edgar reminded her.

Catherine paused in midnibble. "And I don't want you more than an arm's length from me until we leave this place," she said. "I have horrible shivers every time I think of that bucket. And I won't be truly at ease until they find the poor man's head."

Edgar shivered, too. Hurriedly, they blessed themselves. When the spiced wine was passed, they both filled their cups to the brim.

When Solomon heard the butcher's name, his first thought was to rescue the man himself and find out afterwards what he had been accused of. But Edgar's warning made more sense. The Christians of Troyes far outnumbered the Jews and had most of the fortifications. If the man were to be saved, it would be in the time-honored tradition of soft words and hard coins. He headed for the yeshiva.

On his way, he passed the house of Joseph ben Meïr. As he went by, the gate opened and Joseph hissed his name.

"What are the idolators up to now?" he asked, catching at Solomon's arm. "Do they seem likely to riot? I have three houses along the Rû Corde. Are they in any danger?"

Solomon shook him off.

"I know nothing about your houses," he said. "And I care less. One of our brothers is facing the Christians alone and the charge is murder. I'm going for the *parnassim*."

"The elders have gone to Ramerupt," Joseph moaned. "They were having a debate and went to seek the advice of the Rabbenu Tam."

"Are there no *tovim* in this town who will help Gershom?" Solomon glared at Joseph, but the man ignored the slur.

"I told you," he said. "All the elders are gone. Do you want me to get myself killed for a butcher? I have a family. I have property."

He backed away and slammed the gate shut. Solomon heard the sound of the bolt being drawn.

"I'll also see that you have *herem* put on you for your cowardice!" he cried. But the gate remained shut.

There seemed nothing else to do. Solomon went to the place where he had stabled his horse. With luck, he could reach Ramerupt before dark and have the *parnassim* back by morning. He only hoped the countess's justice would let Gershom live that long.

The dinner was slow and conversation sporadic. The poet, when asked for a cheerful tale, could only think of bits from the *Siege of Antioch*, mostly about wading through the blood of infidels. It wasn't a popular choice. But no one seemed eager to leave the table. The darkness grew and the torches and candles seemed to make more shadows than light. Even Catherine was reduced to monosyllables.

"I love you," she said to Edgar.

It seemed necessary to repeat it.

"I love you," he replied, as required.

They held hands and sipped from each other's cups and pretended for a while that there was no one else in the room and that nothing so horrible as murder had ever happened.

But the interlude was short. Nocher returned while they were still lingering over the dried fruit soaked in honey. Behind him, Catherine saw Jehan among the guards. His tired face was streaked with sweat and dirt.

Countess Mahaut got up at Nocher's entrance and motioned him into an alcove to give his report. Noticing Catherine, Jehan came over to the table. She handed him her cup and pushed the bread toward him.

"What is happening outside?" she asked. "Rumors are flying like crows tonight and I've heard nothing so far that I can believe."

Jehan glanced at Edgar, who glared back at him but held his tongue. The knight stiffened for a moment, then his shoulders sagged and he picked up the cup and filled it from the wine pitcher.

"They've discovered who the man was. His father finally identified the body," Jehan said. "He had a mole on his back shaped like a duck. Funny, I've known him for years and never noticed it. I thought it was odd that he didn't join us tonight, but Lisiard was always slipping off to the kitchens to see his *soignant*. Sometimes he doesn't hear the summons."

Catherine nodded, her heart sinking. It was what she had feared all along, even while refusing to admit it to herself. Perhaps she had felt something familiar about the body when she first saw it. But had Lisiard been killed for speaking too freely to her about Walter of Grancy and the countess Alys or had he made such cruel enemies for other reasons?

"He was the son of a provost and the nephew of a cook," she murmured. "How odd."

Jehan didn't seem surprised that she knew the man. "Isembard has far more wealth than Lisiard's father," he said. "Some people prefer gold to an honorable occupation."

He emptied the cup and poured another.

"Perhaps Lisiard should have been a cook, also," he added. "He hadn't the stomach for fighting."

Edgar remembered the things in the bucket and tried not to think that now Lisiard didn't have the stomach for anything.

Jehan didn't seem bothered by any such thoughts. He cut himself a piece from the cold joint, wiped his knife on the bread and returned it to its sheath. He tore at the tough meat, wincing as he hit a tender tooth.

"Has anyone been accused?" Catherine asked.

"Only the butcher," Jehan said around his mouthful. "But no one here believes Gershom did it, not after what you said." He paused and looked at her in fury. "Damn you, Catherine! You bring evil wherever you go! First Roger, now Lisiard. Do you intend to kill all my friends? You are the most *malastrue* woman I've ever known."

As the knight spoke, Edgar stood and leaned across the table, forgetting that Jehan was twice his weight and well armed.

"Say one more word in that tone to my wife," he told Jehan, "and you will do it through a broken jaw. Is that clear?"

Jehan stared at him, then at Catherine. She looked back, her eyes glowing in the torchlight. Edgar didn't move. He merely waited.

With a curse, Jehan threw the meat across the room, where it was snatched in midair by one of the palace dogs. He then took Catherine's cup and the pitcher and returned to the table where the other knights were now seated.

Edgar sat down again, feeling as if he had just survived a bout with a dragon. He was absurdly pleased with himself. He rubbed the shoulder Jehan had twisted in their last encounter.

"Even enough," he muttered.

Catherine wiped her eyes. "That poor man," she said. "It is my fault. I tried to get him to tell me all he knew. He was so innocent. He just wanted to tell stories. Kitchen gossip is the best, he told me. Do you think they cut him up with the kitchen knives?"

Edgar looked at her sharply. Her voice was distant, soft. He'd heard her speak like that once before.

"Catherine," he said, "Jehan is an idiot. Lisiard would have been killed whether he spoke to you or not. He knew something and couldn't be trusted to keep it secret. But, if you hadn't been here today, they might have killed the butcher despite the countess's authority. So you saved a man's life. You are not to blame for Lisiard's death or anyone else's, do you understand?"

Catherine took a deep breath and returned. "Yes," she said. "I understand. But I can't help but feel responsible. I think that his murder is connected with what happened to Alys, don't you?"

"Yes, I do." Edgar spoke with such certainty that Catherine was startled. "But not just because you asked about her."

He went on. "Did you see who spoke for the tanners? That same deacon who owes Abbess Hélöise twenty marks. Doesn't it seem strange to you that he should have been here at all? He owes Joseph ben Meïr, as well. I wonder if he also does business with Raynald of Tonnerre. This affair has more twists to it than a bloom of fresh metal, but somehow, it's all connected."

"Peter of Baschi," Catherine said. "I wonder why Mother Hélöise loaned him money in the first place. It's not as if the convent were rich. Some winters we can barely feed ourselves."

"Clearly he's not from a church that's adopted the rules of reform," Edgar said. "He probably has his own house and a concubine. Perhaps he's amassing a fortune to buy his sons a place at the count's court."

Catherine was exhausted. She had forgotten to dilute the wine. Just as well Jehan had taken her cup or she'd have been under the table with the dogs by now. She tried to piece it all together. Alys, Raynald, the Paraclete, Lisiard, Walter of Grancy, who seemed to have vanished, Constanza and her husband, Peter of Baschi, Paciana. Paciana who was so gentle and humble and who had given her a wedding gift of hate. And who else was part of all this? What was so secret and so important that people would be killed for it, that Raynald would risk damnation by attempting to abduct a woman from the convent, that a human body would be treated like an animal's?

"I don't understand anything," she said at last. "I need to go to bed."

Edgar smiled.

"That's an excellent idea," he said. "I think I'll join you."

By keeping his horse at a killing pace, Solomon managed to reach Ramerupt early that evening. He had no trouble finding the home of the Rabbenu Jacob Tam. The house was large and surrounded by vineyards. Near it was the school where the finest Talmudic scholars of northern Europe came to study. As in the schools of Paris, men of all ages and from all corners of the world came to Ramerupt to learn from the man considered the greatest authority on the Law.

Jacob ben Meïr ben Samuel, Rabbenu Tam, agreed fully with this judgement.

As Solomon approached the house, he saw the elders of Troyes sitting in a disconsolate circle in the courtyard next to the wine press. By their faces, their mission had not been successful.

Solomon went up to a man he knew.

"Yehiel," he began. "There's trouble in town. You all need to return."

Yehiel stood, brushing the dirt from his tunic.

"There's trouble here," he said. "The Rabbenu won't change the ruling on accepting wine as payment from the Christians. He says it doesn't matter if it isn't meant for their sacrifices, it's still not *halakah*. His grandfather decreed it and so it shall be."

Solomon looked around at the arpents of vines.

"Perhaps Rabbenu Tam has his own reasons," he commented.

Yehiel followed his glance.

"There are those who say that, also," he said. "But not to the man's face. Now what is the trouble?"

"Gershom the butcher has been accused of murdering a Christian man," Solomon said.

Yehiel paled. "Gershom? That's nonsense!"

He turned to the other men.

"This man brings evil news," he said. "We must return to Troyes at once."

Solomon explained as much as he knew.

"Our families!" one man exclaimed. "Is this accusation known in the town?"

"The streets were full when I left," Solomon said.

No one needed to hear more. They called for their servants and their horses and left.

"By the way," Solomon asked Yehiel as they rode out, "which of the Christian debtors wants to pay in wine?"

"Several do," Yehiel answered. "But the worst is that deacon at Saint-Aventin, Peter. And I suspect that he was trying to repay us with wine he had stolen from the church."

"In that case, the law is clear."

"Yes, then it would be for sacrifice and we couldn't accept it. That may be why the elders didn't argue the point more strongly," Yehiel agreed. "You don't seem surprised. Have you had dealings with this man, too?"

"I have heard of him," Solomon said. "His reputation among his own people is not good, either."

After that, they reached the main road, which was smooth enough for speed. The elders spurred their horses on through the growing darkness, driven by fear, and Solomon had no more breath for questions.

The shouting began in the hours before dawn.

At first it blended in Catherine's mind with a dream about being lost in Paris, hunting through the streets for Edgar and finding only empty cloaks or bland-faced students. Then the cloaks filled with hoofed demons that were chasing her through the twisting alleys of the Île. She could feel their fiery breath on her neck.

With a scream, she woke.

"Edgar!" she cried. "I thought you were lost!"

She reached out for him and felt only empty blankets. In a panic, she pulled on the first piece of clothing she touched and hurried into the corridor. That was when she

realized that the screams and clanking were coming from
the Rû Corde, outside the window on the other side of the
riverbed. She rushed down the stairs and into the Great
Hall.

There was chaos there as well. Countess Mahaut was
directing the accumulation of buckets and blankets by one
group while Nocher shouted orders to the knights and
men-at-arms.

"Just keep them from entering the palace grounds," he
told the men. "And be on the watch for fires. Half of those
people are drunk and the other half insane. They won't
care what they burn."

He strode over to the countess.

"We've had a messenger from Bishop Hatto," he told
her. "He's sending out his men to protect the synagogue
and the streets around it, but he wants to know if you'll
take in the women and children here, until he's sure it's
safe for them. It seems most of the men have gone off
somewhere."

"Yes, of course," Mahaut said. "Ebeline! Don't soak all
the blankets! We need some for warmth. No, you can't use
the salt cellars for buckets! You have enough. Go and soak
down the roofs and cover the henhouse and the dovecote
with wet blankets."

She waved the people out. Nocher started to order his
men to go bring in the threatened Jews.

"Wait," she called to him. "Make sure they understand
that they don't have to come if they don't want to. Tell
them I only want to keep them safe, not make them convert. Is that clear?"

Nocher bowed. "Of course," he said. "Gunther! Jehan!
Hear that? See that your men don't scare them more than
the mob."

Catherine shoved her way through the scurrying people, hunting for Edgar. In the crush, she bumped against
Jehan, who was waiting for his men to gather up their
equipment.

"*Avoi!*" he said. "Watch where you're . . ."

He stopped upon recognizing her. A slow grin spread

over his face as he looked her up and down. Catherine followed his glance. Her mouth dropped open in horror.

She was standing in the middle of the Great Hall of the palace of Troyes dressed only in Edgar's *chainse*. The sleeves fell far below her fingertips but the hem came only halfway to her knees. She could feel her braids tickling the backs of her legs.

"Well?" Jehan's grin widened.

"I was looking for my husband," Catherine said, crouching a bit in an effort to cover herself more.

"I saw him a moment ago, in the other half of your costume, helping wet down the outbuildings," he answered. "You two can only afford one set of clothes?"

Catherine didn't bother to explain. She ran out into the courtyard, bumping against people until she collided with Edgar, wearing only his *braies*.

"What's happening?" she shouted over the commotion.

"Someone in a tavern decided there was a plot to kill all the Christians and take over the tanneries," Edgar answered. "The next thing anyone knew, there were fifty or so drunken men breaking into the Jewish shops and heading for their houses with torches and cudgels. The countess had the gate to the old city shut, but it didn't hold. And now they're throwing flaming rags over the walls."

He stopped and looked at her.

"Why are you wearing my *chainse*?"

"Do you want it back now?" she asked, annoyed.

"Saint Melania's mantle! Of course not!" he answered. "But go cover yourself before you get raped."

It was good advice, but Catherine was not about to go up to their alcove and root about for her own clothes. She went back inside the hall and looked around. There, in a corner, was the pack of the travelling poet. He was nowhere to be seen. Catherine went over and found, as she had hoped, his extra pair of *braies*. Quickly she slipped them on. Her hips were a bit wider than the underfed performer's and the *braies* stayed up without the need for a belt. Satisfied, she rejoined Edgar, who was making up part of a bucket brigade.

His eyebrows rose when he saw her.

"'Oh, that's *much* better," he said. "Here, take this."

She grabbed the full bucket and passed it on to the next person.

"Have you seen Solomon?" she asked. "Is he all right?"

"He's not come back," Edgar answered. "Careful!"

An empty bucket fell from the roof and landed on the ground next to Catherine. She picked it up and passed it on, took a full bucket from the person next in line and passed it to Edgar, over and over, soon falling into the rhythm. She had grown up in Paris and knew the constant fear of fire in towns made largely of wood. If one of those blazing rags caught on a roof or even a pile of straw, Troyes could be cinders by morning. Her arms began to ache but she didn't stop.

A few moments later the palace gate opened as the guards herded in a frightened group of women and children, clutching the few belongings they had had time to gather up. They stood close together in wary silence. Nocher shouted at them to go on into the hall but no one moved.

"What is it now?" he called. "You all know me. We buy wool from you, Bella! Go on in!"

The woman he had addressed stepped forward.

"We know everyone out there, lord," she said. "They buy wool from me, too. We get our water from the same well and our children skin their knees playing at the same games. And, tomorrow, after they've burnt our homes and stolen all their pledges back, they'll be very sorry, but it's our fault for not believing in your god, what else should we expect?"

"By the sword of Saint Maurice," Nocher muttered. "What else *should* you expect?"

He spoke more loudly. "You are under the authority of the bishop and the count. They have sworn to protect you and your property. No one in here will harm you. Just go in to the hall and wait until we can restore order."

Bella conferred with the others. Finally, with shrugs of resignation, they followed Nocher's order. Bella stayed behind, stopping to speak with him privately. But Catherine was close enough to hear.

"My son and some of the other boys have gone to the yeshiva to protect the holy books," she told him. "They will fight anyone who dares attack them. If the bishop and the count aren't able to control the people of this town, there will be Christian blood as well as Jewish spilt to-night."

Nocher took off his helm and wiped his forehead. "There will be no more murder done," he said. "And those who break the count's peace, whoever they are, will be punished."

"Then tell the bishop to look to his own for those who set men to violence," Bella countered. "That deacon of Saint-Aventin and his partner were in the streets tonight, preaching holy destruction."

With that she turned her back on him and joined the others in the hall.

Catherine's body continued swaying even after someone had taken her place in the line and gently pushed her away. She and Edgar stumbled toward the cookhouse, where someone was dishing out squares of cold, congealed porridge. They ate it avidly, licking their fingers.

"Edgar," Catherine said, sucking the last of the grease off her thumb, "it just occurred to me; we haven't had a whole night's sleep since we were married. I might as well have stayed at the Paraclete and recited the night office."

"And missed all this fun?" he asked, putting his arm around her.

She leaned her head on his shoulder.

"Catherine?" he asked after a moment. "Are you asleep?"

"I was just thinking," she said.

"About what we should do next?"

"No," she yawned. "I was just thinking that you have a wonderful nose. I'm so fond of your nose."

It was the nicest thing anyone had ever said to him. Edgar adjusted her more comfortably on his shoulder. They fell asleep leaning against a cart in the courtyard and didn't awake until well past dawn.

Bishop Hatto had gone out himself that night, leading the knights and showering his wrath upon the rioters. Whether through fear of excommunication or of the swords of the knights, the people were finally convinced to disperse without completing the destruction they had planned on. When the *parnassim* arrived the next afternoon, they found their wives at home, putting away the valuables, and their sons in the square in front of the church of Saint-Frobert, treating the knights of the count and the bishop to a barrel of their best wine.

The elders gave this move their approval and divided the cost among the families. Then they selected a delegation to the court to negotiate the release of Gershom, the butcher.

Catherine had been greeted, upon awakening, by an angry poet, demanding the return of his pants. When that and other matters had been sorted out, she returned to her concern about Solomon.

"I think we should go out and look for him," she told Edgar.

"Catherine, Solomon is better able than either of us to defend himself," Edgar answered. "He proved that when he saved me from your friend, Jehan, last winter."

"All the same, he may need help," she answered. "And, anyway, I want to see if we can discover just what, or who, worked everyone up again. I thought things were calm in the town after we proved that Lisiard was killed here in the palace."

"You think it was Peter of Baschi, as that woman told Nocher, don't you?" Edgar asked.

"Yes, don't you? But I keep wondering who his partner was. It couldn't have been Joseph," Catherine said. "Do you think it was someone else from Peter's church?"

"Somehow I got the impression that the other man wasn't a cleric," Edgar said. "If that woman knew him, perhaps others do. Shall we go to the square by the tanneries and see what we can overhear?"

The streets were littered with debris from the night before, broken crockery, wooden stalls smashed in, puddles of spilled beer, covered with flies. On their way to the square, they were nearly tripped by a handcart being pulled into the road.

"Watch where you're going!" Edgar shouted.

But instead of getting out of the way, the man pulling the cart stopped and studied them. Catherine studied him, as well, and found little to interest her. The man was stooped and had a leg so twisted he seemed to be walking on his ankle. He was unshaven and his hair was matted.

"I don't know you," the man said. "I know everyone in Troyes. You're strangers. Wellborn by the look of your clothes. You'd be the people who ruined it for the ones who killed Lisiard, wouldn't you?"

Edgar let his hand slide casually over his knife, unhooking the sheath.

"What would you know about that?" he asked. "Who are you?"

The man smiled. What teeth he had were brown.

"I'm Lascho," he said as if that explained everything.

They waited.

"I'm the dung collector," he went on. "And I saw the man who put poor old Lisiard in Gershom's shop."

Fourteen

The Great Hall of the palace, Feast of Saint Leo,
Thursday, April 11, 1140

ve'ilu shekufin 'oto lehotzi': mukkah shechin ... vehamekametz,
vehametzaref nehoshet vehaburesi ...

And these are those who are compelled to free their wives:
one who suffers from boils on the skin, ... and the
collector of dung, and the smelter of copper,
and the tanner ...

—*Mishnah Ketubot 7:10*

I'm the best dung collector in Troyes, my lady," Lascho told the countess. "I can tell just by looking what sort of animal left it. The horse and cattle droppings I sell to the farmers, the dog dung to the tanners. Human's good for nothing. I just dump it in the canal. But I keep it nice and divided in my cart. And I get it all. When was the last time you stepped into a pile on your way to Mass?"

The countess Mahaut regarded the man standing before her as if he were another species. He was brown all over, with wisps of hay sticking to his hair and clothes. He and his occupation seemed to have merged. Yet his identity and honesty had been vouched for by the required number of people of the town. So his testimony must be listened to.

"I'm pleased to hear that you perform your job so well," she said. "I will bring it to the attention of Count Thibault when he returns. Now, these people say you have information regarding the murder of the man, Lisiard?"

Lascho's forehead creased in his effort to form his answer. He had been warned of the dangers, here and in the hereafter, of giving out misinformation.

"Well, not about the murder, exactly," he hedged. "I didn't see the man killed. I'd have gone to the bishop or Count Nocher, here, if I'd seen that. But I did see them who took him away and hung him up like a poor dumb beast. I did see that."

He stood alone in the middle of the hall, a mixture of terror and bravado. It was the grandest place he had ever been in. Since the death of his mother, he had rarely been allowed inside a house. The tanners let him use their sheds on cold or rainy nights or he slept in the entrance to one of the churches. For food he paid when he could and begged when he couldn't. He was the least noticed human in Troyes.

And now everyone was looking at him.

"Tell us what you saw, then," Mahaut prompted.

Lascho took a deep breath. "It was nearly dawn, only a few stars left, on the night before last. I was sleeping in the porch of Saint-Urbain but I knew the canons would be along soon and I wanted to be gone before they came and tripped over me."

He paused. "They do that sometimes. They don't see me. Then they swear and that makes them angry so they kick me for good measure. I was crossing the court to Saint-Jacques, where it's not as warm but they don't get up so early, when I saw these two men, dragging something."

"It was still dark," the countess said. "How could you see what it was?"

"Oh, I couldn't," Lascho said. "But it didn't seem honest to me, dragging things about before the sun rises, so I ducked behind a row of barrels and watched. They passed right by me and I heard one say, 'Christ, he's heavy!' and the other one answered, 'Damn *bricon* spent all his time in the kitchens. We'll never get him up on that butcher's hook.'"

Catherine joined in the collective gasp at this revelation. Poor Lisiard! Mocked even by his murderers. But there seemed no doubt that the dung collector was telling the truth. He couldn't have known about Lisiard's preference for food over fighting. He wouldn't have been allowed close enough to a kitchen to hear the gossip.

Mahaut waited for the exclamations to subside. Then she leaned forward in her chair and asked quietly, "Did you recognize the men?"

Lascho twisted his fingers through his beard in his nervousness. He spent a minute in the effort to untangle his hand. Then he shook his head.

"It was too dark," he said. "One was tall and broad in the shoulder; the other much smaller. They said nothing else; I didn't know the voices. I'm sorry. Do I still get a loaf of bread?"

"What?" Mahaut was polite, but puzzled.

"Those two said if I came with them and told the story, that I could have a whole loaf, not ever dripped on by anyone, and a mug of beer."

He pointed at Catherine and Edgar. Edgar stepped forward.

"I did promise him food if he told you what he had told us. Forgive my presumption, my lady countess," he said.

Mahaut nodded and gestured to her chaplain, Conon.

"Have this man taken to Isembard," she ordered. "Tell him that Lascho has been most helpful in the search for the murderers of his nephew and that he is to be given whatever he wishes to eat and drink."

The dung collector was stunned to tears by this largess.

"Thank you, lady, thank you," he repeated. "May Our Lord reward you for your kindness."

Mahaut smiled as he was led out.

"The blessings of the poorest reach God's ears first," she said. "Are the men of his community here to testify for the butcher?"

"Yes, my lady," her chamberlain said. "They have spoken with Gershom and are waiting outside to give pledges as to his innocence."

As the *parnassium* of Troyes came in, Catherine was relieved to see Solomon among them. She and Edgar, their part over, moved back to a seat against the wall and she signaled her cousin to join them.

She hugged him. "I was so worried about you last night," she whispered. "You should have stayed with us."

Solomon disengaged himself.

"You keep forgetting, Catherine," he said. "I'm not one of you. My duty was to my brother, Gershom. I may not keep to the Law like the *tovim* of this town, but I wouldn't hide under a false name and let you Christians kill one of my people. Nor would I cower behind barred gates."

"Of course you wouldn't." Catherine sensed that his rebuke wasn't for her, alone. "You've proved that many times. I was only concerned for you."

Solomon nodded and squeezed her hand.

"It was kind of you, Catherine," he sighed. "Forgive me, I haven't slept at all. Of course the elders refused to rest when one of their own was in danger. My throat is full of road dust and my backside is sore from riding."

"I still have some of that goose grease salve left," Edgar offered.

"Keep it," Solomon laughed. "You may have need of it again."

He got up.

"When the *parnassim* have finished negotiating, they want to meet the two of you," he said. "They would like you to come to the house of Rabbi Samuel this afternoon."

Catherine was aware of her own exhaustion and the fact that it had been some time since her hair had seen a comb. In the Paraclete now they would be putting away the manuscripts and writing tools and preparing for Sext. It seemed impossible that it had only been a few days since she left. She was in another world.

She had missed an exchange between Edgar and Solomon.

"Fine," Solomon was saying. "I'll return for you then."

Edgar took Catherine's arm.

"We must thank the countess for her hospitality," he said. "Solomon says we can stay in the Jewish quarter tonight and leave tomorrow with some wine traders."

"But what about Lisiard?" Catherine asked. "And finding out about the land for Mother Héloïse and . . ."

"We can do that this afternoon," Edgar said. "The elders may be able to help us."

He was hurrying her up the stairs almost roughly, his fingers pressed into the flesh of her upper arm.

"Edgar, what is it?" she asked. "What's wrong?"

He didn't answer until they were back in their alcove. Catherine noticed with regret that the bed had been dismantled. Their things were in a pile on the floor.

"Carissma." He held her close. She could feel his heart thumping against her chest. She ran her fingers along his ribs. He was too thin; she could feel each one.

"Dilectissime," she murmured.

He drew his hand down her jawline. She had proved herself strong many times, but to him she would always seem fragile. He tilted her face to his.

"Catherine, we came here because your father wanted you someplace safe," he said. "We were supposed to ask a few simple questions quietly and inconspicuously. On every level we have failed." He kissed her. "My dear, you are not an inconspicuous sort of person."

Catherine thought of Count Raynald and his father. She had made herself all too memorable to them.

"So, are you telling me we should run away?" she asked.

"Of course not," he answered. "Never. but there is little more we can do here. It's up to Nocher and to Lisiard's family to find those who killed him. If, as we believe, his death was connected with that of Alys and the disposition of her property, then all this should be brought to the attention of Abbess Héloïse as soon as possible. Don't you agree?"

"Yes . . ." She was still unconvinced. "But why shouldn't we stay here a few more days to get the information we came for?"

For answer he reached out and pulled open the curtain across the alcove. As he did, there was a rustle and they caught a glimpse of a shadow as someone rushed down the winding stairs. Catherine nodded, her eyes wide.

"Of course. Those who would not fear to kill a man who lived here, who had family and friends all around, wouldn't hesitate to murder a pair of strangers with no kin nearby," she said. "I wish I knew what this was all about."

"At the moment, Catherine, I don't care," Edgar said. "Abbot Bernard says that a curious person is an empty person. I don't think he meant empty to the limit that Lisiard was taken, but all the same, I prefer to live in ignorance a while longer."

"How much longer?" Catherine wanted to know. "I don't believe curiosity is a sin if it leads to the truth."

Edgar smiled. "I don't either. I am as much a student of Master Abelard as you. But I think we should control our thirst for knowledge until we are safely away from the palace and whoever it is who is watching us so intently."

Catherine shivered as if a cold hand had suddenly clutched at her neck.

"Shall we wait in the courtyard for Solomon?" she said as they gathered up their things. "No one can come upon us unawares out there."

Upon entering the home of Rabbi Samuel they were given water to wash in and then honeycakes and wine with mint sprigs in it to drink. After they were made comfortable, the other elders came in and thanked them.

"Without you to speak for him, poor Gershom might have been killed before we could arrive," Samuel told Catherine. "You are a true child of our lost brother Hubert. *Todah robah,* to you both."

Another of the elders added, "Solomon says you have come here to find out about some land in the forest of Othe. We have noticed a certain interest in this area recently, ourselves. Peter of Baschi and Raynald of Tonnerre's father, William, have both wanted to know if we held pledges of land in that region and what they could redeem them for."

"But Joseph ben Meïr said that Peter was in debt to him and we know he also has borrowed from the nuns of the Paraclete," Edgar said. "How could he redeem anyone else's pledges when he has so many of his own?"

"That, I cannot tell you," the elder said. "But Nicholas of Montièramey, Bishop Hatto's chaplain, has indicated to me that there are those in high authority who would be willing to stand security for him."

"Really?" Catherine said. "I wonder why they don't want to deal with you directly."

The man shrugged. "There are many who don't wish it known that they do business with us, especially those of the Church for whom anything smelling of usury also smells of sulfur and brimstone. We have always admired Abbot Suger of Saint-Denis for his open honesty in his dealings with the Jews. Most clerics refuse to risk the stigma."

"And yet, they seem willing to risk their souls to acquire this land," Catherine said. "What could there be about it? Have you been to the forest?"

Rabbi Samuel nodded. "I've passed through it. It's only a forest. The Othe is mostly unused. It contains great stands of oak and chestnut. It may be that they think they can make a profit from the wood. With the new fashion in building, long beams will be needed for roofing. Suger had to perform a miracle to get enough wood for the roof at Saint-Denis."

Solomon laughed. "You mean he had to go out himself to find it. His builder tried to tell him that there were no trees left tall enough for his needs and he had to buy further away. He didn't count on the abbot hitching up his robes and scrambling through the forest, himself, to mark the trees tall enough for the beams."

Rabbi Samuel laughed, too. "More than one man has regretted equating the abbot's size with his shrewdness. Rather than confront the builder with his trickery and cause resentment, Suger simply announced that it must be a miracle. The trees had grown overnight in answer to his prayers."

"Perhaps they did," Catherine said. "You may be right that Raynald and the others want the forest land to sell the wood. Henry Sanglier is looking for material, I hear, for his new cathedral at Sens, but that isn't enough to explain why they would kill for it. Most of the world is covered by trees."

"We can't answer that," Rabbi Samuel told her. "Nor do

we know why poor Gershom was brought into this Christian situation. He does no money lending. He's simply a butcher."

"It may be that his was the first shop the men came to," Edgar suggested. "Lascho said that the men were staggering under the weight of the body."

"No, Gershom's wasn't closest," Rabbi Samuel said. "They chose him for some reason."

"If the body had been found in one of your homes, what would have happened?" Catherine asked.

There was a brief consultation in Hebrew.

"The Law on that is fairly clear," Rabbi Samuel told her. "We would have searched for his family. If we found no relatives, we would have paid for his burial among his own kind."

"But would there have been such an uproar?" she continued.

"Perhaps," Rabbi Samuel said. "Who knows? Certainly he wouldn't have been discovered by Christians. We would have had time to go to the proper authorities. Of course, it would have been just as difficult to prove we had nothing to do with his death. You think that his killers intended to start a riot against us?"

"Well, it occurred to me, . . ." Catherine hesitated. Now that she had thought of it, the thing seemed obvious and she didn't want to embarrass these scholars. However . . . "If the object was to find pledges for property, a riot in which your homes were ransacked would be a good opportunity to search for them."

"But all our pledges are in Hebrew," Rabbi Samuel pointed out.

"There are Christians who can make out some Hebrew," Catherine argued. "Even Abbess Héloïse reads it a little. She studied it in Paris when she lived with her uncle. That was one of the reasons she left Argenteuil, where she was a boarder. She wanted to study Hebrew as well as attend the lectures.

"Of course," she added, trying to imagine Héloïse so long ago, "then she met Master Abelard."

Rabbi Samuel was not interested in Héloïse's background but was clearly startled by the notion that Peter may have had some understanding of Hebrew.

"Peter of Baschi did study in Paris and Melun, both of which have Hebrew scholars," he said. "It's possible. We have had a number of Christians come to us. I never considered Peter the sort who would, but still . . . when I think of the times we spoke in front of him and the things we said . . . I've been a fool."

"Can you help the women of the Paraclete recover what they loaned Deacon Peter?" Edgar asked.

"I would like to," Rabbi Samuel said, "if only to repay you for your service to us. But he has powerful friends. What you need is to go to one of them. The Paraclete is under the jurisdiction of Bishop Hatto, isn't it?"

"Yes."

"Why don't you ask him?"

"I don't know," Catherine admitted. "Mother Héloïse didn't suggest it. Perhaps he's one of the powerful people also seeking control of this land."

"I'm sorry," Rabbi Samuel said. "I don't have the authority to make this man pay us, much less your abbess. In the end we may have to turn to the bishop, ourselves, or Count Thibault, to get some return on what we've loaned him."

"I wish we at least knew who owned the property adjacent to the pieces Alys left the convent," Catherine said.

"Joseph, the wine seller, could have told you part of that," Rabbi Samuel said. "He holds a pledge there as well. In the forest of Othe, the land is divided between the count of Tonnerre, Walter of Grancy and the monastery of Vauluisant."

"Well, we know that both Vauluisant and Raynald of Tonnerre have shown some interest," Edgar said. "And if Walter could be proved to have attacked Alys, his lands might be forfeit. I wish we could find him."

Rabbi Samuel brightened. "There, at least, we can help you," he said. "Walter is hiding in the forest with the hermit of Lailly."

"He's what?"

"The who?"

"How do you know?"

Catherine, Edgar and Solomon all spoke at once. Rabbi Samuel seemed delighted to have made such an impression.

"Yehiel saw him last week when he stopped by to visit Gaufridus," he told them. "Yehiel, come here."

Solomon's friend stepped forward. He was about thirty, so "elder" must have been an honorary title. He was built like a blacksmith rather than a scholar, all but his hands, Catherine noted. They were soft and white. Only the middle finger of his right hand had a callus. Catherine had one just like it, from hours of holding a pen.

"I'd have told you, Solomon," Yehiel apologized. "I knew he was hiding from Raynald and William; I didn't realize you were looking for him, too. He's staying in a hut near the hermit's cottage. He seemed quite happy when I saw him. Says he might take up the contemplative life."

Rabbi Samuel nodded in satisfaction. "I should have thought of sending you there, myself. I don't know what the murders of the cook's nephew or the countess of Tonnerre have to do with us, but if the links are there, then Gaufridus will have found them. He may not seem to be aware of it, but nothing happens concerning the forest that he isn't told. If someone intends to chop it down to build cathedrals, he'll be the one to tell you. He grumbles enough about the damage the charcoal burners do. Yes, that's the man you should see."

Catherine and Edgar looked at each other. Edgar spoke for them both.

"Is there no one else?" he asked. "Catherine and I have not had great good fortune consulting with hermits."

Rabbi Samuel laughed. "You may not with this one, either," he said. "It depends on his mood. But if you want to unravel this tangle, then you will need his help."

"Where can we find him?" Edgar asked.

Yehiel answered, "His hermitage is in the forest about a mile from the village of Lailly. Anyone who lives there can direct you."

"If you can be ready to leave in the morning," Rabbi

Samuel added, "there is a party of brethren from Lyons, who are on their way to Sens. You can travel with them."

Edgar turned to Catherine. "What do you think?"

"We have no choice," she answered. "We have vowed to find the answers. We can't ignore someone who might be able to give them to us."

"It's settled, then." Rabbi Samuel clapped his hands. "In gratitude for your help, Gershom has roasted the first of the spring lamb. Last autumn's wine should be ready for tasting. Tonight we shall feast. You will join us?"

Lamb and new wine. Catherine's mouth watered.

"We would be honored," Edgar said.

That night Solomon sat with them. Tables had been set up in the courtyard of Rabbi Samuel's home and all the Jews of Troyes were there to celebrate. Solomon ate until Catherine feared he would burst.

"I've never known you to be a glutton," she told him.

"That's because you usually see me when I have to eat *trafe*," he said. "It's so good to have real food again."

He ripped off another piece of bread, soaked with juice from the lamb.

"I never thought of that," Catherine said. "I always knew Jews wouldn't eat at Christian tables, but you do. Why?"

"I eat what's there," Solomon said in annoyance. "Would you rather I starved? For one thing, sometimes it's safer for me to be Stephen and it would be odd if I didn't eat whatever was on the plate. But not pork. I never did that, no matter what. I couldn't. It won't lie on our stomachs. It's a known fact."

Catherine thought of her father, eating hugely of the soups flavored with salted pork. In the winter, it was often the only meat they had. How had he survived? Did baptism, even forced, change one's stomach as well as one's soul? She would have to ask Master Abelard his opinion.

Just before they were shown to their bed, Rabbi Samuel came over to Catherine and Edgar.

"The people of the community want you to know that we are not unconcerned about these matters you are seeking answers to," he said quietly. "We live among you. We speak the same language, sell at the same markets and what happens in the courts of your kings and the abbeys of your monks affects us, too. We are worried that these deaths and this struggle for land are part of something more. And it is especially frightening that we are apparently being made scapegoats. We want you to find out who killed Lisiard. Poor Gershom won't feel safe in his shop again, in any event. The experience of being dragged through the streets has unsettled him greatly. He has vowed never to sell to Christians again, even if it ruins him. None of us will be completely at ease until those who are responsible are brought before the count and shown to the people of Troyes. It's not enough to say we're innocent unless someone else can be proven guilty."

"We'll do what we can," Edgar promised. "But I don't know how much that will be."

Rabbi Samuel smiled at him.

"You are a most interesting young man," he said. "Catherine grew up in Paris and, even before she knew of her father's family, she knew us. But for you we must seem completely alien. And yet you sit and eat with us and offer your help. It amazes me."

Edgar shrugged.

"Everything about France is alien to me," he said. "I was raised to hate Normans and Danes, and several of the families in the neighborhood, not Jews. We have only so much animosity and we spend it on the enemies at hand. It's not amazing that I have none left for you."

Rabbi Samuel shook his head. "Nevertheless, I am pleased and ask you to accept my appreciation for your kindness. Good night."

When he had left and they were settled in bed, Catherine turned to Edgar.

"Do you really think we should waste our time with this hermit?" she fussed, drumming her fingers on his chest.

"I think we need to find Walter of Grancy," Edgar answered. "If he is staying with this Gaufridus, it wouldn't hurt to speak with him also."

"I suppose," Catherine said, unconvinced. "It just seems

that we're getting farther from the answers. I wanted a chance to speak with Alys's mother again. I would swear she was utterly taken aback by Raynald's charge that Paciana was still alive. And her comment that Alys was only interested in worldly matters was very strange. That's a very odd thing for a mother to say about her dead child, don't you agree?"

"Mmmm?" Edgar was more than half asleep. "Oh yes, I agree completely."

There was a moment of silence.

"Catherine?"

"Yes, *carissme*?"

"If you're going to continue moving your fingers like that, would you mind doing it further down?"

Catherine moved her hand. There was another moment of silence.

"Actually, Edgar," she said. "I don't think it will be necessary."

Edgar was feeling much less sleepy. He rolled toward her.

"You may be right," he whispered. "Can we forget Alys for a while?"

Catherine wrapped herself around him.

"I've no objection," she answered.

Fifteen

The forest of Othe,
Tuesday, April 16, 1140

*Il a trové l'ermite son cortil encloant, . . .
'Amis' dist le ermites, qui fu de bone vie
Et de grant carité, 'hui mais n'en irés mie;
De la moie viande arés une partie, . . .'*

He found the hermit in his enclosed garden, . . .
'Friend,' said the hermit, who was a man of good will
and great kindness, 'You will go no further today,
Of my food you will have a share, . . .'

—*Elioxe* Laisse 56–57

*T*ravelling with a party of merchants made Catherine feel a little girl again. She had always loved the laughter and singing and the stories the men told as they rode. In those days, she had laughed and sung along and dozed against her father's back and never noticed that the men all rode with one eye to the forest and one hand on their knives.

Now she dozed against Edgar, delighting in the feel of the sun on her back and oblivious to the rash on her cheek from his woolen cloak. The light was slanting through the trees in golden ribbons and the forest was bright with fresh baby leaves. All the tales of monsters, wildmen and outlaws who were known to roam the woods seeking the weak and unwary seemed impossible on a day like this. Catherine had never seen monsters in the forest; in her experience they were more likely to roam through city streets and dark castle halls.

They arrived at the village of Lailly in the early afternoon. There were no Jews in the town to put them up for

the night, so most of the party decided to continue on to
Sens. Yehiel offered to stay behind.

"I can introduce you to Gaufridus," he said. "With him,
it's always better to have someone he knows vouch for
you."

"How do you know him?" Edgar asked. "Is he also a
trader?"

"Of course not," Yehiel answered. "He has no interest
in such things, would never dirty his hands with money."

"Then how could you have come upon him?" Catherine
asked.

"Oh, through a friend who brought me to meet him, in
the same way I'm bringing you."

They looked at him with suspicion. Yehiel was clearly
not telling them something. He was so full of suppressed
laughter that he was in danger of exploding.

Solomon had intended to continue on to Sens with the
others and then take a barge to Paris. He was more worried than he had admitted about the attack on Eliazar and
wanted to reassure himself that his uncle was recovering.
But, watching Yehiel, he decided to stay with Catherine
and Edgar instead. Yehiel was known to be a trickster and
he had the look of a man preparing a joke. Solomon felt
a familial obligation to be sure Catherine wasn't the butt
of it.

The path from the village up to the hermit's hut was
well-worn. Someone had even placed a series of logs
across a stretch of mud, a courtesy not often found even
on the roads maintained by the local lords. As they approached the hut, they could hear the disputations of a
number of quarrelsome goats.

"He keeps goats?" Catherine asked.

"No, his sister does," Yehiel answered. "She lives in the
village with her family and sends one of her children over
every day to weed the garden, milk the goats and give the
hermit his dinner."

"I see," Catherine said. But she didn't. This didn't
sound like the usual sort of hermitage. Wasn't he supposed
to have exiled himself far from his home to subsist on
roots and rainwater?

The hut of the hermit was rude but sturdy, built of stone and wood. Around it was a garden, fenced with brambles to keep animals from getting at it. The roof of the hut was thick with new *esseules* to keep out the rain. In the door, a small slit had been made in the form of a cross. Yehiel knocked.

They waited.

He knocked again.

"Perhaps he's not home," Catherine suggested.

"He's in there," Yehiel said and pounded the door with his fist.

Finally they heard a scraping as the bar on the other side of the cross was lifted. A sleepy voice greeted them.

"A blessing on all who come here," it said. "What the devil do you want?"

"Gaufridus!" Yehiel shouted through the door. "It's Yehiel. I've come to visit you. I've some friends with me who are in need of your assistance."

There was a mumbling from the other side. It sounded to Catherine like, "How can I ever be expected to find the way to heaven with all these interruptions!"

Finally, the door opened. A man of indeterminate age peered out at them. He was thin, but not gaunt; nor did he show any of the signs of excessive disdain for the body that some hermits affected. His robe was worn, but clean, as was his face.

His sister must see that he washes, Catherine thought with approval.

"*Diex vos saut,*" Gaufridus said in resignation. "Weren't you just here, Yehiel?"

"May the Almighty bless you, as well," Yehiel responded. "I'm glad to see you again, too. These are my friends, Solomon, of Paris, Catherine, late of the Paraclete, and her husband, Edgar."

Gaufridus looked sharply at Edgar and Catherine and tried to slam the door. Yehiel's foot was in the way.

"I've taken in all sorts for you, Yehiel," the hermit said. "But I won't be harboring any runaway nuns, do you hear?"

Edgar reached for the leather bag around his neck. Why

did everyone seem to doubt that he and Catherine had been properly wed?

"I have the contract," he began. "Abbess Héloïse . . ."

"I don't need harboring," Catherine interrupted. "We've come to beg your help. We need information about Count Raynald and Walter of Grancy. It's very important."

Through the gap in the door, Gaufridus looked at each of them in turn. At last he sighed and opened the door all the way.

"I hope so," he said with resignation. "I suppose you might as well come in."

The single room contained a table that doubled as a bed, a bench and stool and various baskets and wooden bowls. A lantern hung from a hook by the door, next to it a bucket. That was all. But there was a window in one wall covered with greased cloth that let in light and produced a myriad of patterns that gave the room the appearance of being part of a constantly changing tapestry.

Catherine decided it was a good place from which to search for heaven. But she was still doubtful as to the status of Gaufridus as a hermit.

"I can only offer you water," he said as they entered. "And maybe a bit of rough bread, and perhaps a little cheese, I think."

He peered into one of the baskets.

"Yes, cheese," he said. "And new onions."

He placed a pitcher, the cheese, the green onions and a hunk of bread on the table.

"You'd get better hospitality from the monks, you know," he hinted.

"This is a feast," Edgar said. "You honor us."

"None of your court talk here," Gaufridus told him, but he seemed mollified by the praise. "Now, what was it that brought you to me?"

They all began speaking at once. The hermit covered his ears.

"Take it in turn," he ordered. "Murder, monks, butchers, charters and counts! *Quelle briche!* How can these matters concern me? I'm only a poor hermit, I know nothing of such things."

"You begin it, Catherine," Solomon suggested. "It all started with Alys."

Catherine explained about how Alys was brought to the Paraclete to die and the outrage over her bequest. She was in the middle of describing the problem of who had the right to the land when she noticed a young boy standing in the doorway. He was about twelve and had an aureole of golden hair that appeared to have been cut with a sickle.

"Forgive me, Uncle," he said to Gaufridus. "Mother wants to know if she can have some of your radishes."

"Yes, take what you want." Gaufridus waved him away.

The boy didn't move.

"And Father Vincon would be grateful if you would preach for him on Sunday. He says his throat feels odd."

"Tell him to stop swearing so much when he loses at draughts and drink wine infused with peppercorns." He rooted around in another basket and came up with a small packet of pepper, which he handed to the boy.

"You may say, yes, if that doesn't work I'll preach for him."

The boy still didn't leave.

"What else?" Gaufridus barked.

"Granny needs some more dockroot. She wants you to come with her tonight to help dig."

"She doesn't need me!" Gaufridus exploded. "I've told that woman it doesn't matter when the stuff is dug up, as long as you say three *paternosters* and make the sign of the cross over the spot before the root leaves the earth. It's pure superstition about having to dig it under a new moon. She could get it at midday and then you could help her."

His nephew waited. Gaufridus sighed.

"Tell her I'll come for her after I've said the evening psalms."

"Thank you, Uncle." The boy grinned and finally left.

Gaufridus returned his attention to his guests.

"Now, where were we?"

Catherine wasn't sure. Oh yes, the land.

"The donation lies in the forest of Othe, just east of here. We can't understand why it's so important. Everyone involved has other property. No one will starve if the Paraclete receives the bequest."

Gaufridus shook his head.

"I can't imagine why anyone would care about this forest particularly. There is a rumor that Henry Sanglier wants to build one of those 'new towns' and settle some of the serfs who've run away to Sens in it. He thinks they're dangerous, too likely to join communes and riot. But that's only gossip, and he'd probably settle them nearer the river. I've seen no sign of land clearing, except for those *desfaé* charcoal burners. I don't understand it; they never used to be so thick. Why would anyone need all that charcoal?"

"Are you sure there are more than usual?" Edgar asked. "All forests have people hiding in them who make charcoal to survive. Was the winter here harder than normal?"

"No, and we take care of our own in Lailly," Gaufridus said. "These are strangers and the forest is full of them."

"Has no one sent men to clear them out?" Edgar asked. "My father would drive them from his forests at the point of his spear."

"No, the monks have apparently given them permission to use their land, as has the count of Tonnerre," Gaufridus sighed. "No one asked us."

"It seems we are left with another mystery instead of answers," Solomon said. "So you have no idea why the forest would be important enough to kill for?"

"I can think of nothing important enough to kill for," the hermit said. "Now I really can't see how I can help you any more. If you don't want another piece of cheese?"

He stood and began edging them to the doorway. As she got up, Catherine heard a giggle at the window.

Gaufridus heard it, too.

"Annali!" he said sternly. "Have you been listening?"

There was a scurrying and more giggles. A moment later, a little girl appeared in the doorway. She was about six, with long thin legs and large brown eyes. Behind her were two other children, a little younger.

"Annali!" Gaufridus repeated. "I am horribly offended by this breach of manners!"

The children did not seem in the least alarmed. They squirmed past the visitors and circled round the hermit, clinging to his robes.

"Story!" they shouted. "We want our story!"

"Have you cleaned the dovecote?" he asked.

They nodded.

"And filled the goats' water trough?"

"To the very top," they assured him.

"Very well," he surrendered. "First I must say farewell to my guests and prepare the oratory for evening prayers."

He led the others out, the three children still attached to his legs.

"The oratory is just up the path, here," he explained. "It's only a small place to pray, not consecrated or anything. And, of course, Yehiel, you wouldn't want to have anything to do with it."

Yehiel extended his hand to Gaufridus.

"No," he said. "But if anyone could convince me to, it would be you. We thank you."

"I've done nothing," Gaufridus said. "Oh, yes, in the middle of all that tale, wasn't there something about Walter of Grancy?"

"Yes," Edgar said. "We must speak to him. Do you know where he is?"

Gaufridus sighed again, with deep emotion.

"I should have said nothing," he looked at them sadly. "You may as well follow me. Walter is staying near the oratory."

As they followed him up the path, Catherine fell behind, catching at Edgar's hand to keep him with her.

"What kind of hermit is this?" she whispered.

"Not like any I've ever met," he whispered back. "I've known tavern keepers who spent more time alone than he does. He might as well have built his hermitage at a crossroad."

Catherine shook her head in bewilderment. She knew now why Yehiel was so eager to come with them. He must be laughing inside this very moment at their confusion.

Hermit indeed! She wondered what Saint Anthony and Saint Athanasius would think of this hermitage.

And yet, . . . She looked around at the hut and the goats and garden and the children. Gaufridus was carrying the smallest one on his shoulders now. It was almost sunset and the light cast an odd aura around the man and his burden.

One who gives what he has to the poor, takes in weary travellers, offers comfort and solace and suffers little children has already found the path to heaven.

Catherine sniffed. Her voices had never chastised her so softly or so thoroughly.

"Walter!" Gaufridus shouted as they reached the top of the hill.

"Walter! Walter! Walter!" the children echoed.

"Hush," Gaufridus said. "Or no story. Walter! You have visitors!"

The oratory was no more than a pile of stones, clumsily daubed together and covered with branches and skins. A wooden cross at the top was all that distinguished it as a place of worship.

"Don't move."

The voice was chillingly out of place in this forest. Catherine started to turn to see who it was and then froze. The sound she had just heard was unquestionably the click of a crossbow being armed.

Gaufridus set down the child.

"Walter," he spoke quietly, "I have not betrayed you. You should know that. These people are here to discover the truth behind the death of Alys of Tonnerre. They want to help you. Look, here's Yehiel. He's an old friend of mine. You've met him before. Put that hideous instrument down and come talk with them."

Catherine heard every sound of the evening; birds, wind in the trees, insects, the bleating of goats and, at last, the sound of the bolt sliding and the arrow slipping out to the ground.

She turned to face Walter of Grancy, furious at having been so frightened. She was about to let him know in no uncertain terms that the pope and the Lateran Council had outlawed the crossbow last year as too dangerous a weapon to ever be used against Christians. She opened her mouth and shut it again.

In the hands of Walter of Grancy, a crossbow was a child's toy. He held it easily as if it had no weight. He was the largest man she had ever seen. She was tall for a woman and Edgar nearly six feet, but Walter was a mountain, an oak in an apple orchard. He towered over them all and was as broad as Edgar and Solomon put together. How could such a man have anything to fear from someone like Raynald of Tonnerre?

"I had nothing to do with the attack on Alys!" Walter told the world at large.

Catherine covered her ears. His voice more than matched his size.

"We believe you," Edgar answered. "But why would Raynald of Tonnerre try to make people think you were responsible?"

"He's a pompous idiot, of course," Walter answered. "Who are you to be asking?"

It took some time for satisfactory introductions to be made. When Walter was finally convinced that Catherine and Edgar both wanted to help and might have an opportunity to do so, he welcomed them both effusively.

"I'm sick of these woods," he admitted. "I only agreed to come here because Bishop Hatto begged me to prevent the effusion of blood during Lent. The only way I could think of to do that was to become a hermit, myself. But come with me where we can sit and discuss the matter thoroughly."

He started to lead them past the oratory to what, presumably, was his hermitage. Solomon stayed behind.

"If you'll excuse us," he said, "Yehiel and I would have little to contribute to this tale. We're going back to the village for the night. Gaufridus's sister, Ermogene, has offered us a bed and we still have the food Yehiel's mother packed for us. Will you be ready to go on to Paris in the morning?"

Edgar and Catherine looked at each other. If they weren't, they would have to find another party to travel with, which might take days. But what if Walter could help them sort out all of this?

"If we could convince him to come with us, we would need no other protection," Catherine said.

"Yes, and we can't keep Solomon waiting for us," Edgar agreed.

"We'll meet you in Paris," he promised. "By the kalends of May. Tell Catherine's family we'll go first to your uncle's home and wait for instructions from them."

"That's over two weeks!" Solomon said. "You could be there in four days!"

"We may arrive sooner," Edgar said. "But I think we may need to return to the Paraclete first. It depends on what the lord of Grancy, here, has to say."

"Very well," Solomon agreed. "Is there any message for your father, Catherine?"

"Only that I'm happy," Catherine said. "And that I love him."

The two men left, hurrying down the path before they were overtaken by the night.

Gaufridus regarded Catherine, Edgar and Walter gloomily.

"I suppose this means you will be staying the night?" he asked.

"We have blankets in our packs," Edgar assured him, lowering his to the ground. They had left their horse for the night in Lailly.

"We can decide the arrangements later," Gaufridus told them. "For now, I must attend to my evening prayers."

He disappeared into the oratory.

Walter of Grancy had been standing impatiently through this. Now he turned and continued into the darkening forest. Catherine and Edgar followed closely. They weren't sure if there were already a trail or if Walter were simply creating one as he stepped. Both of them felt, however, that wherever he took them, they would be in no danger.

They soon arrived at a place where the trees grew so sheltering that the floor of the forest was clear of undergrowth. Walter vanished beneath a curtain of branches and, taking a breath as if about to dive into unknown waters, Catherine and Edgar followed.

They surfaced inside a natural tent. Although the darkness was now almost complete, they knew by sound and smell that Walter had brought his horse with him into his self-imposed retreat.

"I dare not light a fire here," Walter's voice boomed in the enclosure. "But sit where you are. I have a jug of beer we can share."

Catherine and Edgar did as they were told. The ground was soft with centuries of fallen leaves. There was room for them to place their packs behind their backs and stretch their legs without bumping into their host.

"May we also share what we know about Alys of Tonnerre and Raynald?" Catherine asked.

There was a sigh and then a gurgle from Walter as he drank from the jug, then held it out until it touched Edgar's hand.

"Raynald and I have been fighting for years; generations, really," Walter said. "Our land is too close and our families have wed each other too many times. The Church is right to prohibit marriage even between distant kin. No fight's as bitter as that between cousins. Look at Matilda of Anjou and Stephen of Blois."

Catherine took a sip of the beer. It was sour, probably made from rye. She edged the jug back toward Walter's voice.

"So you believe Raynald blamed you for the attack on his wife simply because you were old enemies?" she asked.

"I don't know," Walter said. "It doesn't make sense, now that I consider it. We've always both followed the rules; only fought each other's *serjanz*, no peasants slaughtered for fun, no burning of churches and no attacking unarmed parties, especially of our families."

"You don't believe Raynald might have beat her, himself?" Edgar said. "And then accused you to cover his deed, when he saw how badly he had hurt her?"

"Raynald?" Walter gave a humorless laugh. "He may have hit her now and again, but not repeatedly or to punish her. His anger is the cold kind that waits for perfect vengeance. And he had a hundred better ways of hurting her."

His voice had dropped almost to a whisper.

"He didn't love her, then?" That wasn't the question Catherine wanted answered, but she could think of no way to ask the one she did.

"Of course not, why should he?" Walter said. "She irritated him. Poor Alys didn't know how to handle a man like Raynald. She always looked as though she were expecting a blow, probably was, poor girl. She didn't have the presence to be a countess and manage the land while Raynald was gone. But I don't believe he killed her or that he would naturally blame me. Someone must have denounced me to him."

"Do you know who?" Catherine asked.

"No," Walter said, after a pause to drink. "It would have to be someone he trusted, though."

"Alys's mother, perhaps?" Catherine had not warmed to the countess Constanza. She seemed a perfect instigator.

"Hardly," Walter snorted. "Raynald doesn't trust her. He never forgave her for taking Alys to Paris and leaving Paciana behind to die of the fever. He did love Paciana. I think he would have married her even without her father's land. Only sign the *questre* ever showed of being human."

"So he married Alys for the land she inherited because of her sister's death?" Edgar turned Walter away from speculation about the fate of Alys's sister. He had already figured out who Paciana was and didn't want Catherine tempted to break her promise.

"His father, Count William, arranged it," Walter said. "What was it, five, six years ago? My mother had tried to get Alys for me, but Raynald has Tonnerre and is heir to Auxerre and Nevers if his brother dies and I have all the property I'm ever likely to. There was never much of a chance."

Now Catherine had her answer.

"When did you last see Alys?" she asked softly.

There was a long sigh.

"A year ago. Holy Week. Troyes," he said. "She was on

her way from Mass and stopped to speak to me. She had that *avoutre* monkey on her arm."

"I suppose it was kind of Raynald to get such an expensive pet for her," Catherine said uncertainly.

"He heard the queen had one and thought his wife should, too," Walter said. "She was terrified of it. The thing bit and pulled her hair out to tease her. But that's the way she was. She'd endure almost anything for the sake of peace. So she carried that damn animal everywhere she went. I believe it was the devil, himself."

"So, you don't think,"—Catherine hesitated—"you don't think she would have tried to run away from her husband, or defy him?"

"Never," Walter said. "She knew her duty. And, so do I. Don't be surprised. I could tell from your tone that you wanted to ask it. The answer is no, the child she lost wasn't mine. It was Raynald's or no man's. Alys was a saint, you know, but not the kind that goes about preaching or fighting the infidel. She was the kind who suffers and prays and endures to the end. She *is* in heaven now, isn't she?"

"She must be," Catherine said. "I know we can do nothing more for her, besides pray, but don't you want to help us find out why she had to die?"

"No, I don't. But if you do catch the one who killed her," Walter said, "I'll be happy to slit his throat for you."

He drained the jug.

"It's late," he announced. "I'm going to sleep. Do you have enough quilts with you? The nights are still cold."

"We'll be fine," Edgar said.

He heard the intake of breath as Catherine began another question and quickly put his fingers over her lips.

"In the morning," he whispered. "Trust me?"

A second's hesitation, then she closed her mouth and kissed his fingers.

"May Our Lady protect you until the morning," she said to Walter.

"And you," he answered.

There was a certain amount of rustling as they arranged

their beds. Then silence. But questions still darted like fireflies in Catherine's head.

If Walter didn't kill Alys and Raynald didn't then who? And what about Paciana? Remembering his voice when he saw her at the Paraclete, Catherine could well believe that Raynald had loved her, but had she loved him? If she hadn't, that would be a reason to pretend to be dead and run away to the convent rather than face a forced marriage. But hadn't someone said that Constanza had forbidden the match? She had apparently wanted Raynald for her own child. And yet, the property only came to Alys through Paciana. As the elder, she was her father's heir. That would have been a good reason to kill Paciana, not Alys.

Catherine sat straight up, causing Edgar to gasp as the cold air hit him.

"Edgar!" she whispered. "We must get back to the Paraclete, as soon as possible."

"I know," he whispered back, pulling the quilts back over them. "Now that it's known she's alive, Paciana is in terrible danger."

As she drifted to sleep, Catherine realized, with some annoyance, that Edgar had understood the situation even before they had heard Walter's story. He had told Solomon that afternoon that they would be going to the Paraclete. She had been so involved in the hermit and his charges that she had paid no attention.

She wondered if she would like being married to someone who analyzed events more quickly than she did. She supposed it would depend on how often he did so and how smug he was about it. And, she thought, as she snuggled closer to him, on how cold the nights were.

Sixteen

The Paraclete, Commemoration of Saint George,
dragon slayer and martyr,
Tuesday, April 23, 1140

Ut enim insertum clavum alius expellit, sic cogitatio nova priorem excludit. Cum alias intentus animus priorum memoriam dimittere cogitur aut intermitere.

As driving in one nail forces out another, so a new thought drives away the old. When the mind is intent on other things, it is forced to lessen or interrupt the memory of prior things.

—Héloïse to Abelard,
Letter VI

*H*éloïse was praying. She prayed most of every day, not only when reciting the office, but also when teaching the nuns, supervising the work of the convent and dealing with the outside world. Especially when dealing with the outside world. She prayed for compassion and forbearance and to be free of envy, that they could come and go as they wished while she was left imprisoned in this cage of her own making.

"My lady abbess?" The voice was soft with concern.

"Yes. Astane? What is it?" Héloïse raised her face from her hands. Her eyes were dry. *One day,* she thought. *One day I will be able to shed the tears of true repentance. Then I'll know I've finally been forgiven.*

"Is there something you need?" she asked the prioress again.

"I've been talking with Brother Baldwin, about the late planting," Astane began. "It's nothing urgent. He wants to try a second season of vegetable marrow. He thinks we can harvest it well into the autumn if it's set out in the shelter of the apple trees."

"That's up to you to decide, Astane," Héloïse said. "I trust your judgement and that of Brother Baldwin. Was there something else?"

"There has been a messenger from Lady Constanza," Astane continued. "She would like to visit her daughter's grave and make a donation for the repose of her soul."

"As is proper," Héloïse conceded. "How many retainers do you think she'll bring?"

"At least two maids, I should imagine." Astane counted on her fingers. "Four or five men-at-arms. Perhaps her chaplain, who'll probably want to say Mass for us. I do hope he won't insist on preaching. The man can't construct a sentence in French, much less Latin. His style is fit only for calling cows."

Héloïse hid a smile. She quite agreed with the evaluation.

"Charity, humility, patience," she murmured.

The prioress blushed. "I know, Héloïse. But either of us could produce a more elegant sermon than Father Deol. You give better instruction in chapter each week and you don't get it all from a manual!"

"Thank you," Héloïse said. "But, if he offers to preach, we will accept with humble gratitude."

Astane sighed. "And will attempt to truly feel grateful."

"With success, I'm sure," Héloïse said.

There was a sudden clamor outside, shouts and the neighing of horses. Astane ran to the window.

"Where is it coming from?" Héloïse asked.

"Not this side. I see nothing," Astane answered.

The noise was compounded by the slap of running feet and the startled cries of women. There was a sharp tap on the door, which was opened without pause for permission. Sister Thecla appeared in the doorway.

"There are armed men in the vegetable garden!" she cried. "They're trying to abduct one of the lay sisters. Brother Baldwin is doing his best to fend them off and I've sent for help, but I don't know . . ."

She broke off, panting.

Héloïse jumped to her feet, her lips set in fury.

"How dare they commit such an offense!" she cried as

she began running toward the garden, followed by Prioress Astane. "They risk the wrath of the Holy Spirit, the Holy Father, and me!"

Of the three, Thecla thought the last was the one whose wrath they should fear most.

"Lady Abbess!" she shouted. "Héloïse! You mustn't! You could be killed!"

As they raced across the field, they were greeted by the horrifying sight of two mail-clad knights on horseback and the body of a woman on the ground. Brother Baldwin was standing over her, thrashing with his hoe at one of the marauders. There was a yell of pain and anger as the hoe bit into the horseman's leg. He raised his sword and slashed deeply into the old man's shoulder. Baldwin dropped the hoe and fell to his knees.

Seeing that the people of the convent were converging on him, the knight wheeled about and raced through the garden. He nearly lost his seat, leaping the low spot in the hedge, but landed in one piece on the path to the road, his companion close behind. Héloïse, calling for someone to fetch Sister Melisande and bring litters, fell to her knees next to Brother Baldwin.

He leaned against her a second, then fell forward into the mud. Héloïse bent and rolled him gently to her lap. Blood was streaming from the wound in his neck and onto her skirts. He opened his eyes.

"Montjoie et Saint Denis," he whispered. *"We'll take Jerusalem today. I see the gates!"*

His head lolled sideways in her arms. Prioress Astane knelt beside Héloïse. She crossed herself, murmured a blessing, then reached out and gently closed the old man's eyes.

"Requiescat in pace," she said.

"Amen." Héloïse had found her tears.

She wiped her eyes with the back of her hand and eased the old man's body to the ground. Then she turned to the woman Baldwin had died to protect, who was lying on her stomach. The back of her tunic was soaked in blood. Héloïse felt the side of her throat.

"She's still alive!" she called to the lay sisters who were coming with the litters. "Hurry!"

They lifted her as gently as they could. Astane took her sleeve to clean the mud from the woman's face.

"It's Paciana!" she said.

"I feared as much," Héloïse replied, her fury now turned on herself. "I should have been more watchful of her. I guessed there was danger, but I couldn't believe anyone would have so little fear of God. This is a place of safety! A haven from the wickedness of the world."

Melisande arrived as the women were carrying Paciana to the infirmary. She took rags and pressed them against the wound.

"Keep her face down," she told them. "Unless she starts choking on the blood. You! Put pressure on the wound with this. We've got to stop the flow."

She paused and looked beyond to the body of the lay brother, then to Astane, who shook her head. Melisande crossed herself and then took over for the woman holding the rags.

"Will she live?" Héloïse asked.

"I can't tell," Melisande answered. "It's flowing, not spurting, so we might have a chance to save her. I will use all the skill Our Lord has granted me."

"What can we do?" Héloïse asked.

"You know," Melisande answered as she let up on the pressure a moment, then changed hands.

Héloïse and Astane followed behind.

"Pray," Héloïse said, trying to keep the bitterness out of her voice. "Entreat, supplicate, beg. God knows how far my prayers rise. If only I could cry!"

"You are crying, my lady abbess," Astane said gently. "Forgive my presumption, but only God knows how far our prayers rise, so perhaps we should make them as best we can in our ignorance and have faith that they will be heard."

Héloïse walked a little faster, leaving the prioress a step behind. Then she took a deep breath and faced Astane, her head bowed.

"I stand rebuked," she said. "You're right. Where faith is concerned, you are my superior. Thank you."

"Anyway," she added, "there is more I can do. Send a messenger at once to Anseau of Trainel and to Bishop Hatto, informing them of this outrage. Then find out if anyone recognized these men, these beasts. The Paraclete must not be allowed to suffer such injury without receiving justice."

"Even if no one saw their faces," Astane said, "one of them should be limping for quite a while from the bite of that hoe, if he doesn't lose his leg altogether. Brother Baldwin may have wanted to end his days in tranquillity, but he had not forgotten how to fight. I must confess I feel proud that we had such a defender."

"I agree," Héloïse answered. "I will petition the bishop to let us bury him in a place of honor, as his deed deserves. Now, we have much work to do."

They had reached the gate and were about to enter the cloister when Prioress Astane happened to glance down the road.

"Saint Thecla and the bears!" she cried. "Abbess Héloïse, our Catherine has returned and I believe she's brought us a new protector."

Walter of Grancy thought that escorting Catherine and Edgar to the Paraclete was a wonderful idea. Gaufridus wasn't so sure.

"Raynald's men will spot you as soon as you're on the main road," he argued.

"That's nothing to me," Walter answered. "I only promised not to spill their blood during the Lenten season. I'm tired of living in the woods; my back is tortured from sleeping on leaves and roots and, not to put too fine a point on it, I need meat!"

"You'll not get that from the nuns," Gaufridus said.

"Of course not," Walter said. "But I should be able to find something between here and there, or never dare to show my face in my own castle again."

He patted his bow.

"That's not to say I'm not grateful to you," he added

quickly. "But a man my size simply can't live on greens and cheese."

Gaufridus waved off his explanations. He vanished into his hut and shut the door. Walter nodded.

"I think we should be on our way," he said.

Just then the door opened again and Gaufridus came out with a parcel wrapped in waxed cloth.

"I thought the sisters might like some candles," he said. "The children and I make them."

He handed the package to Catherine.

"May the Lord keep you safe," he said. "Now I really must get back to contemplating heaven!"

The door shut again. This time they all heard the thunk as the bar dropped across.

"A very odd hermit," Catherine commented as she stowed the candles in her pack. "But I like him."

Solomon had left their horse in the village with Ermogene, the hermit's sister, before he and Yehiel went on to Sens. He had also left word that he would meet them in Paris according to their agreement.

"And he added," Ermogene told them, "that if you weren't there when you said, he'd come looking for you."

They thanked her and set out.

"Our road takes us through the property of Vauluisant," Catherine said. "Will we be given free passage through?"

She spoke to Edgar, but nodded toward Walter. Vauluisant seemed to have sided with Raynald in this conflict. What would happen if one of the dependents of the monastery saw their companion and notified the abbot? Since Constanza's brother was prior, he might want to have Walter detained.

"Perhaps instead of taking the road north that passes by the abbey, we should start west, following the river, and turn north at the border of Champagne." Walter suggested. "I don't want trouble from the monks. My quarrel isn't with them and I don't like to risk offending those whose prayers I may one day need."

They agreed.

The path that went along the Vanne twisted with the

river. In some places the spring floods had overcome the banks and made the way treacherous. They had to dismount and lead the horses through the muddy pools. Sometimes it was necessary to leave what had once been the road and make a trail through the woods, above the bog. By the end of the day, they had only gone about seven miles.

"Is there no village nearby?" Edgar asked Walter.

"No." Walter thought a moment. "No, not even a monastery. I thought we'd be farther along by now."

"There's someone nearby," Catherine said. "I can smell smoke."

Walter looked at Edgar.

"Do you know how to use a crossbow?" he asked.

"We have nothing that modern where I come from," Edgar replied. "But I can use a knife and I can stay alert through the night."

Walter still looked worried.

"We'll both need to stay alert," he said. "I think it's better if we find shelter in the forest and light no fire. Those charcoal burners would kill us for our horses alone. And I had so set my heart on fresh meat tonight."

They followed a deer trail a little way from the river until they came to a clearing. They stopped in surprise.

"What happened here?" Catherine asked. "I've never heard of charcoal burners cutting down a whole stand of trees. And what's that grey mound over there?"

"A slag heap," Edgar told her, but he was equally puzzled. "And that pile of clay seems to be the remains of a bloomery. It looks as though someone's been smelting iron."

"For what?" Catherine asked.

"I have no idea," Edgar said. "Lord Walter, do you?"

"Not a clue," Walter answered. He walked over to the broken pile of clay and put a hand to it.

"It's still warm," he said. "That would be the smoke you smelled. But the fire has been put out now. They seem to have abandoned the place. We'll stay the night here."

Walter, Edgar and Catherine unloaded their packs and saw that the horses were rubbed down and tethered where they could reach a good supply of grass. Then the three of them sat on the fresh tree stumps and tried to puzzle out what had been going on.

"I've never heard of poachers mining iron," Edgar said. "Is it a common occurrence in France?"

"Of course not," Walter answered. "The smoke, the smell, the weeks of work to build the bloomery and smelt the iron, all of these would be impossible to do in secret. Are we still on lands belonging to the monks?"

"I'm not sure," Catherine admitted. "Where are we?"

"The Nosle joins the Vanne a mile or so east of here," Walter told her. "My lands, such as they are, are on the other side of the forest."

Catherine thought, trying to remember charters she had copied. She knew the places where the land of the Paraclete touched that of the monks. There were even a few spots where a piece given to the convent was totally surrounded by Cistercian land. If they were at the joining of the Vanne and the Nosle, the Paraclete was north, Vauluisant west, and south lay the forest of Aix-en-Othe. But the actual donation had been in an area just north of here, near the town of Planty.

"You know," she said slowly, "I think we may be just on the edge of the property that Alys gave us."

"This donation that everyone is trying to claim?" Walter asked. "Well, there must be gold on it, then. No one would cut throats over a bit of iron. People have been digging it out of this area for centuries. It takes days to get a few pounds of the stuff to release itself from the rocks, I'm told."

"And half the time it's mostly cast iron and is useless," Edgar added.

"Where did you read that?" Catherine wanted to know. Edgar had such a strange variety of learning.

Edgar shrugged. "I heard it somewhere. Not everything of value is in Boethius. Anyway, I don't see how this could have been done without the monks knowing about it."

"I don't understand how it works," Catherine said,

studying the remains of the oven. "What were these clay pieces for?"

"The chimney, most likely," Edgar said. "See, come here and I'll show you. First they dug a hole and lined it with rocks and clay. Then they built up the chimney with more rocks and clay. There'd have been a hole at the bottom for the tuyere; that's the pipe that lets the air in. Then they drop in charcoal from the top, light it and then drop in more charcoal and the iron ore, little by little. It takes at least two people, one to put in the ore and another to step on the bellows."

"I see, and the bellows are set next to the, what was it? The tuyere—to keep the fire going." Catherine tried to construct it in her mind. "But how do they get the metal out?"

"They pull out the tuyere and the ash and clay wedged around it and scrape out the iron. Then they have to pound out the excess slag at once. And then you have a bloom of iron."

"We call it a *luppa*," Walter said unexpectedly.

"What is it in Latin?" Catherine asked.

"I don't know," Edgar told her.

"Then how did you learn all this?" she demanded.

"I watched and asked questions," he said.

"Oh." Catherine subsided. It seemed an odd thing for a nobleman to do. Or a scholar. Vulgar somehow. And who would have told him? All craftsmen held the techniques of their art to be secret. And yet, when she had met him, Edgar was doing a credible job of pretending to be a sculptor's apprentice.

He was examining the rubble left of the smelting oven in the dwindling light, clearly intrigued. He was pale in the twilight, like some moon spirit. He seemed as remote. Catherine shivered, realizing again how little she knew of this person she had promised her life to.

"Look!" he called to them. "See here, where it's all cracked? I think that happened first. These people didn't know how to build the kiln properly. It must have split open under the heat. That's why they abandoned it."

Satisfied with the answer, he rejoined Catherine on the stump.

"What is there to eat?" he asked, putting one arm around her and rooting in the pack with the other.

"Hard bread, cheese and green onions," Catherine said.

She rubbed her cheek on his shoulder. Solid and warm. She sighed in relief.

Walter sighed, too. "And water," he muttered. "I knew a man once who died from drinking water. I've fasted long enough. Tomorrow we will eat!"

The next morning was grey with drizzle. Catherine woke up slowly, trying to understand why her face was wet and her feet freezing. She buried her nose in the back of Edgar's neck, making him yelp in shock.

"Catherine, never do that!" he said, when he realized what had happened. "I thought it was one of my brothers, waking me with a frog again. I nearly gave you a black eye."

"Sister Bertrada told me you would, one day," Catherine said. "I would hate to see her justified in any of her predictions for me. But my nose was cold."

"Catherine, where's Walter?" Edgar said, looking around. "His horse is gone."

"He wouldn't have abandoned us here, would he?" Catherine said.

"Of course not," Edgar's voice lacked confidence. "Wait, it's all right. He left his pack and his crossbow. He wouldn't go without that."

"Perhaps he just got up early to contemplate Nature," Catherine said.

Edgar nodded. "No doubt. I feel a bit contemplative myself. I think it's the onions. But most people don't take their horses with them at such a time."

There was a sudden crashing in the woods and Edgar instinctively picked up the crossbow with one hand and shoved Catherine out of harm's way with the other.

It had just occurred to him that he didn't know how to load the thing when Walter appeared at the edge of the clearing, gleefully holding up a brace of rabbits.

"Let's find out if we can get a fire going in all this damp," he cried. "Marauders be damned. Fresh meat for breakfast!"

Despite her eagerness to reach the Paraclete and make certain that Paciana was safe, Catherine made no objection to the time it took to build the fire, roast and eat the rabbit.

"I still wish we knew who had built the forge," she said as she licked the grease from her fingers. "It seems that instead of finding answers all we ever encounter are more questions."

"You found me," Walter reminded her.

"That's true," she conceded. "And you have at least convinced me that you aren't responsible for Alys's death. But, there's still so much that almost makes sense, but won't."

Edgar nodded. "That was always my problem with theology," he said. "I would have made a terrible bishop."

"Who wanted you to be a bishop?" Walter was skeptical.

"I'm the fifth son. My uncle is a bishop and my mother's cousin is abbot of the family monastery. Those were my choices. Then I met Catherine."

"I'm so glad you did," she said.

They smiled at each other and neither noticed the look of intense pain that swept over Walter of Grancy.

"Alys," he whispered.

They reached the main road, the trade route between Troyes and Provins, later that morning. There the surface was well maintained and they often overtook carts and other travellers. At first Catherine worried that someone would recognize Walter and start a hue and cry. But she soon realized that everyone they met was involved with their own affairs and only concerned with arriving safely at their destinations. No one cared about a feud between lords, especially when one of the lords was as large as Walter.

As they approached the turning to the convent, two men on horseback came racing down the path. Edgar, who was leading the horse, jumped out of the way. Walter half rose in his stirrups as the riders passed, his bow poised. But, after one glance, both men veered well away from him and continued on their way.

Catherine nudged Edgar and pointed to the ground.

"One of those men was leaking," she said.

Edgar knelt and rubbed his fingers in the damp dirt. They came away red. He sniffed.

"Blood," he said. "We're too late."

Seventeen

The Paraclete,
Feast of Saint Mark the Evangelist,
Thursday, April 25, 1140

Item placuit, ut si quis suadente diabolo hujus sacrilegii reatum
incurrit, quod in clericum vel monachum violentas manus injecerit,
anathematis vinculo sujaceat; et nullus episcoporum ilum
praesumat absolvere, nisi mortis urgente periculo; . . .

If anyone, at the Devil's inspiration, commits the crime of
the sacrilege of laying violent hands on a clerk or
monastic, let him be subject to the bonds of anathema,
and let no bishop presume to absolve him unless
he is at the point of death, . . .

—Canon 15, Second Lateran Council, 1139

I never told them about you, Paciana, I swear. I said nothing."

Catherine wondered if Paciana heard her or, if she did, cared. She was pale as death already, but Catherine could see the slow rise and fall of her chest. For the present, she still lived.

"The wound is deep, but not poisoned," Sister Melisande had announced. "However, the loss of blood has upset her humors profoundly. I have cauterized the wound and bound it with a poultice of wheat and turnips. We're rubbing her hands and feet with a compound of olive and almond oils. All these things are hot and moist and may help restore her, but if the imbalance is too great, she will die."

So they sat in rotation, watching, changing the poultice as it dried, keeping her hands and feet warm with oil. Father Guiberc brought holy oil and anointed her in the presence of the community. Sister Beatriz said that for hours afterwards she could see the lines glowing golden on Paciana's white skin.

Héloïse was as concerned with the insult to the convent as the assault on the woman and the slaying of Brother Baldwin. No word had been received from the bishop, but Anseau, lord of Trainel, six miles away, whose land bordered that of the convent, came himself, at once. He brought a dozen men from the area, all armed.

"Do you know who did this?" he asked. "Did you recognize either of them?"

Héloïse shook her head. "They were mounted and wore helms. I was too far away to see their faces, in any case. I have some visitors whom the men passed on the road as they made their escape. They might have more information. Shall I call them in?"

Anseau nodded and Héloïse motioned to Sister Thecla to admit Catherine, Edgar and Walter of Grancy. Upon seeing Walter, Anseau jumped to his feet, his hand grasping for the sword he had left at the door.

"My lady abbess," he exclaimed. "Do you know who this is?"

"Of course," Héloïse said.

"Don't make an ass of yourself, Anseau," Walter said mildly. "You know I would never have hurt Alys. You don't trust Raynald and his family any more than I do."

"Is that why you've been hiding?" Anseau asked. "More than one person thought you were guilty when you didn't challenge Raynald's accusation."

Walter sank onto a bench, which creaked in protest.

"That's what happens when you try to preserve the Peace of God," he muttered. "Now I have to fight everyone who said I was a coward."

"I withdraw my comment," Anseau said quickly. "And I will be happy to proclaim your piety to any who should ask. Now, the abbess says that you and your companions saw the men who attacked Sister Paciana?"

"Who?" Walter straightened suddenly, which caused the bench to bend.

"I promise to explain later, Lord Walter," Héloïse said. "For the moment, can we please concentrate on these men who have no fear of God's judgement? Did you recognize them? Was one of them Raynald?"

"No, I'm sorry to say," Walter told her. "I've fought him often enough to know his gear and the way he sits his horse. Neither of these men were trained for true combat."

Anseau accepted the judgement without comment but Héloïse wasn't sure. The men had certainly appeared warlike to her.

"How could you tell?" she asked.

"The way they rode, of course," Walter said shortly then remembered whom he was speaking to, "my lady abbess. It would have been clear to the lord of Trainel, here, if he'd seen them, but, of course, it's not the sort of thing you should have to know. It's not proper."

"It wasn't in my education," Héloïse admitted. "But I would like instruction now. We need all the information we can obtain to identify these men and bring them to justice."

"Of course." Walter closed his eyes, the better to remember. "Their shields were dangling from their arms, like pilgrim's scrips, giving no protection, and neither one of them could have spared a hand to slash at an enemy. Even in retreat, a real warrior would never leave himself so open to attack."

"Is that all?" Héloïse asked.

Walter scrunched his eyes shut more tightly.

"No," he said, opening them. "They didn't grip their horses with their knees. Their legs flopped all over. Looked absolutely *sotoart*. I'll wager my best saddle that neither of them was used to riding at more than a priest's trot. Now, what is this about Paciana? You didn't give the name before. It's not the same woman, is it?"

Catherine went and sat next to Walter.

"Mother?" she asked Héloïse. "I know we promised, but Paciana may die because someone wanted to keep her secret."

"You have my permission," Héloïse agreed. "You are released from your oath."

"Paciana is the elder sister of Alys," Catherine told Walter. "She didn't die of the fever; she came here. I don't know why or how. She wanted everyone to believe she

was dead. But Count Raynald saw her when he was here
at Easter. He knew she was alive."

"Saint Genesius's tombstone! Poor old Raynald," Walter
said. "I never thought I could pity that *questre*, but I'm
honestly sorry for him."

"He wanted to marry her," Catherine explained to the
abbess.

"I know, dear," Héloïse said. "She told me so when she
came to me. That was one reason she wished her presence
here not to be known. She wanted the world to believe she
was dead since she wished to be dead to the world. I saw
no reason not to respect that wish, until now."

"I agree, it's not a time for secrets," Lord Anseau said.
"This has not been only an attack on one person but an attack on God and the honor of the Church. These men must
be captured. Can you remember anything else about
them?"

"The one who was wounded was slight," Edgar spoke
up. "Not only short, but thin. His legs were flopping because the stirrups were set too long for them."

"That's right," Walter said. "I remember that, too."

"The other one was taller and broad in the shoulder,"
Catherine said slowly. "There were rings under his gloves.
One had ripped a seam. What does that remind me of?"

"The men who killed Lisiard," Edgar said. "You were
right, Catherine. His death must be connected with this."

"Poor foolish man." Catherine blessed herself. "He told
me nothing and yet they murdered him. It does sound like
the men the dung collector described. My lord, these same
men may have also horribly slaughtered Lisiard of Troyes,
just a few nights ago."

"Can any of you give names to these monsters?" Anseau asked.

"I would know them again," Walter said, "if I saw them
on horseback. But I think they were strangers to me."

"If Paciana awakes, might she name them?"

"I don't know," Héloïse answered. "She may not have
known them. Also, she has taken a vow of silence. They
tell me that, when the men rode toward her, she didn't

even scream. If her conscience says not to speak, I will not force her."

"Even if it means letting murderers go free?" Anseau asked.

"In this life, yes," Héloïse told him.

Anseau stood.

"As you wish," he said. "I will leave several of my men here to keep watch in case there is any further trouble."

Héloïse rose to walk him to the gatehouse entrance.

"Thank you," she said. "You have always been our friend in times of need."

"And always will be," he promised. "I have the greatest respect for you and for Master Abelard. Is there any word from Paris?"

"They say Abbot Bernard doesn't want to debate him, but Abelard and his students want the matter settled and Bernard's friends are encouraging him to accept the challenge," Héloïse told him. "I have also heard that the abbot will preach to the students later this month."

"That may rid Paris of its infestation of scholars," Anseau laughed. "His preaching could convince the devil, himself, to become a white monk."

"Yes, I know," Héloïse smiled. "But Peter Abelard is not the devil, no matter what some people think."

"I will be at Sens, if the debate takes place, to stand by him," Anseau said. "Actually, I will be there in any case. The archbishop has made it clear that he expects everyone to aid in the building of the cathedral."

"I am grateful for your help, now and in the past," Héloïse said.

"It is my honor to do what I can to aid those who protect and intercede for me with their prayers," Anseau answered. "My men will stay as long as necessary."

Héloïse thanked him again. But as she walked back to the cloister, her heart was troubled to think that the world had come to such a state that women of God had to rely on knights to protect them from other Christians.

In the guesthouse, later that afternoon, Catherine was hunting through her pack for her comb. She tossed out other bits of clothing, ribbons, pins, her spoon and knife. Edgar watched her with amusement.

"I can carve you a new comb," he offered.

"It's in here; I know it," Catherine insisted. "I did my hair yesterday. I'm sure I put the comb back."

"Can't you borrow one?"

"I want mine!"

Edgar took a step back. "Is something bothering you?" he asked.

Catherine rocked back on her heels.

"Of course," she snapped. "Everywhere I go people are stabbed or beaten or having their gullets slit. And I can't do one thing to help them or catch the men responsible. Doesn't it bother you?"

"Yes, but . . ."

"And now I can't find my comb!" she finished, starting to cry.

A piece of advice his father had given him surfaced in Edgar's mind. Sometimes, he had said, it's better just to keep quiet and think with your heart. Edgar looked at Catherine sitting on the floor, her things in a pile next to her, sobbing. One hand was clutching the cross he had given her. Edgar knelt next to her and put his arms around her. She leaned against him and, gradually, the crying stopped.

"I'm sorry," she sniffed. "It's only that it's happened here, where nothing wicked should be. This is supposed to be a refuge from the evils of this world."

She smiled up at him, then wiped her eyes with her sleeve.

"Until I met you, it was *my* refuge," she added. "Do you think Jehan was right? Do I curse the people I love?"

"Jehan is a *flearde æsul*!" Edgar said firmly.

"What does that mean?" Catherine asked.

"It means he doesn't know anything," Edgar told her.

He began fiddling with the things in the pile, holding up a pair of linen pants, about knee length, tied with a drawstring.

"What are these for?" he asked. "Do you intend to wear the *braies* in the family?"

She snatched them from him and stuffed them back in the pack, blushing.

"Unless you fulfill my father's expectations of you, I will," she said. "At least for five days a month."

It took him a minute to work that out.

"Oh," he had said at last. "Do you think you'll need them soon?"

"If my emotions are any indication, imminently," she said. "It's hard to tell, though. What with Lenten fasting and then all that's happened in the last two weeks, I'm not in my usual pattern. Normally, I'd ask Sister Melisande for an herb tisane to help things along, but it wouldn't be a good idea now, just in case."

"In case I have fulfilled your father's expectations?" he grinned.

"So many women have trouble conceiving," she said. "I don't want to risk it. The herbs to start the purgation are very strong."

She started to move away, but he stopped her, his fingers slowly tracing the line of her jaw and down her throat.

"Catherine," Edgar said, "I know this isn't logical, but I suddenly have a terrible need to take you to bed."

"Now?"

He nodded.

"It's the middle of the day."

"I know."

She was very still for a moment. Then she kissed him. "You'd better bar the door," she said.

Walter of Grancy had been granted permission to visit Paciana, but only in the company of Abbess Héloïse. He knelt next to the bed and took her limp hand in his paw.

"She hasn't changed that much, even in ten years," he said. "It must have been horrible for Raynald to see her again, after marrying her sister, and all. I hope she lives. It's not right that she and Alys should both be gone."

"She's resting more comfortably now," Héloïse told him. "We've begun to hope."

Walter left, shaking his head.

"I don't understand why she was attacked," he muttered. "It can't be the land. She gave up all right to it when she entered the convent, didn't she?"

"Of course," Héloïse told him. "As far as the inheritance goes, she may as well have died of the fever ten years ago."

"Then why couldn't they leave her here in peace?"

"I don't know," the abbess said. Her face was as sad as his, but there was also anger. "However, it seems to me that it's time we found out."

Walter went out to make sure the men left by the lord of Trainel were doing their duty. Assuring himself that they all had their eyes fixed on the road and woods and not on the windows of the dorter, he began a circuit of the buildings, himself, pacing around and around the walls of the convent, thinking. And the more he thought, the faster he walked, and the faster he walked, the angrier he became. Finally, he stopped in his circumambulations and veered purposefully toward the guesthouse.

"*Avoi!* You in there!" he pounded on the door. "Someone's locked me out!"

There was a scuffling from the other side, a sound like a stool tipping over, whispers turning to laughter. At last the bar was lifted and Edgar's face peered out. He held his *chainse* in one hand and his pants up with the other.

"Back already, are you Walter?" he said. "How is Sister Paciana?"

Walter looked past him, to Catherine, whose *bliaut* was rumpled and who still hadn't found her comb. He grinned.

"Glad to see you've learned *le ju françois*," he said. "Good work, lad!"

"We have it in Scotland, too," Edgar said mildly. "We just use other words for it."

"I'd like to learn them, someday," Walter said. "But not now. If you've got your belt tied, come out for a minute."

Edgar finished dressing and followed Walter outside, leaving Catherine to continue her search.

"I want to see what's so important about this piece of forest," Walter told him, when they were out of earshot of any building. "After all, it seems my honor depends on finding the truth of this. I'm going back there, the first thing tomorrow. Do you want to come with me?"

"I would," Edgar said, "but I don't know how much help I'd be if we run into Raynald's men. I'm not trained to fight."

"It doesn't matter, I am," Walter said. "But I'm not trained to read or to understand things the way you do. Where *did* you learn about the workings of a forge?"

Edgar looked away from him, at the knights keeping watch around the convent.

"I'm interested in how things are made," he said. "That's all. Is it important?"

Walter shook his head. "I guess not. It just seems strange for a nobleman to care about such things. I only learned the bit I do know from watching while my horse is shod. Will you come with me?"

"What about Catherine?"

"We'd only be gone a week, perhaps less," Walter said. "Leave her here."

Edgar leaned back to look Walter in the eye.

"You haven't known Catherine very long, have you?" he said.

"Look, I'd sooner go through wolf-infested forests with fresh meat hanging from my boots than travel with a woman," Walter said. "On the main roads, with other people about, it's safe enough, but there are *ribaux* who wander the forest paths. You and I might fight them off, or scare them, but we couldn't protect her, too."

Edgar sighed. "Yes, you're right. Catherine will understand . . . perhaps. I will go with you."

With that he squared his shoulders and went back to the guest house, marshalling every argument he could think of just in case she didn't understand.

Catherine didn't look up when he entered. She had found the comb at last and her hair was unplaited, hanging like a cloud of midnight across her face and to the floor.

"What did Walter want?" she asked.

He explained.

"You will be careful, won't you?" she said, starting to braid one side.

Edgar came over and held the unbraided hair away from her fingers.

"Thank you," she said. "It always gets in the way. Maybe I should cut it."

"Not while I'm alive," Edgar said.

She smiled. "Then I repeat, don't try to be a hero. That's Walter's place. Defend your life, if you have to, but I'd rather you didn't have to."

"Then you don't mind waiting here for me?" He was suspicious.

"Of course not," she said. "Walter is quite right; I'd only be a hindrance."

He thought about asking when that had ever bothered her before but decided that was unfair. She had never meant to be a hindrance and, at least once, she had saved his life. All the same, it wasn't like her to acquiesce so easily.

Catherine sensed his skepticism.

"You're just lucky it's almost my phase of the moon," she explained. "I don't want to spend the next week on a horse, wandering about in the woods, wondering if I have enough clean rags to last the day out. By the time you return, it should all be over and we can return to Paris together."

Edgar was fascinated. "It never occurred to me that such a thing would be a problem."

Catherine laughed. "Of course it didn't. It's not your problem."

Edgar and Walter left the next morning, Catherine having been granted permission to be a guest of the Paraclete until his return. When she saw him astride his horse, he looked so frail next to the ursine lord of Grancy that Catherine almost regretted letting him go.

"Remember," she told him, "you promise to be prudent and cautious and not risk your life."

"I'm not going on a crusade," he reminded her. "Just a little hunting trip."

"Just see that nothing catches you," she finished.

Catherine waved until they were out of sight, then asked if she could speak with Abbess Héloïse.

When she was admitted, she paused for a moment, looking around the room. It was strange. Somehow, it seemed different. How could it have changed in only two weeks?

Nothing has changed, Catherine, her voices said. *You are looking at us differently now.*

She nodded sadly. She had made the only choice she could make in good conscience, but she knew that she would never again be part of the Paraclete in the way she had once planned.

Héloïse came over and patted her cheek.

"Don't worry," she said. "He'll be back soon."

"I know," Catherine said. "It was you I was missing, Mother."

The abbess turned suddenly and went to the window. She took a deep breath.

"Thank you, Catherine," she said. "What was it you wanted of me?"

"The lady Constanza is coming here soon, isn't she?" Catherine asked.

"In the next day or two, I believe," Héloïse answered. "Why?"

"Edgar and Walter are doing what they can to try to unravel this mystery," she began. "I truly meant it when I said I would only delay them. But there are things that I can find out, where Edgar's presence would hinder me. But I need your help, and Sister Emilie's. Will you give it?"

Héloïse sat down and motioned for Catherine to do the same.

"Perhaps you had better explain," she said. "I make no promises in the dark."

The next day, the lady Constanza arrived to mourn her only child.

She travelled in her own sedan chair, slung between two mules. Around her rode her men-at-arms and serving maids, as well as other ladies for companionship. Her chaplain, Deol, was with her, and her cook. She had also brought her own bed, dishes, footstool and pillows, which were packed into a cart followed by three other guards. Since the pace was set by the cart and the sedan chair, the journey from Troyes had taken her over a week, instead of the normal two days.

Since Constanza presumed without question that she would have total use of the guesthouse and any other lodging she might need, Catherine was once again sent to sleep on the infirmary floor.

When Constanza and her party had settled in, she asked for a private audience with the abbess. After that, she wished to be taken to Alys's burial place.

From the door looking out from the infirmary to the garden, Catherine watched the procession to the cemetery. Emilie peeked from behind her shoulder.

"One would think she'd refrain from dying her hair when going to her daughter's grave," she whispered to Catherine.

"That's five *paternosters* for spiteful thoughts," Catherine teased her. "We're all supposed to believe that she was born that shade of blonde."

"My belief doesn't stretch that far," Emilie said. "No one in all the world was ever born with that color. It's unbefitting to her present state as well as unbecoming generally."

It did look odd, Catherine admitted. The countess was dressed somberly, her *bliaut* rent in several places. She wore no jewelry and her unnatural hair was down and dishevelled. Father Deol supported her as she walked. Constanza was the image of grief. Why did Catherine feel so strongly that it was only an image?

They could hear her cries and shrieks of anguish from where they stood. Despite her reservations, Catherine had to admit the sorrow sounded genuine. But then why hadn't her mother come the short distance from Quincy to see Alys during the week she lay dying? Why had she said that Alys was flighty and not terribly pious? It was an awful thing to say of the dead. And why had she hinted that Alys had some grave sin to repent of? From Walter's description, Alys didn't have the backbone to sin.

There were too many questions. And there was only one way Catherine could think of to find the answers. She still wasn't sure she had convinced Mother Héloïse of it, though.

"Emilie," she said. "Do you think Countess Constanza can be persuaded to take me back to Quincy with her?"

"Do you mean, will I help you persuade her?" Emilie asked. "Yes, to both. But I don't agree with Mother Héloïse. It would be better simply to recommend you to her without any deception about your position here."

"It was for my safety," Catherine said. "She worries that, if anything should go wrong, I might need the protection of the Paraclete."

"But you could also cause the convent great embarrassment," Emilie reminded her. "Please be circumspect in your actions."

Catherine smiled ruefully.

"I think that is another reason the abbess wished me to seem a member of the community," she said. "Concern for your reputation might keep me from acting rashly."

"She is taking a great risk," Emilie said, shaking her head.

"I don't need reminding of that," Catherine sighed.

Despite, or because of, her overwhelming anguish, Constanza only remained at the Paraclete overnight. The next morning, she met with Héloïse, Prioress Astane and Emilie and decided she would be pleased to have the boarder, Catherine, come to her for a week or two of instruction in the art of maintaining a secular household, as she was about to be married to a lord in Ponthieu and needed the sort of advice the convent was ill-equipped to give.

"It would be my honor," Constanza told them. "I will be happy to impart to her what little I know."

And so, that afternoon, Catherine joined the entourage as a temporary attendant of Constanza of Quincy.

"I will try to return before Edgar does," she told the abbess. "If I don't, you'll explain, won't you?"

Héloïse gave her a look Catherine knew only too well.

"You will return before he does," she said.

Catherine bowed her head.

"Yes, Mother."

After Catherine had left, Héloïse returned to her duties. It was not until just after Vespers that she suddenly realized that Constanza had said nothing about the presence of extra guards at the convent and had never asked about Paciana, despite the scene with Raynald that Catherine had witnessed in Troyes. Perhaps grief had driven all other thoughts from her mind.

Perhaps.

Or, perhaps Constanza had always known that Paciana was at the Paraclete and was well aware that she had been recently attacked. Perhaps she believed that this time her stepdaughter was really, finally, dead.

Héloïse bowed her head over clasped hands.

"Forgive me, Lord," she murmured. "I never should have let Catherine go. It was my own curiosity I wished to satisfy, not hers. Twice now, I've sent her in to danger. If they harm her, I will . . ."

What? What possible penance could she set herself for allowing Catherine to be put in jeopardy?

"I will leave it to you, Lord," she continued. "I beseech you, keep her safe."

Eighteen

The forest of Othe,
Monday, April 29, 1140

Ce que n'i est, ce ne pouet on trover.

One cannot find that which is not there.

—Old French Proverb

*W*alter, I know you're skilled in woodcraft," Edgar said. "And I have followed you without question so far. But any human being who would make this trail has to have been deranged. We've doubled back on ourselves a dozen times in the last two miles. I don't think we're more than a few yards from where we started."

He swatted at a low-hanging branch and winced as he realized he had also hit a clump of stinging nettles. Their first day in the forest had convinced him that there was nothing wondrous about it. It was identical to every other forest in France, except it seemed to be even more full of thorny bushes and quagmires.

Walter swore as his horse's mane was caught in a bush thick with burrs.

"You're right," he said. "It's an animal trail, deer most likely. At first it seemed to me that men had used it recently, but not this far in. Perhaps they were deceived by it also. It's getting late; we may as well make camp."

"I héar the river," Edgar said. "Shall we try to find a clearing near the water?"

"Yes, but not too near, the insects are starting to hatch," Walter said. He raised his head and sniffed the air. "Charcoal burners again. I wonder how many and how well armed."

"Do you think it would be wise for just the two of us to approach them?" Edgar asked.

"No," Walter said. "I'll go alone. You wait here."

Edgar boiled over.

"Do you think I'm a coward!" he demanded.

Walter seemed puzzled. "Of course not. You asked me a question. No, I don't think it would be wise for the two of us to go. If there's a band of them, with weapons, then one of us should be ready to create a diversion."

"I see," Edgar said. "In that case, I should go. I'm not as formidable as you."

They argued back and forth for a few more minutes before finally agreeing that Edgar should approach the charcoal burners and Walter should stay back in the woods, his crossbow armed.

They crept carefully toward the scent of the smoke. As they drew closer, they also heard the sound of voices. Edgar motioned for Walter to stay back as he stepped out of the cover of the trees.

There were two men standing next to the charcoal pit. A felled oak lay on the ground, a worn crosscut saw leaning on it. One of the men had an axe in his belt. Beyond them, on the other edge of the clearing, a woman sat on the ground, a baby at her breast. She was stirring something in a pot as two other children hung over it eagerly. Edgar took another step. The branch under his foot cracked like thunder. Everyone in the clearing froze. Then the man with the axe pulled it out.

"Who . . ." he began, then saw Edgar with his pale hair and skin. "Saint Eloi save us! What are you?"

"A demon, father!" one of the children cried, hiding its face in its mother's skirts.

"No," Edgar said quietly. He raised his hands, palms open. "I am a man, a traveller, lost in the forest. I only ask your hospitality."

"He's lying," the other man said. "He's been sent to drive us out."

"Why would I do that?" Edgar asked, taking another step forward. "Do I look like a bailiff? It's nothing to me what you do here. My friend and I only want company for the night. These woods are dark and forbidding. We have fresh meat, if you will share your fire."

The two men conferred. Edgar could see that, beneath the filth, all of them were starving. Axes and broken-toothed saws don't bring down game. The children wore only torn cloaks. He could see their naked skin showing underneath, their legs spindly and bowed. Their shoes were made of strips of bark, tied with twisted vines. He wondered how these people had survived the winter and where they had found the strength to cut down the tree they were burning.

It was the woman who made the decision.

"I don't care if he's a poacher or the Devil himself," she said. "If he has meat, welcome him."

"Where's your friend?" the man with the axe asked. He still held it poised to throw. "What kind of meat?"

"Walter!" Edgar called without moving. "We've been invited to dinner."

As Walter came into their view, the woman screamed and gathered the children closer. The man dropped his axe from nerveless fingers and crossed himself.

"Saint Salvian, protect us!" he cried. "They are monsters!"

Then he saw what Walter carried.

"May the Virgin bless and keep you in health, my lord," he said. "Look, Eva! He's shot a boar!"

Walter leaned back and belched in long and melodic resonance. The others responded with respectful silence.

"I'd sell my Aunt Matilda to the Saracens for a mug of beer just now," he continued. "Nothing washes down fresh boar like beer."

"I'm sorry, gracious lord," the charcoal burner said nervously. "We have only water. Really, we have nothing to repay you for such a meal, unless you want to sleep with my wife."

Walter regarded the woman. To the dirt had been added a layer of boar grease. The children lay in a heap at her feet, the baby balanced on her lap.

"I would not dishonor you so," he smiled.

"Have you been living in these woods long?" Edgar asked.

"Since the beginning of Lent," the man told him. "My wife, my brother and I had a plot of land near Tonnerre, but we were overrun by the lords of Tonnerre and Grancy during one of their disputes."

Walter started. The man didn't notice. He was staring into the past.

"In their fighting," he went on, "they set fire to the house and killed the pigs. Their horses trampled our fields. We had nothing left. I thought I could find work in Sens, but the winter was hard. There was nothing there for a man without a trade or a relative in town. The chapter house of Saint-Stephen fed us a while, and after that, the monks of Saint-Pierre-le-Vif, but there was never enough. Then we heard that we could live in the forest, make charcoal and sell it for a good price."

"And it wasn't true?" Edgar asked. Their poverty was obvious.

"Oh, no, it was," the man said. "We made enough the first week to fill two barrels. We took it to the river to wait for the buyer, but the *ribaux* came and stole it from us. This happened twice. Now we only make enough to keep ourselves warm. We search the forest for food. Next winter, we'll have to live by the charity of the monks again, or starve."

The man stared at the glowing coals.

"I always wanted to give alms, not receive them," he said.

Walter shifted his position. He opened his mouth to speak, then closed it. Let Edgar finish with his questions first.

"Are there many people like you in the forest?" Edgar asked.

"Too many," the man said. "We thought we could survive here and make enough to rebuild the house, at least. There are others who were also lured by the same false promises. But most either died or joined the *ribaux*."

"But who does this land belong to?" Edgar said. "Does no one patrol the forest for poachers?"

"I've seen no knights or soldiers, except you," the charcoal burner said. "We heard that this forest belongs to the countess of Tonnerre, but she's dead now, they say, and the count is going to give it to the monks."

"Which monks?" Walter said sharply.

"The ones over by Lailly, white monks, they are."

He began to smother the coals with damp earth, lest they burn to nothing. Edgar moved out of the way. He wondered where the rumor started that Vauluisant would be the new owner of the forest. He had one last question.

"Do you know who it is that's been buying the charcoal, and what they want it for?"

The man shook his head.

"I saw the man who does the buying," he said. "I don't know whose service he's in. Didn't look like a cleric. The barge was loaded with rocks, too, reddish ones. Rocks and charcoal, it means nothing to me."

"And they send it down the river?" Walter asked. "Where?"

"Who knows? Someone said once it was all for the mill, but I ask you, what sort of mill is it that grinds stones?"

"I don't know," Edgar said. "But it's a wonder I must see."

"Good journey to you then," the man said. "The earth over the coals stays warm through the night. We've learned to sleep circled close. We'll show you."

"No." Walter got up. He went over to his pack and pulled out his spare cloak. It was English wool, lined with catskin. Then, after a moment's hesitation, he also took out his other tunic and *chainse*.

"Here," he said. "Cover your wife and children. Come to Grancy. I'll see your property is restored to you."

He forced the clothing into the man's arms, then went

back to the edge of the clearing. He sank down under an oak tree and leaned against it.

"Sleep," he told them. "I'll keep watch."

The charcoal burner stood looking in stupefaction at the bundle in his arms.

"Is he mad?" he asked.

"Most probably," Edgar said. "But you can believe he will do as he says. He's also the lord of Grancy."

Walter was unusually quiet as they made their way downriver the next morning.

"That was very charitable of you," Edgar remarked. "Especially since one of your tunics could cover all of them with ease."

"It wasn't charity; it was penance," Walter muttered.

"Same thing," Edgar told him. "Caesarius of Arles says that alms wipe out sin, a belief that is echoed in . . ."

"I'm not interested in what your dead priests say!" Walter bellowed. "I can't even remember why Raynald and I were fighting last year. I have always fed the poor. I do not create paupers."

"Of course not, Walter," Edgar said. "Do you want to go back and give them your horse, too?"

"Do you think I should?" he asked.

"Saint Walter of Grancy?" Edgar laughed, then realized the man was serious. "You must do what your conscience tells you."

They rode on a while longer until they came to a crude quai built on the bank of the river.

"This must be where they bring the charcoal," Edgar said. "But I think we should go on to discover where it's taken. I want to find this miraculous mill that grinds stones into flour and then uses the charcoal to bake it into bread. That would be a way to feed all the beggars in Christendom."

Walter didn't answer.

"What do you think we should do?" Edgar asked. "I have the feeling that discovering what happens to the material that comes out of the forest is essential to understanding why everyone wants the rights to it."

Walter raised his dark shaggy head and shook it, making his resemblance to a bear even more pronounced.

"I think that when we have completed our mission, I will go back to the forest and bring those people home with me," he said. "How else can I be sure no one will harm them?"

Edgar smiled. "Walter, I believe that hermit has converted you. Next you'll be turning your keep into a leprosarium. Is that a village ahead?"

They both looked down the river path. It had begun to widen and there were signs of recent cutting. As the trees thinned, they could see a collection of huts climbing up from the river. And, at the place where the river was fed by an inrushing stream, there was another larger building which jutted out over the water. It had a clay chimney from which acrid smoke was pouring. The creak of the turning wheel sounded above the rush of the stream.

"By all the heads of John the Baptist!" Edgar gave a long whistle. "It is a mill!"

Meanwhile, Catherine was wishing, for the hundredth time, that she had gone with Edgar and Walter, or even just stayed at the Paraclete. Her prediction had proved accurate and now she was sitting in the women's room at Quincy with cramps from navel to knees and trying not to scream as Constanza and her ladies lectured her on the upkeep of a castle.

"Never let men above the second floor, especially if you have rugs," Constanza was saying. "They don't look where they step when they're out and they track in all kinds of dirt."

"Of course, you can just insist that they remove their boots at the bottom of the staircase." The speaker was a relative of Constanza's but Catherine had already forgotten her name and rank. "The duchess does that and it seems to work, except with her husband, of course."

"But then you just have them sneaking about silently, surprising the girls at their work," Constanza objected. "No, my way is best. Don't you agree, my dear?"

"Oh, yes, of course," Catherine said faintly. "No boots above the steps."

"No, my dear." Constanza's voice was a touch impatient. "No men above the second floor, unless you only have two floors, of course, then they don't .. : are you quite well, Catherine?"

"Umm ... no, my lady," Catherine said. "I'm indisposed. I would be grateful for a tisane."

"Of course, you poor thing!" Constanza leaned forward and patted her hand. "Like ice! That time again, is it? You should have spoken sooner. I always have my box of herbs with me. Samonie! Get my medicine box."

The other woman bustled over, feeling Catherine's forehead and stomach as well as her hands.

"I always have a warm herbal bath made up for me," she said. "And I just sit in it until the pain lessens. Does the convent make up bags of herbs for those days? I have a wonderful mixture that I got from a friend who got it from the abbess of Saint-Disibod. It is most soothing. She would be happy, I'm sure, to send your abbess the recipe."

The maid had returned, but without the box.

"I'm sorry, my lady," she said. "We must have left it at Troyes, or perhaps the Paraclete. I can't find it anywhere."

"You stupid girl!" Constanza shouted. "It's your duty to keep track of these things. I ought to whip you!"

"Constanza," her friend spoke quietly. "I'm sure someone here has the necessary herbs. Your cook can make up a draught of mint, valerian, thyme, spikenard, artemisia, licorice and raisins. Those condiments should all be available."

"Yes, that will do for now, but what if there were serious illness?" Constanza replied. "Her incompetence could cost someone's life."

The maid threw herself at Constanza's feet.

"Please forgive me, my lady," she begged. "I am truly filled with remorse for my negligence. I can only implore your mercy!"

"Very well," Constanza said grudgingly. "I will pardon your mismanagement, this time. Send messengers out at once. I expect you to see to it that the box is recovered."

At that moment another maid rushed in, carrying a wooden box edged in gold leaf. Upon seeing it, Constanza stiffened. Even through her own pain, Catherine could tell that the woman was furious.

"How dare you touch that!" she said. "That was my daughter's medicine box and is sacred to her memory. I'll not have it used by anyone. Samonie, take it and put it in the chest with Alys's clothing!"

With obvious effort, she controlled herself and turned again to Catherine.

"Since you are feeling unwell, perhaps we should have a bed made up for you in the corner now instead of to-night," she said, trying to smile. "I will have the infusion of herbs brought to you. Rest for the afternoon. Don't feel obligated to join us in the hall this evening."

Catherine stood and thanked her hostess. Constanza also rose and with her companion left the chamber.

When everything had been prepared, the maid took Catherine's arm and led her over to the bed. Within a few minutes she found herself in her *chainse*, tucked in among the quilts, with a warm poultice of mustard and cress on her stomach and a hot cup of wine infused with herbs in her hand. As she sipped it she felt the warmth drawing out the pain and she begun to relax.

Samonie hovered over her, fussing with the covers.

"I know just how you feel," she whispered. "I heard you were about to be married. That's good. It's not nearly so bad after you've had a child."

"I've not heard that," Catherine said. "How do you know?"

"My children live with my cousin, in Troyes," Samonie told her. "I have three."

Catherine opened her mouth to ask about Samonie's husband, then shut it. The maid was pretty and bright, with golden-brown hair, green eyes and dimples. A woman like that in a keep full of men, with no kin to protect her, wasn't likely to keep her virtue long.

Samonie saw her look and smiled.

"They're beautiful children," she said. "They look just like their fathers. Does that offend you?"

"It's not my place to be offended," Catherine said.

"Good," Samonie stopped fussing. She looked around. It was the middle of the day and the women's chamber was empty except for them. But, to be sure, she pulled aside the curtains and checked behind the screens. Then she returned to the bed. Catherine sat up straighter.

"Is something wrong?" she asked.

"Many things," Samonie spoke quietly. "Are you the woman from the Paraclete who found Lisiard's body?"

Catherine nodded.

"My sister was betrothed to him," the maid said. "At least they saw it that way. They were going to run away to the south. His uncle, Isembard, said he would help them."

"I'm so sorry," Catherine said.

"So am I," Samonie's face grew hard. "Lisiard was a kind man, but he had a loose tongue. So does my cousin. She loves passing on all the court gossip she hears. It never occurred to her, until now, that some knowledge is too dangerous to possess. Do you think Lisiard was killed because of what happened to Countess Alys?"

"Yes," Catherine said. "I'm sure of it. Do you also have dangerous knowledge?"

"Of course not," Samonie replied. "But I have questions too dangerous to ask."

"Perhaps you should forewarn me of them," Catherine suggested, "so that I don't unknowingly put myself in peril."

Samonie sat on the bed and leaned close to Catherine.

"That's very wise," she said. "There is one thing I have been wondering ever since Alys was found. And that is, what happened to the monkey?"

"The monkey?" Catherine hadn't even thought of it.

"It's not at Tonnerre or Troyes or here," the maid said. "I presume the nuns don't have it. Did it run away? Was it slaughtered by whoever attacked her? Did she even take it with her when she left for Tonnerre?"

"Do you think it's important?" Catherine asked.

"I think it is strange that no one has mentioned it, or tried to find it," Samonie answered. "Now, I must return to my work. I'll come up again before evening to see how you are."

She left Catherine alone in the tower room. For a while Catherine contented herself with lying still and enjoying the softness of the quilts and the luxury of being pampered. Outside the window, crows cawed raucously, fighting over something thrown into the midden. Nasty, noisy, evil-eyed things.

The monkey. Alys's stepfather, Rupert, had said the monkey was nasty. Walter told them Alys had hated it; Constanza said she doted on it, fed it from her own dish. But they all agreed that she took it with her everywhere. Samonie was right, it did seem strange. What had happened to Alys's pet? Catherine wondered how much it had cost Raynald. Such a rare beast had to have been worth a fortune, more than what most of the people she knew could afford. Why hadn't anyone searched for it?

The poultice had cooled by now. Catherine pulled it off and laid it on the floor beside the bed. The herbs had worked and she was feeling almost normal again. Perhaps she should get dressed and join the others in the hall below. The drawstring of her *braies* was chafing. It reminded her that it was probably time to change the rags.

Catherine looked around for a bucket in which to soak the used rags. In one corner was a large chest, made of yew. There was a lock on it but it had not been carefully closed.

"I wonder," Catherine said as she tiptoed over to it. "Is this where Alys's belongings have been stored?"

The hinges had been oiled recently and the lid opened without a sound. Inside were a number of lengths of cloth, some wrapped around other objects. Catherine picked up one and unwrapped it. It was a small casket of ivory carved with a scene from the wedding at Cana. She shook it and was rewarded by a rattle. Prying open the top, she found a large ring set with rubies. Too large for a woman's hand. The only other thing was a silken purse. In it was a lock of dark hair, almost as black as her own. She thought she could name the head it had come from. Raynald's hair was russet brown.

"Poor Alys," she said. "Poor Walter."

Carefully she replaced the jewel box. The shape next to it was larger. The cloth had been draped over it carelessly. As she lifted it, Catherine recognized Alys's medicine box. Actually, it was odd that Alys hadn't taken it with her when she left for Tonnerre. It was part of the household supplies every woman kept always in her possession. Constanza had been no more than just when she had berated Samonie for misplacing hers. There would be mixtures of herbs and spices that could only be made once a year. The recipes might have been in a family for generations. There was one that her mother had always carried. Catherine supposed her sister, Agnes, used it now.

"I should see about getting one of my own," she considered.

For some reason, that brought home to her more than anything else that she was truly a married woman, with responsibilities. She opened the box.

In it lay the bags of herbs, some linen cut in strips, a small, sharp knife and some smooth stones. Catherine sniffed at the herbs, trying to guess what they were for. Most of them were dried herbs and garden flowers; daisies and roses, iris root, chamomile, comfrey, thyme, different worts, and so on. A few were exotic substances like pepper, sandalwood, myrrh and cinnamon. There was nothing special about it, but Catherine could see that Alys had assembled it with care. Catherine put it back gently.

The rest of the articles in the chest appeared to be nothing more than clothing, shoes, belts or hair ribbons. Catherine rummaged among them, feeling as though she were looting a reliquary. At the bottom of the chest there was a small packet, a leather bag, crudely stitched together. Cautiously, Catherine opened it.

Another smell of herbs rose from the bag. The mixture was familiar; tansy, rue, hyssop, scammony, dittany, and something else, bull's gall, perhaps, or nard. It was the sort of combination she had just been given in her wine, only much stronger. It was designed to bring on the menses when they were delayed. Among the herbs, there was something hard. Catherine took it out. It was a cloth about as long as her middle finger, stuffed tightly and sewn shut. The thread had not been cut but a long cord left instead. Catherine dropped it, rubbing her fingers in distaste. She knew what that was, too—a pessary to be used if the herbs were ineffective.

This was a dangerous compound. A certain amount could cause a pregnant woman to abort. Too much could kill her as well. A woman trying to find the right dosage would have to be very careful. She would probably start out with a weak dilution of the formula and then increase the strength slowly until she achieved the desired result. It might take several days, but if she were careful, no one would know. Each person drank from her own cup.

But the monkey drank from Alys's cup. It ate from her dish; she took it with her everywhere. Was that what had happened to it? Had it been poisoned by the herbs Alys was dosing herself with? And had the unexpected death of her pet frightened Alys into trying the suppository instead?

"Why, though?" Catherine muttered. "Why would Alys want to abort a child that was by her own husband?"

"What do you think you are doing?"

Catherine dropped the bag back into the chest. She looked up in horror.

Constanza stood in the doorway, her ladies just behind her. Their expressions were varying degrees of shock and contempt. But it was Constanza's face that terrified Catherine the most. There was no surprise in it, rather a kind of grim triumph.

"A spy after all," she said calmly. "I think we'll have to find out just how much she knows. Ingeltix, you and Doda tie her to the bed. The rope we used for Alys is still under the table there. Remember, my dear, if you scream, I'll have to kill you."

Catherine had no doubt that she would.

Nineteen

A new village in the forest,
Feast of Saint James, brother of Jesus,
first bishop of Jerusalem,
Wednesday, May 1, 1140

Fasting empties the soul of matter and makes it, with the body, clear and light for the reception of divine truth.

—Clement of Alexandria

I must get inside to see what this mill is for," Edgar said. "I have a guess but it seems impossible. How do you think we could arrange to do it?"

"We could ask that monk over there if he would show us his mill," Walter suggested, gesturing for the man standing outside one of the crude huts to come over to them.

Edgar wasn't amused.

"Aren't you worried that you'll be set upon and turned over to Raynald of Tonnerre in chains?" he asked.

Walter laughed. "I don't see anyone here likely to attempt it. I'm not so dangerous or evil that monks would feel it necessary to attack me."

The monk approaching them certainly showed no signs of hostility.

"Welcome!" he greeted Walter. "How may I serve you, my lord?"

"A mug of beer and a blessing are all I need," Walter answered, dismounting. "But my friend, here, is curious about that strange building by the stream."

The monk's eyes lit and he beamed at Edgar.

"Of course, of course," he said. "It's not quite complete, as yet. I'm still having a small problem with regulating the action of the bellows. But I would be delighted to show you."

"Bellows?" Edgar said with growing excitement. "You've adapted a water mill to pump bellows? For what purpose? Show me."

He slid down from his horse and followed the monk toward the mill, forgetting Walter entirely.

With a shrug, the lord of Grancy took the reins dangling from Edgar's abandoned horse and set about acting as squire.

As they entered the mill, Edgar took a deep breath. The air was redolent of fresh cut wood, burning charcoal and the tang of metal and lime.

"It's only a model, you understand," the monk told him. "The abbott wants proof that this will work before wasting our funds to build in stone. My name is Brother Ferreolus, by the way."

"Mine is Edgar. This machine is beautiful," Edgar said, going over to the contraption of stone and clay. "How does it work?"

"Well, you know how iron is usually separated from its rock, don't you?" Brother Ferreolus said.

"Of course," Edgar said. "The heat of the coal releases the iron imprisoned in the rock and it melts to the bottom of the forge. The problem in the procedure is with maintaining a steady flow of air over the coals to keep them hot enough, but not so hot that the iron metamorphoses into a heavier, useless form."

"Yes, that's one of the problems," Brother Ferreolus agreed. "But another is that it's costly to pay or feed the number of men necessary to keep the bellows working at any speed. And, since we white monks believe that we should not hire others to perform manual labor for us, we have been trying to provide for our needs for iron through our own efforts. As you can imagine, it's very difficult to do this and keep up our other duties, even with the help of the lay brothers."

"Why don't you simply buy the iron from the smiths in the villages?" Edgar asked.

"What villages?" Ferreolus replied. "We build our monasteries in deserted land, far from any other habitation. At least, we attempt to. The world has a way of following us. Still, it is part of our philosophy to be self-sufficient and it was to that end that I designed this."

"You did?" Edgar was amazed. "I thought your order also frowned on novelties, and this is certainly new."

"Oh, this is no novelty, not at all," Ferreolus insisted. "Everything here is a perfectly common tool. I have just arranged them differently to make them work better. That is not new, nor is it frivolous."

"And," he added, "as I explained to Abbot Norpald, if Our Lord hadn't wanted this to be built, He wouldn't have illuminated my mind with its image."

"That is a quite reasonable argument," Edgar said. "This work does bear the mark of divine inspiration."

He examined the stone and clay oven, with the bellows inserted in two places and attached to the workings of the mill so that one opened to take in air as the other blew it over the coals. It was elegant, but the wood building wasn't safe. They would need to build in stone if they intended to continue or expand the operation. He noted that there was an opening at the bottom for the molten iron to run out into a mold. It was fairly primitive. They must have a finery nearby also. Then something clicked in his mind.

"Abbott Norpald?" he said. "Of Vauluisant?"

"Yes, do you know him?" Ferreolus asked.

"I have heard of him," Edgar admitted. "I didn't realize that this land was part of the monastic property."

Ferreolus seemed embarrassed.

"Actually, there has been some dispute on that point," he said. "But I'm sure it will be resolved soon. Do you want to see where I'm going to put the water-driven *martinet*?"

Edgar allowed himself to be diverted from further questions about the land. That could be delved into later. It was the beauty of the machine before him that consumed his interest.

"You've found a way to power a tilt hammer with a waterwheel?" He was doubtful. "That's much more complicated than a double bellows."

"I know," Ferreolus agreed. "I'm having a little trouble with the cam and the balance. But if I pray long enough, I'm sure the answer will come to me."

"I would dearly love to see the result when it does," Edgar said.

"I hope you shall," Ferreolus said as he led Edgar back out into the clearing.

Walter was sitting under a tree with a mug and a hunk of bread, talking with another of the monks. He waved the mug happily at them.

"Your squire seems very astute regarding the working of the forge," Ferreolus said to him. "Is he an engineer?"

"Not my squire," Walter mumbled through the bread. "Says he's English but comes from Scotland; his father's a lord and his great-aunt a saint. Probably all a story. It's nothing to me. I like him. Want some food, Edgar?"

"I could do with something," Edgar said. "You should see what this man has created, Walter. They could make enough iron in a week to shoe a hundred horses."

"Ah, so they're not grinding rocks into flour?" Walter said. "A pity. So much famine in the world."

Ferreolus seemed distressed by this thought. He shook his head sadly.

"That would indeed be wondrous," he said. "But God only granted me illumination, not a miracle. Not that I would ever consider myself worthy of receiving one, of course. Please, allow me to fill a cup for you."

He went to the barrel for more beer. Edgar sat next to Walter, full of excitement over the machine he had just seen.

"You must come look at it," he told the castellan. "It's so much better than the old method. He's even put an extra hole on the side of the forge so that one doesn't have to lean over the chimney to put in the charcoal and rock."

"Fascinating," Walter yawned. "But what has it to do with Alys?"

Edgar thought. The mill was on the property the countess ceded to the Paraclete. But this was, as yet, a minor operation. It was not as if gold had been found there. Iron was necessary to any building project, however, and a ready constant source would be useful. Also, the property was convenient to Vauluisant and the monks had been known to pay well for land they wanted, if they couldn't convince the owner to donate it. Ferreolus had given the impression that Raynald would transfer the land from the Paraclete to Vauluisant. Had the monks promised him a countergift in exchange for it? But why would Raynald need payment? He seemed wealthy enough. And how valuable was the land? Without the efficiency of the water-powered forge, the amount of iron one could capture from the rocks was not enough to bother with. That was why it had always been done by villagers, with little interference from the great lords.

Edgar sipped at his beer, certain that the answer was close. He went through the steps in his mind. First one gets the iron ore from the earth. Then, usually, the smelter is built nearby, the charcoal prepared and sometimes lime is added, if it's available. The metal is extracted and taken to the finery, usually also nearby, to be hammered into a usable shape, strips or bars.

Now, how would this use of water power change that?

The only thing that Edgar could think of was that one couldn't build and destroy the smelter as casually as before. It wasn't just a clay oven, but a complicated set of instruments. That was a drawback. But, if there were sufficient iron ore in the area and enough wood to build the mill and make the charcoal, it would be possible to produce an enormous amount of metal of high quality with very few laborers. That would increase the value of the forest.

Edgar had been at the ongoing rebuilding of Abbot Suger's church at Saint-Denis. He knew how much material was needed for such an endeavor. Iron, wood, stone; it seemed that most of the church was of stone and the worry that there would not be enough in neighboring quarries was constant. But wood was used even more, for a hundred things; beams like those the abbot had miraculously found, huts for the workmen, scaffolding, and, of course, charcoal. And the archbishop of Sens was contemplating building a new cathedral to rival Saint-Denis.

Yes, Edgar concluded. This forest might be valuable enough to fight over. But to kill someone? That seemed rather drastic. And why Alys? She may have held the rights to the land, but her husband would have had the final say. If Raynald had wanted to make an arrangement with Vauluisant or if he had wanted to use the land, himself, he had plenty of ways to coerce his wife to agree. There had to be something more.

He wondered if Catherine were right and Raynald had beaten Alys because she wouldn't renounce her gift to the nuns. He might have gone farther than he had intended and been frightened when he realized what he had done. But why then bring her to those same nuns for care? No, there was still something missing. But they had found all they could here. It was time to return to the Paraclete for Catherine. The thought warmed him. And then to Paris, where it seemed that other clouds were forming around Master Abelard.

Edgar took the last swallow of beer. Beside him, Walter snored peacefully in the afternoon sun. Edgar leaned back against the old chestnut tree and closed his eyes. The slap of the water against the creaking wheel was soothing. Perhaps just a short rest. He wondered what Catherine was doing now. Probably playing happily with the convent accounts. He hoped she wouldn't have become too content with life there by the time he returned. Despite recent events, he suspected that the normal peace of the convent could be quite alluring.

His head dropped forward and his hand released the empty cup. Soon his gentle whistling snore gave a counterpoint to Walter's bray.

Catherine twisted her hands once again, desperate to work loose from the ropes. There didn't seem to be much point in trying to escape unnoticed, as they never left her alone, but not having the use of her hands was pushing Catherine close to hysteria and so she continued the effort.

Constanza's visitor, who had finally been identified as Marcella, a recent widow making the tour of her less fortunate friends, smiled thinly at Catherine's struggle.

"If you can't endure a few days bound to a bed," she smirked, "how do you ever propose to survive years of being bound to a man?"

Catherine didn't respond. She had learned on the first day of her captivity that neither argument nor protestation had any effect on these women. Apart from slapping her a few times in their first moments of fury and fear, they hadn't touched her. But their incessant tales of the bitterness of marriage were torture enough. Marcella continued, her voice grinding into Catherine's ears.

"How would you like to be lying in that bed, night after night, knowing that someone was coming to torture you, to poke and prod and bite and drool all over you and you with no hope of freedom, no one to save you. A man with his horrid scratchy face and stinking breath, hands like wooden planks, leaving splinters in whatever they touch," she snorted. "What we've done to you is nothing to what you'd experience once you wed. It would be a mercy to let you die now."

Catherine kept her eyes turned away. If she gave no sign of hearing, maybe that horrible woman would stop.

But she didn't.

"I remember how I used to watch my husband go off on one of his hunting trips, and the saints only know what he was really hunting." Her words were still thick with resentment. "Every time I would wave and smile and pray he'd break his ugly neck."

She paused. Her voice calmed. "And, one day, my prayers were answered."

Catherine still refused to look. She heard the clink of the pitcher against a cup and the sound of liquid pouring. She tried to swallow, but her mouth was too dry. She wouldn't acknowledge her tormentor, not even to ask for water. They had allowed her a cup a day, but no food.

Why? What did they want from her? They had asked her
no questions, not what she was doing or who had sent her,
nor why she was there. They had only kept her prisoner
and tried to drive her insane with stories of the horrors
done to them by men. She couldn't understand it. What
was their reason? Did they plan to convince her to stay
with them rather than marry? Or that whatever they had
done was justified by the treatment they had endured?
They couldn't hope to keep her incarcerated forever;
Héloïse knew where she was.

"At least your husband was young and good for something." Constanza had returned to add her recital of hard-
ship. "He gave you sons who have to take care of you
now. I was sold off to an old man who could barely drib-
ble and already had a daughter he doted on. I had to wipe
up after him and listen to his maunderings about his first
wife and kiss his spongy lips and know that, when he finally died, I would have nothing but a pitiful bit of dower
land that couldn't support a mouse."

It was beginning to make Catherine's stomach turn.

"But finally you had Alys," Marcella reminded her.

"And what I went through for that isn't fit for Christian
ears," Constanza said.

Catherine wondered what could be more unsuitable than
what they had been drilling into her for the past several
days. She felt confident that they couldn't surpass her
mother for gruesome childbirth stories. Those had been
Catherine's final incentive to enter the convent. It was
proof of Edgar's charisma that he had made her forget
them all for him. Now she only hoped these harpies would
let her live long enough to find out for herself how awful
it was.

Her thoughts drifted as the drone continued. She wondered what kind of children she and Edgar would have, if
she ever got out of this place. Would they look like Sax-
ons? She had a vision of a row of pale, blond infants with
grey eyes, staring mournfully at her, accusing her for being their dark foreign mother, locking her in a dark dower
house with no windows.

Catherine forced her mind back in focus. It was the lack

of food. Her empty stomach was too light to keep her brain anchored. Hermits always fasted in order to allow their minds to ascend to spiritual realms. But she didn't want her mind to go anywhere if her body couldn't come, too.

Catherine?

Oh, no. She refused to believe those voices were anything divine. Nothing could be more annoying.

Lie quietly, child, they whispered. Why, she didn't know. No one else seemed able to hear them. *Let them think you're sleeping. Then listen. They've not been pouring water but undiluted wine.*

Marcella was speaking again, her voice overly loud.

"I still don't know why you married Rupert," she said, "after your first experience. He's hardly better than a dodderer, to my mind, and owns hardly anything of his own."

"He has his uses," Constanza answered.

Catherine heard the pitcher clanking again.

"He must keep them all in his *braies* then," Marcella laughed. "The man can't even ride his own fields without mishap. Takes to his bed after a little fall. Personally, I think you should have tried to get Raynald for yourself. You're not that much older than he; you haven't dried up yet. Once Paciana died, there was no reason to make him wait for Alys."

"Yes, there was," Constanza said.

"Oh?"

"You don't have to know everything," Constanza snapped.

There was a pause.

"I know more than you think," Marcella said softly. "For instance, I know where you were the afternoon Alys was conceived and who was visiting."

There was a crash as the table was knocked over. The pitcher smashed on the stone floor.

"Don't try your tricks with me, Marcella!" Constanza shouted. "You have no more than the suspicions of your foul mind."

She made an effort to gather her dignity.

"Obviously," she began again more carefully, "I've kept

you too long in my company. You must be fatigued with our chatter. I'm sure you have duties at your own home to attend to."

"Really?" Marcella sounded overconfident. "Of course, I'll leave at once, if you wish it. I may stop by the Paraclete on my way and tell the nuns how your guest is doing."

"You should," Constanza agreed, unfazed. "I was about to send a messenger there. They will have to know that she isn't well at all. I'm afraid she might have a quartan fever. I should have sent word when she collapsed but it's very contagious, I fear. We don't dare risk sending her back to infect the dear sisters. As a matter of fact, Marcella, *you* seem a bit flushed to me. I do hope you haven't contracted it also."

The room was very still. Catherine's heart was pounding so loudly that she was afraid she would miss something. Finally.

"I understand, dear friend," Marcella said quietly. "Perhaps I should go to my own lands at once and not risk catching this dreadful illness."

"Especially since you've seen how dreadful it is, with the poor girl delirious, shouting wild accusations and forcing us to tie her down to prevent her harming herself," Constanza said. "I only hope we can save her."

"I shall pray constantly for her deliverance," Marcella said.

"As do we all," Constanza replied.

There was a rustle of skirts and then quiet. For the first time in days, Catherine was alone.

But not for long. There was another step on the stairs. Catherine turned and opened her eyes in fear.

It was the servant Samonie, carrying a pail of water.

"I was sent to wash you," she announced. "And give you clean clothes."

"Why?" Catherine asked. "They've let me lie here bleeding all over the blankets since Monday. Has Constanza suddenly become a gracious hostess again?"

Samonie put down the pail and began untying Catherine.

"I have no idea," she said wearily. "Can't you just be grateful that you don't have to lie in this mess anymore?"

"I suppose," Catherine said, "I could, if I wasn't afraid it meant I was being cleaned to be put in my winding sheet."

"Oh, why did you have to do something so stupid as rummage through Alys's things?" Samonie moaned. "Didn't they teach you anything useful in that convent?"

"Prying into the affairs of others wasn't in any of the lectures," Catherine said tartly. "Neither was escaping from tower rooms. Why won't you help me get out of here? You must know that Constanza is planning to tell Mother Héloïse that I died here of a fever. How does she plan to do it, poison? Or perhaps a fevered slip on the staircase?"

"And what do you think she'll do to me if I help you?" Samonie replied, helping Catherine out of her filthy clothes. "Who will feed my children if I'm dead, you?"

"Anyway," she added less angrily, "I don't think she has decided yet to kill you. She seems to be planning it so that when you return, gaunt and clearly just over a terrible illness, no one will believe anything you say about her."

"The truth is, I haven't heard enough to say anything incriminating about her at all," Catherine admitted. "Only to guess. But I'm sure now that the monkey died before Alys did. That's what you wanted me to discover, wasn't it? It drank the potion she prepared for herself. Did Constanza find out?"

"Yes, she was furious," Samonie told her. "She took Alys up here. If you think you are being treated badly, you can't imagine what they did to her."

"Constanza killed her own daughter?" Catherine wanted to believe anything of this evil woman, but that seemed too much.

"No, at least not here," Samonie said. "Alys was alive when she left and not seriously harmed, at least not that one could see. No more than a few new bruises. Constanza knows how to hurt in other ways, as well. I wasn't there that last day, but I think Alys told her mother something that frightened her and caused her to stop the punishment and send Alys back to her husband."

"But what?" Catherine asked. "Do you know why Alys took the potion in the first place? Why wouldn't she want to bear Raynald's child? It would have guaranteed her security."

"I don't know," Samonie answered. "Here, put this on. I don't think she hated Raynald the way Marcella did her husband. She was afraid of his scorn. A child could only have improved her position in any case. William of Nevers would have been delighted to have another grandchild. The family is dwindling, at least the part that's legitimate. I've heard William has enough bastards to create a new town just for them. But that may be no more than male bragging."

Catherine was losing interest in the family as a whole. Nothing she had learned made any difference to the bequest to the Paraclete. Even if Alys's baby had lived, it would not have inherited land already donated. Of course, if Raynald had murdered her in a rage for aborting his child, that would diminish his prospects for recovering anything from the convent.

"Samonie," she said. "I refuse to just lie here and wait for Lady Constanza to decide if she's going to kill me or not. I'm hungry, I'm thirsty and I've been abused and degraded by these people. If I ever do get my hands free, just pray Constanza is no where in my reach."

The maid picked up the reeking clothes and the pail, its water now pink.

"Well, don't ask me to help you any more," she said. "If they try to kill you, I'll do what I can, but I can't risk myself for your discomfort. By the way, I don't think you should let them know you're not a virgin."

Catherine looked up, too astonished to dissemble.

"How did you know that?"

"I told you, my sister works in the kitchens of the count of Champagne. She told me that, when you were there, you were sharing a bed with a man who claimed to be your husband. If Constanza discovers that, she'll be able to threaten you with exposure and your life will be worth much less to her."

"No, she won't," Catherine said, reaching to stroke the talisman cross Edgar had given her. "He is my husband, and, despite all the vicious tales of those women, I will do anything necessary to be with him again."

She might not have been quite so eager to rejoin him if she had seen Edgar's face the next afternoon when he arrived at the Paraclete to discover her gone.

"We didn't expect you back so soon," Sister Thecla explained at the gate. "She wished to visit Lady Constanza at Quincy for a few days. We'll send for her at once."

"It's not that far," Edgar said. "I'll go get her now, myself."

The portress hesitated.

"I don't think that would be wise," she said, biting her lip. "We felt it would be better to employ a slight subterfuge, for Catherine's sake. It would be difficult to explain if you came for her."

"You've not put her back in a habit, have you?" Edgar asked.

He was trying to keep his temper. It would be unforgivable to yell at the portress. He hadn't realized until that moment just how strong his anger could be, or how imperious. Catherine had been left in the care of the nuns and they had let her leave, possibly to go into a place of danger. It was inexcusable.

"It was Catherine's idea to insinuate herself into the household of the lady of Quincy, wasn't it?" Edgar already knew the answer. "She thinks she can get them to tell her all the secrets of Alys's life. She never considers the risks she's taking. I swear, when she comes back, I'll kill her for making me worry in this way!"

He did not know how much, at this moment, he resembled Catherine's father and his own.

The portress was not impressed with his histrionics.

"Catherine is a very sensible person," she told him. "She will do nothing intentionally to put herself in jeopardy."

"I think you should be proud of Catherine, Edgar," Walter said suddenly. "If Alys had had her courage, she might still be alive. She should have come to me, no matter what they said her duty was. By the time she sent word, it was too late."

Edgar sighed and sat on a bench by the convent gate.

"I wouldn't have Catherine anything but what she is," he said. "But I don't like *where* she is."

"I'm sure she'll return in a day or two," Thecla said. "I'm afraid it might spoil her plans to ask her to come back now."

Edgar and Walter were still arguing the matter when a rider came to the gate.

"I have a message from the lady of Quincy for your abbess," he announced.

"Tell me what it is and I will see that she gets it," Thecla answered.

Edgar's stomach seemed to invert in the pause that followed.

"The lady Constanza sends her deep apologies," the man began. "The guest she brought back from your convent was taken suddenly ill, with a fever. In her delirium, she ran out of the keep and vanished into the forest. We have been hunting for her all day, but have found no trace. My lady wishes to know if you would care to send some of your people to aid in the search."

"That's ridiculous!" Edgar said. "I don't believe a word of it."

He got up to confront the messenger but Walter held him back.

"Wait," he cautioned. "It sounds as if they are trying to arrange for her to be found as Alys was. If you challenge them now, we may never know the truth."

Edgar froze. "You don't think they've killed her already, do you?"

Walter wanted to say something reassuring but had no store of platitudes to draw on.

"I don't know," he said. "But I think we should go find out."

"No, Walter," Edgar decided. "You're too well known to them. This time, I am going alone."

Twenty

The keep at Quincy, Saturday,
Feast of Saint Monica, widow and mother, May 4, 1140

Steadfast is she who resembles a flower in the wind: if she
sways, she does not fade away; if she is confounded,
still she does not fall.

—Peter of Celle,
On Conscience

Catherine stared listlessly at the ceiling. A diet of water and verbal abuse for nearly a week had brought her to unwonted lassitude. She was beginning to wonder if there were a world outside the room she lay in. She was on the verge of believing it didn't matter, because she would never see it again, in any case. Her fingers found the ivory cross Edgar had given her. She held it tightly and pressed it to her cheek.

" '*Ego dormivi et soporatus sum; et exsurrexi, quia Dominus suscepit me, non timebo . . . ,* ' " she recited softly, " 'I lay down and slept and woke again, for the Lord sustains me, I will not fear . . . ' "

Catherine smiled to herself. It was strange, but the most useful thing she had learned in her years at the Paraclete wasn't to question and analyze, although she was grateful for the training. It was the hours and hours of reciting the psalms, so that now, when she needed comfort more than logic, they came to her as gifts.

She knew what Constanza planned now. It horrified her that the other women all either agreed with her or were too afraid of her to rebel. They spoke in front of Catherine now, believing she was past listening. Her body would be found in the forest, starved, and they would weep and do penance for their lack of care of her. Or possibly she would never be found at all and Edgar would have to wait years before he could marry again. Poor Edgar! They might have had such interesting children.

Catherine! her voices were shouting at her. *For shame! Did we raise you to surrender? Think of all the saints who fasted years and remained steadfast. Where's your resolve? Where's your faith? Where's your blasted stubborn perversity?*

"Go away," she murmured, waving at them as at flies.

As she did, a small spark lit in her mind. The ropes, not untied since Samonie had given her fresh clothing, were looser than before. Even though she hadn't been able to undo the knots, the cords themselves had stretched. Perhaps, in the night, if they let her live another night, she could slip out of them and creep past the guards.

Very good, my dear, the voices cheered. *It's one thing to die, and we all must, someday. But one should do it in God's time, not Lady Constanza's.*

So Catherine took a little hope. She tried not to think of the difficulty of getting past the women guarding her and a keep full of people. She ignored the fact that she was now too weak to raise her head without dizziness. She would make the attempt to escape and at least die trying, rather than passively submitting to their plans.

She tucked the cross back into her *chainse*. The cool ivory warmed to the touch of her skin. She still lived and so she decided to hope.

Héloïse was more than disturbed at the message from Constanza. She was outraged.

"That woman must think my intelligence as weak as her own," she fumed. "Ran off into the woods, indeed! With a houseful of people to stop her! If she ran anywhere, it would be to us."

Walter reached for his crossbow, then remembered he had left it in the portress's lodge. He looked incomplete without it.

"I will ride for Anseau of Trainel," he offered. "Between us, we can get enough men together to take the keep or certainly frighten them into giving her up."

Héloïse looked at him sadly.

"That is not acceptable, not yet, anyway," she said. "There has been too much violence done already, to Alys and to Paciana, and, of course, poor Brother Baldwin. I won't risk Catherine, also. There must be a way to get her back without more bloodshed."

"God forgive me," Edgar said. "I had forgotten Paciana. Does she still live?"

"Yes, *Deo gratia*," Héloïse said. "Sister Melisande believes she'll recover fully."

"Has she named those who attacked her?"

Héloïse shook her head. "No, she refuses to, but I am sure she knows who they were. Perhaps, for Catherine's sake, she might."

"If she wouldn't for her own sister, why for Catherine?" Walter asked. "Paciana cares more for her damned silence than the lives of those she loves."

"Walter," Héloïse said gently. "It's not your place to judge her."

Edgar was losing patience.

"That doesn't matter now," he said. "We have to find Catherine before they kill her."

If they haven't already, everyone added silently. But no one dared say it aloud.

"My lady abbess," Edgar said. "May I have the loan of one of your mules? Or, better, a horse in its declining years? Something humble, befitting a poor trader with few wares."

"Most of our animals are in that condition," Héloïse told him. "You may take your choice."

"They won't allow a peddler as far as the women's rooms," Walter said. "And, if you try to sneak up there, they're sure to slit your throat, if not worse."

"I know that," Edgar said. "I only want to get an idea of where everything is, how secure the watch, and how many people are there. I'll go at first light tomorrow, then come back and report.

"And if I am discovered," he added, "the rest doesn't
matter. If Catherine is . . . dead, then I might as well be,
too."

He closed his eyes. In France they might leap into tears
for any reason, but his father thought this showed weakness. "Only weep before God, son," he had told Edgar.
"Never in front of mere men." Edgar swallowed hard and
then exhaled. He rose and put on his cloak.

"Where are you going?" Walter asked.

"To the woodpile," he said. "I need a few blocks of pine
or other soft wood. May I take what I need?"

"You may have every piece of it, if it will help to find
Catherine," Héloïse said.

Curious, Walter followed Edgar out.

"Not enough to construct a siege engine," he said. "Do
you intend to burn down the keep?"

Edgar was busy examining the logs, peeling away the
bark with his knife, testing them for insects. The wood had
to be dry, but not decaying. The work would be crude, he
knew, but, if he could keep at it all night, he would have
two or three pieces of sufficient quality.

At last he found two pieces that satisfied him. He took
them over to the guesthouse and, planting himself on the
stool outside the door, started carving.

Walter watched in amusement.

"I've seen you doing that before," he said. "All that
whittling, does it help you to think better?"

"No," Edgar answered, his eyes on the wood. "Well,
yes, it does. But that's not why I'm doing it. If I'm going
to be a peddler, I need something to peddle."

Walter crouched to get a better look.

"I don't think a few bits of scraped pine will get you
admitted to the keep," he began.

Then his jaw dropped in amazement. The block in Edgar's hands was transforming under the action of his knife.
Shapes were appearing in the grain, a leaf, a snake, the
head of a swan. Quickly, he crossed himself.

"Love does work miracles," he breathed. "You
shouldn't be able to do that."

Edgar scowled. "I know it; I've been told so often

enough. It's not fit work for a descendent of the kings of England. But I can't see a bit of wood or bone or a block of stone without wanting to release the beauty hidden inside. And I feel the same way about a well-crafted machine, like that iron mill. Are you going to laugh at me now, refuse to be seen with me?"

Walter shook his head, looking at Edgar's fingers move so swiftly and carefully over the pine. He held up his own huge hands, wrists and arms distorted with muscles developed during a lifetime of training in battle. He could no more carve a design than he could hold a pen.

"You are a strange man," he conceded. "And this is craftsman's work, not fit for a lord. But it is marvelous, indeed, to watch you. I'm not inclined to laugh."

"Thank you," Edgar said. "Now would you mind moving out of the light? I have much to do."

The horse they found him was perfect, swaybacked and spavined. It had been donated to the convent by a knight who had overloaded it with armor and other gear for too many years. The poor thing was so patient and pathetic that Prioress Astane hadn't had the heart to refuse the gift, although the animal ate far more than it could produce by its labor.

"Will he take my weight?" Edgar asked.

"Assuredly," Walter said. "But you might get there faster if you led him."

"Right." Edgar tied the pack onto its back. It was light enough not to burden the horse unduly; a change of clothes, a warm cloak with a few holes, borrowed from one of the brothers, his cup, bowl and spoon and knife and the trinkets he had made. He had tried a cross like the one he had given Catherine, but that took too long, so he decided to settle for hair combs and a couple of long stirring spoons. They wouldn't get him past the kitchen, maybe not even past the courtyard, but that should be enough.

"If you don't return by this evening," Héloïse warned him, "I shall go myself to Quincy and search every corner, whatever protestations Rupert and Constanza make. We must have both you and Catherine back."

"Don't worry," Edgar told her, "I will find her."

Despite his fears, as he set off Edgar couldn't help feeling a bit like one of those knights in disguise that the travelling minstrels told about. Off to rescue the princess locked in the tower. The feeling lasted until the first bend in the road. After all, the knights always had a magic talisman, a sword or shield or a horn to summon help. They could slash their way up staircases and leap from tower windows, the lady in their arms.

He would have been happy to do all those things for Catherine, but he was too logical not to realize that such adventures belonged only in winter tales. In real life, the knight rarely got his lady and the rescuer was skewered before he reached the tower.

So he and the horse plodded the three miles to Quincy, nervously fording the river Ardusson, now high with spring rains, arriving an hour later at the keep of Rupert and Constanza.

There seemed to be nothing out of the ordinary there. A few people lounged in the courtyard, others came and went about their duties. Edgar saw no sign of a frantic search for a delirious woman, or of any alarm at the idea of possibly infectious illness about.

"I'm not too late," he told himself. "She's in there. She's alive. She must be."

There was a maid crossing the courtyard with a basket of *maslin*, mixed wheat and rye for feeding the geese. Edgar approached her.

"*Diex te saut,*" he greeted her. "Would there be any in this place needing a lovely new comb, or a fine spoon, the handle smooth and polished?"

The woman stopped. Edgar held up one of the combs. She took it from him with her free hand and turned it over.

"It's good workmanship," she said. "And the pattern one I've never seen. Wait here until I've given the geese their meal and I'll have a look. That is, if your price is not too dear."

"Half a penny of Provins," Edgar said, then seeing her hesitate, "or a hot meal and some oats for my horse."

The maid regarded the horse and laughed.

"He's not worth feeding oats to," she said. "But we can argue it later."

She looked over his shoulder. Edgar turned. There were some other women, taking baskets of linen down to the river.

"You might show them your wares," she suggested. "When they've finished spreading out the clothes."

Edgar followed the women down to the bank, where they rinsed the soapy clothes in the river and then spread them out on the grass to dry. He waited, watching idly until he noticed a pair of short grey *braies* being shaken out. Next to them was laid a *chainse* in light wool, a large brown stain not wholly removed, and finally a *bliaut* of convent grey. Stumbling, he walked toward them.

"I'm too late," he whispered. "They've killed her."

There was a tap on his shoulder. He swung around, ready to strike whoever it was with all his might.

A woman stared up at him, pretty, blonde, with dimples and sad eyes.

"What do you want here?" she asked.

Numbly Edgar handed her a comb. The woman examined it.

"A beautiful design," she said. "And unusual. I've only seen it once before. A guest of the lady here wears a cross with leaves and birds twined on it just like this. How much?"

"What?" Edgar said. He felt his body jerked from despair to hope so quickly that his thoughts couldn't maintain the transition.

"How much for the comb with the design like the one my lady's guest is wearing now," the woman spoke very slowly. "Keep your face still, and for heaven's sake don't hug me. You're her husband, aren't you? My sister told me he was the palest man she had ever seen."

"Everyone here says that," Edgar said. "She's alive?"

Samonie bit her lip.

"Just," she said. "Constanza is starving her. If you have a plan, I will help you."

"If I come back later in the day, will you let me in and give me a bed for the night?" Edgar asked.

"Yes, but you won't be allowed near her," Samonie told him.

Edgar knew that. There must be a way. He looked around wildly. Two of the women were anchoring bed linens with rocks to keep them from blowing away. He had an idea. Not exactly the sort of disguise a knight would choose, but, after all, he was just a simple wood-carver and philosopher.

"Can you leave the bed linens in a pile somewhere near the stairs tonight," he asked.

Samonie looked puzzled. "I suppose I can see to it," she said. "They are usually left in the washhouse until we put them through the mangle, but I could think of a reason."

"Thank you," Edgar said. "Now, how many sleep in the room where Catherine is being held?"

"Lady Constanza is up there now, since her husband is in their bed, recovering from his accident." Samonie counted on her fingers. "Me, two other maids. But I think one of them has planned a tryst for tonight. We haven't had many visitors since Lady Constanza's daughter was killed."

"Good. I'll be back before sundown. Here, take the comb. A gift."

Edgar took the reins of his horse, who had followed him down to the river with great docility. It would have been nice to leap into the saddle and gallop off, but Edgar settled for wading back across the river, dodging the flowing linen, and practically dragging the poor animal back to the Paraclete.

He did hug Sister Thecla, whirling her around until the old woman slapped him and told him not to act insane.

"She's alive!" he shouted.

"Deo gratiae," Thecla murmured. "Where is she?"

"Still in the keep," Edgar sobered. "And very weak, I fear. I have a plan to free her tonight. Will one of the lay sisters loan me some clothes?"

He explained. Thecla nodded slowly.

"It might work," she said. "Rub dirt on your face or, better, ashes, to make yourself look older. And you'll have to stoop. You're too tall. In the dark, one would think your hair already grey. But still, what reason could you give for being about after dark?"

"I hope to go up after the torches are lit but before the household retires and the gates are locked," Edgar said. "The laundresses are all women from the village. It shouldn't seem too odd for one of them to be seen leaving with a bundle."

"I think we should discuss this with the abbess," Thecla said. "Perhaps it should be one of us who goes. I could be a senile old woman a lot more convincingly than you could."

"Sister!" Edgar was shocked. "I would never let one of you take such a risk."

Thecla looked him up and down.

"You, young man," she said finally, "would have nothing to say about it."

However, Héloïse did.

"It is a kind and brave offer, Sister Thecla," she said. "But, Edgar is the one who should go. If we can teach him to move humbly and to wind his scarf properly, he might be able to get past the guards. Yes, you could do it more easily, but you couldn't carry our poor Catherine out and you couldn't defend her, if necessary.

"And also," she added fondly, "we cannot spare you."

"So, you think it will work?" Edgar asked.

"I think it's the greatest example of sheer folly I've ever heard," Walter said. "Dressing as a woman. How could you even consider it?"

"Didn't Hugh of Crecy disguise himself as a prostitute to get back into his castle when it was under siege?" Edgar asked.

"Yes, but he . . ." Walter caught the amused expression of the abbess and blushed. "I'll tell you the story another time," he promised Edgar. "I withdraw my objection."

"Then, if you will be so kind," Edgar said to Héloïse, "show me how to drape this lovely widow's head scarf."

Catherine had decided to pretend to be worse off than she really was, in order to delude Constanza into watching her less closely. The trouble was, she was a lot worse off than she believed. The Lenten fasting, the rigors of the trip to Troyes, the stay in the forest, the normal loss of blood, added to a week with only a cup of water a day, had left her with little in reserve. She found it easy to hum psalms and wander in her speech. Over and over, a lullaby ran through her head. She hadn't heard it since her sister, Agnes, was a baby. So long ago, when her mother was still alive to the world and to her. The tune was so clear, but she couldn't remember the words.

"Lullay, lullah, lullay, lullah," she sang, half asleep.

She was brought to complete wakefulness by a hard slap in the face.

"Stop making that dreadful noise, you horrid *jael*!"

Constanza stood over her, poised to strike again. Catherine only stared in dull confusion.

"I sang that to Alys," Constanza said in a more normal voice. "I won't have her mocked."

Catherine could feel the marks of each of Constanza's fingers reddening on her cheek. Why should a song have upset her so? The woman had beat and tormented her child, forced her into an unwanted marriage, perhaps killed her. What did a lullaby matter?

Nevertheless, Catherine sang no more.

She could feel the day ending. The light in the room grew dim. Unless, she thought, I'm going blind. They say that happens when you starve.

She was reassured when Samonie came in, bearing the oil lamp.

"There was a peddler here today," she said casually. "I got a comb from him. Do you want to see it?"

"Not really," Catherine answered, thinking of the last time she had braided her hair and how Edgar had held it for her so that it didn't tangle.

"He was an odd-looking fellow," Samonie went on. "Looked as if he'd fallen into a pot of lye and bleached himself."

Catherine turned her head and tried to reach out to the maid for the comb.

"Don't tease me with hope, Samonie," she said. "Hope can break the heart."

"I don't know how much hope I can give you," Samonie told her softly, looking over her shoulder to check for listeners. "His plan is chancy at best. But I would try to stay awake tonight.

"My lady!" she said, quickly tucking the comb under Catherine's head and then turning to face her mistress. "Do you wish me to help you prepare for dinner?"

Constanza swept in, looking unusually pale and tired herself. She snapped orders at Samonie and the other maids and found fault with everything they did.

"I have no idea why I'm bothering," she complained. "Rupert just lies in bed, moaning on about his pain. Really, he was hardly scratched. No one except dreadful people like Marcella ever comes to visit. We haven't had decent entertainment here in months. I swear, as soon as this business is over"—she nodded toward Catherine—"I'm going to spend a month in Paris. I'm going to see what the queen is wearing and hear some new stories and talk with people who don't snivel.

"There, leave me alone!" Constanza pushed the maid away as she tried to adjust her robes. "Are you sure there's been no word from Raynald or his father?"

"Yes, of course, my lady," Samonie answered. "There's been no one at all."

"*Questres!*" Constanza muttered. "They think I don't know what they're up to. Just wait. Well, hurry up! Do you want to eat or not?"

She swept out again, shooing the maids before her.

Catherine felt the comb under her cheek. She twisted until she could see it, tracing the pattern with her eyes, birds, leaves, twisting vines and, yes, here in one corner, or was it just fancy? No, she would believe it. The vines twisted into two letters, a ℭ and an ℰ.

He hadn't believed her lost or dead. He had forgiven her for leaving the convent where he had thought her safe. He wasn't going to let her die abandoned here in the tower. But how could he get up here? There was no safe way.

She had to do what she could. Once again she began working at the rope.

Hours passed. The noises from below were more raucous now. Someone must have ordered another cask of wine opened. That might help Edgar or it might make things worse if he were found above the first floor and challenged by a drunken guard. It was almost full darkness, one star twinkled through the narrow window. There was no one about. She would have to try. It was maddening to think of him so close.

She slid the ropes over her hands and tried to get out of bed. That didn't work. Her head spun so that she couldn't find her footing. She sat on the floor with a thump.

Sister Bertrada always said you had no fortitude, the voices taunted.

Catherine gritted her teeth and began crawling across the floor to the staircase. The rushes crackled under her hands and knees. Her head was hanging. She didn't hear the person enter, didn't realize anyone was there until she ran into the skirts.

She looked up. Looming above her was a tall dark figure with a hood. It held a large bundle in its arms. As her arms gave way and she fell to her elbows, the form bent. She had a glimpse of a face streaked with black. Death had come for her.

"Catherine."

Odd, Death spoke to her in Edgar's voice. Maybe it wasn't so fearsome after all.

"Catherine," he said again. "I'm going to wrap you in this blanket and carry you down. Don't wiggle."

It wasn't as easy as he had planned, making a woman look like a sack of laundry. Edgar threw the blanket over her and tried to lift her to throw over his shoulder. He looked down. Her feet stuck out. He tried to cover them and felt her arm flop loosely down his back. He pulled at one corner and her feet showed again. Edgar sighed. There was nothing for it. He would have to go as fast as he could and pray they met no one.

He started down the staircase.

They made it as far as the Great Hall. Edgar could see

the passageway out into the courtyard. The door had not yet been barred for the night. He hurried out and started down the outer stairs.

"You!" someone shouted. "What have you got there? Halt! Stop at once!"

The voice came from behind him, but now there were stirrings from below. The space from the bottom of the stairs across to the gate seemed a thousand leagues. A man ran up the stairs and faced him.

"Thief! Put that down at once," he commanded.

Catherine was roused by the noise and motion. Still confused as to what was happening, she tried to twist around.

"Catherine! Hold still!" Edgar yelled.

But it was too late. Her foot had connected with the man's chest and he went tumbling backwards into the manure pile next to the keep.

Edgar kept heading down, tensed for the blow from the guard above them. But instead, he heard a cry of anger and intense pain and, as he reached the bottom of the stairs, slippered footsteps followed him.

"Here," Samonie said, reaching for Catherine. "Swing her around, we'll drag her between us."

"What happened to the guard?" Edgar panted as he did as she ordered.

"Hot poker, well aimed," Samonie panted back. "Hurry!"

Each grabbing her about the waist and putting her arms across their shoulders, Edgar and Samonie dragged Catherine through the partially open gate. Behind them, they could hear the cries and rattle of weapons as the keep was aroused to follow them. Once through, Edgar scooped Catherine into his arms and started down the road, staggering a little from his exertions and Catherine's weight. Samonie followed. There was a scrape and a slam as the gateway opened completely and the men-at-arms poured out. Edgar kept going although he knew there was no way he could outrun them. He didn't bother to waste energy looking back as the men of Quincy came after them.

The angry shouts were cut off as the men were suddenly

confronted by a huge apparition, a giant in full armor, crossbow in one hand, sword in the other. It loomed out of the night, the river mist curling around its legs. A second Goliath come to challenge them.

None of the men had thought to bring a slingshot.

The guard, armed only with lances and swords, none of them magic, and not having taken the time to put on mail, backed slowly through the gate. A moment later the bar dropped with a satisfying thud, putting wood and iron between them and the monster.

Slowly, the giant backed toward the river, until it was hidden by the darkness.

The first thing Catherine was aware of as she regained her senses was the sound of deep chuckling from nearby. She raised her head from Edgar's shoulder and beheld the dark demon of Quincy grinning at her.

Walter of Grancy had come to rescue the princess.

Twenty-one

The Paraclete, very early, Sunday, May 5, 1140

A mother who kills her child before the fortieth day shall
do penance for one year. After the quickening, she shall do
penance as a murderess. But it makes a great difference
whether a poor woman does it on account of the difficulty
of supporting the child or a harlot for the sake of
concealing her wickedness.

—Eighth Century
Penitential

*S*ister Thecla was roused from honest sleep by a pounding at the gate. Hastily throwing a scarf over her head, she leaned out the window to inquire who would disturb the peace of the convent at such an hour.

"Open the gate quickly, Sister!" Walter called back in what he thought was a whisper. "We've brought Catherine; she needs you."

A few moments later, Catherine was wrapped up in a bed in the guesthouse with Sister Melisande pouring warm broth into her as quickly as she could be made to swallow.

"Enough," she sputtered finally. "I'm better now. I feel fine, except my left hand. It's numb; I can't move it."

"Oh, I'm sorry, *swete.*" Edgar let go of her hand.

"Héloïse is coming to speak with you," Melisande said. "If you feel up to it."

"Yes, of course." Catherine tried to sit up, but the room swam around her and she let her head fall back on the pillow.

Héloïse entered then. Upon seeing Catherine, her welcoming expression changed to one of firmly controlled fury. She said nothing for a moment, only looked down at Catherine with terrifying eyes as Catherine tried to smile a reassurance.

"I'm fine, Mother," she said. "I wasn't very clever, I'm afraid."

Héloïse bent down and kissed her forehead. When she stood again, the anger was conquered.

"To have you back and safe is quite enough," she told Catherine. "Perhaps we weren't meant to know the secrets of the house of Quincy."

"But I did learn something." Catherine tried to rise once more. "Oh, I hate being dizzy like that! Alys didn't miscarry as a result of a beating. She aborted the child on purpose."

"Are you certain of this?" Héloïse asked.

"I can confirm it," a soft voice interrupted.

Héloïse turned and for the first time noticed the woman standing quietly outside the ring of lamplight.

"Who are you?" she asked. "What do you know of the matter?"

"I am . . . was the servant of Lady Constanza, my lady abbess," Samonie told her. "I was there when Countess Alys miscarried. I mopped up the blood and found the pessary and the bag of herbs. I was the one who hid them," she added to Catherine.

"Do you know why she did this?" Héloïse asked.

Samonie shook her head.

"Had the child quickened?"

Samonie shook her head more decidedly.

"Oh, no, of course not!" she assured the abbess. "Alys would never have done anything after the quickening, no matter what. It was far too early, I'm certain. She wasn't showing at all."

Héloïse nodded, reassured. It was still a terrible thing to be driven to, but at least not a mortal sin.

"Catherine," she said gently. "Do you think Alys died because someone else discovered what she had done?"

"I'm afraid it's possible," Catherine admitted.

Behind her, Walter groaned. His fist thumped the wall. "That bastard! To do that to her and then accuse me. It had to have been Raynald's. She would never have killed a child of mine."

He slumped down onto a bench and buried his face in his hands.

Catherine waited until his weeping subsided. She looked up at Edgar and took his hand again.

"And I fear that Paciana was attacked not only because someone discovered she was still alive, but because she knows who murdered Alys and why."

Héloïse was silent a moment. In the lamplight, Catherine was suddenly aware of the lines around the abbess's eyes and mouth. Lines of worry and responsibility. Catherine felt a wave of guilt. Héloïse had so many cares already and she had only brought her more. It seemed a poor recompense for all the Paraclete had given her.

Finally, Héloïse sighed and straightened.

"I will speak to Paciana in the morning," she said. "No secret is so dark that one should die or let others die to protect it. For now, Sister Thecla, can you find sleeping places for these people?"

"Of course, Lady Abbess," Thecla assured her. "You go on back to sleep. Everything will be fine."

Héloïse half laughed at that likelihood. But she started back to her room. At the door, she stopped and looked at Samonie.

"You've run away from the lady Constanza?" she asked the woman. "Are you a serf?"

"No," Samonie answered indignantly. "I'm freeborn, as was my father and his."

"Good," Héloïse said. "Very good. Then we needn't fear she'll demand your return. Sister Thecla, should anyone else desire admittance tonight, for any reason, call me at once, but don't unbar the gate."

She left. Samonie sat on the bench next to Walter, who had recovered somewhat.

"I wouldn't have gone back anyway," she muttered.

Sister Melisande had been watching Catherine.

"I think you should all go find your places for the night," she told Walter, Samonie and Edgar. "Yes, even you, young man. Catherine needs rest now, not the sort of solicitude you'd provide. I'll give her more broth each time she wakes. You can see her in the morning."

Sister Thecla put Edgar and Walter in the other guest room, Walter promising to be ready to help her keep anyone coming from Quincy from forcing their way in. Thecla took Samonie up to her room over the gate.

"What will you do now?" she asked the maid.

Samonie shrugged, too tired to think.

"I have to feed my children somehow," she said dully. "I suppose I'll have to go and stand outside the mill and grind for the men waiting there with their grain."

If she had thought to shock the old woman, she was disappointed.

"You can't trust those men to pay enough," Thecla said. "It's not like the young lords, who'll give you a brooch you can sell."

It was Samonie's turn to be shocked.

"How would you know of such things?" she demanded. "What were you before you came here?"

Sister Thecla smiled. "I'm convent bred, my dear. My parents gave me to Argenteuil when I was eight years old. But I have listened and heard the tales of many sad lives. Enough to be grateful my mother and father loved me enough to give me to God."

She patted Samonie on the shoulder.

"Come along," she said. "The middle of the Great Silence is no time for such worries. Say your prayers, child. A way will be found for you."

Samonie was too tired to argue. She did as she was told and fell asleep in the middle of a mumbled *nostre pere*.

In the room below, Walter was equally dormant. His snores soon resounded through the building. But Edgar lay awake until the bells for Vigils cut through Walter's blasts. He was beginning to realize the ordeal he had taken on in valuing another person's life more than his own. In the moment when he had thought Catherine dead, he had felt the loss of all hope, all reason. It was something his rational mind loathed and feared. What had he done to himself? How could humans survive such pain?

The bells ended and the lilt of chanting floated from the chapel. Edgar reminded himself that Catherine was fine, sound asleep in the next room. He didn't need to answer those questions tonight. With a long sigh, he closed his eyes and, pulling the blanket over his head, slept.

The next day Héloïse went to see Paciana.

The lay sister was better now, allowed out of bed for short intervals. When she saw the abbess, Paciana signed a request to be allowed to return to work.

"Not yet," Héloïse said. "Sister Melisande will tell you when it's time."

She motioned for Paciana to sit and then stood over her.

Reading the intent in Héloïse's eyes, Paciana set her jaw and folded her hands tightly in her lap.

"Paciana," Héloïse said. "There are many forms of silence. There is the quiet we maintain so that we may better hear the message of Our Lord. There is the silence of good manners, that we might not disturb others. There is the silence of expiation, that we might be constantly forced to recognize our sins."

Paciana's head bowed. Her hands loosened.

"But there is also a silence of fear," Héloïse went on, her voice becoming harsher. "And of selfish cowardice. There is no virtue in that. You came to us for protection. We have given you that. When you had told me of your plight and your fear, I asked nothing more of you. But, because of you, the security of this refuge has been breached and, in trying to discover the reason for the attack on you, Catherine has put her own life in danger."

Paciana looked up again. Her hands moved furiously.

"Yes, I know you didn't ask her to," Héloïse said. "But she cares about you and the other women here, enough to try to find the truth. She cares about your sister, too. Apparently more than you did, when you ran away and left her to her fate."

Paciana's expression at that moment chilled Héloïse. She was smiling. It was the coldest, most bitter, despairing look Héloïse had ever seen outside a mirror. The woman's hands shook as she explained.

"I didn't think they would make her marry him," Paciana signed. "I was stupid. Now it's too late. If you wish, I will leave. But I will say nothing more."

Héloïse stared at her for a long moment.

"When you have recovered, the question of your continuation here will have to be decided in chapter. I am very disappointed in you."

She left the room. Paciana sat on her bed, staring at her fingers until Sister Melisande came to change the dressing on her wound.

Héloïse went back to the guesthouse and was relieved to find Catherine sitting up at last, with a bit more color in her cheeks.

"Paciana refuses to help?" Catherine asked.

"Nothing I say will change her mind," Héloïse sighed. "Has no one come from Quincy?"

"We had no other visitors last night," Sister Thecla said.

"It's very odd that they should let her be taken without some sort of attempt to retrieve her, or at least some explanation as to why she was kept against her will. Perhaps I should send someone there to protest her treatment." Héloïse sat on Catherine's bed and put a hand to her cheek. Catherine felt the misery of the last week fade. She was home.

"Mother, I think we should wait," Catherine said. "I suspect that Constanza has to report to someone else before doing anything more. She may be afraid to tell that person that I got away."

"Perhaps." Héloïse considered. "I think that I may send a formal complaint, though, to their lord. Don't they hold from William of Nevers?"

"I believe so, although Quincy is part of Nogent," Walter answered.

"Lady Abbess," Edgar interrupted. "I was so occupied with Catherine that I forgot to tell you. I think Walter and I have discovered why so many people want the property Alys gave the convent."

"I don't know that I care anymore," Héloïse said. "Let

Raynald or Vauluisant take it all. It's not worth anyone's death. We can survive without it."

"Well, I still care," Catherine said. "What did you find out?"

Edgar told them about the amazing invention of a smelter and forge run on water power. He described the process in loving detail, even the part of the monk, Ferreolus, had yet to solve.

"But when he is able to control the speed of the hammer," Edgar concluded, "then they will have the ability to produce a large amount of high-quality iron and steel with very little labor."

"But why do they need this piece of forest, particularly?" Héloïse asked, intrigued in spite of herself.

"It has a good supply of ore and wood for charcoal. There are even lime pits," Edgar explained. "And, it's not far from the monastery or the river Vanne. It's a perfect setting."

"But it's still not worth the attention of a nobleman like Raynald," Catherine said. "And, as we've said, he could have forced Alys to assign the land somewhere else, if he had wished."

"It may be," Edgar said. "With all the building going on, high-grade iron would command a good price. But you're right. I don't think that's all. There's still a piece missing."

Catherine leaned against his shoulder, going over in her mind all the other pieces, trying to make them form a picture.

"Edgar," she said at last. "When you were at Quincy, did you happen to see Rupert, Constanza's husband?"

"Rupert?" Edgar thought. "I don't know. I can't remember ever seeing him."

"He kept to his bed the whole time I was there. He had had an accident," Catherine said. "Constanza's friend was taunting her for marrying a man who couldn't even keep his seat on a horse."

"Do you think the accident was an encounter with Brother Baldwin's hoe?" Héloïse asked. "But that doesn't

make sense. He was the only one who always knew Paciana was here."

"What?"

"As her stepfather, he gave the permission for her entry," Héloïse explained. "I couldn't let her in without the
consent of her legal guardian."

"But I'm sure Constanza didn't know," Catherine said.
"Why did he tell her Paciana had died?"

"To protect Paciana from Constanza, perhaps? Or to be
sure her property came to Alys without questions?" Edgar
guessed. "He may have believed he would have more control over his wife's daughter than Paciana. But if he knew
she was here all along, why harm her now?"

They all sat in frustrated silence. Finally Héloïse rose.

"Somehow," she said, "we have to find that final piece.
Three people have been killed. I don't think it was merely
for a piece of forest land, no matter how valuable it might
be. There is a deeper secret. When we know that, everything else will come clear."

Walter had come in while she was speaking.

"I'm ready now to return to Quincy and make them tell
me," he offered. "It would be a great pleasure to reduce
the place to rubble."

"I couldn't countenance that," Héloïse told him. "And I
don't think it would help, in any case. The fact that no one
from the keep has come here to protest the abduction of
one of their guests makes it clear that they are mired in
guilt and, perhaps, fear of what we may know."

"Edgar and I won't give up the search," Catherine said.
"Where should we go from here?"

"First, we're going to Paris," Edgar said firmly. "We
certainly will have no luck returning to Troyes and we've
discovered all we can in the forest. I want to find Astrolabe and see if Master Abelard's health has improved. I
want to find Solomon and be sure Eliazar is mending and
learn if the attack on him has anything to do with this."

"As do I," Catherine said.

"And," Edgar added, "I want to visit your father and
give him the opportunity to laugh at my expense for not
having listened to his warnings about marriage."

"You may do that, too," Catherine said coolly. "If you give me the chance one day of letting your parents do the same."

Edgar was dumbfounded.

"But they're in Scotland!" he argued. "No one wants to go to Scotland. Why do you think King David keeps invading England?"

"We don't need to go today," Catherine said. "Just sometime."

Edgar shelved this idea in the back of his mind and hoped it would stay there.

"I agree," Héloise said. "You should go to Paris. As soon as Catherine is strong enough."

She paused.

"If you can," she added, "send me word. Master Abelard is determined to face Abbot Bernard and debate him in Sens. If he does, I would be grateful if you would go with him and report to me everything ... everything that happens."

"Of course," Edgar promised. "Walter? Will you come with us?"

"I have no interest in Paris or debates," Walter said. "I'm going home to see if my land and my horses are being properly cared for. I'm going to bring that family of charcoal burners back with me and see that they are given a house and a plot of land again. Then I'm going to let Raynald of Tonnerre find me."

"Walter," Héloïse cautioned. "What about the Peace of God?"

"Easter's over," Walter said bluntly. "I've done all that should be asked of a Christian knight. My duty on this earth is to maintain order and justice. Running a lance through the gut of Raynald of Tonnerre will be a most fitting way to ensure both those things."

"That's not justice, Walter." Héloïse fixed him with her glare. "That's vengeance, and vengeance belongs to God."

Walter was unmoved. "True enough, but there's nothing in the Bible that keeps me from being His instrument. Thank you for your hospitality. When I get home, I'll send a dozen laying hens to repay you."

He forestalled any further argument by picking up his pack and his crossbow, bowing and leaving.

"And now, my lady abbess, do you have any wisdom for me?"

Héloïse had not forgotten Samonie, but she had not had time to think of a solution to her problem.

"You are welcome to stay here as long as you wish," she told the maid. "You may even become a *conversa*."

Samonie chuckled. "Thank you, no. Hair shirts give me a rash. Anyway, I have three children and what I want most is to be able to have them with me again."

"Come with us to Paris," Catherine told her. "My father knows many people there, even more than he does in Troyes. You saved my life, in spite of the consequences. I will find an honest way for you to live and keep your children. I promise."

"It frightens me to go even farther away from home, but I have no choice but to believe you," Samonie said. "I will come. I would be grateful, should the abbess be sending a message to Countess Mahaut soon, if she would include one for my sister in the kitchen there, telling her where I am."

She appeared neither grateful nor hopeful, but that made Catherine even more determined that this, at least, was one person she could do something for.

Four days later, the barge they had boarded at Nogent arrived at the Gréve, the unloading dock on the right bank of the Seine, upstream from the bridges and tolls of Paris proper. Catherine was still a bit wobbly but the river trip and several good meals had improved her health almost to normal. Edgar was relieved. He seemed to have a habit of returning Catherine to her family in less than perfect condition. Last time she had nearly had her throat slit. This time Catherine simply resembled a blue-eyed wraith. He smiled at her.

She smiled back, wondering what her father would say when he heard what she had been doing. She hoped he had taken the time to have a room set up for them above the counting house. She hadn't brought up the subject with

Edgar but they hadn't had a real bed to themselves alone since Troyes and she, at least, was getting impatient to find one.

Samonie sat and watched them with a sadness that bordered on resentment. Did they have any idea how rare and fortunate they were? She looked across the river to the left bank, where the houses weren't so thick. They had passed the abbey of Saint-Victor a while ago, with its dependent village cuddled against its walls and the field of grain and vines spreading out around it. That wasn't as foreign as this city of Paris, much larger than Troyes, that spilled through old fortifications and stretched itself out fearlessly through the countryside. New faces, new customs, strange accents, men who would think her pretty and alluring for a night or two and then remember they had something else to do; Samonie was sorry she had agreed to come so far from her family.

Catherine could see the roof of her father's house on the other side of the Place de la Gréve. It was a narrow three stories, backed by a court with a small garden and surrounded by a wall. A stream flowed through the property and down to the Seine, giving them fresh water for washing. She hadn't realized how much she loved it until now. She wondered if her father would let them use the curtained wooden tub. She had promised to wash Edgar's hair.

"Catherine, you wait here with Samonie," Edgar said. "I'll find out if it's safe for you to go to the house."

The two women sat on a couple of barrels that had just been unloaded. Samonie looked around nervously.

"Why shouldn't it be safe?" she asked.

"Not that sort of safe," Catherine sighed. "It's a very long story, but my mother is a bit . . . confused. She thinks I'm with the saints. It would be very dangerous to her mind if she saw me alive."

"She thinks you're dead?" Samonie asked. "Can't you just explain to her that it's a mistake?"

Catherine blushed. It was so embarrassing.

"That would be hard," she sighed again. "Mother thinks I've been assumed into heaven. She's built me a shrine."

"But that's blasphemy!" Samonie was horrified.

"No," Catherine said sadly. "It's madness."

She got up and walked along the riverbank. The air was heavy with the smell of blossoms. The fruit trees were in bloom, cherry and apple and almond, planted by the merchants and tradesmen in the long lawns from their houses to the river. She inhaled the scents of her childhood; the brackish, slightly fishy water, the flowers, a faint drift of woodsmoke and pork being turned on an outdoor spit. She heard the cries of the street hawkers, and the slow, dignified chant of the wine caller. As the man came closer, she realized that it was one of her father's workers.

"Let it be known to all that Hubert LeVendeur has opened a fresh barrel of new wine from Burgundy!" The man's voice resonated in the afternoon bustle. "Any who would sample this fine wine, made by the monks of Cîteaux themselves come to the Bluewinged Duck this evening."

The chant began again as the man passed her. It was no one she knew. He father had hired a number of new people in her time at the convent. His business seemed to improve every year. She wondered how many barrels he had bought from the monks and if they were from Vougeot, one of their best wine-producing priories. Oh, it was good to be home!

"Catherine, get down!" Edgar grabbed her elbow and pulled.

"What is it?" she gasped as she sat down with a squish. "Oh, Edgar you've put me in the mud again!"

"It's your mother," he whispered. "Your father warned me. She's on her way home from Saint-Gervais. Over there, see? She's just left the Rue Mariroi and is crossing the Gréve now."

"Where?" Catherine tried to see in the small space Edgar allowed her between the boxes they were hiding behind. "No, that couldn't be. Oh, Mother!"

She didn't look mad. Her clothes and hair were all in place. She didn't scream or foam at the mouth. But Catherine could see the change. Madeleine was wrapped in widow's purple, a long veil wound about her face that flut-

tered behind as she walked across the Gréve, full of carts
and stalls and people. She gave no indication that she saw
any of them. Three times she stopped, guided by some in-
ternal sign, and fell to her knees in prayer. Each time, her
attendant waited a few moments then gently helped her to
her feet. No one else paid her any attention. Everyone had
their own private rituals of devotion. It was ill-bred to notice.

Catherine turned away, her throat burning with shame
and guilt. For a moment Edgar watched the boats pass by
on the river, then he put his arm around her.

"Your father suggests that we go to your Uncle Eliazar,"
he said. "He'll try to come by this evening to see you."

Edgar paused. Was she listening?

"He wants to see you very much," he continued.

"Yes." Catherine tried to brush the mud from her cloak.
"I wonder if Aunt Johannah has soup tonight."

Edgar knew better than to pursue a conversation until
Catherine had collected herself. He got Samonie and their
packs and they walked along the bank, past the walled gar-
dens, to the Grand Pont. Underneath the bridge they could
hear the constant creak of the mills. Once across, they
headed for the Juiverie.

"I just remembered," Catherine said suddenly. "It's Friday afternoon. We have to hurry."

"Oh, that's right," Edgar said as he stepped up his pace.
"I'm surprised Hubert didn't remember."

"What?" Samonie asked.

Edgar hesitated, then told her. "The household we're
going to is Jewish. Their Sabbath starts on Friday."

"Is that all?" Samonie asked. "They'll have the soup
and beans in the ovens and the candles lit in plenty of
time. What are you worried about? Do you think they'll
have chicken with barley?"

Edgar and Catherine stopped so abruptly that Samonie
ran into them.

"What do you know about it?" Catherine demanded.

Samonie rolled her eyes in exasperation. "My family is
from Troyes," she reminded them. "My grandfather tended
vines for Rabbi Solomon, himself. My brother does the

same for his grandson, Rabbi Jacob. A hundred years ago or more, the market day was changed from Saturday to Sunday afternoon so all the craftsmen and traders would be there, especially the wine merchants and the tanners and makers of vellum. I know about *Shabbos*."

She stomped on ahead of them, muttering.

"They're all the same, think the world begins and ends in Paris and the rest of us are all *bricons de champaigne*."

Edgar walked more slowly behind her. He glanced at Catherine, who was trying not to laugh.

"I believe we've been put in our place," she giggled.

"I do hate feeling a fool," he said.

Catherine patted his arm.

"It's all right, dear," she said. "God loves fools, too."

They reached the home of Johannah and Eliazar in plenty of time. Johannah was still in the kitchen, overseeing preparations. One of the servants was putting out the freshly polished silver candlesticks. Solomon greeted them, eyeing Samonie with curiosity and approval.

"If you're going to stay to eat," he told them, "you'll have to sit through all the prayers."

"Is there chicken with barley?" Edgar asked.

"In saffron sauce."

"We'd be honored," Edgar decided. "May we see Eliazar? Is he well enough for visitors?"

"He'll want to see you both," Solomon assured them, still staring at Samonie.

"I would rather wait in the kitchen," Samonie said, glaring back at Solomon.

Catherine explained who she was. More respectfully, Solomon had one of the other maids take her to meet Johannah.

"My uncle will tell you he's fine," Solomon said as he led them up to Eliazar's room. "It was just a robbery, except his purse wasn't cut. Don't believe it when he says he's well. He nearly bled to death. He is mending, but slowly. If we tire him, you can forget about the saffron sauce. Aunt Johannah will feed us only the chicken *boële* with river water."

Catherine's stomach turned. She couldn't think of intestines without remembering the bucket in Troyes.

He knocked softly at the door.

"Come in, come in!" Eliazar said. "Don't fuss, nephew, I'm not dying. Catherine! I'm glad to see you again! So you convinced those nuns to let her go. Good work, boy! Now, tell me the news. What is this about the Christians trying to implicate the brethren of Troyes in a murder?"

He didn't look like a man who had barely escaped death. He was thinner than Catherine remembered, but his color was good. She wasn't surprised that he had already heard about the murder of Lisiard. The merchants they had travelled with must have reached Paris with the story several days ago.

Edgar told him what they knew.

"I don't think it has anything to do with the attack you suffered," he concluded.

"Of course not," Eliazar said. "That was simply some lunatic looking for demons in the shape of men."

"Yes," Edgar said. "Solomon told us about that. Catherine, don't you want to greet your aunt?"

"If you mean, do I want to leave so you can tell them how you really got that bruise, the answer is no," Catherine said.

"You may as well tell us," Solomon said. "You can see she's not leaving."

Briefly, Edgar told them about the man who tried to stick a knife into him and how the gold deflected the blade.

"I was coming from your house at the time," he ended. "I thought there might be a connection."

He avoided Catherine's accusing look.

Eliazar stroked his beard thoughtfully.

"It does sound like the same man," he admitted. "But why? No one would ever believe you one of us."

"Uncle," Catherine said. "Are you and Father doing secret business with Abbot Suger again?"

"Again? Still!" Eliazar threw up his hands. "The man is a whirlwind. You can't believe how quickly his church is progressing. He has sent for artisans from Rome and Spain and even Constantinople, for all I know. But we are discreet, not clandestine. We are doing nothing wrong. There are those who resent us, always. Just as in Troyes, it amuses some to make trouble for us. I am heartily sorry if you have been caught in this spitefulness."

A maid appeared at the door, with a tray of covered dishes.

"It's almost sundown," she told them. "The mistress would like you to join her for Sabbath prayers. She also said to remind you not to tire the master."

"Master!" Eliazar laughed. "Not in this house. Go on, tell Johannah I will eat my dinner and sleep like a good boy."

"There seems to be no connection between this and what happened in Troyes," Catherine said as they went down.

"Probably not," Edgar agreed. "But it does seem strange that so much happens when we're around."

They entered the dining hall just as the candles were being lit. Johannah, hands over her eyes, was reciting the blessing. As they waited for her to finish, Catherine looked around the room. Standing at the other end of the table, watching her with blurred eyes, was her father.

Unmindful of manners, she ran to him. He held her as if he thought she would fly away should he loosen his grip.

"You're so thin, child," he murmured. "Nothing but bones and braids. What have you done to my daughter?" he snarled at Edgar.

"He saved my life, Father," Catherine defended him. "And he loves me."

"I see." Hubert released her and apologized to Johannah for the interruption.

When the prayers had ended and they sat down to eat, Hubert continued. "I understand you have become entangled in the affairs of the Paraclete again."

"It began there," Catherine said. "But it's gone much farther."

"Well, I think you should leave it for now," Hubert told

them. "Your Master Abelard is in enough trouble, without scandal at the convent rubbing off on him."

"What's happened?" Edgar asked. "Has the archbishop of Sens refused to allow him to debate."

"Much worse," Hubert said. "He is permitting it and Abbot Bernard has finally been persuaded to attend. All over Paris people are drawing up sides. And it doesn't help Abelard that one of his strongest supporters is that Italian rabble leader, Arnold."

Catherine's heart sank. Arnold of Brescia had been driven out of Rome only a few months ago for his preaching. He encouraged the communes and the guilds to challenge those in power. A dangerous supporter to have. Even those favorably disposed to Abelard, like Count Thibault, might withdraw if it meant protecting Arnold as well.

Edgar was thinking much the same.

"At first light," he whispered to her as the soup was brought in, "we are going to Sainte-Geneviève. If we can't help Abbess Héloïse find who killed Alys and why, we can at least fulfill our promise to stand by Master Abelard."

Catherine took out her spoon.

"I only hope we have more success there," she said. But her confidence in succeeding in either endeavor was fading quickly.

Twenty-two

Paris, Sainte-Geneviève, Saturday, May 11, 1140

Utique par est sine derogatione personae sententiam impugnare,
nihilque turpius quam cum sententia displicet aut opinio, rodere
nomen auctoris.

It is proper to disagree with the views of a person
without maligning him; nothing is more contemptible
than to smear the name of an author only because
his ideas are not to our liking.

—John of Salisbury,
Metalogicon

The boys moved out of earshot. Catherine and Edgar hurried on to Abelard's rooms near the abbey.

They wove their way through the crowd along the route. Other teachers were giving lessons in everything from basic grammar to astronomy. Their shouting created a cacophony that was almost as bad as that of the street vendors and animals.

Abelard's rooms were, if anything, worse. Men of various ages and habit were crowded around a table, all talking at once. Catherine recognized a few of them. She spotted John, the tall serious Englishman whom she had met the previous autumn. She heard he had gone to study at Chartres, but perhaps he had returned to Paris when master Gilbert de la Porée had resigned as chancellor there and come to Paris to teach. Yes, Gilbert was also in the room, sitting across from Abelard, pounding the table and looking as though he wished it were Abelard's head.

"I never said you were a heretic, Peter," he insisted. "You're a stubborn ass who won't admit that I'm right, but you're no heretic."

Abelard looked better than he had in months. His skin was free of the red patches and his eyes were alive as he returned to the debate. He and Gilbert were back on their old quarrel about *deus* and *divinitas*. Catherine knew she should care deeply about the nature of the Trinity, but at the moment, she could only think of the nature of the person who had killed three other people. What prize could be so great or what secret so dark that one would murder? To her it was more unfathomable than the composition of the universe.

She looked around. There were others she didn't know, a boy of about sixteen who was clearly one of Abelard's uncritical disciples. He sat as close to the master as he dared and hung on his every word and gesture. Sitting in the corner was a stranger of about forty, ascetically thin, in the clothes of a priest, a humble priest, Catherine thought, from a poor country parish. She wondered how he could have wandered into this group. His dark hair was shot with grey and his brown eyes seemed to laugh at her as he caught her watching him. He stood and bowed to her. Astrolabe, sitting next to his father, noticed and came over to introduce them.

"Catherine, Edgar," he said. "This is Canon Arnold, late prior of the Augustinians at Brescia. Master Arnold, Edgar and his wife are students of my father. Catherine also has been a pupil of my mother."

"A rare honor, lady," the man smiled. His Latin rolled out like music. "I shall feel tongue-tied in the presence of such erudition."

Catherine felt a bit tongue-tied, herself. This was the reformer and rabble-rouser who had just been run out of Italy by Pope Innocent? He looked as meek as a newborn kitten.

"Welcome to Paris, Canon Arnold," Edgar said. "Are you here to preach?"

The man smiled. "I had thought to teach for a while," he said. "Some consider it a form of preaching. I also wanted to see my old master. It seems he has also had his share of troubles from the authorities. I'm afraid I haven't helped."

"Abbot Bernard already knew that you and my father were friends," Astrolabe assured him. "His seeing you here last week won't make any difference."

"Abbot Bernard was in Paris?" Catherine said. "I always seem to miss him. I wasn't at the Paraclete yet when he visited the sisters and I've been very few other places since then."

"Then you must come to Sens," Arnold said. "You will have the opportunity to hear him there, since the good abbot wasn't successful in his attempt to persuade Abelard to cancel this debate of theirs."

Edgar's jaw dropped. "Abbot Bernard and Master Abelard met! I would have liked to have heard that conversation."

Astrolabe laughed ruefully. "I'm afraid most of Paris heard my father's side of it. I haven't seen him so angry in years. It only made him more determined to refute Bernard in public."

"What did he say to your father?"

"The abbot explained," Astrolabe said, "in a gentle,

kind, fatherly manner, that Father had made of number of errors in his study of theology. The abbot offered to teach him the orthodox interpretations and assured him that, if he desisted in his heretical teaching and repented, all would be forgiven."

"He didn't!" Catherine and Edgar were stupefied. Catherine shook her head.

"I'm surprised Master Abelard's reaction wasn't heard as far as Rome," she said. "For a man ten years his junior, of the same rank both in society and the Church and far less educated than he, to say anything so condescending . . ."

Catherine stopped. She couldn't imagine an equally insulting event to compare it to.

"You would think the abbot wanted a public debate," Edgar said. "Such condescension would only incense Master Abelard more."

"In my opinion," Arnold said, "Abbot Bernard was astonished by Abelard's response. He's so accustomed to being listened to and obeyed that he finds difference of opinion incomprehensible, and, therefore, heretical."

"That's what I don't understand." Astrolabe rubbed his forehead as if it ached. "Bernard admits that he doesn't understand the subtlety of many of Father's propositions. He's not trained in this sort of disputation. He knows it would be an unequal debate. I'm sure he's only doing this because his friends have convinced him that Father is wrong and only he can refute him."

"But how?" Edgar asked.

"I suspect," Arnold said. "That he intends to stand up and let God speak through him."

"*That* sounds heretical to me," Edgar commented.

"At the very least, somewhat arrogant," Catherine amended.

"This debate will take place the day after the octave of the Pentecost?" Edgar asked.

"Yes, along with the showing of the relics," Astrolabe said. "There's a rumor that the archbishop has received a donation of a piece of another saint and plans to unveil it then, but I don't know which one or from where."

"If it wasn't named it may be nothing special," Edgar said. "No more than a finger or tooth of some local saint to excite curiosity and bring in more donations."

"Personally, I hope it's someone important," Astrolabe said. "I can't imagine anyone coming to Sens just in the hope of being cured by the relics of Saint Saverin and the little they have of Saint Stephen."

Catherine disagreed. "I think that's exactly why most people will be there. I fear that the debate between Master Abelard and Abbot Bernard will be nothing more than an extra entertainment."

"You don't think the master will be given serious consideration?" Edgar asked.

"I don't see how," Catherine said. "If someone with more training, William of Saint-Thierry perhaps, were to debate him, then something might be resolved."

"William has become a white monk at Signy and won't be budged," Astrolabe said. "Also, I think that he fears Father would spin verbal webs around him that he could never cut through."

"But at least they would use the same language, the same rules," Catherine said. "A debate between Master Abelard and Abbot Bernard makes as much sense as one between me and Lady Constanza. There is no point for their thoughts to intersect."

The room was beginning to empty now. Canon Gilbert got up, followed by John.

"Peter," Gilbert pleaded. "You are out of your mind. You can't dispute theology with someone who simply smiles and forgives you for your temerity or tells you to stop analyzing words and look for answers in flowers and rocks."

Abelard stood also.

"I can't let these slanders go unanswered," he replied. "My work is meant to instruct and enlighten, to lead young minds to the questioning that results in wisdom. I won't let all that I've done be lost. Not without fighting for it."

"I wish you well, Peter," the canon sighed. "But I fear

you may only bring more disaster on yourself by forcing the issue."

"So you've said," Abelard answered. "Will you be there, all the same?"

"Assuredly," Gilbert said. "I wouldn't miss it. If you like, you may practice on me. Monday afternoon, at my *schola*?"

"Agreed." They shook hands and Gilbert left with John and two of his other students.

Abelard finally became aware of Catherine and Edgar. He greeted them with enthusiasm, hugging them both.

"Let me see, married a month now," he said. "Are you starting to regret leaving the contemplative life, yet?"

"Not at all, Master," Edgar said. "Although I'm not sure that our honeymoon has been typical."

Abelard grew serious again. "Héloïse wrote me about the death of Brother Baldwin. It was a hideous deed, which shows no fear of God or man. Have you discovered the perpetrators?"

"We think so," Catherine said. "But we have no proof as yet and the men we suspect have powerful friends."

"That is always dangerous," Abelard said. "But it shouldn't keep you from pursuing the truth."

"You've taught us that, if nothing else," Edgar told him warmly.

Abelard suddenly seemed exhausted. The color drained from his face and he swayed, as if dizzy, and sat down again. Astrolabe knelt beside the bench.

"Let me get you some wine, Father," he said. "And your medicine."

"No, I need nothing," Abelard grumbled. "That concoction doesn't work anyway, probably made from cat liver and pigeon droppings; it certainly tastes like it. I'm only tired. Trying to make a hardhead like Gilbert see reason would wear anyone out."

"Yes, of course." Astrolabe was unconvinced. "Why don't we let you rest, Berengar?"

The boy Catherine had noted earlier got up at once. He looked like a puppy being trained to fetch. Catherine half expected him to yip excitedly.

"How may I help?" he asked eagerly.

"Come with us and let my father sleep," Astrolabe told him. "If you like, you can go to the baker's and the wine shop and do some other errands."

"Anything!" Berengar's expression implied he was ready to wade rivers of fire to procure the master's sausage rolls.

Astrolabe gave him some coins and the boy shot off in the direction of the shops. That left only Catherine, Edgar, Astrolabe and Arnold. The Italian also rose to go.

"My support may not be of much use, Master," he told Abelard. "But, if you wish it, I, too, will be at Sens."

"Are you certain, old friend?" Abelard asked him. "At the moment, you are only charged with sedition. Would you add heresy to the arrows your enemies shoot at you?"

Arnold shrugged. "Like you, Master, I am shielded with the armor of truth."

"May it protect us both," Abelard answered.

They left him stretched out on his cot, one arm over his eyes. Astrolabe closed the door softly.

"I don't know if this business is killing him or keeping him alive," he told Catherine and Edgar as they walked back toward the Île. "I think he's having nightmares about the council at Soissons, where they made him burn his own work and recite the creed in public. He'll never let anyone shame him so again."

"That council was the year I was born," Catherine said. "Why are they still pursuing him after so long? All his writing has been done to uphold orthodoxy, not destroy it. The monks of Saint-Gildas tried to poison him in return for his efforts at reform. One would think he'd receive praise instead of censure."

The spring day was clouding over and the wind picking up. There would be rain by nightfall. Edgar put up the hood of his cloak. He decided he was not meant for the life of a *gyrovagus*, wandering from one place to another. He wanted his own table and fire and bed. Abelard had never really known that. Edgar wished he had the courage his master showed, but he was coming to the sad conclusion that he was not a brilliant philosopher, but someone much more ordinary. He put an arm around Catherine to guide her around the obstacles in the road. She never would look where she was going. Her mind was always somewhere else. Would she be happy with an ordinary man?

Catherine fell against him as she stumbled on a brick, fallen from a wall into the street. She smiled at him gratefully.

After that she tried to watch her step, but her thoughts kept chasing down other streets, the crooked streets of Troyes, for instance. A slight man and a larger one, carrying a body. A slight man and a larger one attacking Paciana. Rupert, who hunched over and looked away when one spoke to him and let other men command in his household, could he be brave enough to murder? But why? What did he gain? Or, what did he have to lose?

She tripped again. Thank goodness for Edgar. What he must think of her, clumsy, always stained with mud or ink, or worse. Dragging him into situations that could get them both killed. She was sure that wasn't the life his family had had in mind for him. Could he be happy with someone so maladroit?

As they started across the Petit Pont, Edgar asked, "Astrolabe, where are we going?"

"I'm going to the cathedral school to talk with another of my father's old pupils, who's about to return to the papal curia. I want to see if he will still give us his support. My father has been deeply hurt by the way old friends and students have turned on him. Where are you going?"

"I believe we will go back to the home of Eliazar," Edgar said. "Their Sabbath will be over just after sundown. Merchants hear all the gossip. Perhaps he can give us the information we lack to bring these murders home to Rupert of Quincy."

Catherine squeezed Edgar's arm. All this time, he'd been speculating on the same problem she had. And kept her from absentmindedly walking into the river as well. Now, what could she do for him in return?

"Edgar," she said. "Did you know that Eliazar also has a covered tub in his garden, and next to it a charcoal bra-

zier to heat water? At the convent, Saturday was always
the day to wash hair."

"Really?" he said, quickening the pace. "Well, the best
of luck, Astrolabe. We'll come Monday to hear Master
Abelard and Canon Gilbert debate."

Astrolabe bid them good-bye and headed for the south
end of the Île, where the cathedral school lay. Catherine
and Edgar went on to the Juiverie. Edgar was having almost as much trouble as Catherine watching where he
stepped. All at once, his imagination seemed to have overtaken his common sense. Steam, soap and a curtained tub.
Finally. He imagined Catherine's braids undone. What had
he done to deserve such contentment?

Nothing.

When they reached the house, they found Hubert waiting for them. He greeted them briefly, then came at once
to the point.

"The countess Mahaut wishes to see the both of you,"
he told them.

"The countess?" Catherine said. "But she's in Troyes,
isn't she?"

"Count Thibault has sent word to her that he and King
Louis are returning from Reims and he wishes her to meet
him here," Hubert explained. "Apparently, the countess
has also learned a great deal about your activities. More,
I might add, than anyone has bothered to tell me."

He glared at them both and Edgar felt his bath evaporate under the heat of his anger.

"Abbot Suger has given the countess the house the abbey keeps for his visits to Paris," Hubert continued. "She
would like you to meet with her privately before the evening meal."

"But I have nothing appropriate to wear!" Catherine
moaned, thereby proving she was not entirely alien to
Constanza.

"Samonie and I will find you something," Johannah told
her. "I've discovered that she has been trained to do the
finest embroidery, so I'm sure she can stitch you into a
pair of sleeves."

"I will be there, as well," Hubert told them. "The countess was kind enough to invite us to eat. Agnes is particularly looking forward to it."

"Agnes! I'm so glad," Catherine said. "I didn't know if there would be any way for me to see her, and I've missed her so."

"One reason I am going to see the countess," Hubert said sadly, "is to petition her intercession with the abbess of Tart, that your mother might be admitted there. Your sister has borne the burden of her care too long."

"Tart? Will mother go?" Catherine asked.

"I believe so," Hubert said. "She isn't . . . that is, she'll be happier there. The women will care for her and let her pray whenever she likes. And I can't bind Agnes and your brother's wife to her much longer. They have their own concerns."

"Father, are you sure?"

"Yes," Hubert said. "We have all discussed it. This is for your welfare, too. Remember, as long as she remains, you can't come home."

Catherine paid little attention to the clothes she was being sewn into that evening. Johannah had no children and she was delighted to finally have the chance to bring out her old finery and share it.

"Yellow, I think," Johannah said. "And red. You've been in quiet colors too long, Catherine. Don't you agree, Samonie?"

"Yes, I do," Samonie said decidedly. "If you are going to dine with the countess, you need to stand out."

"I think I stood out quite enough the last time," Catherine shuddered. "I'm surprised she wants to see me again."

"Hold still," Johannah told her, "or we'll stick you. So your sister will be there. Does she look like you?"

"I forgot, you've never met her," Catherine said. "No, Agnes is nothing like me. She looks more like Samonie, pretty and small and much fairer than I am. More like our mother."

Poor Mother! Catherine was quiet again. Agnes had been left with most of the work, not only of caring for Madeleine, but also attending to the duties of the mistress of a household. She was nearly seventeen. She must be eager to have a household of her own. She thought again of Paciana and Alys. What would have happened if Paciana had stayed and married Raynald, as he had wished? Would Alys still be alive? What would have happened if Catherine had remained at the Paraclete as Madeleine had wished? Would her mother be still running the household and Agnes settled in her own home?

Speculations are pointless, Catherine, her voices interrupted. *What will happen is all that matters.*

"There, all finished," Johannah got up from the floor, where she had been kneeling to adjust the length of the *bliaut*. "You look beautiful, my dear. I think I have a gold band to put over the veil. It will rub your forehead a bit, but it will set off your coloring perfectly."

Hubert was waiting impatiently below for them to be ready. Edgar had put on his black *braies* and red *chainse* again. He had not had a chance to shave, but he had washed his face and combed his hair. With his gold chains and black boots, he looked like a courtier again. Hubert raised his eyebrows in approval. The change in Catherine's appearance left him speechless.

"What do you think of your beautiful daughter?" Johannah asked.

Hubert's eyes filled. "You look just like your grandmother," he told her. "I have no higher praise. Now, shall we see if you can reach the countess without falling in a puddle?"

"That may be difficult," Edgar said. "It's starting to rain."

They wrapped up tightly in thick wool cloaks. Catherine sat sideways on the horse in front of Edgar as they crossed the river back to the right bank. Around them, there were others on horseback similarly bundled. As they approached the house, Catherine noted a figure that seemed familiar. She nudged Edgar.

"The man over there, by the gate, just arriving, do you see?"

Edgar nodded. "Yes, I don't know him, though."

"Are you sure?" Catherine said.

The man was still hooded. One servant had taken the reins and another stood beside the horse to assist the man, who dismounted gingerly, moving with obvious pain. He leaned heavily on the servant, who gave him a stick to aid him. Even with that help, it was clear that every step was agony. His right leg dragged as he walked.

"Poor crippled man," Edgar said. "No, I don't recognize him."

"He doesn't deserve your pity," Catherine said. "He wasn't crippled the last time I saw him, but a deep cut from a hoe must take a long time to heal. Edgar, I'm sure that's Rupert of Quincy."

"Rupert? What's he doing here?" Edgar tried to get a better look, but the rain and deepening twilight made it impossible. "Do you think Constanza is with him?"

"She tried to murder me!" Catherine was shocked at the thought of seeing her again. "How could she dare show her face?"

"I don't know," Edgar replied. "But I think we are about to find out."

They entered the courtyard, where an ostler waited to stable the horses of the guests. Edgar dismounted and lifted Catherine down. Hubert had already arrived and was waiting for them in the entry.

"Did you see the man who just entered?" Catherine greeted him.

"The one with the limp?" Hubert said. "Yes. He seems familiar, but I can't place him. Is he a friend of yours?"

Catherine was spared the need to explain by the distraction of a shriek in her ear.

"Is that you, Catherine?" Agnes grinned in disbelief. "Not a spot of ink! You never dressed yourself in that!"

Catherine grinned back in relief. Agnes was as beautiful as ever. She didn't look bowed down by duty or, thank goodness, resentful. She hugged her sister, thinking again of Alys.

"Oh, Agnes," she said. "I'm so glad you're safe."

Agnes returned the hug. "That's a very odd thing for you to say to me. Why shouldn't I be safe?"

"Never mind," Catherine turned to Edgar. "You've

never properly met my sister. Agnes, this is Edgar. We're married now."

"So I heard," Agnes said. "At the convent. You couldn't even have a normal wedding. But I'm glad you're back. I hope you'll be home more, now. I've missed you."

Agnes smiled at Edgar. "I think I remember you," she said. "You look much better without a layer of dust."

"Thank you," Edgar said.

"We're supposed to meet with the countess before dinner," Catherine said. "Do you know where?"

"Of course, I'll show you," Agnes said. "Father, are you coming, too?"

"Yes," Hubert said. "Countess Mahaut seems to think I might have to stand surety for Edgar."

"For me? Why?" Edgar's hand went instinctively to his knife. He suddenly remembered that he was in a foreign country with no kin to defend him.

"That's why you've been summoned. There have been charges brought against you," Hubert told him. "That you and Walter of Grancy abducted two women by force from the keep of Rupert of Quincy."

They had reached the door to the countess's chamber. A guard stood outside, waiting for them to give their names. Catherine ignored him.

"You can't be serious, Father!" she said. "How could Rupert and Constanza have the audacity to make such an accusation? They must know that I'll tell the countess the truth."

Edgar tapped the handle of the knife. "It's very clever, you know, to accuse first those who might incriminate you. It will confuse the issue. What if you do tell the countess that I rescued you? You wouldn't be the first woman to abet her own abduction. What puzzles me is, how do they know me? Someone might have recognized Walter, but I'm a stranger to them. And who told them Catherine was your daughter? Héloïse gave them nothing but her name."

"Countess Mahaut knows who we are," Catherine said. "But she never told Constanza, at least not in my presence."

She had another thought.

"Father, you aren't really worried by this, are you? You know that the countess doesn't believe the charge. Why is she letting them make it?"

"I can't speak for her," Hubert answered. "I only know what her messenger told me. Why don't you ask her, yourself?"

"Very well." Suddenly, Catherine was nervous. She adjusted her headband and smoothed her skirts. "Guard, would you please announce Hubert LeVendeur and his family?"

The door opened and they were led in. The countess Mahaut was seated again with her advisors, Girelme and Father Conon, at a long table. On the far side of the room stood the lady of Quincy. Next to her sat Rupert, his injured leg propped up on a cushioned stool.

"Sieur Hubert," the countess greeted him. "It's good to see you again. Thank you for coming."

Hubert bowed deeply. "I am always at your service, my lady, and that of your husband. You remember my daughters, Catherine and Agnes?"

Both curtseyed to the floor. Catherine wobbled a bit, but Agnes steadied her.

"And I believe you have met my son-in-law, Edgar," Hubert continued. Edgar bowed, not quite as deeply.

Out of the corner of her eye, Catherine saw Constanza start. So, their information wasn't complete.

Mahaut acknowledged them all with a nod. She glanced at Girelme, the chamberlain, who rose, holding a piece of parchment.

"The countess wishes to inform you that she is in receipt of a letter from the abbess of the Paraclete," he announced. "Complaining of the treatment of her guest, Catherine LeVendeur, at the hands of Constanza of Quincy. The letter states that it was only through the efforts of Walter of Grancy and Edgar of Wedderlie that Catherine escaped with her life."

"That is a forgery!" Constanza shouted. "Or the good abbess has been taken in by lies. Our home was infiltrated by ruffians, and both dear Catherine, who was still delirious with fever, and my serving maid were viciously abducted. My husband was grievously wounded in the attempt to save them, as you can see."

"Catherine?"

"I was not sick my lady countess," Catherine said. "I was starving. Lady Constanza invited me to her home and then kept me prisoner in the women's rooms. Without the help of the maid and the courage of my husband, I might have died."

"I see," Mahaut said. "Of course, if you were as ill as they say, your memory of the event might be incorrect."

"But I wasn't!" Catherine couldn't understand what was happening.

"You can see, my dear countess,"—Constanza came closer to the table—"that her statement can't be given credence. In her illness she imagined many things. I see now that this is simply a misunderstanding. Although my family has already suffered greatly from the deeds of Walter of Grancy and we intend to continue our search for him, I would be willing to settle this problem without a formal charge. Perhaps if you would allow us to discuss this privately, we might be able to reach an agreement that you could relay to Abbess Héloïse."

Hubert bit his lip. This smacked of extortion. He feared that Constanza and Rupert had learned more about him than his name.

"Lady Countess," he said. "For the sake of peace, I will agree. However, may I request that Agnes also be allowed to leave. This has nothing to do with her."

Agnes faced the table. "My lady, please, let me stay. This is my family. It has everything to do with me."

She went to her father and knelt before him.

"I have always obeyed you, Father," she said. "I have never questioned your decisions. But I am grown now and I have a right to know the truth about us. You trust Catherine. You have a secret that has driven my mother to the refuge of the saints. She weeps about it constantly. Should I weep, too? At least, give me the right to decide."

Hubert drew her up into his arms.

"Forgive me," he whispered, his voice fearful. "You may stay and listen and I pray you will understand."

Countess Mahaut stood. "I will allow you a few minutes to come to a peaceful settlement. But I warn you, my guards will be just outside the door."

Her chaplain and chamberlain preceded her. As she went through the doorway, the countess looked back. Her expression was warning enough.

When she had gone, Hubert turned and faced Constanza, who moved forward, leaving her husband in the shadows.

She laughed at him.

"We know who you really are, Hubert," she said. "And we plan to tell the countess so that she knows that your word and that of your family is not to be trusted. You were born in Rouen, the son of a Jew. A benevolent Christian took pity on you and had you baptized and taught the True Faith. But we also know that you have spit on your benefactors and returned to your old beliefs like a dog to its vomit."

"No," Agnes said. "That's a horrible lie. Tell her, Father. She has no right to defame us so!"

Twenty-three

A few seconds later, no one has moved

What is more against reason than, by reason,
to transcend reason?

—Bernard of Clairvaux,
Letter CXC

*H*ubert shook his head. "Later, my child."

Agnes said nothing more but took Catherine's hand, holding it so tightly that her nails sliced into her sister's palm.

If Constanza had counted on Hubert to react with fear or anger, she was disappointed. He only watched her.

"Well," she goaded. "Have you no response?"

Finally Hubert spoke. "Of my birth and my baptism, you may have proof. But you will find no one who will swear to my ever having been anything but a good Christian. Of course, in my business, I would prefer my parentage were not known, but it isn't that much of a detriment. However, I don't think it is your intention to expose my past. If your desire were to save the countess from contamination by apostates, you would have told her immediately. What do you want?"

Constanza lifted her chin. "We want only to give you the opportunity of confessing privately, repenting your wickedness and returning to the True Faith."

Catherine opened her mouth. She had a few similar sug-

gestions for Constanza. Hubert forestalled her. His voice
was still even, unconcerned.

"I see," he said. "I am astounded by your charity.
Surely there is something else you desire? Our silence,
perhaps, for yours?"

Constanza smiled. Then out of the shadow, Rupert
spoke.

"What have we to fear from you?" he said. "You have
nothing to keep silent about. We have already explained
how your daughter was taken by a fever while in our care.
Her ramblings must have deluded the simple maid who
sent word that she was being held captive. If her husband
had only come and asked for her, instead of entering the
house in disguise and stealing her away, all would have
been made clear."

Edgar had a sudden remembrance of Catherine crawling
desperately across the room in the keep. His hand went
again to his knife.

"For what you have done to my daughter," Hubert said,
his voice for the first time showing his anger, "you will
pay, either here or later. But I am more concerned with
what you did to two innocent men and, even more despic-
ably, to your own daughter."

"That's not true," Constanza snapped. "She was alive
when she left us. Walter of Grancy killed her."

"Constanza!" Rupert's warning was cold as steel. He
addressed Hubert. "We have proof of your perfidy, Hubert
of Rouen. You have nothing but speculation and wild as-
sumptions about us."

Edgar longed to yank the man out of his chair and into
the light, but he saw, as Hubert did, that to give in to anger
would be to admit defeat. He stepped to the edge of the
darkness and spoke directly to Rupert.

"Walter of Grancy is willing to face you and Raynald of
Tonnerre in open court to deny that he is responsible for
the death of your stepdaughter," he said. "Do you have the
courage to refute him?"

Rupert indicated his injured leg.

"I am hardly able to meet Walter in combat, but

Raynald will do so, gladly. I will swear any oath you like, before anyone you name, that I did not kill Alys."

"And what of your charges against my father-in-law?" Edgar continued. "Are you prepared to show your proof?"

Rupert smiled. "I might consider waiting before making them public. Perhaps Sieur Hubert has kept to the faith, after all. I should give him time to demonstrate his belief."

Edgar moved back to stand next to Hubert.

"Things are different here in France," he said casually. "At home, if a man came to my father with such lies, he would find his tongue in the next day's soup."

"A fascinating custom," Rupert responded. "I would be interested in continuing the comparison of our countries over dinner."

He reached for his crutch. "Countess Mahaut will be happy to learn that we have agreed to settle the matter between ourselves," he said. "As for Walter, if he dares show his face, we will meet him in Sens. Raynald and his father plan to attend the display of the relics. We leave Paris the day after Pentecost. Constanza, help me up."

Constanza hurried over to obey him. Until that moment Catherine had been unaware of the pressure of her sister's fingers. Now the pain hit. She pulled her hand free and held it up.

There were three thin red slices in her palm where Agnes's nails had dug in. Catherine showed her. Agnes looked without seeing.

"It's not true, is it?" she asked. "You wouldn't have kept such a thing from me?"

Catherine looked away. "I only learned of it last year," she said. "It wasn't my place to tell you."

Agnes held her arms across her stomach.

"I can't stay here," she said. "I'm going to be sick."

She rushed from the room, passing the guards, and down the staircase, nearly running into the knight, Jehan, who reached out to stop her.

"Agnes! What is it?" he called after her.

He saw Catherine at the top of the stairs.

"What have you done this time, *lisse*?" he demanded. "Is no one safe from you?"

Catherine paid no attention to him, but ran down the stairs after Agnes. Hubert and Edgar followed close behind.

Jehan looked after them, then continued up. He reached the council room just as Rupert and Constanza left.

"Countess Mahaut has sent me to tell you that the bell has rung for dinner," the knight said, ashamed to have been sent on such a servile mission. "She hopes all of you will be able to join her."

Rupert thanked him with a self-deprecating bow. "We are grateful for her consideration, and yours," he said. "My wife and I will be pleased to dine in her company. As for Sieur Hubert and his family, I fear they have become suddenly indisposed. We shall inform the countess that they will be unable to attend."

Lord Rupert spoke mildly and with humility. But for some reason, Jehan felt a shiver at the back of his neck and had a strong urge to make the sign of the cross, putting it between himself and this poor limping man.

Agnes ran past all the guards and the other guests, out across the court into the rainsoaked street. Catherine ran after her. She caught Agnes at the corner, leaning against the stone wall, retching her stomach empty. Catherine held the veil away from her face.

"Please Agnes, you mustn't react so," she said. "This doesn't change anything, not who you are or who Father is."

"How can you say that?" Agnes wept. She coughed and gagged again. "It changes everything. No wonder Mother feels she must do so much penance. I don't see how she can bear it!"

Catherine grabbed her sister's shoulders.

"Agnes," she said fiercely, keeping her voice low. "Father is a Christian, as much as he can be. So are you, as much as you wish to be. There is no disease hiding in you. His parents weren't lepers; they were Jews. And do you know how his mother, *our grandmother*, died? She was murdered by noble crusaders who couldn't wait until the Holy Land to start killing the infidel."

Agnes pushed Catherine away. She wiped her mouth on the sleeve of her *bliaut*.

"I don't want to hear it," she said. "You always have some fine talk to make sunshine seem moonlight and wrong right. If Father feels no shame about his birth, then why has he kept it secret?"

"I did it for you, Agnes." Hubert had stopped long enough to get her cloak. He wrapped it around her and held her in it. "I kept silence for you and Catherine and Guillaume and your children and theirs, that there would be no stigma on them in this Christian land. But I could not abandon my brothers, either. I tried to balance myself between the worlds. I'm sorry, Agnes. I wanted to protect you."

Agnes stood stiffly in the circle of his arms.

"I don't want to be protected with lies, Father," she said. "Take me home."

She broke away from him and walked away toward the stable. Hubert watched helplessly.

"Maybe I am cursed," he sighed. "Edgar, Catherine is soaked. Will you take her back to Eliazar's? I'll come as soon as I can. Tomorrow, or the next day, when Agnes is better."

He didn't wait for an answer.

Catherine stood in the rain, ringlets plastered against her cheeks.

"I don't know how to help her," she said to Edgar. "It was different for me. Father took me travelling with him; Solomon and I played together even though I didn't know we were cousins. Mother always insisted that Agnes stay with her. She never knew Jews as people. Even when I went to the Paraclete, there were no sermons about those who crucified Our Lord, only the glory of the Resurrection. Abelard and Héloïse have great respect for the Jews. Héloïse was teaching me the rudiments of Hebrew. I was better prepared to accept this. Agnes had no warning."

"I had no warning, either," Edgar said. "But I've accustomed myself to it. I like Solomon and your aunt and uncle. Agnes will, too, if she allows herself to. Come along, Catherine, before you freeze."

They arrived at the Juiverie, dripping and miserable.
Johannah bustled around, getting dry robes and warm
drinks, all the while clucking under her breath at their
story.

"The poor child!" she said, when she had settled them.
"I hope Hubert can comfort her; I only wish I could."

"She needs you now," Catherine agreed. "I only wish I
knew how Rupert and Constanza found out about Father."

"They live part of the time in Troyes, don't they?"
Johannah asked. "The brethren there all know Hubert,
though I can't imagine one who would betray him."

"I can." Solomon had heard them return and had come
down from Eliazar's room. "Joseph ben Meïr. His talk
about staying away from the Christians has more fear to it
than piety. If he were paid enough or threatened enough,
he'd betray us all."

"But would he have gone to Rupert on his own and told
what he knew?" Edgar wasn't convinced.

Solomon frowned. "I can't see him doing that. It would
be too big a risk."

Catherine raised her face from her steaming wine pos-
set.

"It was the deacon," she said.

"What deacon?" Johannah asked.

"Peter of Baschi," she said. "I can't prove it, but I'm
sure it was he who told Rupert. He's clearly a man with no
principles. He borrowed money from Héloïse and didn't
repay it. He borrowed from Joseph. He was in the mob
that captured the butcher and spoke up for his accusers. He
dresses above his station and far too luxuriously for a deacon. He's the sort who uncovers secrets. He's tall and
broad in the shoulder. He might be strong enough to hang
a body like a slaughtered sheep."

"Why would he murder Lisiard?" Solomon asked. "Or
attack Paciana? All we know of him now is that he's venal
enough to steal from nuns."

Catherine had no answer to that, but she was certain she
was right. There was something about Peter of Baschi that
reminded her of Rupert. Both of them were the sort who

deferred to others so that they could walk behind softly, with a knife.

The cup nearly dropped from her fingers. Johannah took it and set in on the table.

"You can do nothing tonight," she told them. "You are tired and sad. As soon as the sun set, I had your room prepared. It's just a corner and you'll have to share it with boxes of spices and bolts of silk, but it's quiet."

She kissed Catherine and patted Edgar's cheek.

"May the Holy One keep you through the night," she said.

The mingled scents of myrrh and sandalwood, combined with a dozen other spices, filled the room.

"I feel as if we've been put in a reliquary," Catherine said as she snuggled into the feather bed.

Edgar blew out the candle and climbed in beside her. "I hope that doesn't mean you're going to pray all night."

Catherine rolled over to face him. She knew just where her cheek would fit against his collarbone, his chin resting on the top of her head, his arm across her back. She had already memorized the curve of his spine, the smoothness of his skin. It was odd how something so new could have become indispensable to her life. She twisted her head to kiss the underside of his chin. He lowered his so he could reach her mouth.

"What did you say?" he asked a moment later.

"I said"—she ran her hands down his back—"we can pray in the morning."

Catherine was awakened the next morning by the bells of the Île: Saint-Étienne, Sainte-Marie-Nôtre-Dame, Saint-Denis-du-Pas. They were calling her to Mass. She stretched and rolled over, draping her arm across Edgar's stomach. He opened one eye, then closed it.

"What's wrong?" Catherine asked. *"Defututus es?"*

Edgar opened both eyes wide, eyebrows raised. "Catherine! I'm shocked at you!"

She grinned. "That I've read Catullus?"

"I'm sure they didn't teach that at the Paraclete," he answered. "But no, I'm shocked that you could believe one night could wear me out."

"It was a most energetic night," she said.

"Oh, I see." He reached over her shoulder, took one of her braids and began tickling her with the end of it. "What you mean is, *tu defututa es.*"

"Not at all." Strange, she'd had braids all her life and never thought to do that with them.

"Prove it."

She took the braid from his hand and tossed it over his shoulder, looping it behind his neck so that his face was drawn to hers.

"Libenter," she said. "As often as you like."

The bells had stopped. There were clanks and thumps through the rest of the house that assured them everyone else was up and working. Catherine wasn't inclined to join them. She had never felt so completely relaxed in her life. But, even as she tried to push them away, thoughts of the previous evening and Agnes kept intruding.

"Father should have told us," she muttered. "Keeping secrets like that only makes the pain greater when they're discovered."

"Mmmph?" Edgar said.

"Agnes should have been told about our grandparents," Catherine went on. "There are many converts who are good Christians, even priests. It needn't have made that much difference. And now she's so terribly hurt. She feels betrayed."

"She was," Edgar was awake now. "What could be worse than denying someone the truth of their own ancestry? Didn't you feel so when you found out?"

Catherine searched her feelings. "I think, somehow, a part of me always knew. Solomon and I are so alike. It was upsetting, at first. I didn't know who I was, anymore. But I understood why Father had hidden it from us. And, the day I found out, you were with me."

"That made a difference?"

"Yes."

Edgar had so many possible responses that he made none at all.

"We're back at the old questions," he said finally. "We assume it all began with Alys, because that's where you came in. What if her death were really the end of something much older?"

Catherine thought about it, reordering the known facts in her mind.

"Secrets?" she asked. "It would be logical. Constanza and Rupert seemed very sure Father would do anything to keep his secret from being revealed. Perhaps they thought that he would react as they would."

"Or have," Edgar said.

"It was my finding the abortifacients that frightened Constanza into trying to kill me," Catherine went on. "Everyone says that Alys was docile, obedient. She'd been beaten into submission. Why would she risk so much to rid herself of a child that was presumably her husband's?"

"Perhaps it wasn't," Edgar said. "Maybe she'd been seduced, or even raped."

"But there was no way Raynald could know that, unless he'd been away during the time of conception and no one has suggested that he was. She could have passed the child off as his."

"It's certainly been done before," Edgar agreed.

"I can see why Rupert and Constanza would be furious," Catherine went on. "The property all belonged to Alys, through her father. If she had no children, it would pass to Raynald. They would have no say in it at all."

"Then why would they kill her?" Edgar asked. "I can understand that they would want Paciana out of the way, especially if they think they can profit from using the land. One could become wealthy if this new method of producing iron works. And Paciana had a better claim to that land than Alys. As for Lisiard's death, I suppose he simply found out one piece of gossip too many and Rupert felt he had to silence him. It's the ritual horror of it that I can't comprehend. And I can't understand how the death of Alys would benefit her mother and stepfather. Nor can I fit Deacon Peter into it all."

The sun was shining directly onto the bed. Catherine threw off the quilt and reached for her *chainse*.

"I think you're right," she said. "Alys wasn't the beginning. But she's the center around which all of this turns. I'm sure of that."

"Are we getting up?" Edgar asked sadly.

"We don't want to be accused of the sin of *luxuria*," Catherine said. "We have much work to do. Apart from the problem of Alys and the donation to the Paraclete, apart from Agnes, there are still the accusations against Master Abelard. We promised Mother Héloïse we'd stand by him."

Reluctantly Edgar got out of bed and pulled his *chainse* over his head. He picked his *braies* off the floor.

"Those are all good reasons," he admitted. "But I'm only leaving this bed for one."

"What's that?"

His stomach rumbled, answering for him.

"I'm starving," he said.

Hubert appeared that evening. He slumped into the chair Johannah offered him and took the mug without thanking her. He drained it before speaking.

"Agnes won't listen to me," he said. "She spent all day in the churches with Madeleine. I don't know what to do."

"Will she see me?" Catherine asked.

"I don't know." Hubert poured more wine into his mug. "Not yet, I'm afraid. She's terribly confused and angry. I've never seen her like this. She was my tranquil child."

Catherine winced. Hubert noticed and reached for her hand.

"I never wanted you to be different, Catherine," he told her. "Only more careful."

He sighed. "She told me she wishes I weren't her father. I think she would be relieved if she could believe I weren't."

"She doesn't mean it, Father." Catherine knelt by the chair. "She's only angry. She loves you. She would be devastated if she thought you weren't really her . . ."

Catherine broke off, a sudden light flooding her mind.

"That's it," she said. "I've been so stupid."

"What are you talking about?" Hubert asked.

Catherine stood. "Edgar, we have to get a message to Walter and be sure he's coming to the display at Sens. I think I know why Paciana came to the Paraclete and why Alys risked her life to avoid having Raynald's child. It's so simple. Any kitchen maid with an ear to the door would have figured it out ages ago."

"Catherine, you're babbling again."

"Yes, Father, I know." She kissed him. "I must see Samonie at once. If Rupert killed Lisiard and tried to kill Paciana for what they knew, then her life may be in danger as well. Sometimes gossip isn't as idle as it seems."

Samonie was startled by Catherine's question.

"It's possible," she said. "It never occurred to me. But yes, Lord Rupert was his clerk at the time the lord of Quincy died. I never understood why Lady Constanza married him, a man in minor orders, with no land and no prospects. It makes sense now."

"Might Lisiard have known about it?" Catherine asked.

Samonie shrugged. "Who knows? He loved collecting information. I don't think he put it together, though. If he had discovered something this dangerous, even he would have had the sense to stay quiet. Unless, . . ." She put her hand to her mouth. "Oh, you poor stupid man!"

"Unless what?" Catherine prompted.

"Lisiard wanted to run away with my sister," Samonie said. "They had no money. He might have been foolish enough to try to sell his silence, or his knowledge. Either way, his death would warn anyone else who might think of revealing what they know. Like my sister."

"Would you be willing to stay here until after the council?" Catherine said. "After that, I believe we can depend on Countess Mahaut to find a place for you in Troyes, so you can be with your children. I hope that by then there will no longer be any danger to either you or your sister."

Samonie nodded. "If Dame Johannah is willing, I would be happy to stay here. It's the children I'm worried about. If Rupert and Constanza can't find me, I'm afraid they'll try to harm them."

Catherine hadn't thought of that. The lord and lady of Quincy were quite capable of such infamy.

"They won't have time," she decided. "The display of relics is in less than two weeks. They are in the entourage of the countess and so obligated to be in attendance, especially after Count Thibault arrives. And afterwards, if everything works, they won't be in a position to harm anyone, ever again."

She went to find Edgar.

"Have you found someone who will go to Grancy for Walter?" she asked.

"Your father is sending Solomon," Edgar said.

"That's good. Walter already knows him," Catherine sighed. "Poor Solomon! He does seem to be everyone's errand boy."

"This errand is worth it," Edgar reminded her.

"Yes, if Walter isn't there, to force them all to meet together, I don't see how we'll ever get Constanza to admit the truth."

Edgar took her arm. "Are you sure it is the truth?"

"Yes," Catherine said. "It's the only thing I can think of that would explain everyone's actions. The only thing that hurts me is that the one person most to blame for everything that's happened is the one least likely to suffer."

Twenty-four

The city of Sens,
Feast of Saint Petronilla, virgin and martyr,
Friday, May 31, 1140

*Tu es diaboli janua; tu es divinae legis prima desertrix tu es quae
eum persuasisti, quem diabolus aggredi non valuit.*

[Woman,] you are the devil's door, you are the first
deserter of divine law, you are the one who persuaded
[Adam] whom the devil was not strong enough
to overcome.

—Tertullian

*O nimis infide! Cur sic mentire super me? Exemplaris Adam qui
culpam vertit in Evam!*

Oh, wicked betrayer, why do you lie so about me? You are
the same as Adam who put all the guilt on Eve!

—*Poem of Ruodlieb*
Part VIII 11.35–36

sure that man over there and that woman are currently discussing the possibility of the Holy Spirit having been perceived by Plato as the *anima mundi*."

"Ah, yes," Astrolabe said. "That must be what he's looking for under her skirts. With such serious-minded people in the audience, the meeting on Monday won't be a debate; it will be a debacle."

Looking at the devout or dissolute crowd—actually, everyone he saw seemed a bit of both—Edgar was inclined to agree with Astrolabe. These people couldn't recognize dialectic if it appeared in flames over their heads and weren't likely to be convinced even if it did. On the other hand, Abbot Bernard's clear, emotional exhortations could convert anyone from that legless beggar, dragging himself by on his cart, to the king, himself. Edgar had heard that Queen Eleanor was not yet under the abbot's spell, but she was certainly one of a very few remaining.

Edgar tried to keep his mind on the debate. That, after all, was the larger, more important issue. This business with the Paraclete, the ownership of a stretch of forest and the reason why three people died, these didn't matter when placed beside the eternal issue of faith, reason and truth.

But in reality, he was much more concerned about the meeting with Count Thibault that had been arranged for Saturday morning. Walter of Grancy had arrived the night before with his men, all fully armed and ready to defend his innocence. Raynald was already in Sens with his father, who, as count of Nevers, was required to attend the council. With some badgering from Thibault, the men had agreed to put their differences before his comitial court for judgement. Of course, if the matter weren't settled to their satisfaction, they reserved the right to lay waste each other's land until their need for vengeance had been sated.

"I wouldn't worry, Astrolabe," Edgar said finally, pulling his mind back to Abelard. "The master has spoken under worse circumstances. He's been challenging others in open debate since long before either of us was born. He knows how to lecture hecklers better than anyone. I've watched him."

Astrolabe picked up a handful of pebbles from the road

and began pitching them at a stone water trough nearby. They bounced against it with a sharp *ping!* and then fell back, leaving no mark. He threw them one after another until his hand was empty. Then he stood, wiping the dust off on his tunic.

"My father used to be like that," Astrolabe said wearily. "Nothing they did to him could stop him or change him. Even castration didn't affect who he was. I think Mother was the one who suffered most from that. But they've been throwing stones at him for his entire life. It seems to me that he's covered with chips and cracks. The rash on his skin is a symbol of what's happening inside. If one more thing hits him, even a pebble, he's going to shatter."

Edgar had no comfort to offer for that. He feared it was true. While in Paris, Abelard had seemed his old self. He had enjoyed a spirited argument with Master Gilbert and had taken on the questions of the students in the crowd with enthusiasm and humor. But the atmosphere of Sens, or the weather, which had turned warm and humid, seemed to be sapping his energy. His skin problem had returned and the heat on his wool robes made it worse. The prospect of defending his writings before an indifferent audience may have become less attractive than when he had first proposed it.

"Well, Catherine and I will be there." Edgar stood also. "And the students as well as Master Gilbert and Canon Arnold. And he has other friends; Count Thibault, for instance, has given generously to the Paraclete."

"The count also gave land for the expansion of Clairvaux," Astrolabe said. "There are many who feel kindly disposed to Father, but they also respect the abbot, and some, I think, even fear the censure that might come from opposing him. Bernard is more trusted and honored than the pope."

He took a deep breath. "Never mind. The course is set. And you have your own worries. Will you and Catherine eat supper with me tomorrow? I want to know how everything turns out. I don't care about the bequest to the Paraclete. I do care when the sanctity of my mother's convent is invaded. Can you bring this home to Rupert of Quincy?"

"We are certainly going to try," Edgar said.

He and Catherine had found a place with one of the Jewish families of Sens. Word of the threats against Hubert as well as the attack on Eliazar had spread through all the communities and they were more than willing to help combat this danger to their own.

Although they shared the room with their host and his family, Edgar was not about to complain, knowing how many people were crammed three and four to a bed in the inns. But, even though he tried to ignore it, he did feel out-of-place with these people, even more than with the other French. Perhaps it was because Catherine seemed to fit in with them so well.

When he arrived, the women were laughing at her attempts to pronounce Hebrew.

"Reach farther back in your throat," their hostess, Sarah, teased. "Pretend you're choking and cough the word."

Catherine shook her head. "I fear I might spray it across the room. Edgar! I'm glad you're back. We've been preparing for the Sabbath. Did you see Master Abelard?"

"No, he's resting." Edgar kissed her chastely, aware of all the feminine eyes. "Astrolabe would like us to dine with him tomorrow."

"If we survive the morning," Catherine said lightly. But her eyes were worried. "I hope I haven't made a terrible error in deduction."

"We can't think about that now," Edgar said. "I saw no errors when you explained it to me."

"But this isn't a schoolroom. People's lives are at stake," Catherine fussed.

"If we don't speak, Brother Baldwin and Lisiard and Alys will have died for nothing," Edgar reminded her. "Their killers will be allowed to enjoy the profits of their iniquity. Perhaps they will pay in hell, but, since I don't plan to be there to see it, I find that little comfort."

"Nor do I," Catherine said. "You're right. I only needed you to remind me."

"I promise I'll always be here to do it," Edgar said.

"Now, tell me again all the rituals for eating here. I can never remember."

After discussing the matter, separately, with both Hubert and Constanza and conferring with Héloïse by letter, Countess Mahaut had convinced the count that the fewer people to attend the meeting, the better. Justice was paramount, but it should be achieved without unnecessary scandal. So the meeting took place in a private hall, donated by the archbishop. Walter and Raynald had left their men outside with severe threats about disturbing the peace. Raynald's father, William, came with him. Rupert and Constanza arrived, Rupert having to be carried up the stairs, cursing the men who jolted his leg. Constanza was dressed plainly, in dark colors, as if to remind the count that she was the mother of the victim, not one of the accused.

Catherine and Edgar wore new clothes that had been made for them in Paris. Catherine was in green and gold, with the ivory cross and earrings shaped like gold bells as her only jewelry. Edgar contrived to look vaguely clerical, but wellborn. His gold chain shone richly against his blue tunic.

At the bottom of the steps, Catherine stopped.

"You told my father that you would train for the law," she said to Edgar. "Do you think you're ready to begin?"

"Honestly, I only said that so he'd let me marry you." Edgar looked up the stairs nervously. "I don't think I've the temperament to argue in court."

"But you will," Catherine said, "for Alys and the others?"

"But I will," he answered. "Mostly for you."

They started up.

They had almost reached the top when they heard someone rushing after them.

"Edgar!" Astrolabe was taking the steps two at a time. He was waving a bit of paper. "Here. Mother sent it. I don't know if it will help you."

"What is it?" Edgar took the letter. " 'My beloved son, you and your father are . . .' "

"No, this part"—Astrolabe pointed—"about Deacon Peter."

Edgar read the indicated passage. " 'I have just received a letter from Bishop Hatto telling me that Pope Innocent has, in his great benevolence, and as one who takes notice of even the humblest of his flock, issued an order, commanding that Deacon Peter reimburse the Paraclete the twenty marks of silver that he borrowed. I believe the Holy Father included other instructions for the bishop concerning the deacon's financial activities. . . .' "

"Does that help you?" Astrolabe asked.

"It might," Edgar said. "May I keep this until evening?"

"Of course," Astrolabe said. "May all the saints be with you."

"Thank you." Edgar stowed the paper in his sleeve and, taking Catherine's hand, entered the chamber.

Count Thibault, fresh from dismantling the commune of Reims, was seated on a raised platform. He had no need for advisors. Since André de Baudement had left, he hadn't even bothered with a seneschal. He was past fifty now and had been governing an area larger than all of the territory of the kings of England and France combined since he was little more than a child. He had so much that he had allowed his younger brother, Stephen, to take the throne of England, even though he could have claimed it. Infamous for his violent temper and rapacious behavior, he had been partially tamed in recent years by the sudden loss of five family members in the wreck of the *White Ship* and the influence of a pious wife.

He still intimidated Catherine. She and Edgar went quietly to a bench against the wall. She sat up straight, her hands folded in her lap, and studied the others.

Raynald and his father were on one side. William of Nevers occasionally glanced at Constanza and Rupert, who sat behind them, ready to give their evidence. On the other side of the room, near where Catherine and Edgar had been put, Walter of Grancy stood in solitary confidence.

Despite the lack of a weapon, he seemed completely at ease, even peaceful. He felt Catherine watching him, turned to her and smiled reassuringly.

The count began the proceedings, brushing aside ceremony with a gesture.

"We are here today to seek the truth," he began. "Heinous acts have been committed, the first being the deadly attack on Alys, the wife of Raynald, count of Tonnerre. For this, Walter of Grancy has been charged and will answer the accusation."

Walter said nothing. He merely nodded his agreement.

"I have been persuaded that this attack is connected with two others," Thibault continued, "both of which resulted in murder, but more importantly, which violated the sanctity of a place of God and of my own home. Walter of Grancy has accused Rupert of Quincy and another, unnamed, person in these deeds."

Rupert's cane thumped on the floor, but he made no other response.

"Finally," Thibault said. "Walter has also been accused of aiding in the abduction of a woman who was a guest at Quincy. I understand this charge has been settled by the parties involved, but it was brought to my attention to point out the violent nature of the lord of Grancy.

"Which is rather stupid," he added, "since I've known Walter all his life, as have the rest of you. Now, we have no clerics here today. I don't want your oaths of innocence or offers of trial by hot iron or combat. I want to know what happened, and then I will personally wring the neck of the man who had the effrontery to use my latrine as an abattoir. Is that clear?"

His tone never varied, but Catherine cringed. The old Thibault was not entirely tamed. She wondered again if this meeting were wise, although Countess Mahaut seemed to think it was the best hope for revealing the truth.

As the first injured party, Raynald began by describing how Alys was found in the woods near Tonnerre, beaten and left for dead.

"Where were her guards?" Thibault asked. "She certainly didn't leave Quincy alone."

Raynald pointed dramatically at Walter.

"They were found nearby," he said. "Two had been killed, shot with a crossbow. The other two were severely wounded. Both have since died as a result. They reported that the attacker was a huge man, alone. They believed him to be a demon."

Everyone looked at Walter. It wasn't difficult to imagine.

"It is well known that Walter wished to marry Alys, himself," Raynald went on. "I contend that he tried to abduct her and, when she resisted, he killed her. He said he was nowhere near Quincy, but I can bring witnesses who saw him there. My lord count, I want justice for this atrocity. I want him hanged like the common murderer he is."

In her corner, Constanza sobbed loudly.

Thibault turned to the lord of Grancy.

"Walter," he said. "How do you answer this charge."

"I am innocent," Walter declared. "I would never have touched Alys."

He bit his lip and looked guiltily at Catherine and Edgar.

"I was near Tonnerre that day," he admitted. "Alys had sent word to me that she needed my help. She didn't say why. I came as quickly as I could but I arrived too late. I should have spoken of it sooner; I didn't think anyone would believe me. I suppose, once she was dead, I didn't care. I had nothing to do with her death or anyone else's. I don't need to kill in secret and I was on my way to the Paraclete with Edgar and his wife at the time of the attack there. They are here now and will swear to this. I saw the men who did it and would know them again, if I saw them on horseback. One was wounded in the right thigh, just as Rupert of Quincy is."

Everyone looked at Rupert.

"I received this in an accident near my home," he said, looking more vague and feeble than ever. "I am hardly the sort of man who would take violent action against anyone."

Thibault motioned for Edgar to approach.

"Young man," he said. "I understand you are here on behalf of the Paraclete."

"Yes, my lord count," Edgar answered. "They don't have a formal *advocatus*, so Abbess Héloïse requested that I speak for them. The abbess is concerned, not only by the attack on the Countess Alys and the lay sister, Paciana . . ."

Here Constanza gasped. "She's dead, I tell you! Why must we go through this again? Rupert, you swore to me she was dead!"

"Quiet!" Thibault ordered.

Edgar continued. "There is also the problem of a bequest that the countess left to the convent. Although her husband agreed to it, there is some dispute now as to who has the right to this land. Raynald claims it is his as her survivor. Lady Constanza says it was part of her dower from her first husband. I believe that the value of this property could be considerable, but I have revised my earlier conviction that it would be grounds for murder."

Catherine was, for the moment, so impressed with Edgar's style that she forgot her fears in pure pride. Thibault, however, felt no wifely partiality.

"Then why mention it at all?" he asked.

Edgar swallowed. He was about to throw the thunderbolt. If only it didn't bounce back and strike him.

"After much investigation," he said carefully, "we have come to the conclusion that the countess of Tonnerre had no right to the property in question, either to keep or to dispose of it. She was said to have inherited the land through her father, Gerhard of Quincy."

"If you're going to say it should have been Paciana's, you won't get far," Count William broke in. "Whether she was killed by a fever or entered a convent, it makes no difference. She still renounced all claim to her inheritance."

"I know that, my lord," Edgar said. He wondered if they could tell how fast his heart was beating. "Our assertion is that Alys, countess of Tonnerre, had no right to the property because she was not the daughter of Gerhard of Quincy."

Constanza rose in fury.

"How dare you!" she screamed. "I'll have your head over my hearth for such a slander!"

"Sit down, Constanza," Thibault said. "That is an odious accusation to make, young man. And, I think, almost impossible to prove."

Suddenly Catherine remembered that Thibault had inherited the county of Champagne from his uncle in just such a case. Count Hugh had been presented with a son by his young wife after several doctors had told him he was sterile. Hugh did not believe his wife's statement that God had granted him a miracle, especially since he had been on crusade at the time of conception. He repudiated the wife and had her sent away. The baby was rejected. But there were still people who argued that the boy was the true count, although not in front of Thibault. Catherine hoped the memory of this would dispose the count to listen further.

"Can you prove your accusation?" Thibault asked.

This is where the earth threatened to become a bog beneath their feet. Edgar tried to remember who was patron saint of lawyers. He couldn't, so he just breathed a quick supplication to the Virgin to protect and guide his path.

"Evidence has been found to indicate that all the murders were committed with the sole purpose of hiding the true parentage of the countess Alys," he told the room, trying to sound as assured an orator as Master Abelard. "I would like to request that my wife be allowed to speak, as she is the one who discovered what really happened."

Thibault looked at Catherine, who stood, blushing. Countess Mahaut went over to her husband and whispered something in his ear. Thibault pursed his lips, then nodded.

"Your name?" he asked her.

"Catherine LeVendeur," she answered. "Daughter of Hubert LeVendeur and Madeleine de Boisvert, of Paris."

"Oh, Hubert's girl," he surprised her by saying. "I thought you'd gone to the Paraclete."

"I was there," she said. "I left to be married. I never took my vows. But I was present the night that countess Alys was brought to the convent and I have known the lay sister Paciana for several years. I was also the one," she added, glancing nervously at Rupert, "who discovered the body in your privy."

Thibault's eyebrows raised.

"An unfortunate coincidence?" he asked.

Catherine bowed her head. "No, my lord," she said. "I fear that Lisiard was slaughtered because of what he knew about the family of Quincy. He told me some of it the night he died. I believe he also mentioned it elsewhere and those he gossiped about decided he should be silenced."

"I'm still waiting for proof," Thibault told her.

"If I may beg your indulgence, my lord," Catherine said. "It might help if I explain how I discovered this."

"I haven't forbidden it," Thibault said, with some impatience.

"No, my lord." Catherine reached for Edgar's hand, but he had retreated to let her tell her story. Instead she clasped both hands together, almost in supplication.

"While in Troyes, I observed several things that puzzled me about the family of the countess Alys," she said. "There seemed to be little grief concerning her death. Also, there seemed to be no agreement about the sort of person she was, only that she was timid. I was unhappily present at a confrontation between Count Raynald and Lady Constanza. What they said convinced me that Alys was beaten by someone in her own family, not an outside attacker."

"Lies!" shouted Raynald. "This girl is only seeking to advance her own family in your regard."

"I don't see how," Thibault said. "Continue."

"I told Mother Héloïse what I suspected and she arranged for me to visit Quincy." Catherine noticed that Constanza sat up straighter at the mention of the abbess. "While there, I discovered evidence that Alys did not miscarry as a result of the attack, but before she left Quincy and through her own machinations."

She explained about the herbs, the monkey, and the pessary.

Raynald's jaw was tight and his fists clenched. He turned to Constanza.

"You were supposed to watch her," he muttered. "None of this would have happened if you'd done your job."

Thibault leaned forward, fascinated.

"She aborted the child herself?" he asked. "Whose was it?"

"That's what confused me," Catherine admitted. "Everyone agreed that it had to have been her husband's."

"Oh." Thibault leaned back, disappointed. "Now I'm confused. Why would she get rid of a legitimate heir?"

Catherine braced herself. "I thought about that a long time. Alys hadn't wanted to marry Raynald; it took a number of tortures from her mother to convince her to do so. But once she did, she seems to have been resigned to her duty. And, no matter how much she hated him, having a healthy child could only improve her position. Also, she was very devout. It was her greatest wish to become a nun at the Paraclete. I know that she aborted before the quickening, which isn't as severe a sin, but I still couldn't believe she would do such a thing simply for her own comfort."

She glanced around to be sure Walter was ready to protect her.

"The only reason I could deduce from what I knew, and I didn't believe it until I saw the lady Constanza in Paris, . . ." Catherine looked at Constanza now. She realized with a thrill of horror that all her speculations had been correct. Constanza was glaring at her in pure hate and terror. Catherine paused, trying to keep her voice steady. "The only reason would be if Alys had found out that to have the child would be a greater sin than to kill it."

Raynald leaped to his feet. "I won't listen to this!" he shouted. "The woman is raving! She is spinning lies for some maliciousness of her own."

"Raynald," Thibault said. "I will decide if she is lying. When she is done, you may refute her. Have you finished, Catherine?"

"Almost," Catherine couldn't keep from shaking now. "At first I thought that Alys's mother and stepfather had beaten her when they discovered what she had done. They had. But the maid swears Alys was alive when she left for Tonnerre. That left one possibility."

She face Raynald.

"Alys returned to Tonnerre and told you that she could no longer live with you," Catherine said softly. "I think she was trying to get back to the Paraclete. Your guards weren't out there to protect her, but to help catch her. And when you found her, and she resisted, you hit her, over and over."

She tried to stop the tears, but couldn't. She had to finish.

"When you saw what you had done, you had to dispose of the guards, too." She ended. "Why? Why not let her go? The property she brought to you was nothing."

Raynald started toward her. "You will burn at the bottom of hell for your foul lies," he began.

Suddenly, Constanza stood and lunged at him. Raynald was taken by surprise as her nails raked his face. He managed to push her away. She fell against Catherine, who caught her by the arms.

"You killed my baby!" she shrieked at Raynald. "You cold, arrogant bastard. She wasn't good enough for you, not well enough born! You only married her to help your own schemes, because William wanted you to. You didn't want her any more than she did you and yet you hated her for not respecting your exalted rank. You sneered at her and at me. She was all I had, you filthy beast! I did everything for her."

William, who had heretofore been a silent observer, abruptly stood, strode over to Constanza and slapped her.

"She's hysterical with grief," he said icily. "She'll say anything. I've had enough of this. I will not have my family denounced by persons of inferior birth."

Constanza lifted her head and spit at him.

"Inferior!" She could barely force the words out, her rage was so great. "It was you who thought they should marry. You laughed when I protested. What did you think their children would be, wax copies of you?"

William raised his hand once more. Catherine tried to turn Constanza from the blow.

Walter didn't have his crossbow, but he didn't need it. He caught Count William by the shoulders and lifted him off the floor.

Raynald slowly came forward. He looked at his father, dangling in the air in impotent rage. For the first time, Catherine saw the count of Tonnerre uncertain.

"What is she saying, Father?" he asked. "What have you done to me?"

Catherine pulled Constanza upright, tightening her hold on the woman's arms.

"Tell him," she commanded. "It's too late for lies."

Constanza glared at them all, especially Raynald. Only Catherine's grip kept her from flying at him.

"You think yourself so fine and noble." She tried to laugh but choked on it. "The perfect schemer, arranging everything for your own gain. Well, you are nothing next to your father."

She spat again.

"I married an old man who was going to die and leave me with nothing. I needed a child. You didn't think I was insane then, William. You were so sympathetic and helpful."

The doubt in Raynald's eyes turned to horror.

"Father?" His voice trembled. "She can't be saying that . . ."

"Don't listen to her!" William begged.

But Constanza went on and no one else tried to stop her.

"That's right, you pompous fool!" she shouted. "Alys was William's child, your sister! And he knew it! You married your own blood kin and then murdered her. And may you be cursed for the rest of your life for it!"

Constanza collapsed on the floor and Catherine let her go. She had worked the problem out logically, step by step, and she had been proven correct. But she felt no pride in the victory. She only felt sick.

Walter let William down. He moved away from the count, wiping his hands as if he had touched a leper. Raynald stood still, frozen in horror. Slowly he turned from Constanza to his father. He read the truth in William's face.

"I didn't meant to hurt her so badly." Raynald's voice was numb. "She kept whining that we were horrible sinners and she wouldn't live with me, but she wouldn't say why. I thought it was just spite. I thought she'd killed the baby to torment me because she knew how much I wanted a son."

He faced his father with dead eyes.

"What have you done to me?" he whispered. "How will I ever atone?"

Count Thibault finally roused himself from his stupefaction.

"Count William," he said. "You and your son will withdraw all claim to any property that once belonged to Alys of Quincy, and certainly any charge against Walter of Grancy. Anything that would have come to Alys, I take into my custody until its proper disposal can be arranged. Constanza of Quincy, I order you to give up all property you received from your late husband, including dower rights. I am expelling you from any land under my jurisdiction. I don't care where you go. Rupert of Quincy, you I am going to hang."

The thought seemed to please him very much.

Painfully, Rupert pulled himself up to his feet in outrage.

"You have no proof that I have committed any offense!" he shouted. "Raynald beat my stepdaughter to death. Constanza committed adultery and allowed an incestuous marriage. I have done nothing! But because I'm not well-born, you think you can punish me for their deeds."

"Nothing!" Constanza was hoarse from so much screaming. "You manipulated everything! You forced me to marry you as your price for silence. Yet you were the one who agreed with William that Alys marry Raynald, no matter what I said. You have given me twenty years of hell with your unspeakable habits and your disgusting associates. Hang! You should be torn alive with red-hot pincers! You should be ripped apart by mad dogs. You should . . ."

"That's enough, Constanza," Count Thibault said. "Hanging will do. And don't worry. I already have excellent justification. We have proof that he murdered Lisiard. He was seen and his partner has confessed. I allow no one to commit murder in my house.

"Perhaps," he continued, rubbing his chin in consideration, "perhaps I should eviscerate him, first."

Rupert fainted.

Twenty-five

Sens, an inn near the cathedral, that evening

Attendite ergo ne lucem sensuum vestrorum propriae sententiae amor obnubilet.... Quid plane refert ... si vario tramite ad eandem regionem, ... si multicipli itinere ad eandem quae sursum est Iherusalem pervenitur, quae est mater nostra?

Be careful lest the love of your own opinion covers the light of reason.... What does it matter ... if by various paths to the same region, ... by a number of roads to the same goal, we each continue upward to reach Jerusalem, which is the mother of us all?

—Peter the Venerable, abbot of Cluny,
Letter 111, to Bernard of Clairvaux

$\mathcal{D}$on't mix your wine with so much water, Catherine," Astrolabe suggested. "You haven't stopped shaking, yet."

Catherine put down the water pitcher.

"I know I did what was right," she said. "The truth had to come out. Rupert would have continued removing anyone who threatened him. Raynald would have become wealthy from trading Alys's land to the monks. He would even have been honored for his generosity, which angers me more."

"But . . . ?" Astrolabe prompted.

"You know very well," Catherine answered. "All that ugliness. I feel filthier than when I fell into the canal. Even the look on Raynald's face when he realized what he'd done makes me ill to remember. I never thought I would pity him."

"I don't," Edgar said. "And Walter certainly doesn't. It was only the authority of the count that kept him from cutting Raynald down right there."

"So the feud will continue?"

"I don't know," Edgar answered. "Raynald doesn't seem to have the heart for it anymore."

"And nothing can be done to Count William." Catherine poured a cup for Edgar. "It's a family matter. He's a nobleman. He killed no one. But lowborn Rupert will dangle in the town square."

"I doubt it," Edgar said. "Didn't you smell it as we passed him? That leg is suppurating. He'll die slowly, as Alys did, before they can hang him. I think that's fitting."

"I wonder if we'll ever know how far his nets were spread?" Catherine said.

"It frightens me to consider it," Astrolabe said. "At least Father's enemies strike at him in public, in daylight. By the way, did the information on Peter of Baschi help?"

"It wasn't necessary," Edgar told him, giving back the paper. "The count seems to have already known about a lot of Rupert's dealings. Bishop Hatto sent a message to him at the same time he wrote Héloïse. If Deacon Peter has to pay back all those he borrowed from, without being able to draw on the purses of Rupert's victims, he should be suitably humbled."

"Not enough if he was the one who murdered Lisiard," Catherine said. "And, if that's proven against him, he'll claim the protection of the Church."

"Somehow I don't think Bishop Hatto will allow him to escape punishment," Astrolabe said. "I only wish I knew why they tried to put the blame on the butcher."

"My father is worried about that, too," Catherine said. "He thinks there may be a conspiracy to implicate the Jews in these extortions. He even feared the attack on Eliazer was connected to this."

"Don't start on that," Astrolabe warned her. "You'll be as bad as *my* father. He says that he's never been able to hear of a group of bishops meeting together without fearing they were planning to denounce him."

"But, Astrolabe," Edgar pointed out, "sometimes he was right."

He gingerly rubbed his bruised side. He feared that now he would never know why he and Catherine's uncle had both been stabbed. He sighed. Ignorance was probably just another way God kept him from arrogance.

They were distracted from that line of thought by the bowl of fish stew that had just arrived, and were busy for a time spooning it into the hollows in the bread and eating around the thin bones. Catherine was surprised at how hungry she was. It didn't seem proper, somehow, to be slurping stew when one had just destroyed the lives of three people.

People who had spent years destroying the lives of others, her voices reminded her. Odd how mild they were becoming of late. Perhaps they were being softened the longer she was away from Sister Bertrada. And that reminded her.

"What do you think will happen to the land Alys gave the Paraclete?" she wondered. "Count Thibault won't keep it, will he?"

"Of course not," Edgar said. "I would guess that the bequest will be honored, even if it wasn't Alys's by right. I hope that Abbess Héloïse and Abbot Norpald can come to some agreement on it, though. I'd hate it if Brother Ferreolus were forced to dismantle that amazing iron mill."

"Edgar," Catherine said. "I've never seen anything interest you the way that mill does. You should see your face when you describe it."

Edgar shrugged. "I appreciate the ingenuity of it," he said. "It's beautiful, in its own way, like the sculpture Garnulf did."

Catherine leaned over and wiped the gravy from his chin. Her ivory cross swung over the bread and thumped back against her chest. She touched it, letting her fingers trace the intricate pattern.

"You made this," she charged. "Didn't you?"

Edgar examined a backbone from the stew.

"It's just something I do with my hands," he muttered. "It helps me think."

Catherine studied the cross. "What were you thinking about while you were carving this?"

He looked up and grinned. "You, of course. What do you imagine?"

"I imagine you would be a terrible lawyer," she said. "I think you are a brilliant artisan."

Astrolabe suddenly felt very much the intruder at the table.

"I can't carve wood for a living," Edgar said. "Or build machines. I was born in the wrong rank. It's impossible."

Catherine nodded. "That's true. But, Edgar, you and I are together and that was impossible, too."

Astrolabe felt that the evening was becoming a bit tedious. He finished the last of his stew and put his bread on the tray to be given to the beggars.

"I think I'll go see if Father needs anything," he said.

Catherine and Edgar looked away from each other guiltily.

"I'm sorry," Edgar said. "It's early yet. Please don't go."

"I'm not offended," Astrolabe said. "But both of you are more tired than you realize. You'll need to arrive at the cathedral early tomorrow if you want to get in for Mass."

"Are they going to carry the relics in a procession through town or put them on display in the cathedral, itself?" Catherine asked. "I'm curious about this new acquisition. It seems odd that the name of the saint wasn't announced well in advance."

"Doesn't it?" Astrolabe didn't really care, he was more concerned with the following event. "Well, Henry Sanglier has never been a typical archbishop. Abbot Bernard almost had him excommunicated a few years ago. To answer your question, I believe the relics will be displayed before the altar so that the faithful may pass by and view them from a respectful distance."

"We may not be able to find you in the crowd," Edgar told him. "Shall we meet here again tomorrow evening? Unless you'd rather stay with the students or eat with Master Abelard and the canons."

"I'll be here," Astrolabe said. "The enthusiasm of the students for constant argument wears me out and Father is being well attended to. You two are occasionally obviously and embarrassingly besotted with each other, but in general I enjoy your company."

"Thank you, Astrolabe. We like you, too."

As they got up to leave, Catherine kissed him lightly on the cheek. Edgar did the same.

"Peace to you, Astrolabe," he said.

"Peace to you both," he responded, although they all knew it was a forlorn hope. "Good night."

Sunday, the octave of Pentecost, was brilliantly clear, the sun summer bright in an azure sky. The area around the cathedral was already crowded when Catherine and Edgar arrived, shortly after dawn.

"We'll never find anyone in this," Catherine complained as she was jostled by the shoulders and elbows of pilgrims trying to be first in line when the relics were unveiled. "Edgar, I know I need the comfort of the Mass more than ever today, but I can't face being crushed in with those people. Look, even the poor cripples who've come to be healed are being shoved aside."

Edgar gripped her arm tightly to avoid being separated in the throng. It seemed that they were being sucked toward the cathedral. He set himself against the tide and began pushing their way out.

"There are other churches in Sens," he said. "I imagine they will be nearly empty today. Do you need your Host consecrated by the bishop of Chartres for the sacrament to be valid?"

"Of course not," Catherine grabbed hold of his tunic to keep from being dragged away. "I do want to come back this afternoon to see the relics."

"It won't be any better," Edgar shouted over his shoulder.

"I know," Catherine said. "But I just overheard someone say that the new relic was acquired through a trader from Troyes."

Edgar stopped short. Catherine slammed into him.

"You don't think . . . ?" he said.

"I just want to be there," Catherine answered.

They found a quiet little church south of the center of town, near the river. They never did discover who it was dedicated to. It was ancient, with high, tiny windows. In the wall next to Catherine, the stone head of some Roman god peeked out, indicating the source of the building material. The priest had but one assistant and there were only a few old women and children in attendance. The sermon was read from a book. The priest had trouble making out some of the words. It was cool and quiet there and only intense curiosity coerced Catherine to return to the square of the cathedral.

"Are you sure you want to do this, Catherine?" Edgar asked. "You look a bit pale."

"I'm fine," she told Edgar. "My back hurts a bit, that's all. It's about that time again. I think I'll have to make myself a new pair of *braies* soon. I left the old ones at Quincy."

"Very well, we'll dive into the sea of pilgrims. Just don't let go of me," Edgar said as they plowed back into the mob.

The common people were being kept behind the altar rail. The bishops and the nobles had vied for the honor of carrying out the relics. King Louis, barefoot, had one corner of the reliquary of Saint Savarin and Count Thibault another. The king's long blond hair kept catching on the gold leaf and jewels encrusting the coffin. They set it down carefully and joined their wives, seated at one side of the altar. The bishops and abbots had already brought in the relics of other saints, which were arranged before the altar. Finally Archbishop Henry appeared, carrying a box of wood, adorned with silver filigree. He set it reverently on a table, tilting it so that the lid would open downward, allowing the faithful to see.

"The city of Sens and the cathedral of Saint-Étienne have been exalted by the knowledge that many of the saints have chosen to bless us by their presence and protection," the archbishop said. "Recently, we have been honored by the acquisition of an ancient and holy relic, a victim of the persecution of Diocletian, who before he achieved his crown of martyrdom was put into a cell without food or water and made to lie naked on broken glass."

"And I thought I suffered," Catherine whispered to Edgar, who was standing behind her.

"You did," Edgar said.

He circled her with his arms and rested his chin on the top of her head. She was torn between a feeling of security and the desire to stand on tiptoe to see better.

Archbishop Henry signaled to a deacon, who stood next to the box, his hand on the latch.

"It is proper that this relic be unveiled today," he continued. "We will commemorate his feast tomorrow at High Mass."

Catherine was trying to remember whose feast was June second and who had been made to lie on broken glass. She was beginning to feel back in the classroom. The archbishop was still speaking.

"May we all be inspired by the example of this brave priest, beheaded for the faith, whose miraculously preserved remains have come to bless the city of Sens, Saint Marcellinus."

The lid dropped open. All through the cathedral, people fell to their knees in devotion. As the group in front of her knelt, Catherine leaned forward and saw the relic of the Roman saint.

The head was well preserved. The brown hair and beard looked soft still. The skin was darkened as if by great age, but still intact as one would expect of a saint.

"I'm not going to scream," she told herself. "He looks very peaceful there. And, after all, he was a martyr, of a sort."

"We were right. Can we leave now?" Edgar said.

Catherine nodded. In front of them she heard a man in deacon's robes say to another. "But I thought Saint Marcellinus was in an abbey in Germany."

"A fake," the other answered. "Those Germans are all too gullible."

She couldn't help taking one more look at the head in the reliquary. She hoped Rupert would live long enough to hang for such blasphemy. Poor Lisiard! She couldn't stand to see him there.

As they turned to go, she noticed Count Thibault, who was watching the crowd, not the relic. Countess Mahaut had placed one hand on his shoulder and Catherine was sure that it was only her influence that kept the count from bursting into laughter.

"He knew," she said. "Even before he came here, Edgar. He knew what the relic was!"

"Shh!" Edgar warned. "Not here."

Catherine held her peace until they were out of sight of the cathedral, in a narrow lane in the Juiverie.

"How could they do such a thing!" she gasped. "It was Deacon Peter who arranged the sale, wasn't it? Relics ought not to be bought. It isn't proper. No saint would allow such a thing. I wonder what the archbishop paid."

"Twenty marks of silver, perhaps," Edgar said.

Catherine suddenly felt wobbly. She sank down onto a mounting stone in front of an inn.

"We can't let people venerate the head of a minor knight of Troyes who loved gossip and good food," she said. "I thought Count Thibault was supposed to have reformed."

Edgar patted her head. "Well, it does have its humorous aspects," he said.

Catherine glared up at him.

"Don't worry," he told her. "Countess Mahaut was looking at her husband just as you are at me. My guess is that in a few days, Thibault will tell Henry privately how he's been duped and, at the next display of relics, the head of Saint Marcellinus will not appear."

Catherine sighed. "Well, I suppose it's for the best. This must be the crime that Count Thibault knew he could lay on Rupert, and it's wrong, I know, but I really will sleep better knowing where the head is."

Edgar did laugh then and, after a second, Catherine joined him.

Astrolabe was waiting for them at the inn. He had saved the end of a table.

"Did you enjoy the display of relics?" he asked innocently.

Catherine made a sudden noise at the back of her throat. Astrolabe looked at her in concern.

"Swallowed the wrong way," she explained. "We didn't stay long. The heat was too much. Were there any cures?"

"Not that I saw," Astrolabe said. "But there were a number of donations to the new cathedral. I dropped in a coin, myself, after being trapped against the wall for an hour, unable to move."

"Was your father there?" Edgar asked.

"He thought he should go and help carry the relics, to show his orthodoxy," Astrolabe said. "He has the right. But we convinced him it would be better if he rested. His illness is getting worse."

"Astrolabe,"—Catherine put her hand over his—"would you rather be with him now?"

"We discussed this last night," he smiled. "Father hates the way I fuss over him. He'd rather be with people who think he's invincible. Tonight, that's probably the best thing. He doesn't need my doubts."

"Do you think he'll be well enough to face the abbot tomorrow morning?" Catherine asked.

Astrolabe shrugged. "He'll do it in any case. He feels himself as much a martyr as any Christian in the time of Diocletian. He's been called to preach the truth and he is prepared to face death to do it."

He took a bite of his dinner.

"Do you think this is the same stew they served last night?" he asked with deep suspicion.

"Astrolabe! I'm so glad I found you!"

The water pitcher rocked as the new arrival fell against the table, panting. He seemed familiar to Catherine. Oh, yes, Berengar, the young disciple of Abelard's from Poitiers. He didn't waste time on greetings.

"They're holding a secret meeting tonight, at this very moment!" he announced.

"Who is?"

Catherine had visions of Rupert and Deacon Peter plotting with faceless minions to take revenge on her.

"The bishops, of course," Berengar said. "That flatulent abbot is trying to make them swear to decide in his favor tomorrow."

"Berengar! That's no way to speak of him," Astrolabe

cautioned. "Especially in public. Now, how do you know this?"

"They're all together, at the archbishop's palace, having a feast," Berengar sniffed. "Henry's wine cellar will be empty by midnight with that group."

"Of course they're dining together," Astrolabe said. "They rarely meet and have many matters to discuss. I'm sure they enjoy the chance to exchange views over a meal."

Berengar poured himself a cup of their wine.

"How can you be so trusting?" he said. "Bernard has admitted he is untrained in dialectical argument. He's told people that he fears Master Abelard will simply overpower him with intricate wordplay and that the simple people listening will then doubt the faith. Hmph! What he means is that he's so simple, he can't follow a syllogism. He's going to browbeat the bishops with fears of heresy and revolt until they agree to do whatever he says."

Catherine thought Berengar was overinflating the danger. She couldn't imagine anyone intimidating Geoffrey of Chartres, who was not only bishop, but also the papal legate. And the other bishops were men of good conscience, even those who were decidedly loyal to the Cistercian abbot, like Hugh of Auxerre, who had been one of the original monks to come with Bernard to Cîteaux. She ran through the careers of the other men in her mind.

On the other hand, perhaps it wasn't so foolish.

Astrolabe seemed to agree. He got up from the table, taking his spoon and mug.

"Perhaps, I will go back and worry," he said. "I'll see you in the morning."

Catherine and Edgar finished the stew. It did taste the same as the previous night. The cook had simply added more water and herbs. Catherine's stomach felt strange by the time they left.

"Edgar," she said. "Do you think I'm *malastrue*?"

"What caused that thought?" he asked. "Of course not. If I thought you were cursed, I wouldn't be walking next to you."

"It's only that while I was at the Paraclete, intending to

stay, nothing bad ever happened," she fretted. "Now we just seem to fall from one catastrophe to another."

"Catherine, if you start reasoning like that, you'll end up like your mother," Edgar said sternly. "The world is full of disaster. We don't cause it. Anyway, did you ever consider that God sent us here so that we could put some things right?"

Catherine was quiet for a moment.

"No, I never did," she admitted. "Do you think that's why we always seem to be in the middle of chaos?"

"I don't know," he answered. "But I think that, as long as we are, that's what we should try to do."

The High Mass the next morning was the longest Catherine had ever attended. She could barely endure having to stand through the ritual. Her lower back ached intolerably and her legs throbbed as if she'd been running for days.

I must still be recovering from the ordeal at Quincy, she thought. *Or preparing for a terrible purgation.*

But finally the archbishop turned from the altar to bestow the kiss of peace upon his deacon, who then gave it to the subdeacon and he to his subordinate. Henry faced the crowd, then the king, and gave the final blessing. The last gospel was read.

"Ite," Henry intoned, *"missa est."*

But no one left. It seemed as if everyone in the cathedral held their breath at the same time. Even the candles were still.

Then there was a slight motion from among the white-robed monks standing near the altar screen. A man stepped out from the group.

Catherine had thought he would be taller, at least as tall as Master Abelard. And younger; he looked much older than his fifty years. His was reed-thin, his tonsured circle grey as his robe. Slowly Abbot Bernard mounted the pulpit.

A black-robed figure stepped from the group on the other side of the room. The circle of his tonsure was not as great and there were still dark streaks in his grey hair. Héloïse had seen the sudden aging, but from where she

stood Catherine could only make out the aquiline nose, the
straight back. As he stepped to the front, he paused to
whisper something to Master Gilbert, who started guiltily.
Then, standing before the assembly, outwardly calm,
Abelard waited for Bernard to make the first sortie.

The abbot held up a sheaf of papers, stepping back to
focus at arm's length. He cleared his throat and began.

*"Caput primum: Impia Abelardi de sancta Trinitate
dogmata recenset, et explodit, . . ."*

Abelard opened his mouth to refute the charge that he
misunderstood the nature of the Trinity, but Bernard hadn't
finished.

*"Caput secundum: In Trinitate non esse admittendam
ullam disparitatem, sed ominimodum aequalitatem."*

Catherine wanted to shout at him, *Wait, allow Abelard
to explain. You don't understand! That's not what he said.
You're only giving half-lines, unfinished arguments.* But
the abbot didn't wait.

*"Absurdum dogma Abelardi . . . dicit Abelardus. . . .
Arguit Abelardum."* His mellow voice went on and on.
Most of the people in the church had no idea what accusations were being made. A man not far from Catherine
was leaning against the wall snoring.

But Abelard understood every word. Even more, he understood that, once again, he had been judged and condemned without recourse, without being given the
opportunity to defend his beliefs or his methods. The decision had already been made. He would get no impartial
hearing today.

He strode toward the pulpit. The abbot looked up. Everyone tensed in anticipation.

Abelard stopped in midstride. He put his hand to his
chest as if fending off a blow. He looked down, breathing
quickly, then shook his head as if to clear it. At last he
straightened and stood proudly before the pulpit like the
aristocrat he had been born.

"I will not answer these preordained indictments. You
are not qualified to judge me in this manner. I will take
my case to the pope himself!"

With that he turned on his heel and marched out through the west transept, his startled acolytes at his heels.

The shock within the cathedral lasted a full minute. Then, as if nothing had happened, Abbot Bernard continued reading the charges and asked the bishops to decide if Abelard should be condemned for the stated beliefs.

One by one, the bishops nodded, yes.

Catherine and Edgar couldn't believe what they were seeing. Would no one speak for Abelard? And what difference would the condemnation make if the case were appealed to Rome?

At the first possible moment, King Louis rose, looking bewildered, and, giving his arm to Queen Eleanor, left the cathedral, followed by the people of the court. Thibault and Mahaut went with them, looking equally nonplussed. The bishops finally stood and left through the door to the chapter house.

Catherine and Edgar found themselves outside in the hot afternoon sun, wondering what had just happened. They were not alone. The general opinion was that it had been a poor show. But people seemed to be divided as to its significance.

"Is he a heretic or not?" one woman asked. "I brought eggs to hurl at him if he was."

"Why didn't Bernard let him speak?" someone else whined.

"Why didn't they talk French, like normal people?" another voice complained. "I could tell if it was heresy if they'd just use words I knew."

For most people the matter was best settled sitting down with a mug in one's hand. Slowly, the crowd drifted away, to the open spaces where there were freshly tapped kegs and travelling minstrels. Edgar and Catherine sat on the edge of the water trough wondering what to do.

"Mother Héloïse told us to stay with him," Catherine said at last. "We should go find him."

"I only wish I knew what to say when we do," Edgar said.

"Maybe it will be enough that we're there."

When they entered the house where Abelard was staying, they found themselves swept up in a whirlwind of which the accused, himself, was the calm center. He sat by the window, eyes closed. Berengar screamed hysterically to a circle of believers that it was all a plot and the pope would make them pay; every one of those bishops would be forced to give up his see, and as for Bernard, no humiliation was deep enough.

Canon Arnold was sitting with Master Gilbert. Edgar went up to him and bowed.

"I saw you go," he told the canon. "Perhaps you haven't heard that the council also condemned you today, although I can't understand why."

"To tar poor Master Abelard with a blacker brush," Arnold chuckled. "Don't worry, boy. I deem it an honor to be condemned by the like of those bishops with their fine jewels and furs."

Astrolabe was sitting next to Abelard. When he saw Catherine and Edgar, he came to them and led them back out onto the portico. His eyes were red and he wept without awareness.

"He saw it, that it would happen just like before," Astrolabe told them. "He told me it was as if a dark curtain had been dropped around him. His mind went blank of all but the terror of his words being repudiated once again by those who could see that they were suppressed and forgotten."

His jaw tightened in fury. "I only pray that the man is ignorant of what he's doing. Why can't he see that Father's faith is as deep and orthodox as his own?"

They could give him no answers.

"What will the master do now?" Edgar asked.

"What he said," Astrolabe answered. "He'll go to Rome and put his case before the pope. He has friends in the curia who have read his work with more care than the abbot of Clairvaux. I plan to go with him."

Catherine could tell from his face that Astrolabe knew his father was unlikely to survive the journey.

"What about your mother?" she asked.

Astrolabe looked at her pleadingly. "I'll be back," he said. "She'll agree that it's best I stay with him."

Catherine's lip trembled. "Why can't you take him back to the Paraclete?" she begged. "They'll care for him there."

"That's the last thing he wants, Catherine," Astrolabe said. "He has to fight this; if he doesn't, he'll die. But you can go, you and Edgar. He wants to write her, to explain. Take our letters to her. Tell her everything that's happened. Take her our love."

Reluctantly, they agreed. There seemed to be nothing else for them to do there. Astrolabe started to go back in.

"Wait." Edgar stopped him. "Before Master Abelard went before the council, he said something to Master Gilbert. Did you hear it?"

"Yes," Astrolabe said. "And I hope Bishop Gilbert de la Porrée took heed. Father told him, *'Nam tua res agitur paries cum proximus ardet.'* "

" 'It is your business, too, when your neighbor's house is in flames,' " Catherine translated. "Horace."

They walked away, the bright afternoon grating on their eyes.

"What shall we do?" Edgar asked Catherine.

"Go where we're needed," she answered.

Epilogue

The Paraclete,
Feast of the Nativity of Saint John the Baptist,
Monday, June 24, 1140

Soror mea Heloissa quondom mihi in saeculo chara; nunc in
Christo carissima, odiosum me mundo reddidit logica. . . . Quia ut
mihi videtur, opinione potius traducuntur ad judicium, quam
experientiae magistratu. . . . Si irruat turbo, non quatior, si venti
perflent, non moveor. Fundatus enim sum supra firmam petram.

My sister, Héloïse, once dear to me in the world, now
dearest to me in Christ; logic has made me hated
by the world. . . . But it seems to me that they have come
to their judgement by supposition, not by weighing
the evidence. . . . Though the storm rages, I am unshaken,
though the winds may blow, I am unmoved;
for I stand fast on an immovable rock.

—Abelard to Héloïse,
Confession of Faith, the last letter

$\mathcal{H}$éloïse took the letter from them and went to her room to read it alone. There was no point in crying, she told herself. She should take comfort from the fact that his first thought was for her, knowing how worried she would be. Astrolabe's message was briefer, not as polished, smudged with tears. She tied that one carefully in her sleeve. Abelard's she smoothed and left on the desk. She would see a copy was made so that, if things went badly in Rome, future generations would know of the propriety of his beliefs.

Sister Thecla took Edgar and Catherine to the guest-house. She hugged Catherine and gave Edgar a severe stare.

"Are you treating her well, young man?" she demanded.

"He takes good care of me," Catherine assured her.

"At least I try to," Edgar added. It was his private belief that half of heaven needed to be fully occupied with watching out for Catherine.

"How is Paciana?" Catherine asked. "Can I see her?"

Thecla's face grew grave. "Her body has healed, but not

her spirit. The news that those who caused Alys's death are to be punished only grieved her further. Mother Héloïse and Sister Melisande have spent many hours with her, but nothing brings her comfort. She has consented to the sin of despair. I'll ask Sister Melisande, but I don't know if she will see you."

"Do you think I might be allowed a few moments with Emilie?" Catherine ventured.

"Possibly," Sister Thecla smiled. "In Sister Bertrada's presence, of course. Now, why don't you two go for a nice walk. It's a lovely day. I know the abbess wishes to see you both when her duties allow. Before Vespers, I'm sure."

Catherine and Edgar took her suggestion, walking down the hill to the town of Saint-Aubin.

"It still seems vaguely immoral to be outside the convent," Catherine said. "I don't notice it when I'm far away, but within sight of it, I can't escape the feeling that my place is on the other side of the walls."

"Regrets?" Edgar asked.

"No. Mother Héloïse was right. It's better to follow one's heart. Insincere prayers don't rise. When I'm with you, my gratitude is real. God was very kind to let me find you."

They passed by the infirmary garden on their way back and saw a lone figure pulling weeds. She ripped them out of the earth savagely, clumps of mud clinging to the roots, and threw them in a pile with angry force. Catherine watched her with pity and fear.

"Edgar," she said. "Wait for me here. I have to try to speak to her."

Paciana didn't look up as Catherine approached, even when a clod of dirt bounced against her shoe. She continued her work in single-minded intensity.

"Paciana," Catherine said.

The lay sister shuddered, but made no other response.

"Paciana!" Catherine repeated. "Stop. You have to look at me!"

The grimy hands faltered and Paciana straightened. She

stared at Catherine. Her face was gaunt and her eyes empty. Catherine stepped back a pace.

"I forgive you," she whispered. "You believed silence was the only way to protect the secret. You couldn't have known it would lead to such horrible consequences. Can't you forgive yourself?"

For a long moment, Paciana was still. Then she shook her head once sharply and bent again to her task.

Shaken, Catherine walked slowly back to the path where Edgar stood waiting.

When they returned, Sister Thecla informed them that Héloïse had a few moments to spare and wished to see them.

Héloïse rose and hugged them both as they entered. She questioned them first about the council and its outcome, although she had heard most of it from other sources.

"I will pray for the abbot of Clairvaux," she said. "That his devotion to the faith will be tempered by charity and forbearance. Now, Bishop Hatto and Countess Mahaut have both informed me that we may keep the bequest Alys left us. That is welcome news, of course, but I grieve deeply over the manner in which it has come to us. It's odd, Catherine, that you were right all along about Raynald."

"I wasn't, Mother," Catherine admitted. "I was completely mistaken. I thought he had no heart or soul. Now, I think he's the only one who feels any remorse for these crimes. He has made peace with Walter and established alms in Alys's name. He had decided to go on a pilgrimage of expiation. Do you think that knowledge would help Paciana at all?"

"I don't know what will help Paciana." Héloïse sighed. "In some ways, her crime was the worst. She discovered that William was Alys's father. She knew what Rupert was doing. But she ran away from it. When Rupert threatened to kill her, she begged him to let her come here instead. She could have told Raynald the truth of Alys's birth; he would have believed her. Then he never would have married Alys. But Paciana was a coward. She abandoned her sister to her fate. A word would have saved her. Now she believes only eternal silence and mortification will atone. I cannot convince her of her error."

Catherine had never known the abbess to be so hard. Her anger was evident, despite the attempt to control it.

"So Paciana knew that she and Alys weren't really sisters," she said.

Héloïse stood. "Of course they were sisters. Just as much as you and Agnes, or you and Emilie. We are all sisters. If you take nothing else away from your years here, remember that."

She stopped, abashed, then smiled.

"I don't need to tell either of you that," she said. "You both have shown true friendship and loyalty to me and mine. I am very proud of you both, and grateful. You've expended the first weeks of your marriage in helping us. It's time you returned to your own lives. What will you do now?"

"Go back to Paris," Edgar said. "Catherine's sister has taken their mother back to Vielleteneuse. Hubert wants us to live with him. He needs Catherine's help with his accounts. I'm not sure yet what I'll be needed for."

"I thought you would continue with your studies," Héloïse said. "There are many fine teachers in Paris now."

"Yes, of course." Edgar didn't look enthusiastic. "I told Hubert I would study law. I can't disappoint him."

Catherine was unnaturally quiet. Suddenly, she jumped up and ran from the room. Edgar apologized and ran after her.

Catherine was bent over, throwing up in a laundry bucket.

"What is the matter with me?" she moaned. "Convent food never did that before."

Héloïse had followed them out.

"Catherine," she said. "I suspect you did not spend every moment of the last few weeks exclusively on convent business. Has your back been hurting, legs aching? Have you been tired and easily annoyed?"

"That last I can attest to," Edgar answered. "Is there something wrong?"

"If she were still in the convent there would be," Héloïse answered. "One more question; when did you last need your *braies*?"

"Six, seven weeks ago," Catherine said. "Mother, do you think. . . ?"

"All evidence points to that as the logical deduction," Héloïse told her. "Edgar, if you wish to make some radical request of your father-in-law, I think now would be the time to do it. He will probably refuse you nothing when you tell him he's about to have a new grandchild."

A Note on Sources

Of course, *The Devil's Door* is a work of fiction. Catherine, Edgar and their families are pure invention. But the time they live in is not. I have done my best to make it as accurate as possible. This includes not only costume and customs but also attitudes and beliefs.

The story is woven around real events. The Council of Sens did take place, probably on the date I gave. This meeting, so crucial to the life of Peter Abelard, is not well understood. I found little agreement on who was there, why Henry Sanglier was displaying the relics (I guessed it was to raise money for the Cathedral, which was begun the following summer) or even the exact wording of the list of accusations read by Bernard. I have done my best to recreate it according to surviving accounts.

Many of the minor characters in the book also really existed. However, I have created their personalities from little or no information. William of Nevers and his son, Raynald, were never accused of anything worse than trying to keep tithes from the monks of Vézelay. I have no proof that Raynald was even married. And all I know of

Peter of Baschi is that he borrowed money from Hèloïse and the pope made him repay it. I apologize to anyone writing dissertations on these men.

I am particularly interested in writing about the diversity of medieval society, which is only beginning to be studied. There are a number of excellent books and articles now available on Jewish life in Europe, on women, both in and out of the convent, on the poor, on monastic life in general, and many other previously neglected aspects of medieval life. I have assembled a partial bibliography that I will send to anyone interested. Just send me a self-addressed, stamped envelope, in care of the publisher.

My work is intended to entertain first and foremost. But I also truly love this time and these people. My research is ongoing and I would be happy to hear from anyone who has made a special study of any aspect of twelfth century society I may have touched on. Please cite your sources so that I might enjoy them, too.

I have put this note at the end of the book because a number of people have asked me about the research. However, this is not a classroom; it's a novel. I would much prefer that my readers just enjoyed the story. That's why I wrote it.

With thanks,
Sharan

Look for Sharan Newman's new novel

The
Wandering
Arm

Coming in hardcover
October 1995

Prologue

The bishop's palace at Old Sarum,
Salisbury, Christmas 1139

Rogero deffuncto, Rex annisus est Philippum quemdam sufficere
cancellarium suum, sed tam legato quam clero Sarisburiensi
retinentibus destitit ab incepto.

When [Bishop] Roger died, the king strove to elect as
successor a certain Philippe, his chancellor, but he was
robbed of it from the start by the resolute stubbornness of
both the legate [Henry of Winchester] and the clerics of
Salisbury.
—De praesulibus Angliae commentarius

Philippe d'Harcourt, dean of Beaumont and Lincoln, archdeacon of Evreaux, chancellor of England and, in his own mind at least, bishop-elect of Salisbury, was tired of the greasy manners of the Norman nobility at dinner. He leaned back onto the cushion of his personal folding chair and viewed the assorted revelers with annoyance.

His patron, Stephen, King of England, had clearly come to terms with the arrogant canons who had refused to accept Philippe as their new bishop. The king had given them places of honor at the table and they were all dining together in the utmost amicability. Philippe was saddened but not surprised. In return for the unobstructed pillaging of all the secular and some of the ecclesiastical treasure of the see of Salisbury, Stephen had restored property to the canons and donated handsomely to the monastery of Malmesbury. The king had also made a tentative peace with his brother, Bishop Henry of Winchester, who had

had his own candidate for the see. But, watching him from across the hall, Philippe noticed that Henry seemed nearly as irritated as he was, either by the behavior of the gathering or by some secret insult. The realization comforted him.

All the combatants of the recent struggle were at this moment gorging themselves hugely at Stephen's expense. It was a necessary investment. Stephen needed to win all the support he could to keep his throne from the eager seat of his cousin, Matilda, who never let anyone forget she was the last surviving legitimate child of King Henry I, not to mention widow of the Holy Roman Emperor and, lately and reluctantly, countess of Anjou.

King Stephen ordered another cask of wine to be opened. The hall echoed with cheering.

Everyone was content at this joyous season. Even Bishop Henry allowed a page to pour him another cup of wine.

Philippe d'Harcourt was the lone exception. Politics and family connections aside, he *deserved* to be bishop of Salisbury. And he knew how he could prove it in such a fashion that no one would dare challenge him.

He looked down at his plate and felt his stomach turn. Despite his certainty that his cause was just, the enormity of the possible consequences of what he planned destroyed his appetite.

Just as well, he thought. One should fast before encroaching upon sacred space even for the purest of motives.

Eventually the dinner descended to the level of such dissolution that the haughty Norman nobles were challenging each other to Saxon drinking games. By the time the shouts of "*Waes Heal! Drinc Heal!*" began to be interspersed with the sounds of retching, Philippe felt the moment was right to withdraw. He signaled his wish to King Stephen, who waved him out. Philippe was known to be a

serious cleric who preferred his books to an evening of ca-
rousal. No one thought it odd that he would leave early.
Few noticed his departure at all.

It was well past midnight. Those who weren't still drinking were surely asleep or at least otherwise occupied in
bed. Philippe met no one as he made his way from the palace to the church. As he entered, he noticed two men
kneeling before the high altar. He called to them softly. They blessed themselves, then rose and came to
him.

"Did you get the keys?" Philippe asked.

"Yes, my lord."

The younger man held them out and Philippe took them.

"Do you have the other box?" he asked.

The elder opened the sack he carried to show Philippe
the contents.

"Good," he told them. "You are both worthy servants.
I'll not forget you."

"Thank you, my lord," the elder said. "But we seek
only to be remembered in your prayers."

"Of course," Philippe answered. "But I shall remember
you in other ways as well, never fear. It would be better
if one of you stayed up here to watch, but I need you both
as witnesses. Therefore, we must rely, as always, on divine
protection. Are you prepared?"

"Yes, my lord," the younger man said. "We have spent
the entire evening here praying that we might be judged
worthy of this task."

"We have eaten nothing since the host passed our lips at
Mass this morning," the elder said. "Both Father Geronce
and I are resolved to accompany you and support you to
the end."

"I thank you both," Philippe said. "Our Lord must know
that we do this not for vainglory or profit, but only to allow His will to be made manifest to those men of clay
who care only for worldly power."

The three men knelt again for one final prayer. Then Philippe turned the key in the iron gate. It swung open with a grating creak. Father Geronce shuddered and the other priest winced, but Philippe entered without hesitation.

His steps slowed as he reached the reliquary. Motioning to the others to stay back, he tried to swallow. His mouth was suddenly dry with terror. What if he were mistaken?

No. It wasn't Stephen who had intended Salisbury for him. The king was only the instrument. Philippe was sure that it was God's will that he become bishop.

And God had little patience with the faint of heart.

Philippe knelt before the wooden box. He fumbled with the keys until he found a smaller one that fit the lock. He took a deep breath and crossed himself again, his lips moving in prayers of supplication. Behind him, he could hear the murmured support of the priests.

He opened the box.

The jewels glittered in the lantern light: ruby, topaz, beryl, sapphire, all set into brightly polished silver. Looking over Philippe's shoulder, Father Geronce reflected that one of the Salisbury canons must have dedicated his life to seeing that no tarnish ever appeared on the reliquary. Of course, he considered, something in daily contact with the divine might well assume aspects of incorruptibility. The young priest swayed slightly. Hunger was making him light-headed.

Philippe took a pair of linen gloves from his sleeve and put them on. He wanted to prove to the saint that he meant no disrespect.

"Blessed Aldhelm," he addressed the relic. "You who were bishop here before all others, you who brought the heathen Saxon to the Light with your wisdom, show me your mercy. Help me prove that you find me worthy to be your successor. Accompany me to France until such time as we may return here together. I ask you this with a humble heart."

Even though he was convinced of the righteousness of his plea, Philippe trembled as he reached out and opened the reliquary.

Inside the bejeweled silver casket lay the arm and hand bones of a man. Brown with age and brittle, they lay quietly in their place, the earthly remains of a soul now in heaven.

Philippe licked his lips. Would Aldhelm allow this or would he strike at the one who would desecrate his body? The saint had once caused a band of would-be looters to be thrown paralyzed to the ground where they lay helpless until found by the canons. Everyone knew the holy ones needed no guards.

"Oh, blessed Aldhelm," Philippe begged. "Believe my heart is pure."

His gloved hand touched the bones.

The lanterns flickered. Somewhere there was a draft.

Nothing else happened.

Philippe's knees went wobbly and he leaned against the case in relief.

"Quickly! Bring the box!" he ordered.

Father Geronce brought the box and opened it. Inside was another reliquary, made of wood, carved in the shape of an arm and covered in gold leaf.

"Hurry!" the other priest whispered. "I hear someone coming."

The bones were quickly snatched from the silver reliquary and placed in the wooden one. Philippe shut the original box and locked it. The men doused the lanterns and felt their way slowly back into the nave.

"I must stay with my master, the king," Philippe told the priests. "Go under the protection of the good saint who travels with you. Also take with you the box of vessels for the Mass that is in my chamber. I will meet you in Evreaux before Ash Wednesday. Above all, guard the relic closely. You are responsible for it to heaven and to me."

Both priests bowed and swore they would die rather than allow the relic to be harmed. Philippe smiled as they departed, satisfied that the will of the saint agreed with his own. When the canons of Salisbury learned that he had the support of Saint Aldhelm, their opposition to his election would evaporate.

He slept that night with a clear conscience in the sure and certain belief that, with the support of their first bishop, the canons would soon welcome him as their leader.

Saint Aldhelm had other plans.

THE BEST OF FORGE

☐ 53441-7   CAT ON A BLUE MONDAY $4.99
       Carole Nelson Douglas   Canada $5.99

☐ 53538-3   CITY OF WIDOWS $4.99
       Loren Estleman   Canada $5.99

☐ 51092-5   THE CUTTING HOURS $4.99
       Julia Grice   Canada $5.99

☐ 55043-9   FALSE PROMISES $5.99
       Ralph Arnote   Canada $6.99

☐ 52074-2   GRASS KINGDOM $5.99
       Jory Sherman   Canada $6.99

☐ 51703-2   IRENE'S LAST WALTZ $4.99
       Carole Nelson Douglas   Canada. $5.99

Buy them at your local bookstore or use this handy coupon:
Clip and mail this page with your order.

Publishers Book and Audio Mailing Service
P.O. Box 120159, Staten Island, NY 10312-0004

Please send me the book(s) I have checked above. I am enclosing $ _____
(Please add $1.50 for the first book, and $.50 for each additional book to cover postage and
handling. Send check or money order only—no CODs.)

Name _____

Address _____

City _____ State / Zip _____

Please allow six weeks for delivery. Prices subject to change without notice.

THE BEST OF FORGE

☐ 55052-8   LITERARY REFLECTIONS $5.99
                James Michener   Canada $6.99

☐ 52046-7   A MEMBER OF THE FAMILY $5.99
                Nick Vasile   Canada $6.99

☐ 55056-0   MY UNFORGETTABLE $4.99
                SEASON—1970
                Red Holzman   Canada $5.99

☐ 58193-8   PATH OF THE SUN $4.99
                Al Dempsey   Canada $5.99

☐ 51380-0   WHEN SHE WAS BAD $5.99
                Ron Faust   Canada $6.99

☐ 52145-5   ZERO COUPON $5.99
                Paul Erdman   Canada $6.99